In the Heart of the Hills

In the Heart of the Hills
A Novel in Stories

DWIGHT HARSHBARGER

MARTIN AND LAWRENCE PRESS
GROTON, MASSACHUSETTS
2005

In the Heart of the Hills
A Novel in Stories

Published by:
Martin and Lawrence Press
37 Nod Road
P.O.Box 682
Groton, MA 01450

ISBN 0-9721687-5-3

In the Heart of the Hills: A Novel in Stories
by Dwight Harshbarger   1st edition

Cover design by Jennifer Eaton Alden
Printed in Canada

August, 2005

To Bethany, Brynn, and Eric.

May they grow up to be storytellers.

Acknowledgements

My thanks to the storytellers of the West Virginia hills. They have enriched my life. Thanks to my writing group for their thoughtful critiques of earlier versions of these stories. And special thanks to Richard Meibers for his editorial suggestions and publication guidance.

Table of Contents

Chapter 1

Air Raid

In the underground darkness of the air raid shelter I wondered if Momma and I might die, if we'd see our home and Daddy again. An hour later when Daddy met us at the front door, Momma threw her arms around him. "The war has finally come to Kettle," she whispered, and then gave Daddy a kiss. I hugged them with all my strength; buried my face in Daddy's chest and Momma's shoulder. I breathed the sweat of his work, the scent of Momma's perfume.

After I went to bed that night in December, nineteen and forty-two, the events of a few hours earlier jumped around in my thoughts. I wanted to stop thinking about them but couldn't. Next to my family, I loved my little town in the West Virginia hills more than anything. I prayed that German bombs wouldn't destroy Kettle, but after what we'd been through I knew it could happen. A bomb has a job to do and when it lands, whether planned or accidental, it destroys.

When I closed my eyes I felt afraid, wanted to get up and run somewhere, though I didn't know where a twelve year-old boy could go. On the dark sides of my eyelids I saw bombs falling, exploding, on Gruber Feed and Grain and the Kettle Methodist Church, their walls collapsing and smoke rising from fires burning inside the ruins of the buildings. Bombs hitting the tracks of the C&O railroad in the center of town, the heavy steel rails twisted, railroad ties blasted across U.S. Highway 42. Kettle's old nineteen and twenty-eight Ford fire truck would be too puny to step up to the blazes set off by the German bombs. The little brick building that housed the fire truck, headquarters for Kettle's only police officer, Chief Tackett—blown apart. The oversized old silver telephone bell that hung on the outer wall of the building could ring itself off what remained of the wall, but the Chief would have more urgent business. The Kettle Volunteer Fire Department's powerful siren, once mounted high above the building, would lie smashed across Main Street.

Mayor Raymond T. Baumgartner's famous phrase, often quoted in our weekly paper, the *Kettle News Leader*, "You can go from birth to death and never have to leave Kettle for anything. It's all here," would have to change.

A few hours earlier in the day, Momma, my best friend William White Wallace, and I stood in front of the cash register on the old wooden counter in the grocery and meat section of Gruber's Department Store. The counter passed down one long side of the room. I loved to breathe the room's rich aromas of newly ground coffee beans, onions, and fresh baked bread. Outside, in the late afternoon darkness, the street lights had come on. From the room's high and white tin ceiling, lamp globes hung like frosted white glass muffins. The meat counter that stretched the length of the other side of the room had fresh-cut pork chops and steaks behind a glass-front cabinet that steamed up year-round, always hard to see through. My favorite place, the candy counter, occupied the area on one side of the front door. On the other side sat a coal-burning pot-belly stove and four oak chairs. Whit Saunders, wearing his high-topped lace-up boots, wide-brimmed hat, and leather jacket, leaned back in one of the chairs. In the wintertime the front of the store always smelled like coal smoke. So did Whit.

Momma snapped her purse shut after she paid for our groceries. She had no sooner buttoned up her long blue coat and smiled at me and William White, than the wail of the town's fire siren began. The siren sat on top of long metal struts on the roof of the Fire Department building, cattycorner across Kettle's Main Street from where we stood. The siren's powerful sound waves shook the store's large plate glass windows. I held my ears. William White stood motionless but his blue eyes darted around the room like a thief planning his next heist. His stillness reminded me of a wooden cigar store Indian in the Roy Rogers movie we'd seen on Saturday afternoon at the Dixie Palace, though I'd have to over-look William White's skinny frame and wavy blond hair. Everybody in the store, maybe fifteen people, seemed frozen in place—a room full of cigar store Indians.

A few seconds before the first wail of the siren began, Momma had said, "You boys are big strong twelve-year olds. Each of you please take a poke of groceries." But we hadn't yet picked up the big brown paper bags.

In the loud wail of the siren, Momma stood with her eyes closed. William White often said he thought my Momma's height, blue eyes, high cheek bones and curly dark brown hair made her the prettiest woman in Kettle. I told him, "Remember, she was runner-up in the Miss Kettle contest of nineteen and twenty-seven." Daddy often said that I had Momma's long legs and high cheek bones, but I got his brown eyes and curly reddish brown hair. He could've added that I'm skinny and have freckles

A second, then a third wail sounded. A brief pause crammed the air with silence. I'd never thought about hearing silence, but at that moment I could. Also the beating of my heart. The three-wail cycle sounded a second, then after another pause, a third time. Everybody knew what that meant—our groceries would have to sit on the counter for a while.

Kettle Police Chief Arthur R. Tackett, all red-faced, walked in the front door of Gruber's as the third cycle of siren wails ended. He stopped, rested one arm on the glass case of the candy counter and looked around the room. The chief's old red and black checked mackinaw covered the upper half of his khaki uniform and stretched itself tight across his belly. He unbuttoned his mackinaw, and then raised his arms and shouted, "All right everybody, the siren has blowed three times three. You read the paper, it's an air raid drill." Then at a lower volume, a more personal voice, "Y'all got to git yourselves down to Gruber's basement. This won't last long." Then the chief turned to Whit Saunders and said in a confidential way, "I mean it shouldn't last long, assumin' it's just a drill."

"Just a drill—what if it's not?" I wondered.

James Garfield Worthington, owner and editor of our weekly newspaper, stood next to us at the cash register. His silver hair, black topcoat and gray fedora gave him a distinguished look. Last week's special edition of the *Kettle News Leader* had been devoted entirely to Kettle air raid drills. One article described how Kettle town council argued about approval of town-wide air raid drills, what Mayor Raymond T. Baumgartner called the Kettle War Readiness Program. On a split vote, then on a second, unanimous, vote, they approved mandatory air raid drills for the town. The paper announced the signal for an air raid drill: three, three-wail cycles of the fire siren, what we had just heard. Three times three, the *News Leader* called it. Easy to remember. In a photo beside the story, the mayor smiled as he handed Miss Isabel B. Mounts, our high school librarian, not smiling, a World War One helmet. It had been painted white and had the word "Warden" stenciled in black letters across its front.

Town Council also passed an ordinance that required the town to be dark five minutes after the air raid siren ended. Violation of the ordinance would lead to a fine. The paper quoted Mayor Baumgartner, "Don't anybody run to me with appeals to get rid of fines. This is wartime. The town of Kettle, just like the rest of the country, is at war with Germany and Japan." The paper carried other air-raid related articles. One of them contained a list to help folks double-check that all their lights had been turned off. Another one had information about where to take shelter during a drill, and suggested food and supplies to stock up on at home, just in case German bombers showed up and we faced an enemy attack from the air.

Everybody looked at Chief Tackett, then at each other. Wink Winkler unbuttoned the jacket of his blue gabardine suit, the one he called his "good luck sales suit", got a serious look on his ruddy face, and said in a voice full of upset, "Chief, I got me a car, a brand-new Studebaker, to deliver to the Mayor," followed by a wink. His wink always signaled the end of what he had to say, and not a little joke, though folks usually smiled and sometimes laughed after he winked at them. As William White said, "It's hard not to smile at Wink after he winks at me."

The chief raised his voice and put some force into it. "Your delivery will have to wait, Wink. Folks, you heard me. Move along, now! Go to the basement. Time's a-wastin'. We got less than five minutes before the lights here and all over town is goin' out." Then he spelled the word big and loud, "O-U-T!" The chief looked around and added in a serious voice, "Them Germans could be flyin' over us before you know it."

I wanted to get to the basement, pronto, but didn't know where to go.

A few people shuffled towards the back of the store, stopped and milled around. Beverly Shade, a member of our sixth grade class, tall, dark curly hair, stood alone alongside the candy counter. William White motioned for her to join us.

Whit Saunders pushed his wide-brimmed hat back on his head and planted his right foot on top of a small keg of pickles. I always admired how Whit kept his khaki pants legs tucked into the tops of his lace-up boots. He wondered aloud, "Chief, where in tarnation is the door to the basement? We don't exactly live here, you know."

"Uh, understood, Whit. Good question." The chief raised his voice and pointed towards the back of the store, "Everybody, go through the door at the rear of this here grocery section, into shippin' and receivin'. Basement door is on the right. Light switch is outside the door, on the left. Whit, you go first. Make sure the light is on."

13

Miss Hattie McClintock pulled her black wool coat tight around her small frame. The gray curls of her hair bobbed she spoke at such a fast pace, clipping off the end of each word. William White once said she spoke in a sprightly manner. "Chief Tackett, I have a roast cooking in my oven. It's now six PM, pitch dark, and I'm walking, not driving. My roast will be done in exactly thirty-three minutes. I need to get home."

"Please go to the basement, Miss Hattie. You'll get home in due time. If need be, I'll give you a lift."

Miss Hattie continued, "Is it warm enough down there, Chief? Can't be more than forty degrees outside."

The chief sighed, gazed up at the ceiling, and then looked at Miss Hattie. He spoke in a soft but exasperated voice, "Miss Hattie, and everybody, please move to the basement. I'm sure it's warm, warm enough, anyway. You won't be down there for very long."

Momma gently tugged on William White and me, Beverly too, and the four of us lined up behind Whit and James Garfield. Everyone else fell into line behind us. We followed the back of Whit's hat and leather jacket through the doorway into the shipping and receiving area, a cavernous room, two stories high, with dark corners. William White once told me he had seen a foot-long rat in there. The shipping platform, its wide doors closed, took up most of the far end of the room. Above it there was a second-story loading platform, its waist-high wooden gates hanging open. Pulleys and ropes dangled from the platform. Crates of produce and hard goods cluttered the room. We wound our way among them to the basement door. Whit stood beside the door and nodded to each of us as we passed through it, like we had come to visit him.

The basement's moldy dampness and cool air hit me as soon as I started down the wooden stairs. One by one, everybody in the store filed down the steep and dark stairway, holding tight to the shaky wooden banister. William White raked his fingers along the crumbling cement between the bricks in the wall above the banister, and our feet crunched the powder that sprinkled on the steps.

After everybody made it to the basement the chief leaned through the doorway at the top of the stairs and said in a calm voice, "I'll be back soon," and then he closed the basement door.

A single, dim light bulb on the end of a frayed cord dangled above us, a weak light at best, but it would have to do. With no success I looked around for another light. Our little crowd milled around the benches in the center of the store's cellar, surrounded by floor-to-ceiling stacks of packing crates and open waist-high bins of apples, potatoes, and onions. The air carried the aroma of a musty mixture of cider and onions.

Mr. Harlan Roosevelt, known around town as Pappy Roosevelt, walked over to the benches, backless pews in the center of the room. Two brown strings of dried tobacco juice formed lines from each corner of his mouth to his chin. He ran one hand through his unruly gray-brown hair, put his thumbs under the straps of the muddy bib overalls that wrapped around his ample belly, and raised himself to his full six-foot height. His voice sounded like he had charge of us as visitors out at his hog farm, "OK, you ladies take them benches. Y'all set down." William White, who had already sat down, stood up. Pappy's wife, Mrs. Ovieta Blankenship Roosevelt, dressed in a two-piece bright blue suit she wore to church a couple of weeks earlier, Miss Hattie, Momma, Beverly, and two ladies wearing long black wool coats sat down. I stood directly behind Momma.

The door opened and the chief yelled down the steps, "Everybody, sorry but I got to turn out the light. They's basement winders that's lettin' light out on to the street. I thought the sandbags would block the light, but they ain't." Then after a pause he added in a serious tone of voice, "Don't nobody light matches nor a cigarette lighter. In total darkness you can see a match light for miles. We don't wanna give away our whereabouts to them German pilots."

The chief shut the door and the light went out. Pitch-black, total darkness. I felt all discombobulated. I heard Momma's short, quick breaths. That rat William White saw upstairs—he had to have a nest somewhere. The bins down here had food in them.

A man's voice said, "Yep, them German pilots are likely to be searching for Kettle," then he laughed. A couple of other men laughed too.

In the darkness William White made a ghost-like sound, "Whooo-ooo," and a woman let out a little whimper. A deep male voice said, "I don't know which of you boys done that, but don't do it again." Momma elbowed me in the ribs and William White said, loud enough for people to hear, "Freddy, shhhhh." Beverly reached up from the bench and banged my leg with her hand.

Two weeks earlier Momma and I had gone to Huntington to buy Christmas presents. I hadn't wanted to go but Momma said we needed to shop where we'd have more choices in the presents we'd buy. Huntington had a downtown with lots of stores. Along the sidewalks in front of the tall buildings, sand-filled burlap bags had been piled three and four bags high in front of the buildings' window wells. We walked around them. Momma told me the sand bags would protect the people inside if something happened in the war. The sand bags and thoughts of the war made me uneasy. I asked Momma, "Are German planes going to drop bombs on Huntington?"

She didn't answer me right away. "Well, anything's possible, Freddy, but I don't think we need to worry about it, OK?" She spoke in a tone of voice that meant let's not talk any more about this. Then Momma began to walk a little faster. A few days later I watched Buster Whittington's uncle, who worked for Gruber's Department Store, stack sandbags along our Main Street in front of the basement windows of the store.

We sat in silence and total darkness for what seemed like a long time, though it may have been only a few minutes. Across the room I heard a light scratching sound, hoped it didn't turn out to be a…I didn't want to say the word, even to myself.

James Garfield, speaking more to himself as editor of the *Kettle News Leader* than to any of us, said, "Well, maybe there's a story here. Kettle's first air raid drill, seen, or not seen, as the case may be, from the basement of Gruber's Department Store."

No one spoke for a couple of minutes, then a tenor voice that sounded like Wink Winkler, began to sing the hymn, "Leaning, leaning, leaning on the everlasting arms...." Everybody joined in. Next we sang the first verse and chorus of "The Old Rugged Cross." When we hit the second verse, only Wink knew the words and he sang a solo while folks hummed the melody. The warm voices and familiar words of the hymns comforted and calmed me. Things will be all right, I told myself. Momma put my hand in hers. Then she tightened her grip. I said the Lord's Prayer in a voice only I could hear.

We sang "The Battle Hymn of the Republic" in harmony. The song seemed to rouse everybody and we rolled right along in high gear. Momma relaxed her grip. Whit Saunders laughed and said, "Lordy, you folks are as good as any Sunday morning gospel quartet on the radio."

Mrs. Roosevelt yelled, "What about some Christmas carols?" and led us in "O Little Town of Bethlehem." "Silent Night" seemed to fit the darkness of the basement, though after the first verse, except for Wink, most folks didn't know the words and dropped back to humming.

At the end of "Silent Night," William White pulled on my arm and whined like a little kid, "Freddy, when are we gonna get outta here?"

Before I could answer him Miss Hattie jumped in with spirit, "Indeed. We've done our civic duty. My roast is surely done. I need to get home!"

That brought on a general chorus of voices in the darkness. "Yes, let's go home. Enough is enough. War or no war, we got things to do" and words such as that.

I recognized Peyton Gruber's baritone voice, though I hadn't seen him in the store when the siren sounded. I imagined his oval face, bald head, and moustache. "I don't care if Mayor Baumgartner fines me or not, I got to get out of here. My wife will think I've run off somewhere." Daddy had once said that Hanna Mae, Peyton's wife, kept a tight rein on him.

Miss Hattie replied, "I agree, Peyton. Let's go home." Other voices joined in with unsettling comments.

Whit Saunders's deep voice—loud and authoritative—rose above the din. "Folks, take it easy now. I don't like it here in the dark neither, but keep in mind there's a war on. The chief said he'd be back in a few minutes. I'll make my way up the stairs, stick my nose out the door and ask what's happenin'. Everybody just stay calm."

Pappy Roosevelt said in a low voice, "Whit's right, folks. Let's take 'er easy." The din settled down to worried whispers.

Footsteps sounded in the darkness and I counted fourteen creaks of the wooden steps. Then raspy squeaks as the doorknob turned. More squeaks as it turned again. And again. Then the sound of the door being shaken, followed by knocking and then loud pounding on the door.

"Chief, you out there?" Whit yelled.

Silence.

"Hello? Chief? You there?"

More silence.

I whispered to Momma, "Where is he?"

More forceful, loud pounding. "Anybody out there? Anybody?"

Nothing.

With no warning a deep boom pounded the air of our small room, the floor vibrated in a shock wave, and the rafters above us shook. One woman, it may have been Miss Hattie, let out with a shrill scream. Other women screamed. I gasped, along with lots of folks. A man's voice yelled, "What the hell?" Another said, "Oh no!"

Then a second forceful boom stuck. The light bulb hanging from the ceiling flickered on for an instant, just long enough for me to see everybody looking around the room, eyes wide, many with their mouths hanging open, and a cloud of dust in the air. Beverly tottered backwards from the bench and I caught her. She grasped my right hand tightly—her touch felt soft, warm.

The instant the flicker ended and darkness returned, Pappy

Roosevelt yelled, "Hit's an attack. Germans! Thur's got to be a way outta here, maybe a winder er the coal shute." Loud bangs came from among the bins and crates. Something made of glass crashed and splintered.

After a few seconds of the banging, Mrs. Roosevelt yelled, "Harlan—get yourself under control!"

The movement stopped. Silence. Darkness. Momma wound her arms tightly around my left arm and William White hung on to my right arm. Beverly still held my right hand. My heart pounded.

James Garfield muttered in a fretful voice, "This story may be about more than a drill."

I wished Daddy had come with us.

From the far side of the room Pappy Roosevelt said, with a quiver in his words, "I heard that Huntington were number three on the Germans' attack list for America. The way I see it, if a navigator were just a little off in his figurin', Kettle would be smack in a bomber's path." There was a loud single clap of hands and Pappy Roosevelt yelled, "Bull's eye!"

I jumped. Momma, William White and Beverly yanked my arms and hand.

"Damn!" a man yelled.

Nobody spoke. I imagined Kettle as a little pin on a war map, like the one I saw General Omar Bradley and his officers studying in a Movietone newsreel.

The voice of Hartford Wilson, owner of Wilson's Dry Goods, came through the darkness. He said in a worried tone of voice, "My wife Iretta's at home by herself. I pray that she's all right—that God will spare her and, the Lord willing, our store on Main Street." After a pause he continued, "My sister's nephew died when the battleship West Virginia was sunk at Pearl Harbor. I thought that was the closest the war would come to me. Guess I was wrong."

Then a man's voice, at first so soft that I didn't recognize it, said, "I live alone, and there's nobody at my house to turn out the lights." The voice came from near the ceiling, the top of the stairs.

Whit Saunders said, "My lights may've been enough to bring the German bombers to Kettle. I've been worried something like this was going to happen. Ever since Pearl Harbor, almost one year ago to the day, there hasn't been a single day when I didn't wonder how and when the war would come to Kettle. Now I know."

The room remained silent for a few minutes and then a woman began to cry. The crying stopped and Miss Hattie spoke, her voice cracking, "No doubt about it, German bombers it was. And they came after us, not folks in Huntington. It's possible they hit Gruber Feed and Grain to hamper our farming." Her voice got louder, stronger, "Or, God forbid, they may have hit the heart of Kettle, the Methodist Church. I suppose if they really wanted to hurt us, the Methodist Church is what they'd go after."

Wink Winkler spoke up real fast with an edge to his voice. "Miss Hattie, the water-sprinkling baptisms of the Methodists don't hold a candle to the full immersion of the Baptists, and everybody knows it, even the Germans. No maam, it's the Baptist Church they'd hit, that is if they was goin' after churches."

A sudden burst of voices began to argue about whether the Methodist or Baptist churches had target value for German bombers, and the spiritual value of each of their baptisms, a sprinkling of water on the head for the Methodists versus the full-immersion method of the Baptists.

About the time William White chimed in, "What about the Presbyterians? Don't anybody want them blowed up?" Whit Saunders began to pound again on the basement door. The room fell silent.

Her voice low, Miss Hattie said, "I've listened to the broadcasts of Mr. Edward R. Murrow from London, and his accounts of the blitz and the awful destruction from German bombs dropped on the city, mostly at night. What's just happened to us, tonight. I'm not sure I want to see our town after what the Germans have done to it. I'm glad it's dark outside, and we won't have to look at the destruction until morning, except for the flames that may still be burning. Tonight should be a night of prayer, and our giving thanks to God that, unlike so many in London, our lives have been spared." After a pause she added, "At least so far."

The basement door opened. A collective sigh passed through the room when the light bulb flickered on again. From the top of the stairs came the crisp voice of Miss Isabel B. Mounts, librarian turned air raid warden. She said, "All right everyone, it's all over. Come on up."

No one spoke as we filed up the stairs. I felt relief, but fearful about what waited on us.

Miss Mounts stood outside the basement door, wearing a short khaki coat and her white warden's helmet. She gave an official-looking nod to each of us as we passed through the doorway into the shipping and receiving department. After the last of our group arrived, she smiled the kind of smile I had seen her give little kids at Sunday School when they did something she told them to. She said, "Thanks for being so patient—and for being such good citizens."

The faces around me looked solemn. Like me, did they dread seeing a bombed Kettle?

The shipping and receiving area had broken pieces of wood and large rolls of linoleum strewn across the floor. Buster Whittington's uncle pushed a dolly and strained to move one of the big rolls. Another man threw pieces of wood into a pile.

Pappy Roosevelt spoke up. "Looks like they were some damage done here."

Miss Hattie wiped her eyes with a lace handkerchief. She sounded near tears when she asked, "How bad is it, Isabel?"

Miss Mounts pushed her white helmet back on her head. "How bad is what?"

"The damage. From the bomb."

Miss Mounts stared at her for a moment, and then replied with surprise in her voice, "Bomb?"

"The Germans."

Buster Whittington's uncle lowered his dolly, looked over at us and spoke in a matter of fact way, "Miss Hattie, during the dark of the air raid drill one of the boys thought he'd get a step ahead and move a delivery of linoleum around the upstairs storage area. He

21

didn't know the upstairs gate was open, and two large crates toppled over and fell from way up there." He pointed towards the second floor platform at the other end of the room, a full story above us. "Foolish of him to try it, but that's what he done. Down in the cellar you probably heard the crashes when the big crates hit the floor and smashed. Heavy stuff, rolls of linoleum. Could'a hurt somebody, even killed 'em."

Wink Winkler laughed, "Now ain't that a good'n. There weren't no bomb, Miss Hattie. What're you talkin' about?" Then he winked at her.

Everyone, except for Miss Hattie, Momma, and Beverly burst into laughter. Pappy Roosevelt cut loose with a hoo-haw belly laugh and slapped James Garfield on the back. William White elbowed me in the ribs. I laughed and elbowed him.

Miss Hattie looked around the room and asked, her voice rising, "Where's Chief Tackett? I need a ride home. Arthur?"

Chapter 2

MISS KETTLE'S PLACE

The summer heat of nineteen and forty-four took different forms. The common form, the one everybody felt—eighty degrees by seven-thirty in the morning. The uncommon form, felt only by me and my best friend William White Wallace—the passionate love of two fourteen-year-olds for a twenty-two-year-old married woman. Though William White once said to me, "Freddy, she's mine," he never acted jealous. In the dark of night her voice awoke and aroused me, brought on groans of desire.

She had a married name, Lorna Comstock Meyers, but to us she remained Lorna Comstock, Lorna C everybody called her, winner of the Miss Kettle contest of nineteen and forty. In a story on the competition, our weekly newspaper, the *Kettle News Leader,* described Lorna C as "Perhaps Kettle's candidate for movie stardom, with her shoulder-length chestnut hair, brown eyes, and a countenance that brings smiles from all but the most hard-hearted of men." William White once said "She's so trim, you think she's wearing a corset, but she's not." Lorna C's dark eyes had the power of magnets, bringing my gaze to hers. In the dark of night she appeared in my dreams. In the light of day when I looked at Lorna C's face I couldn't put the brakes on the slow downwards drift of my gaze. It would come to rest on her rounded and slightly upturned breasts, perfectly proportioned for her five-foot-nine-inch height. On chilly mornings delicate bumps would rise at their tips, push against her sweater. "Freddy, would you warm us, put us back in place?" they seemed to whisper. Once Lorna C caught me staring and gave me a stern look. My face felt hot and red. Then she surprised me with a tiny smile.

The Miss Kettle Contest took place on the stage of the Dixie Palace, named the Kettle Opera House at the time of its construction in nineteen and twenty. The theatre had a large stage and a pit for an orchestra. When the Opera House first opened it showed silent movies and hosted traveling vaudeville acts. Grandpa Lemley told me Al Jolson played the Opera House one night in nineteen and twenty-one. In nineteen and twenty-six a large group of Kettle Methodists and Baptists, most of them active in the Temperance movement, persuaded town council to pass an ordinance that prohibited vaudeville acts. A year later talking pictures arrived and that led to the building's name change, to the Dixie Palace.

Often when I arrived early, before the lights dimmed I'd stare at the ceiling and soon find myself making-believe that I'd entered another world. The vaulted ceiling had clouds painted across it, and six octagonal chandeliers with amber glass panes and bronze scrollwork dangled like oversized jewelry. Smaller jewels, wall sconce fixtures that resembled miniature chandeliers, glistened. Walnut and oak paneling rose halfway up each wall, below the patterned maroon tapestry of wall coverings. Another of the large chandeliers hung in the lobby. I once told William White that the Dixie Palace seemed like a big room from a castle that had been mysteriously placed on Main Street. Every Saturday afternoon William White and I each plunked down ten cents for admission and enjoyed the Dixie's cowboy movies. Sometimes I liked sitting in our palace more than the movies themselves.

In the first part of her talent presentation in the Miss Kettle competition, Lorna C, who had been a business major at Kettle High School, solved arithmetic problems read to her by the emcee of the contest, Mr. Johnson Weeks. The two of them stood in the center of the stage under bright lights, Lorna C in a tight-fitting red one-piece swim suit and Mr. Weeks in a wrinkled dark blue suit. The lights reflected off Mr. Weeks' bald head. He gave Lorna C a wide smile and his heavy jowls shook as he asked, "Three hundred and fifty seven divided by three?" Before you could say Jack Robinson, Lorna replied, "One hundred and nineteen." Mr. Weeks asked, "Two thousand sixteen, plus one thousand seventeen, plus two thousand one hundred and fifteen?" "Five thousand one hundred and forty eight," Lorna C said without a pause, right on the money every time. No sooner had the math problems ended than the pianist in the orchestra pit struck up a fast-paced rendering of the Glenn Miller tune "In the Mood." Lorna C put on a red, white, and blue top hat, picked up a baton, and began the second portion of her talent presentation, tap dancing. The stage lights dimmed and a spotlight beamed on her. Lorna C's dark eyes sparkled and she flashed her bright smile at the audience, then at William White and me. Lorna C dragged the toe, then heel, of her right foot in a circle while the pianist played the introduction to the tune. As soon as the melody started, Lorna C's left foot jumped out in front of her and led her right foot into an accelerated tapping that punctuated the music. When the music and tapping ended, she received a standing ovation. Later, as Mr. Johnson Weeks placed the crown on Lorna C, he smiled and said with pride, "With her beauty and talent, I believe Lorna C could pass as a sister to Ruby Keeler or Ginger Rogers, except I personally think she's probably a lot smarter than both of them put together."

Lying in bed that night I wondered where I might study tap dancing. Then I thought about Lorna C in her red swim suit. I imagined taking her hands and, like Fred Astaire and Ginger Rogers, dancing with her on stage of the Dixie Palace. After our performance we would walk backstage. Her lips would touch mine, her arms around me.

Lorna C and Wandel Meyers—that's "Wan-del", with the emphasis on the "del"—got married in June of nineteen and forty-one. The wedding took place exactly one month after that rainy morning when Wandel, who had a strong aversion to centipedes, aimed his twenty-two rifle at a solitary centipede crawling on the sidewalk that connected the screened front porch of his Momma's small white frame house to the berm of Route 42 and pulled the trigger. After the bullet passed out of the barrel of Wandel's twenty-two and through the centipede, at a high velocity, it glanced off the concrete beneath the remains of the centipede, ricocheted off the brick steps in front of Wandel's Momma's house, then returned itself to Wandel, and came to rest in his right thigh. He recovered from his wound in time for the wedding.

Everybody knew Lorna C loved Wandel. Still, William White and I, and most folks in Kettle, could not understand what she saw in him. Already, at age twenty-four, Wandel's sandy brown hair had thinned. And Lorna C stood at least two inches taller than Wandel. He still had active remnants of acne and no one knew of his ever having caught a baseball, football, or basketball in any form of team competition. He did not play a musical instrument and had a rough time reading the written word aloud. And Wandel had a problem with centipedes.

On the positive side, Wandel carried a tune reasonably well and satisfactorily sang hymns. In spite of his reading difficulties, Wandel had memorized the Twenty-Third Psalm, which he enjoyed reciting at church whenever members of the congregation testified about their Christian commitments. But none of this mattered. Wandel loved Lorna C and she loved him.

William White and I attended the wedding at the Kettle Baptist Church, though we didn't receive written invitations. But neither did anybody else in Kettle. Lorna C and Wandel's Mommas just called a lot of folks, told them the date and time of the wedding and asked them to please come—if they wanted to bring a dessert, cookies or a small cake, for the reception that would be fine.

That warm June evening William White and I stood beneath the elm trees in the yard of the white frame Baptist Church, its steeple as tall as the trees. The pink-frosted glass windows of the church reflected the glow of the burning candles in the sanctuary. William White said, "It's too hot to go in there." I yanked on his arm and pulled him through the door. Inside, the candles, rows of them placed along the altar and part-way up each aisle, and a sanctuary full of people pushed up the temperature. William White and I sweated in our dark gray wool suits, buttoned-up white shirts and blue knit neckties. We found aisle seats near the front of the church on the side reserved for the groom's family and friends. When the organist hit the first notes of "Here Comes the Bride" everybody turned to look at Lorna C at the far end of the aisle. She wore a white gown, pearl buttons down its front, and so long that it trailed along the carpeted aisle behind her. A lace veil fell across her face. William White jumped up and down to get a glimpse of her until I grabbed his shoulder and held him down. Then he stepped out in the aisle and stared at Lorna C with a dumb grin on his face. She walked down the aisle with William White facing her. When she reached our pew I pulled him back to his seat. As Lorna C passed us she turned her dark eyes ever so slightly towards William White and me and smiled. I wished I could touch her white gown. I wished I was older.

At the reception in the large room the Baptists called The Hall of Joy we drank fruit punch. William White pulled me over to a corner, frowned, and then put on an expression that looked like the one he wore when he got his final word in the spelling bee, the one he couldn't spell. "What has she done, Freddy? What she has done?"

Wandel and Lorna C had a brief honeymoon. Lorna showed us a photo of her and Wandel standing in front of the RC Cola sign beside flat rock-face of the entrance to Luray Caverns in Virginia. After they returned to Kettle and settled into the three-room apartment attached to the back of Wandel's Momma's house, Wandel convinced Lorna C they should buy Jim's Place, a restaurant for sale on Main Street in the center of town. Jim's Place sat opposite the C&O railroad station and next door to Gruber's Department Store. The owner, Jim Ramsay, had decided to retire. He had operated the restaurant his entire life. It had belonged to his father and before him his grandfather and great-grandfather, whose father, Jim's great-great-grandfather, had cut virgin timber and used the logs to build the Kettle Trading Post. The large old green-roofed log building stood until nearly the turn of the century when Jim's dad had it torn down and built the present two-story brick building on the site of the old Post.

Jim never married and had no children to take over the business. In recent years he'd lost his hair, once curly and black, and his once tall frame became stooped. Momma told me she heard he had a serious disease. William White said Jim had ulcers and heart problems from too many years of eating his own greasy hamburgers. Maybe that's why Jim had hired Bertha Benson as chief cook a few years earlier.

The front part of the restaurant, long and rectangular, had four booths with red table tops and black leather seats along its two side walls. In the center of the room sat three red Formica tables, each with four chromium plated chairs. Beside the entrance Lorna C had placed a Wurlitzer jukebox, bright red, green, and blue sections forming an arc above the machine's center-window. After we deposited five cents and made a selection, behind the window a record dropped on to the turntable and music played after a long arm with a tiny needle at its end gently lowered itself to the surface of the turning record. Across the opposite end of the room sat a red counter with five round stools, each with a red-leather top. William White liked to spin them. Behind the counter a wall with tan double doors, each door with a half-moon window, opened into the kitchen. A round illuminated electric clock, "Drink RC Cola," hung beside the door.

William White and I could never figure out how Wandel got Lorna C to agree to buy the place, much less how they came up with the money. But he did and they did, even though everybody in town knew that Wandel had only enough money to stay two jumps ahead of the bill collector. He beamed with pride the day a work crew placed the new rectangular neon sign above the front entrance, perpendicular to the brick building. When lit, one-half of the sign blinked the words "Miss Kettle's Place" in blue neon.

The other half of the sign had a red neon outline of a shapely woman wearing a top hat and holding a baton. When the sign blinked, one red leg raised, then, on the next blink, returned to its original position. Some people said the sign seemed kind of racy. William White and I viewed the sign as a poorly disguised attempt by Wandel to cash in on Lorna C's being a local celebrity. "Just one more reason for her to ditch him," William White said.

Wandel achieved two small places for himself in Kettle history. The first occurred when he became the one-hundredth man from the Kettle area to enlist in the service after Pearl Harbor. The *Kettle News Leader* carried a picture of Wandel and an Army sergeant leaning over a desk in a room at the County Court House as Wandel signed his enlistment papers. The picture appeared in the "War News" section of the paper and carried the caption "Kettle hits 100 with Wandel Meyers."

After his departure for boot camp in the spring of forty-two, Lorna C ran the restaurant alone. This didn't alter things in any major way for she operated the restaurant pretty much by herself even with Wandel present. Wandel enjoyed talking with customers and told Lorna C it meant a lot to them for him to do that. He also liked to sample the food Lorna C and Bertha Benson, who stayed on after Jim sold the restaurant, prepared for customers. Bertha's desserts got lots of compliments, particularly her pecan pies, with their rich fillings made with lots brown sugar and Karo syrup, and their flaky crusts. When she took a break from cooking, Bertha liked to talk with customers. You could tell where she placed herself by just listening for laughter. Sometimes she'd help Lorna C with the restaurant's business ledgers.

Wandel would talk to customers about preparing for the restaurant business as a business major at Kettle High School. He often added that until he and Lorna C bought the restaurant he hadn't determined the right way to apply his education. Wandel had tried such businesses as Wandel Meyers Paperhanging, Wandel Meyers House Painting, and Wandel Meyers Trucking and Delivery, businesses with a couple of things in common. First, Wandel's nineteen and thirty-seven quarter-ton shiny red Dodge pickup truck with whitewall tires and "The Wandel Meyers Co., good work, hydraulic brakes, Phone 3736, Kettle, W.Va." painted in gold letters trimmed in black on each door. Second, Wandel's failure to earn a profit and build a steady income, a problem that may have been created by Wandel's love of fishing.

One day I listened to Wandel express his wonderment at what he could have missed in his business courses at Kettle High, "A fully accredited secondary school," Wandel said. Lorna C served a blue plate special to a customer in the next booth, then took Wandel aside and said, "Honey, remember that period during your senior year when you had the chicken pox? I'll bet that's when they taught business profit."

When William White learned that Wandel had joined the Army he ran out his front door, got on his bike, and pumped the pedals while standing up all the way to the Mount Zion Baptist Church and back, a distance of at least six miles, including Haggett's Hill, top to bottom. Then William White came to my house all hot and sweaty, his blond hair plastered against his head, lacking the little wave in the front that he kept combed just right. He started fixing his wave with the pocket comb he always carried in the right rear pocket of his jeans and said, "Mark this day, Freddy, April seventeenth, nineteen and forty-two. It is the start of my new life with Lorna Comstock."

When William White arrived I had been trimming our front yard hedges next to the sidewalk. Later I would help Daddy paint the dark green trim on the windows of our white frame home, a step I feared would be the first one down the road to the two of us painting the entire two stories of the house. The thought made me sweat even more.

"William White, do you mean Mrs. Lorna C. Meyers?" I said, emphasizing the "Mizzes." He ignored me and went right on talking about plans for his new life, punctuated with comments about Lorna C's beauty.

William White often hung out at Miss Kettle's Place for hours at a stretch. Lorna C didn't seem to mind his being there, particularly during the slow times of the day. After Wandel left for basic training, Lorna C said she liked to have somebody around to talk to, a comment that William White took most personally. "Freddy, it was an invitation," he bragged. "She wants me there."

I often went with him to the restaurant, but just sitting around drinking RC Cola and mooning after Lorna C, though nice, after a while had a dulling quality for me, particularly when Bertha fried lots of hamburgers and the smell of burnt grease took over the restaurant. After I had a long stint at Miss Kettle's Place, my Momma sometimes threw a conniption fit and made me hang my clothes on the back porch to air out.

Most of the time William White shared Lorna C's company with Albert Newcomb, who returned to Kettle in nineteen and thirty-nine after he lost the lower half of his left leg in a mining accident at the Rowena Number Three Mine near Slab Fork, south of Beckley. Because of his disability, Albert had no steady employment and lived with his Mom on their farm. A few years earlier Albert's Daddy had died in a tractor roll-over accident on the farm. Albert, then fifteen, had been riding behind his Daddy when the tractor, a large red Farmall, began to tip over and he jumped clear of it. Before the accident Albert had been a good student at Kettle High. But after his Daddy's death he quit doing his homework and failed one test after another. Everybody knew that when Albert turned sixteen he would quit school. And he did.

After Albert's return to Kettle from Slab Fork, each morning his Momma gave him a ride to town on her way to work in Huntington. He hung around Kettle until her return in the evening. Tall and trim, always wearing his black Stetson cowboy hat, denim jacket and flannel shirt, Albert would stand on the sidewalk in front of the Post Office. The Post Office occupied the ground floor of the red brick building at the corner of Main and Maple Streets, at the opposite end of our Kettle business district from Gruber's Department Store. Albert wore a wooden peg leg, which he fitted on just below his left knee where his leg had been cut off. He doubled up the unused portion of his left trouser leg and pinned it above the straps that held his peg leg in place. On rainy or cold days he'd go inside the Post Office, or to Miss Kettle's

Place, where he'd share the company of Lorna C with the rest of us. All the while Albert made himself available to the community for what he called free-lance work, such as helping with trash hauling, tobacco pruning, tending and harvesting, and his favorite work, taking tobacco crops to auction at the Huntington market, an all-day free-lance job.

Albert had four hand-carved oak peg legs that he had cut, dried, and fitted himself. Each one had a cushioned leather top with leather straps that secured the peg leg to his knee and lower thigh. Albert, it turned out, had a talent for woodcarving, and folks around town appreciated the life-like figures he carved into the surfaces of his peg legs. Each leg's carving featured a different theme. I liked the one he called "Fourth of July." It featured a Winchester rifle, an American flag flying from a flagpole, and a small cannon firing a ball up the length of the leg. Albert's peg leg for Christmas, with a tiny sled, Santa, and reindeer, attracted lots of attention, as did the Easter model with its rendering of the Crucifixion. The fellows who hung out at the Post Office preferred Albert's leg with a hunter and rabbit, "hunting season," Albert named it. Lots of people wanted Albert to enter one of his legs in the woodcarving competition at the Cabell County Fair. Albert always told them, "That ain't no place for a false leg."

In addition to looking for free lance work, Albert and his friends spent each day talking and sharpening the blades of their pocket knives on the stone window sills of the Post Office building. For different reasons the men couldn't serve in the Armed Forces. Some of them had grown too old. Others couldn't pass the physical exam. One day as I walked by, Albert and a couple of his friends talked about the woodcarving competition. One of them said right to Albert's face, "Albert, I believe you are afeard you will win a blue ribbon." I think he had it right.

The leg carvings sometimes created difficulties for Albert. When little children saw the leg carvings they'd say things like, "Mommy, look at the flags on that man's leg," or "Mommy, Jesus is on that man's leg." If the lady didn't know Albert she'd tell the child, "Hesh up." When adults realized that they stood before a work of art, they'd do a double take and stare at Albert's leg. Albert usually ignored them. He'd stroke the blade of his pocket knife on the stone sill of front window of the Post Office and test the sharpness of the blade's edge by slicing a piece of paper.

One day Albert's seventh-grade English teacher, Miss Daisy Watkins, wearing her customary print dress covered with yellow daisies, observed Albert's concentration during a blade test as she walked by. Miss Daisy said, "Albert, I wish you had paid just half as much attention to your studies when you were in school." Albert's face reddened and he quickly removed his Stetson. "How'd do, Miss Daisy," though he said it mostly to the back of her gray head for Miss Daisy didn't slow her pace.

If Albert knew the person looking at his leg, the leg gazing usually brought a "howdy" from him and a comment from the viewer about the model Albert wore that day. Mayor Raymond T. Baumgartner would make a big to-do about Albert's peg leg and call people to gather 'round and have a look. He'd then say in a proud way, "There's so many ways each of us can contribute to the life our Kettle community, just like Albert here does with the art of his peg leg carvings." The mayor usually finished his comments in Albert's absence, for by then Albert would have ducked into the Post Office or the front door of a store.

Albert attended every Kettle High School football game. He loved to watch the team pass the football, and his deep bass voice would rise above the noise of the crowd, yelling for the Kettle Tops to pass the ball on most every down, even though, year in and year out, the team had little strength in the passing department. Albert's friends from the Post Office joined him in repeated calls for passing and loud cheers for Kettle High. Albert always wore a heavy sweater of bright orange and black, our school colors. During the first half of a game Albert and his friends would consume a fair amount of corn liquor produced out at Pappy Roosevelt's hog farm. Along about the third quarter of the game they often made a supporter of the opposing team angry and a fight would break out.

Most people around Kettle knew the danger of a fight occurring near Albert and made a point of looking out for Albert's black Stetson poking above the crowd, then skirting the area. But out-of-town fans hadn't been warned about Albert and what they faced. Albert had achieved some local notoriety as a fighter because of a surprise move he originated. Once into a fight, Albert would reach down and quickly loosen the straps of his peg leg. Then while vigorously hopping around his opponent on his good leg, an act that generally caused his opponent to stare at him gape-mouthed for a moment, Albert would seize the peg leg by its small end and swing it as a club. The blow usually dispatched his opponent in mid-stare and set Albert on a course of finding and dispatching another opponent. Saturday morning's discussion among Albert and his friends at the Post Office might start with Friday night's Kettle High School football game, but would quickly become a replay of the fistfight and Albert's hopping and dispatching of opponents.

Kettle had a joyful Fourth of July celebration in nineteen and forty-four. D-Day had taken place a month earlier and folks sensed that the war in Europe had turned and would be won. Wandel Meyers landed in the Normandy invasion and earned a promotion to sergeant for his leadership in battle. "Wandel Meyers? Are you sure?" some folks asked. Others mentioned the intensity of Wandel's battles with centipedes and allowed that he might have redirected those considerable energies towards German soldiers.

The Fourth of July celebration took place in Riverfront Park, three acres of grass, maple trees, and picnic tables at a bend in Sour Apple River not far from Main Street. At the park's sandy beach we'd swing from a heavy rope tied to a strong limb of an old water maple on the river's bank. When the swing reached the highest point in its arc over the river, we'd drop into the cool water. We didn't have fireworks that Fourth of July; fireworks had to wait until after the war. But in the days leading up to the celebration everybody pitched in and decorated the park with American flags and red-white-and-blue patriotic bunting. On the Fourth of July folks arrived at noon with picnic baskets. Some of the boys chose teams and we played softball games while many of the men, some pulling wide-brimmed hats down over their eyes, pitched horse-shoes. About three o'clock the town band assembled on a platform and folks gathered in front of the bandstand to hear a thirty-minute concert of patriotic tunes. Afterwards Mayor Raymond T. Baumgartner walked to the front of the bandstand. He wore a white shirt, white pants, and a wide red-and-blue-striped necktie. The mayor's shirt had become so soaked with sweat it stuck to his short round body. His thinning brown hair, also wet with sweat, had plastered itself to his head. The mayor, a Roosevelt Democrat, devoted a considerable portion of his speech to reminding every-body "of all that Franklin Delano Roosevelt has done to improve life in the town of Kettle, including the Civilian Conservation Corps dam and pond." He paused for applause, for folks enjoyed Sunday picnics at the CCC dam. "The paving of Kettle's streets with brick by the WPA." Applause again. "A Federal banking system that kept the Bank of Kettle solvent during the darkest days of the Depression." A pause, silence. "And now, along with our cousin Mr. Churchill and our comrade Mr. Stalin, Franklin Delano Roosevelt is leading us to victory in World War Two." A pause followed by enthusiastic applause. The Mayor beamed, raised both arms, and with each hand formed the two-fingered V for victory that we often saw Winston Churchill flash in Movietone newsreels at the Dixie Palace.

In the heat and excitement of public speaking, the mayor's face flushed a deep red. His white cotton britches looked like they could barely contain his ample girth. Although Mayor Baumgartner's speech had been serious, growing waves of laughter from the audience punctuated it. Little kids behind the bandstand had discovered that the entire seam in the seat of the mayor's white cotton britches had failed, exposing his bright red, white, and blue striped boxer shorts. Each time more kids joined their friends to view the mayor's underwear, a new wave of laughter and agitated pointing erupted among them. Adults in front of the band-stand began laughing at the kids. The mayor must have thought some hidden wit and humor in his speech had created all the good spirit, for he seemed to be working himself into a long speech. Mrs. Raymond T. Baumgartner, dressed in a red blouse and a blue and white skirt, walked out on the band-stand and whispered something into the mayor's left ear. He thanked folks for their patriotic spirit, waved and shuffled sideways, stiff-legged, to the bandstand steps. The ended his public appearances for the day.

Rows of picnic tables displayed dishes of mouth-watering food. Sliced ham, fried chicken, potato salad, green beans, chocolate pies, angel food cakes and more. I chose a large piece of the raspberry cobbler made by Beverly Shade's Mom. Beverly and I had classes together at Kettle High. I ate my piece of raspberry cobbler so fast I dripped red raspberry juice down the front of my white shirt.

Beverly found some soap and water and helped me remove the raspberry stain from my white shirt. She rubbed the soapy cloth on the red spot on my shirt. I put my hand on hers to direct it. My heart raced and I didn't want to take my hand away or for her to stop. Beverly's height and high cheekbones put her face even with mine and her eyes became pools of blue that asked me to stare into them. I had an impulse to invite Beverly to go with me to a movie at the Dixie Palace on Saturday night, but decided against it. William White and I already had plans. I'd do it another time.

Later I walked to Miss Kettle's Place to meet William White. Lots of folks drifted over to there after the celebration and ordered the blue plate special. William White and three of our friends, all four of them wearing white t-shirts and Cincinnati Reds baseball caps, sat in a booth playing Rook and eating French fries. Each of them had a bottle of RC Cola. Lorna C had turned on the radio that sat on the front counter and folks listened to Lowell Thomas give a positive account of the war news and wish his listeners a happy Fourth of July. It had been a good day.

Albert, his Stetson pushed back on his head, sat at the far end of the counter near the cash register. I told William White that I wondered if Albert chose that seat so he could look at Lorna C each time she rang up a customer's bill. Sometimes she returned Albert's look and give him a little smile. When that happened

Albert's face would redden and he'd turn and gaze towards the plate glass window and Main Street. The last time William White and I saw this happen, William White elbowed me and blurted out, "Freddy, Albert's trying to come between us and Lorna C."

I pulled the last empty chair in the place up to the booth next to William White and my friends. Shortly after I seated myself, Lorna C asked if I would like something to eat or drink. "Sure, Lorna C, I'll have an RC Cola." She turned and walked to the pop cooler, bent over and reached inside to pull out a cold and dripping wet bottle of RC Cola. When she got good and bent over, William White elbowed me in the ribs. "Look," he whispered. I then surprised myself. As shapely and nice as Lorna C appeared, I found myself thinking about Beverly Shade, though I didn't tell William White.

Later that evening, after I went to bed and turned out the light, when I closed my eyes, I saw Beverly's face. Then the image melted and Lorna C's face appeared. I felt a passion for her surge through my body.

That summer William White and I had a business partnership mowing lawns, earning from fifty cents for small yards to a dollar and a half, and once in a while two dollars, for larger yards on hillsides. We had the use of our families' push mowers and the two of us mowing in tandem would polish off an average lawn in a half-hour. We'd allow another fifteen minutes for hand-trimming around sidewalks and trees. We had rounded up quite a few "contracts," as William White called them, back in March when Kettle had had a warm spell and the grass began to grow. We knocked on lots of doors and gave folks a chance to get in on the ground floor of our business, as William White described it to them. By the end of June we found that if we got an early start each day we could manage our mowing contracts by working only in the mornings. That left us with afternoons to go fishing or swimming, or to work on our now favorite game, basketball.

The local hospital, just outside of Kettle, had a new full-length outdoor blacktopped basketball court with lines painted on it and a hoop and backboard as good as what we had in the Kettle High gym. We never saw anybody on the court, so we began to go there in the afternoons and play one-on-one. Sometimes a few guys joined us to play a real game. We had to hitchhike the three miles from Kettle to the hospital and back. We'd stand beside the highway and look squarely at the driver of an oncoming car, our right arms extended and our thumbs pointing in the direction we wanted to go. Most folks knew us and we got rides quickly.

In the past six months William White had grown to five-foot-nine. He told me that he wanted to try out for the junior varsity basketball team this year and pushed me to play with him almost every day. One day he said, "Maybe I can teach Lorna C to play basketball and the three of us can play two-on-one," a hare-brained scheme if ever I heard one.

Along about the first day of August, a Wednesday, we mowed lawns and then thumbed over to the hospital. We played a few games of one-on-one until it began to rain, and then we headed back to town. I went home—I didn't want to miss "Terry and the Pirates" on the radio that afternoon. At the end of the previous day's program the announcer had said, "Terry has prepared secret plans to blow up a Japanese ammunition factory in Indochina. Tomorrow he'll be ready to strike a blow for freedom. But can he do it? Find out. Tune in, same time, same station."

The stores in Kettle closed on Wednesday afternoons. That, combined with the rain that turned into a downpour, made for a nearly deserted downtown. William White headed for Miss Kettle's Place and a visit with Lorna C. Earlier in the day Albert had gone with Benton R. Kinder to weed and prune Benton's tobacco crop.

William White later described to me the events of that afternoon. "There were no customers in the restaurant and Bertha Benson had gone home when I got there. Lorna C and I sat next to each other at the counter and played 500 rummy for nearly an hour and a half." He described to me the tight-fitting white blouse and pink skirt that Lorna C wore. He said she kept looking at the front door and once in a while would walk to the door and glance up and down Main Street. "She might have been looking for customers or, more likely, she was checking to make sure we'd be alone." No customers appeared and the rain showed no promise of letting up. Lorna C told William White she wondered if she should keep the place open on a day like this. The two of them continued to sit at the counter. Lorna C played her cards and counted her points in the game. William White played his cards and counted his blessings in what had become more than a card game.

What happened next on that rainy afternoon differs, depending on whether the story is told by William White or Lorna C. William White's version—he had just played the eight, nine, and ten of spades. In leaning forward to place his cards on the counter his knee brushed against Lorna C's leg. "She cast the gaze of her beautiful brown eyes first towards my leg that had just touched hers, then slowly turned and looked right into my eyes. She leaned forward, her lips parted ever so slightly and she half-closed her eyes." He paused then said, "I am a human being, Freddy, and I was unable to resist a clear invitation from the woman I love. I kissed her."

Lorna C said, "We were playing 500 rummy and in the middle of the game William White lunged at me and tried to kiss me. I screamed. Then I yelled, 'William White Wallace, you get out of this restaurant! And stay out!'"

William White and I had been best friends since first grade, but I felt Lorna C's rendering of the story had the ring of truth to it.

One evening a few days later, William White and I joined some of our friends for hamburgers at Miss Kettle's Place. After we placed our orders Lorna C said, "I'm sorry, but I can't serve you until one person who will remain unnamed leaves this restaurant." We all turned and looked at William White, whose face had turned crimson. He made a beeline for the front door. I left too. That evening William White and I sat on the front steps of the Bank of Kettle and watched traffic pass along Main Street.

William White suffered through the remaining weeks of August. No more long afternoons for us at Miss Kettle's Place. We continued to do our lawn contracts but I had to double-check William White's work. He often left uncut streaks of grass due to his failure to overlap his paths of mowing, due to a failure of his vision on the job caused by the failure of a dream coupled with, in my opinion, his own stupidity that day in the restaurant. On the positive side, at least I didn't have to listen any more to details of William White's plans for a future life with Lorna C.

About the time the Rose of Sharon tree in our yard began to bloom, William White and I hit our stride at basketball. My play had improved and we had close games most every afternoon. The appearance of the Rose of Sharon's whitish-pink blossoms signaled the coming end of summer and the approach of the beginning of school. William White and I wanted to use every available minute of our remaining freedom to do the things we enjoyed most.

One afternoon after a few games of one-on-one basketball at the hospital court, we stood on the highway and thumbed a ride back to Kettle. A fellow we'd never seen before, alone and driving a black four-door nineteen and thirty-five Chevrolet, stopped and gave us a lift. The car had back doors called "suicide doors." They had the hinges on the rear side of each door. If you drove along at a good clip and for some reason opened a door, the wind would quickly push it wide open. If you happened to have a firm grip on the door handle you had better hang on or you would find yourself out on the road. Or maybe somebody else would find you because you'd be unconscious or deceased.

"Hop in, boys."

William White and I climbed into the back seat of the Chevy. "We're going to Kettle," I said. William White slammed the door shut.

The driver appeared to be in his late thirties or early forties, balding and chubby. In the afternoon heat, sweat dripped from his face. From ours too. He wore a white shirt that stuck to his body, and a black necktie. A white straw Panama hat lay beside him in the front seat. Beside us in the back seat lay two glossy magazines with naked women on their covers. Totally naked. Front views. In color. Beside the magazines some smaller one-inch thick booklets had been stacked, each one with a pen and ink sketch on the cover. One booklet featured Superman and Lois Lane with their hands in each other's private places. William White picked up one of the little books and found that if you held it between your thumb and forefinger and flipped the pages rapidly, Superman and Lois Lane stripped naked and went at it. I could see the fellow watching us in the rear view mirror. He smiled and a gold upper front tooth gleamed. He said, "It's OK, have a look." I don't think even Superman could have done it as many times as we flipped the pages of the little book. A carton on the floor had a printed label, "Drives women crazy. The original French Tickler." William White started to open the carton and I stopped him.

The fellow smiled again, "You boys from Kettle?" He watched us in the rear-view mirror. We nodded. He continued, "I'm wondering if there is a place in Kettle where a man could find a woman, you know, for the afternoon?" I had never been asked a question like that and didn't know what to say. I wanted out of the car, but didn't like the thought of opening a suicide door while rolling along at forty miles an hour. I shook my head, no. William White got a serious expression on his face and looked into the fellow's eyes in the rear view mirror. "Why yes, I believe that's possible." My mouth gaped open.

William White continued, "There's one place you can go. It's a restaurant called Miss Kettle's Place." He paused and gave the man a serious look, then said, "Miss Kettle's Place is in the center town, directly across Main Street from the railroad station. Just go in and sit at the counter and ask for Lorna. You can't miss her. She's very pretty. Dark hair, tall. When you speak with her, tell her you have some time on your hands and show her your wallet—that'll do the trick. She has a room in the back where she entertains."

I kept my mouth shut, but imagined it hanging open. "What's he doing?" I yelled inside myself. For all we knew this guy would come back looking for us after he discovered William White's lie.

About the time William White said "that'll do the trick," the car stopped at Kettle's traffic light. I said, "We'll get out here." We thanked the man for the ride and jumped out of the car.

The fellow flashed his gold tooth in a big smile and replied, "I sure appreciate your assistance."

William White stuck his head in the passenger side window of the front door and said, "Glad to be of help." He winked at the man and added, "I hope you have a good afternoon."

When the car pulled away from the light I felt relief.

At first we walked away normally. But when we got far enough away that the fellow couldn't see us, we began to run as hard and fast as I have ever run in my life. When we arrived at my house we threw ourselves on the floor of the front porch. William White began to laugh in whoops. In between whoops he'd say, "I can hear him, 'time on my hands,' he'll say, then show her his wallet." Another whoop.

I have to admit, the whole thing seemed so ridiculous I began to laugh. Then whoop. Each time we stopped laughing William White'd whoop once more and that would trigger me to start again. The ache in my sides finally got the best of my laughter. Even William White could only whoop for so long.

We waited about an hour then headed for Miss Kettle's Place. We scouted Main Street for the Chevy with the suicide doors. Not seeing it anywhere, we walked to the front door of Miss Kettle's Place. William White said he thought it would be best if he didn't go in, so he crossed the street and sat in the shade of the railroad station platform. I walked in the restaurant and took a seat at the counter. Lorna C's movements wiping the counter top seemed a little jerky, but I thought I might be imagining things. Albert stood just behind the plate glass window at the front of the restaurant and looked up and down the street. I said hey to Albert and Lorna C. After I ordered an RC Cola I asked, "How're things going?"

Lorna C turned towards me with her mouth partly open but no words came out. Albert pulled the brim of his Stetson forward, lowering it towards his eyes, and then said, "I tell you, Freddy, we had a little set-to a while ago. Some feller in a Panama hat come in here actin' real odd, like he knew somethin' we didn't, askin' for Lorna and flashin' a wallet filled with money. About the time she said 'I'm Lorna' I stepped in and said, 'Who wants to know?' He said, nasty-like, 'What's it to you?' and I said once more 'Who wants to know?' and he said 'Excuse me,' in a way that sounded like he wanted me to go fishin' by myself and then rotated his self on his stool towards the counter, turnin' his back to me. I give his shoulders and that stool a good spin. By the time he stopped his spin and stood up I was on my good leg and had my peg leg in my right hand, my arm arched and ready to swing. The feller's eyes got right large. He said, 'I think there's been some mistake,' and high-tailed it towards the door. I yelled, 'Hey, you ain't paid for your coffee' at his backside."

Lorna C looked at me, then at Albert, and spoke in a slow and quiet manner, "I don't know who that man was, or what got into him, but Albert, I'm glad you were here." I had never before seen Albert smile. He had a handsome face. Albert pushed his Stetson back on his forehead and said, "Thank you, Lorna C. I'll always be here." Lorna C gave him a warm smile.

The day after Labor Day Lorna C received a telegram from President Roosevelt. Wandel had been put on a list of men missing in action. For a couple of days folks came in the restaurant and offered Lorna C comfort and support. They told her they'd pray for Wandel. Then a second telegram arrived. Wandel had died in battle and distinguished himself in such a way that he would be awarded a Silver Star—Wandel's second niche in Kettle history. No soldier from Kettle had ever been awarded a Silver Star. The War Department also told Lorna C that because of the explosion that took Wandel's life, there would be no body of Wandel to return home. She learned that Wandel had lost his life when he charged a German machine gun nest that guarded a fuel storage tank. After Wandel had been wounded, he threw a hand grenade into that nest. When the grenade detonated it triggered an explosion of the fuel storage tank and everything went to cinders, including Wandel.

Until Wandel's death, I hadn't known anyone who died in the war. I thought about how we said goodbye twice to Wandel. Once after he joined the Army, the one-hundredth enlistment, and a second time when he left for overseas. Yet Wandel continued to live in my mind. I imagined him driving his truck or talking to folks in the restaurant—all the while a voice in me said, "Wandel is dead and gone." Each time I heard the words "dead and gone" within me, I felt like my insides had fallen into a dark pit. Then I'd have trouble concentrating. Not long after Wandel's death I failed a math test, a subject that had been one of my best.

The evening we received the news of Wandel's death, after I went to bed I thought about him and cried—for Wandel, for Lorna C's sorrow, and for mine too. I got up and went down to the kitchen. Daddy walked in shortly after me. He had on his light blue pajamas and old dark blue bathrobe. I told him I couldn't sleep because of my thoughts of Wandel. Daddy fixed a glass of warm milk for each of us.

We sat down at the kitchen table and Daddy said, "It's hard to understand something like Wandel's death." He told me that at the time of World War One, a war Daddy said people called "the war to end all wars," he knew a young man from Kettle, Sonny, who served in the Army and died in France. Sonny grew up in a family who lived near Daddy and Grandma and Grandpa Lemley. In the summertime Sonny worked for Grandpa Lemley and Daddy worked alongside him, even though Daddy said that as a young boy he probably didn't add much to their getting jobs done. Sometimes Daddy and Sonny would sing hymns while they worked together. Daddy said he cried when he learned of Sonny's death in battle, "I couldn't believe Sonny was gone forever. Grandma and Grandpa Lemley took me to a memorial service for Sonny, and that helped me put my feelings for Sonny in a special place."

"Where'd you put them?"

"At the service I asked God to watch over Sonny. And to help me live in a way that would honor Sonny. I guess God helped me find a special place inside myself to put my memories of Sonny, for I felt a little better after that."

William White and I went to the memorial service for Wandel at the Baptist Church. I asked God to watch over Wandel and to help me put my feelings in a special place.

After the service many of Lorna C's regular customers, including William White, gathered at Miss Kettle's Place. Everybody brought potluck dishes and people reflected on Wandel's life and told stories about him. We laughed when somebody told the story of Wandel shooting the centipede. Lorna C remembered aloud how well Wandel recited the Twenty-Third Psalm. Then she recited it in its entirety just the way he would have done, and we cried.

Buford Vittitoe, a tall and heavy-set man about Wandel's age, dressed in blue jeans and a brown work shirt, talked about fishing with Wandel, recalled the time Wandel caught a fourteen-inch sucker during night fishing on the Sour Apple River. Then he asked "Do you folks remember the Kettle Nativity Scene of Christmas, nineteen and thirty-eight?" People nodded their heads and murmured that they remembered.

Miss Hattie McClintock, her gray curls bobbing as she spoke in her fast and snippy manner, said, "I helped sew the costumes that year, along with the other members of the Women's Club. We put a lot of time into it. The club's top talent did the sewing."

Buford said the town had invested in floodlights that lit up the manger scene set up beside the fire station with Joseph, Mary, the baby Jesus, and the Three Wise Men. "One night," Buford said, "Wandel and me sneaked into to the far station and got far helmets and put them on the Three Wise Men. Then we crossed the street and sat on the Bank steps, waited to see what would happen. Sure enough, a fellow from out of town stopped his car and yelled to us, 'Why are there fire helmets on the Three Wise Men? Don't folks around here know anything about the Bible?' Wandel answered him, 'Well sir, we read our Bible carefully and it says that the Three Wise Men came from a far.' We liked to split our sides laughing."

I laughed along with everybody else, although down deep I felt a great sadness. Lorna C laughed too, but tears filled her eyes. Then she asked me to help her with dessert and get some plates from the kitchen. When I opened the cabinet doors I remembered Wandel standing at that very spot getting plates. My eyes filled with tears and my stomach jerked so hard I gasped.

45

After the potluck, Lorna C closed the restaurant, though not just for the night. I watched for the lights to come on again, but the place remained dark for a couple of weeks. After she reopened the restaurant, Lorna C worked only once in a while. Bertha Benson ran the place. One day I stopped in for a RC Cola. Bertha sat in the first booth, alone. She wore her usual light blue work dress and her heavy body stretched the dress's seams to their limit. She had covered her wavy black and gray hair with a light blue net—Bertha said that health regulations required her to wear it when she cooked food.

I asked about Lorna C and Bertha replied, "Lorna C told me she learned that Union Chemical was advertising in the Charleston newspapers for people to work in the factory. She figured she could do something for the war effort and at the same time honor Wandel by going to work there."

Lorna C put the restaurant up for sale and Bertha Benson bought it. The neon "Miss Kettle's Place" sign came down, replaced by a simple black and white sign with a single light on either side of it: "Bertha's Place." Each side of the sign also had painted on it a large bottle of RC Cola.

Lorna C moved to Charleston and lived near her new job at Union Chemical. After the war ended she continued to live there, though we heard that she got an office job in the State Capitol. Albert Newcomb said, "Half of the men in Kettle put aside work to come in the restaurant and stare at Lorna C. Can you imagine the men in the State House? They ain't got much to do anyways. I'll bet every chance they get they're in Lorna C's office hangin' out and gawkin' at her. I'd give my good leg to have her back here."

Albert surprised everybody and bought Wandel's red Dodge three-quarter-ton pickup truck from Lorna C, a purchase that helped him improve his free-lance business. On each of the truck's two doors he had painted in gold letters trimmed in black, "Albert Newcomb, no job too small." Albert rigged a shoe to fit on the end of his peg leg—that allowed him to successfully negotiate the truck's clutch for the shifting of gears. Otherwise he drove just like anybody else. "The right leg does most of the work anyway," Albert said.

After the war ended William White and I got all wrapped up in our lives at Kettle High School and my memories of the summer of nineteen and forty-four began to take their place alongside everything else that happened over the next four years at school.

About two weeks before graduation in the spring of forty-eight, William White pounded on my front door a little after ten o'clock at night. All out of breath, he told me that he and Billy Joe Wheeler had been at the A&W Drive-In in Charleston. While they sat there eating hot dogs and drinking root beer, in came Wandel's, now Albert's, red pickup truck with Albert Newcomb behind the wheel. A woman who looked like Lorna C sat beside him. We stayed on the front porch until just after eleven o'clock and speculated on the possibility that Albert Newcomb had begun to spark Lorna C, something neither of us could believe.

The next day at noon hour, while William White, Beverly, and I walked to the cafeteria, he mentioned Albert's sparking Lorna C. Beverly threw a steely glance at me then turned to William White and said, "Well, well, a local beauty may be gone. Will Kettle's boys live through their disappointment?"

Our speculation about Lorna C ended late one afternoon about a week later when the *Kettle News Leader* arrived on our front porch. In the lower right portion of page one was a story that Lorna Comstock Meyers and Albert Newcomb had been married in Charleston and would live there. Lorna C and Albert Newcomb? Married? My stomach contracted and my breath grew short. I sat down in a porch chair. Why had she done it?

A few minutes later I walked into the living room. Momma had seated herself in her favorite chair, beside the table with her reading lamp. She first asked me to hand her the paper, then she paused, stared at me for a moment, and said, "Freddy, you look like you just lost your best friend. Is something wrong?"

I went up to my room and shut the door, recalled the evening at Miss Kettle's Place after Wandel's memorial service. How the food and stories we shared had nourished us, lifted each other's sorrow. At the end of the evening, how everybody, even William White, had hugged Lorna C and kissed her on the cheek as they left the restaurant.

I had been the last person to leave. Lorna C turned out the lights and for a moment the two of us stood in the doorway. I put my arms around her to say goodbye and she gently hugged me. Then her arms lingered, stayed around me. The length of her body rested against mine and she turned her face towards me. Her lips gently parted and her eyes closed as her face neared mine.

William White's words echoed inside my thoughts, "She cast the gaze of her beautiful brown eyes first towards my leg that had just touched hers, then slowly turned and looked right into my eyes. She leaned forward, her lips parted ever so slightly and she half-closed her eyes."

I wanted to place my lips on hers and tightly press our bodies together. I wanted to gently undress her. And I knew she wanted me.

Chapter 3

RADICALS

The words chalked on our classroom blackboard carried a disturbing message, one I'd never before read. Or heard—never even thought about. I knew who wrote the words but I didn't know what to do about it.

Just over an hour earlier I had awakened with a start, afraid I'd overslept. The old wind-up alarm clock beside my bed read ten minutes till six. Most days I'd roll over and nap ten more minutes. That morning I jumped up and dressed in the blue jeans and red checked shirt I'd laid out last night; tried without much success to comb my mop of red-brown hair. I'd finished my orange juice and a bowl of Wheaties when Momma and Daddy, still in their pajamas and all sleepy-eyed, came into the kitchen. "You're up early," Daddy said. "Special day?" Momma asked.

The blue sky and crisp air seemed right for election day at Kettle High School. I walked to school at a fast pace. The bright sun lit Kettle High's yellow brick walls and reflected off the building's large front windows. I passed through the columns of the main entrance and thought about how in a few hours, during homeroom period, we'd cast our votes for the nineteen and forty-five Homecoming Queen and her Court. In our class we had a hot contest between Betty Lou Sovine and Cricket Hobson for sophomore class Attendant. I served on the Homecoming Election Committee and had a special responsibility that morning to check the home rooms and make sure the ballots and ballot boxes had been distributed. I did my job. In the center of each teacher's desk sat a stack of ballots and a box wrapped in orange and black crepe paper. Each box had a white sign with red letters, "Homecoming Ballot Box," and the teacher's name.

When I had completed my check of all the home rooms I walked to Mr. Johnson's room for first period history class. I stopped in the hallway just outside the door. Inside Cricket Hobson stood alone, writing on the blackboard. Her height, nearly six feet, placed the top of Cricket's head near the upper edge of the blackboard. To Cricket's left the board still displayed the Mr. Johnson's list of historical events, part of a week-long lesson he called "West Virginia enters the twentieth century." We'd have to memorize his list for a test.

1898 Spanish American War: West Virginia raises two regiments of volunteer infantry
1901 Governor George W. Atkinson requests the Legislature to name a state flower
1904 Davis and Elkins College established at Elkins
1905 Morgantown incorporated
1909 White Sulphur Springs incorporated
1910 Weirton Steel Company begins operations

After Cricket finished writing on the board she walked to her desk, sat down and opened her notebook. Cricket's list went down a different road from Mr. Johnson's list, and told of things we'd not talked about in class—things I'd never heard anybody talk about

.

Real History—The West Virginia Coal Mines Wars
1902 Mother Jones campaigns to unionize 7,000 miners in Kanawha Valley

And men died in underground explosions and cave-ins –

1906   January 4: 22 miners killed at Coaldale mine in Mercer County

       January 18: 18 miners killed at Detroit mine in Kanawha County

       February 8: 23 miners killed at Parral mine in Fayette County

       March 22: 23 miners killed at Century mine in Barbour County

       January 29: 84 miners killed at Stuart in Fayette County

       February 4: 25 miners killed at Thomas mine in Tucker County

       December 6: 362 miners killed at Monongah—worst mine disaster in US history

1909   January 12: 67 miners killed at Switchback mine in McDowell County

I walked into the room and went to my desk. Shortly after I sat down other kids came in. Most days we had lots to talk about before class. But that day everybody stared at the list, though only I knew Cricket had written it. No one spoke. Cricket looked up from her books and gave the list a wide-eyed stare, like she had never seen it before.

Mr. Johnson, in the brown gabardine suit and brown necktie he wore on Tuesdays and Thursdays, walked into the room. He stopped about halfway from the door to his desk, pushed his thick glasses up the ridge of his nose, and joined us in staring at the new list. After a moment Mr. Johnson walked to the blackboard, picked up an eraser, and wiped the right half of the board clean. My gaze stayed riveted to the section of the board where Cricket's list had been, as if the words remained but had become temporarily invisible.

Mr. Johnson turned, faced the class and then, peering through what William White called his Coke-bottle-lens glasses, looked at each of us. His lips frowned downwards and his eyebrows arched upwards. At one point he looked me squarely in the eyes. One by one he did the same to everybody in the room. "I don't suppose whoever among you wrote that… that…," he paused, "that list on the board, will stand up." When he said the word "list" he hissed it, lissst. "Or will you?"

Cricket had no expression on her face. She sat there as cool as a cucumber, her eyes on Mr. Johnson. My insides churned. Should I raise my hand? In the movies James Cagney called anyone who squealed on his friends to the cops "a rat." I didn't want to be a rat. Still, I knew who wrote the list, and it bothered me.

I didn't want to look at Mr. Johnson. But if I didn't look at him, he might think I wrote the list. I eased my eyes back to Mr. Johnson. I first looked at the gold key chain across his brown vest, and then inched my gaze up to his round face. When I got to his eyes my breath stopped for an instant. He had his eyes aimed directly at me. I tried to look like I just remembered something important, ducked my head and studied a page in my notebook. My cheeks heated up.

Mr. Johnson spoke sternly, his voice a deeper bass than usual, "I won't have that radical….lissst…in this room. Don't let it happen again."

He studied some notes on his desk. After a minute he looked up, licked his lips, and gave us big smile so big I could see a thin line of brown stain along the tops of his upper teeth. "Now, we'll get on with American history in the early twentieth century, and West Virginia."

On the blackboard where Cricket's list had been he wrote,

1912   Prohibition becomes effective
       The Beckley fire
1913   Thousands homeless in Huntington and Parkersburg
       due to Ohio River flooding in March

That morning we heard a lot about the Beckley fire. Mr. Johnson had grown up in Beckley and accepted his first teaching job there, the year the fire occurred. The fire took out both sides of Heber Street for quite a few blocks, including Mr. Johnson's school. He told us he lost all of his teaching notes and lesson plans. Most of downtown Beckley had burned, along with many of homes. Mr. Johnson said people believed that radicals, organizers for the United Mine Workers, set the fire to burn down a building that housed the Mountain Coal Company.

I made a decision to keep quiet, at least for now, about Cricket's writing the radical list. But my decision troubled me. After all, I saw her do it. And Mr. Johnson asked, "Who did it?" I didn't want to be a rat, but I didn't like knowing the truth and not telling it.

After lunch hour I walked the long corridor to our homeroom with Beverly Shade. Although the milk-glass globes dangling from the corridor's ceiling were lit, the bright sun shining in the window at the end of the corridor made the hallway seem dark. The darkness got a boost from the dark green paint half-way up each corridor wall.

At the Kettle Fourth of July celebration the summer of forty-five, I had found myself looking into Beverly's blue eyes when the two of us tried to get red raspberry juice stain out of my white shirt. Not long afterwards I invited her to go to a movie with me. We had continued to date, though not every weekend. This coming Friday night we'd go to the homecoming dance together. With the war just over, this year's homecoming would be special. Some of the Kettle boys who had returned from overseas service would be there.

Walking into homeroom, Beverly and I talked about the election. The orange and black ballot box sat on the teacher's desk between the door and the large windows on the far side of the room. My Momma had been elected Attendant to the Queen during her junior year at Kettle High School, nineteen and twenty-five. On our piano we had a picture of her and Daddy at the homecoming celebration. Momma wore a fluffy gown and Daddy a dark suit. Momma held Daddy's arm.

Beverly and I turned towards the sounds of somebody running lickety-split down the hall. William White Wallace ran to us, red-faced and out of breath.

"Freddy, Ralph Persinger just punched me on the shoulder and told me to vote for Cricket Hobson. He said if Betty Lou Sovine gets elected he's going to whip my ass—that my name is first on his list."

I shook my head. "William White, ever since the finalists were announced, Ralph Persinger has been telling everybody, including you and me, to vote for Cricket Hobson, and he'd whip our asses if we didn't. You're just on his list again for today."

Beverly put her hand on my arm and said, "Freddy, what those boys are doing is wrong. I wish you could find a way to stop the whole thing." She walked into home room.

I knew a way to stop it, all right.

I tried to get my thoughts around the possibility of pimple-faced Ralph Persinger beating up on all the boys in the sophomore class. Ralph had a stocky and strong body, but he ate too much candy and carried lots of fat. About then Cricket Hobson walked past us into homeroom. Her coarse straight black hair, cut short with bangs, seemed to form a block around her head. Cricket had long arms and legs. William White once said, "Freddy, remember Olive Oyl in the Popeye comic strip? I think Cricket looks like her."

Shortly after Cricket had been born, her Momma, Orpha Ball Hobson, took one look at her little baby's long arms and legs and big brown eyes, and said, "Honey, you look like a cricket." Cricket is her given name.

The Hobsons lived on a small farm up on Cedar Creek. One side of their farm butted up against Ermil Goad's big spread. Whenever Ermil Goad came to Gruber's Store, always wearing his brown derby and blue-and-white-striped coveralls, he'd take a seat by the stove and folks would hear about his lingering bother with Cricket's Daddy, Pinetar Hobson. Ermil Goad would lean forward in his chair, push the old dusty derby back on his head, and say to anyone who would listen, "I told him, whether through design or neglect, Pinetar Hobson, your farm is a breeding ground for tobacco worms. A sinkhole full of green and yellow slinkys, that's what it is. And them worms are a direct threat to my cash crop."

One summer evening before school started, Daddy and I sat after supper in the glider on our front porch. That afternoon I had bought some eggs for Momma at Gruber's. Ermil Goad had been there, sitting in a chair beside the pickle barrel and complaining about Pinetar Hobson. I asked Daddy about Mr. Goad's problem. Daddy stretched out his long legs, ran his hands through his reddish-brown hair, and told me that during the growing season everybody who raised tobacco had problems with tobacco worms. "Maybe Ermil Goad just wanted to blame somebody," he added. Daddy said as far as he knew, Pinetar minded his own business and took care of his tobacco crop and vegetable garden.

Then Daddy squinted his eyes and continued, "Freddy, in the early winter of nineteen and twenty one, after some trouble in the coalfields down around Logan as well as in Mingo and McDowell counties, some miners and their families, including Pinetar Hobson, moved up here and settled on Cedar Creek. Pinetar was a young man then. As I recall his first wife had died before he moved here. He worked on farms around town, and then bought his small farm. Some of the kids from those families were in classes with your Momma and me at Kettle High.

"The miners who moved up here had been through a difficult time. They'd been trying to organize the union in the coalfields and fighting had broken out, though it wasn't the first time fighting had occurred."

I remembered the times Momma, Daddy, and I drove the curvy roads through the steep mountains of Logan County to visit relatives. Sometimes I got carsick from all the sharp turns. "What were they fighting about?" I asked.

"The mines were unsafe places, Freddy. Still are, though not as bad as back then. Down in the mines there was bad air and dangerous work. Sometimes there were explosions from methane gas. At other times, roof-falls and cave-ins. Many men died. Lots of men were injured."

"Like Albert Newcomb losing his leg in a mine?" I asked.

"That's right, though I think Albert got run over by a coal car. And to make matters worse, miners were paid low wages and then had to shell out money to buy their own tools. Sometimes they even had to buy the dynamite to blast out the rock and coal underground."

"They paid for it out of their own pockets, I mean their own money?"

"Yep. And the coal companies built towns with small homes they rented to the miners who worked for them. And they built company stores to sell the miners groceries, clothes and tools. Most of the miners' wages went right back to the company.

"How'd the miners ever get a little ahead?" I asked.

"Lots of them, maybe most, never did. In eighteen and ninety-three there was a miners' uprising over wages and safety. A company of National Guard troops ordered to deal with the miners made their camp right here in Kettle and traveled by rail down to the coalfields.

"Where'd they camp?"

"In the flat land just on the other side of Sour Apple River, on the road to Broke Hill."

I made a mental note to tell William White about the camp. We might find bullets or camp items the soldiers left behind.

"Things quieted down until nineteen and twenty-one. That year miners and coal operators fought skirmishes along the Tug River, between West Virginia and Kentucky. Then the fighting spread. Many of those miners had served in World War One, and were no strangers to armed combat. A year earlier, nineteen and twenty, the coal operators had called in outside help from the Baldwin-Felts Detective Agency. The agency's men assembled in Matewan, a town where the miners were well organized.

"We went to Matewan one time, didn't we?"

"Yes, we drove right past the place where the Baldwin-Felts men tried to serve what they said were arrest warrants on some of the miners. The local police chief, Sid Hatfield, took the side of the miners and stood up to the operators and Baldwin-Felts men. He said the warrants weren't legal and they couldn't arrest anybody. Nobody knew who fired the first shot, but there was a shootout. Didn't last three minutes, but ten men were killed, including the Mayor of Matewan, Cable Testerman.

"Ten, shot dead?"

"That's right. And a couple of months later, on the front steps of the McDowell County Court House, a Baldwin-Felts man shot Sid Hatfield dead. He claimed self-defense, but eye-witnesses said otherwise. That triggered serious fighting and it came to a head at the Battle of Blair Mountain.

"I know where Blair Mountain is, but I never heard about a battle there," I said. The highway from Boone County to Logan, the county seat of Logan County, passed down a valley overlooked by Blair Mountain.

Daddy's face reddened a little and his face grew tense as he described how Logan County Sheriff Don Chafin had hired and deputized large numbers of men. Local men out of work, college students home for the summer, even teachers. Hundreds of men came in by train, some from other parts of the country. In late August of nineteen and twenty-one Chafin commanded an army of deputies, Baldwin-Felts detectives, and the Volunteer State Police of West Virginia, along with much of the West Virginia National Guard. The U.S. Army's 10th Infantry Division had arrived too, though not authorized to fight.

Daddy said that Chafin's army, thousands of men armed to the teeth, defended the Logan County side of Blair Mountain. Thousands of miners had organized themselves in Boone County and set about to march to Logan and take on Sheriff Chafin and his men. As they approached Chafin's army, the miners spread out through the thick woods and climbed the steep Boone County side of Blair Mountain. Both sides opened fire and fought on the mountain.

Daddy's long face became even longer, and drawn. He told me that the U.S. Army had brought airplanes with them—that the Battle of Blair Mountain had been the only time in American history when our government dropped bombs on U.S. citizens.

"The battle lasted three days. On the third day President Harding authorized the Army to enter the conflict. When the troops arrived the miners drifted back into the woods, then off the mountain. The mine owners' victory made it possible for them to keep the United Mine Workers out of southern West Virginia, at least until after Franklin Roosevelt was elected president."

"Was Pinetar one of the miners at Blair Mountain?" I asked.

"I think so. Most of the miners who moved to Cedar Creek were at Blair Mountain."

Pinetar, short and thin, had coarse black hair that he slicked down and combed straight back. He had dark eyes and high cheekbones. Some folks around town said they thought he had Indian blood in him—Cherokee, Hartford Wilson claimed. One Saturday afternoon on Main Street, Pinetar walked past William White and me and we spoke to him. Folks customarily greeted each other when passing on the streets of Kettle. But Pinetar looked straight ahead and walked on. William White leaned towards me and said in a low Indian-like voice, "Still water run deep, ugh."

Cricket, the youngest of three sisters, had been a member of our class since first grade. But even by the tenth grade I didn't know her very well. Each day, year in, year out, Cricket rode the early bus to school, attended classes, and then rode the bus home. In class she rarely spoke unless a teacher called on her. Cricket liked to read and had done well in her studies, though on exams she hadn't placed at the top of the class. If we had class projects Cricket joined a group of her friends from Cedar Creek. William White called them "The Cedar Creek Gang." The girls wore cotton print dresses made from the large bags that feed and grain came in. At noon the little group ate together at a table on the far left side of the cafeteria and kept pretty much to themselves.

Miss Isabel B. Mounts, librarian at Kettle High School, taught the junior high girls' bible class at the Kettle Methodist Church Sunday School. One Sunday morning she said something about Cricket to her Sunday School class that Beverly Shade passed on to me as a direct quote from Miss Mounts. Beverly even tried to make her voice go into a high-pitched sing-song tone, like Miss Mounts, though she fell a little short of an exact copy. I helped her out by imagining Miss Mounts's round face, bobbed brown hair, black dress, and wire-rimmed glasses. "When I think of a good example of a young woman who leads a life of dignified simplicity, a young woman who is clean, moral, and in her proper place in the natural order of things, I think of Cricket Hobson. Her life is, perhaps, uneventful, but it is one in which a girl, indeed all girls, can take pride."

At four o'clock that Tuesday, election day, William White, Susie Mac—that is, Susan MacLendon—and I walked into the Kettle High School library. The library had nearly a thousand books placed on the light oak shelves that lined the room's walls. Oak tables, each seating six students, had been placed in rows of two the length of the large rectangular room. Miss Mounts positioned her desk near the front door, along with the index card files, wooden drawers crammed with cards bearing information on each of the library's books.

William White, Susie Mac and I had been appointed the ballot counters for the election. William White volunteered himself for anything that put him close to Susie Mac, and in this case he volunteered me too. Susie Mac had curly blonde hair and sparkling blue eyes. But most of all she had a well-endowed figure. William White said he knew for a fact that she wore the largest bra of all the girls in the sophomore class. I wondered how he knew.

When we walked into the library, Miss Isabel B. Mounts sat behind her desk carefully wiping the lenses of her glasses with a tissue. Miss Mounts sometimes interrupted study halls in the library to remind kids who wore glasses to clean them—she maintained that unclean glasses lens had been proven to be a prime cause of pinkeye.

We stood in front of her desk while Miss Mounts completed her lens cleaning. She held the glasses up to the light for inspection, then wiped them some more, held them up, back and forth. Her glasses had thin gold wire frames, the only color other than black or white that adorned Miss Mounts. Finally she gave us an approving smile, placed her glasses on her nose and with each hand pushed the temple pieces over her ears. Then she placed the tissue inside the front of her black dress, behind the lace at the center of her ample bosom, with one corner of the tissue sticking out of the lace. I got so caught up in Miss Mounts' lens cleaning and tissue placement that I nearly forgot why we had come to the library.

"Let's get started," she said, then took a deep breath, "and remember that whether in a school, town or state election, what you are about to do is a bedrock practice in our democracy." She pushed the three large square boxes covered with orange and black crepe paper across her desk towards us. One box had the label, "Queen Ballots," and the other two boxes had labels of "Junior Class Attendant Ballots" and "Sophomore Class Attendant Ballots."

Miss Mounts then pursed her lips, which she often did whenever she studied on something, and watched us count. We first counted the ballots for election of the queen, though I had no doubt about the outcome. June Ann Morris had been the favorite to win over Lola Sue Murrell, and sure enough, she won in a landslide.

At the school assembly when the candidates had been introduced, June Ann's curly black hair, bright blue eyes, and warm smile gave her a special beauty. When June Ann's opponent, Lola Sue, stood up, her red hair had glistened under the stage lights and her face turned a deep crimson. Her lower lip quivered and she thanked everybody for making her a finalist. Then she paused and flashed a big smile and said, "I myself am voting for June Ann Morris, and I hope you will too!"

For a moment the auditorium remained stone silent. Then the large room filled with a sudden burst of applause accompanied by whistling and stomping of feet. It continued for nearly a full minute.

Miss Mounts introduced the junior class finalists, Ruthie Southworth and Vera Mae Bledsoe, majorettes in the Kettle High marching band. Both of them had long black hair and wore their orange and black majorette uniforms with short skirts to the school assembly. At a distance I could hardly tell them apart. Ruthie and Vera Mae grinned and hugged each other, and then each of them pointed to the other and said "Vote for her." Everybody laughed, even our principal, Mr. Lawton.

We tallied the votes with special care. The Ruthie-Vera Mae contest ran neck-and-neck. Ruthie won, but by only a few votes.

William White, Susie Mac, and I then turned our attention to the sophomore class ballots, our class's representative in the Queen's Court. Betty Lou had let everybody know she wanted the honor and I figured that a lot of kids at Kettle High would feel she deserved it. William White and I sometimes wondered how Betty Lou Sovine always got selected for one or another honor. William White argued that Betty Lou had to be a born leader, at least among girls. Last year she had been voted "Freshman Girl Who Has Done Most for Kettle High School." At the sock hop the week before the homecoming election Betty Lou had danced with each of the girls and every boy who would dance with her.

She'd drawn the attention of boys since early in the sixth grade when she began to develop pretty curves. Her blue eyes, blonde hair, always carefully styled, and near-perfectly formed lips gave her a look of beauty, though the look was offset a little by her long thin nose.

One time in the sixth grade I stood in line at the pencil sharpener, just behind Betty Lou. When she bent over to pick up a scrap of paper I peeked over the front of her dress. She stood up and stared hard at me. My face felt all hot and red. Then Betty Lou broke into a big smile and said, so loud that everybody in the room could hear her, "Like what you see, Freddy? Take a picture, it'll last longer." A couple of kids in line giggled. Harley Cremeans, chubby and sweaty, stood in line right behind me. He pointed at me and let out with a big laugh, and then everybody in our class joined in.

At the assembly, after Betty Lou Sovine had been introduced she faced the audience, raised both arms waist-high, and motioned for kids to be quiet. She waited for complete silence in the auditorium. Betty Lou's face was so down-turned I thought she might cry.

Betty Lou spoke softly. Some kids leaned forward in their seats to hear her better. "Thank you for this great honor. I love Kettle High School. It will be my life, at least through my senior year, and after that I will come back to visit. And when I am dead and gone I will return to haunt these halls." Betty Lou paused, then sang in a slow romantic whisper, the first two lines of the Kettle High School Fight Song, "Let's give a cheer for Kettle High School, for the colors orange and black ...." Her voice trailed off. She raised her right arm, put her fist in the air and yelled in a feisty voice, "Go, Tops!" Everybody cheered.

Cricket Hobson's election as the other sophomore class finalist surprised me. After Miss Mounts had introduced her at the assembly, Cricket stood, smiled, and nodded to everyone. She looked at the audience, stood a while longer. I wanted her to give a speech, say something. Anything. Finally Cricket said, "Thank you for this honor," then sat down.

After a period of silence, Miss Mounts brought her hands together with a loud smack and began to clap. Other teachers joined her, and then the student body joined them in what I'll call polite applause. In the background Ralph Persinger and members of the football team laughed and yelled, "Go, Cricket!" and "Way to tell 'em, Cricket!" and things like that. Mr. Lawton whirled around with a scowl on his face and scanned the audience. I hoped Cricket didn't hear Ralph and his friends, but her smile had disappeared. Later one of the girls in the Cedar Creek Gang said to her, "Cricket, you done real good."

We counted the ballots and stacked them on Miss Mounts's desk beside the name of each candidate. To my surprise, Betty Lou Sovine lagged way behind Cricket Hobson. I couldn't believe it. From "Most Popular Freshman Girl" to just a handful of votes in the tenth grade—Betty Lou Sovine?

Susie Mac held the last ballot above the name of Cricket Hobson, and then released it. We watched the rectangular piece of paper float downwards and come to rest on top of Cricket's large stack of ballots. During the downward movement of the ballot, the pursed lips of Miss Mounts ceased to purse. Her full lips parted so slowly they stuck together in places for a few seconds, like an old Band-Aid being pulled off my arm. Miss Mounts's jaw moved downward and her mouth dropped fully open the moment the ballot came to rest on the stack. Eyes wide, she stared at the pile of ballots and gaped, a full, open-mouthed gape.

William White and Susie Mac fixed their gaze on the pile of ballots. Susie Mac's arm remained extended over the ballots and she swayed sidewise in the slow rhythm of the falling paper. Susie Mac's movements resembled the hula dance of Esther Williams in a movie at the Dixie Palace when she pretended to be a native Hawaiian dancer in order to fool Ricardo Montalban who pretended to be a wealthy trader from Spain. Susie Mac, swaying, William White, staring, and Miss Mounts, gaping. For a moment I wondered if some invisible force had us in its power, suspending everything except swaying, gaping, and staring.

The spell ended when Miss Mounts sucked in a wad of air then forcefully exhaled it, saying, "Well, I never..." Her mouth slammed shut and her lips locked as tight as the little curls on the back of her head.

Cricket Hobson—elected sophomore class Attendant to the nineteen and forty-five Homecoming Queen? I tried to imagine her posing for a *Kettle News Leader* photograph. Or riding on our sophomore class float in Friday afternoon's Homecoming parade. Or standing in the center of the football field during the half-time ceremony at Friday night's game. A member of the Queen's Court at the Homecoming dance?

My thoughts turned back to the minutes before our first-period history class and Cricket's writing what Mr. Johnson called a "radical lissst" on the board. Should I tell Mr. Johnson? Miss Mounts? Should I tell anybody? Daddy once told me that when I had doubts about telling something, I probably shouldn't tell it. So far, that's what I had done—had I done the right thing?

Cricket had written the list for her own reasons, and kept it to herself. If I told her secret most likely I would bring trouble to her, maybe even cost her the election. Cricket hadn't been a close friend, but I felt a responsibility to protect her secret. But I had a responsibility as a Kettle High student too—to tell the truth to teachers, even Mr. Johnson.

Cricket's surprising election had been part of a plot fertilized, incubated, and hatched by Ralph Persinger. Ralph had joined our class after his Daddy retired and his family moved to Kettle about a year ago. He had brown hair and a muscular but chubby body, and acne spread around his face. Ralph had an older brother in the Army. Ralph's Daddy had owned and operated two coal mines down in Logan County. Sometimes Ralph bragged about how his Daddy bossed the miners around and showed them a thing or two when they tried to bring in the union. "I'll do the same thing if I ever get a chance," Ralph always added.

Last year, shortly after he had entered Kettle High, Ralph met Betty Lou Sovine and decided right then and there that he wanted to marry her. "Betty Lou is the prettiest girl in our class, and she's mine," he told the boys. Ralph told his friends that he and Betty Lou should date some so she could learn to feel the love for him that he felt for her. Ralph said to Billy Swan Ronk that he believed way down deep Betty Lou really liked him a lot, maybe already loved him. Billy Swan, short and skinny, had come to admire Ralph. Although he and Ralph claimed each other as best friends, Billy Swan told William White, who told me, that Ralph had asked Betty Lou to go to a movie four times, and each time she said no.

In September, right before we had nominated girls for Homecoming Queen and her Court, Ralph had sat alongside Betty Lou in art class. Very politely he said, "Betty Lou, would you please pass me the art gum eraser?" When she handed him the eraser he leaned over and with a loud smack planted a wet kiss on her lips. Betty Lou screamed, wiped her lips and yelled, "Yuck!" Then she ran to the teacher, who told Ralph to go to Mr. Lawton's office.

Ralph walked to the classroom door, then stopped and turned to the class. In a loud voice he said, "I was just givin' her a little of what she wanted. Right, Betty Lou?" then he slammed the door behind him.

Later that afternoon William White and I had been in the boys' locker room getting dressed for phys-ed class. A couple of lockers away, Ralph stood naked, holding his jock strap in one hand. He grinned and yelled at everybody to watch, and then put his jock strap on backwards over his head, with the strap around his forehead and the pouch on the back of his head. Then he said, "Betty Lou winked at me in art class—I believe this here is what she wants." He put one hand underneath his privates and rubbed his member until it began to come to life. He acted like he had a new friend who wanted to meet everybody. With the guidance of Ralph's hand, his long friend nodded his head up and down in a greeting to each of us.

William White and I pulled on our shorts and gym shoes and got out of there. He said, "Sometimes Ralph scares me."

Ralph scared me too. One day he had pushed me out of his way as we came in the front door of Kettle High. Then Ralph turned towards me, like he expected me to do something back to him. I yelled at William White, a few steps ahead of me, to wait and then ran past Ralph. I wondered if I should have stood up to Ralph. Maybe if I had, and if other kids had, he'd have gotten tired of bullying everybody and doing the dumb things he did.

For a couple of days after he kissed Betty Lou, Ralph would buttonhole anybody who would listen and talked about how, down deep, Betty Lou liked, maybe loved, him. None of us had the courage to call him a liar. Ralph weighed nearly two hundred pounds and as a sophomore he had won the first team center position on the Kettle High football team. Sometimes Ralph would walk up behind a guy smaller than him and grab the back of the fellow's underpants and jerk them tight up against the guy's crotch. He did it so hard and fast the guy would gasp and yell, and Ralph and his buddies would laugh. Most of the fellows he grabbed never stuck around after Ralph let go of them. Ralph liked a fistfight.

Ralph kept his hair in place with liberal doses of oily Vaseline hair tonic. One time, sitting in a booth at Bertha's Place, he had leaned his head against the wall while he talked to his friends. When he sat up the wallpaper had a big oil spot. Bertha saw it, got all upset and told him to never do that again. After she had turned to walk to the front counter Ralph made a face at her and gave her the finger. All the guys in the booth laughed.

William White told me he had learned from Billy Swan that Ralph decided to get even with Betty Lou after what happened that day in art class. Ralph's first idea had been to find a girl to run for sophomore class Homecoming Attendant who could beat Betty Lou in a one-on-one contest. But he hadn't been able to find the right girl to do it.

Then, and William White said Billy Swan beamed when he told this part of the story, Ralph developed what he called his reversal strategy. "We'll elect a girl whose victory will bring the high and mighty Miss Betty Lou Sovine—Miss Betty Lou Bovine—off her throne. The plainest, simplest girl in our class. A girl who hasn't never done nothin' for Kettle High School, and who isn't ever likely to." Billy Swan said Ralph spoke just two words, "Cricket Hobson."

When Cricket's name first had appeared as a candidate, everybody smiled and acted like it was a nice thing. "After all," Betty Lou Sovine said, "Cricket has never had an honor, and this is awfully nice for her."

At the introduction of candidates in classes or school assemblies, Cricket smiled and seemed proud. She always had her hair combed and wore a clean dress. Afterwards the girls in the Cedar Creek Gang would tell her, "You done real good," and Cricket would smile.

Ralph had convinced the sophomore boys on the football team to join him in his campaign. He told them to do whatever it took to get votes for Cricket or they'd answer to him. Lots of the players took smaller boys aside and said, "You better vote for Cricket or Ralph'll getcha." The junior and senior football players had laughed about it, but still told kids to do it as a joke.

And Ralph had done his part. Before school each morning he had gone around telling the boys in our class, "You, and your girl friend too, better vote for Cricket or I'll whip your ass."

At lunch in the cafeteria the day after Mr. Lawton announced the finalists in the election, I sat at a table near Ralph and some boys on the football team. They laughed about Cricket's making it to the finals and spouted a lot of pride in their political handiwork.

We finished our count of the ballots. Cricket had won the election—she would be the sophomore class Attendant in the Queen's Court. Miss Isabel B. Mounts nodded at Susie Mac, William White, and me. Behind the lens of her glasses her eyes closed and opened in two prolonged eye-bats. "This is quite a surprise," she said, "one I am not sure is in the best interests of Kettle High School." She turned and walked at a fast pace to the black intercom speaker mounted on the wall, pushed the toggle switch down and spoke into it in a slow and serious manner. "Mr. Lawton, Mr. Lawton." Miss Mounts then returned the toggle switch to its up position, and held it between her thumb and index finger as though it had a life of its own.

In a few seconds we heard an electronic squeak and the voice of Mr. Lawton. "Yes, Miss Mounts?"

"Please come to the library as soon as possible. I think we have a difficulty—a problem in the order of things."

After she had toggled the switch to its up position, Miss Mounts let her fingers rest on the toggle switch for a moment and stared at the intercom speaker.

What problem did we have in the order of things? Sure, Cricket lived up on Cedar Creek where those former miners settled, but like it or not she had been elected. Maybe if I had spoken up about what happened in Mr. Johnson's room the outcome of the election would have been different. But I didn't, and the results stood. Leaving Ralph Persinger out of it, Cricket won something important. Tall, skinny, and shy, Cricket didn't have the good looks of Betty Lou Sovine. But she won.

When Mr. Lawton walked in the door of the library, his grey suit coat unbuttoned and his salt and pepper hair mussed. Miss Mounts asked us to leave. I could have stayed and told Mr. Lawton about Cricket's list, but I didn't.

The morning after the election, a Wednesday, when I walked into Mr. Johnson's classroom Cricket and the Cedar Creek Gang had taken their seats. The word must have gotten out about Cricket's winning the election. She had a big grin on her face and her friends beamed. One of them held Cricket's hand. Betty Lou Sovine rested her head on her desk.

The blackboard still had Mr. Johnson's list: Prohibition, the Beckley fire, the Huntington flood. Beside it another "radical list" had been written, covering the identical years as Mr. Johnson's most recent list. It had the same handwriting as the list on Tuesday.

Real History—The West Virginia Coal Mines Wars

1912 Paint Creek and Cabin Creek miners strike to get recognition of the United Mine Workers of America
Governor Glasscock declares martial law three times, sends troops
March 26: 83 killed in underground mine disaster at Jed
September 21: Mother Jones leads march of miners' children through Charleston

1913 February 12: Mother Jones leads protest of mine conditions and is arrested
May 8: Mother Jones released from jail

Mr. Johnson walked in, looked at the new list, and erased it. Then he made us hold out our hands, palms up. He walked around the room inspecting us for chalk dust. He didn't find any.

"We seem to have a secret radical here among us. One who wants to be a history teacher." Mr. Johnson jabbed his American history book towards us and lowered his voice, "Maybe it's one of you that done this, maybe it isn't. But sooner or later I'll know. You can count on that, just like the sun rising tomorrow morning. It's only a matter of time. Count on it."

By then he had walked to his desk at the front of the room. He paused and his expression softened. He looked around the room, licked his lips and smiled a narrow and stretched out smile that reminded me of a fox eating yellow jackets. "And once the truth is known, I'll deal with the child who did this. Only a child would consider this sordid side of our great state's history worthy of even mentioning." His voice began to rise. "And I'll deliver to our wayward child the one thing a child understands, or my name is not Veloit Velmer Johnson." He paused and cast his large eyes around the room. A loud crack sounded as he slammed his history book on the desk with so much force the floor shook.

After a brief silence, Ralph Persinger raised his hand.

"Yes, Ralph?"

"Mr. Johnson, everybody knows we had Reds, Communists, among the UMW organizers down in the coalfields. Maybe there's one here at Kettle High. A Red, I mean. When you find out who wrote this stuff on our blackboard I hope you'll have 'em arrested. That's what my Daddy done when he found some organizers who was working in his mines."

What if I'd reported Cricket to Mr. Johnson—would she have been arrested? Had Cricket broken the law when she wrote her lists? Had I broken the law by not speaking up? Would I be arrested too? A little shiver ran deep inside of me.

All through the day my secret about Cricket weighed on me. I needed to talk to somebody. I could tell William White but I didn't think he'd be able to help. And he might blab the whole thing to somebody. My Daddy might know what to do, but I wondered if he'd punish me for breaking the law. One time after I broke a neighbor's window with a baseball, Daddy told me I had to go tell what I'd done and then buy them a new pane of glass. And, worst of all, I couldn't play baseball for a week. Daddy knew right from wrong.

That evening after supper I helped Daddy rake some leaves in the yard. When it got too dark to rake we came in the kitchen and sat down. Momma poured each of us a glass of cold cider and went upstairs. Daddy took off his heavy sweater. He grinned at me and held up his glass in a silent toast. I did the same.

Then I described to Daddy what I saw early on Tuesday morning in Mr. Johnson's classroom, and how Ralph had engineered Cricket's election. What Ralph had said about the person who wrote the lists on the board being a Red—somebody who should be arrested.

Daddy leaned back in his chair and gave me a serious, not angry, look. He took another sip of his cider then told me what Cricket had done in writing her lists hadn't been against the law. He said, "Maybe she broke some rules at school, but not the law." For a moment Daddy looked down at his glass at cider, and then he looked at me. "You're on the front side of a tough choice, Freddy. How do you see it?"

We talked about my responsibilities—to the school and to my friends. I told him I felt loyal to the school, but just couldn't be a tattletale and turn Cricket in. "Still, I'm uneasy about not telling the truth when asked."

"I know you are, Freddy, and I'm proud of you. But I think you've done the right thing by keeping it to yourself, at least for now. Give it a little time. Sometimes hard knots work themselves out in natural ways."

The next morning we had no new—radical—list on the blackboard. Just another Thursday with Mr. Johnson in his brown suit. Mr. Johnson announced, "Today, our lesson is a look at the Great War, and West Virginia before and after it. Nineteen and fourteen to nineteen and twenty four." He picked up a stick of chalk, turned to the board and began to write his new list.

He no longer had to tell us to copy his lists into our notes. While everybody wrote down Mr. Johnson's new list, William White leaned over and whispered, "I'll never remember all this stuff. Maybe I should move to Kentucky."

1914 A glass manufacturing plant, later part of the Owens-Illinois Co., begins operations in Huntington

1915 Supreme Court rules West Virginia owes Virginia more than $12.3 million a debt from the time of separation from Virginia

1916 Amendment allowing suffrage for women rejected in November

1917   US enters World War I. 45,000 West Virginians see active service, 624 are killed in action

1919   Governor Cornwell signs a bill creating the Dept. of Public Safety (W.Va.State Police), the fourth in the nation

1920   Hull of the second West Virginia (Battleship No. 48 to the Navy) was laid

1921   KDKA broadcast the first football game ever on radio, WVU vs. University of Pittsburgh
West Virginia becomes the first state to have a sales tax

1922   International Nickel Company plant begins operations in Huntington

1924   Beckley's first daily newspaper, the *Evening Post*, begins publication

William White and I stayed up late that Thursday night helping our class decorate the gym for the Friday night Homecoming dance. Cricket's election as sophomore class Queen's Attendant seemed the only topic anybody would talk about. Two of Betty Lou's friends made fun of Cricket by pinning their hair up in a box-like shape.

We hung red, white and blue bunting along with crepe paper—mostly orange and black—all over the gym. William White climbed a ladder and dropped crepe paper streamers of all colors from the ceiling lights, and then attached narrow rolls of orange crepe paper to the seating area above one side of the gym floor to the stands on the other side. Once done, the many connecting strands of crepe paper created a new and colorful ceiling over the area of the gym floor where we would dance. One of the teachers smiled and told us the gym looked like a set for a Judy Garland movie. Kids grinned with pride.

On Friday morning William White ran up to me just outside the door to Mr. Johnson's room, all excited. "The radical struck again, Freddy—we got a new list."

71

I muttered, "Dear God, please end this. Make her stop. Amen."

We walked into the room. Not a sound, quiet as church. Everybody stood at the front of the room reading the huge new list that started and ended with the same years as Mr. Johnson's long list from yesterday.

Real History—The West Virginia Coal Mines Wars
More men die underground in explosions, cave-ins—
1914 April 28: 192 killed in mine disaster at Eccles
1915 March 2: 112 killed in mine disaster at Layland
1917 Department of Special Deputy Police, wartime internal security force, established
1919 September: miners march in Logan County to unseat Sheriff Don Chafin, federal forces called in
November, nationwide coal strike
1920 May 19: "Matewan Massacre"—ten people shot to death after Police Chief Sid Hatfield tries to arrest "detectives" (thugs) working for the coal operators. One of the dead is Mayor Cable Testerman (a good man)
Martial law in Mingo County
1921 Three day battle along shores of Tug River
"Volunteer State Police" organized by coal operators
Women and children gunned down in raids on miners' tent settlements
August 1: walking to his trial, Chief Sid Hatfield is shot and killed on steps of McDowell County Courthouse
August 21: National Guard activated
August 25: federal troops and military planes called in
September 3: Battle of Blair Mountain, bombs dropped on miners
May: "Treason Trial" of miners who were in march on Logan and Battle of Blair Mountain

1924   April 28: 119 killed in mine disaster at Benwood
        Number 9

During the time we read the new list, Mr. Johnson had walked into the classroom. He stood behind me and whispered, "Sweet Jesus." Then his bass voice boomed, his words moving air across the back of my neck. "Everybody take your seats."

Everybody sat down and Mr. Johnson stood in front of our class. He looked at us and didn't speak. I checked the clock on the wall above Mr. Johnson's desk, opened my notebook and wrote down the time. I studied "8:07" like it would to be on a test. Mr. Johnson continued to look at us, one by one. Kids shifted around in their seats. I stared at the curly hair on the back of Harley Cremeans head until I got tired of it. I looked up at the clock again and found two minutes had passed—I wrote down the new time and double underlined it.

Finally Mr. Johnson spoke. "I started teaching in nineteen and eleven, just in time for the Beckley fire the following spring. That fire didn't stop me though. I wrote new lesson plans and kept at it. And while us honest, God fearing folks was out there working, the miners was organizing, preparing to shut down all," he raised his voice and repeated, "all," then paused, "of the mines in southern West Virginia. Of course most of us didn't know that. We thought the miners was just going to work like everybody else. But in the darkness underground, and in the darkness of night above ground, serious crimes, even treason, was afoot.

"When the Great War came, I was not allowed to serve. My vision was too poor, the doctors told me. I told 'em it was good enough to play football in high school and I wanted to fight in the Army. But they wouldn't listen." Mr. Johnson told us his opportunity to serve came after the war, in the summers of nineteen and nineteen, twenty and twenty-one.

"I went to Logan County and worked as a deputy for Sheriff Don Chapin. I packed a sidearm and we showed the miners—the radicals, troublemakers, and rednecks with red bandannas around their necks—a thing or two. The law is the law."

His words, "the law is the law," echoed in my thoughts. If Mr. Johnson had been on the side of right, by not speaking up had I put myself on the side of wrong? Daddy's words about hard knots working themselves out came to me.

Mr. Johnson spoke with a touch of pride. "In August and September of twenty-one I lugged supplies up one side of Blair Mountain and carried men, most of 'em wounded and a two of 'em dead, back down the mountain. I sent up smoke signals directing planes towards the rednecks. I hit the ground when the bombs exploded.

"But all that I did, and everything on that radical list you see before you, was just a tiny chirp in the symphony of our great state's history. A tiny and off-key chirp. Hardly worth the space it occupies on the blackboard, or the time it has taken this morning in this classroom."

Mr. Johnson paused and his magnified eyes surveyed the room. "Now, open your books to page one hundred and twenty-three and we'll start today's lesson." He turned to the blackboard. The eraser in his right hand had just touched the first word on the radical list when a soft voice called out from the back of the room, "Mr. Johnson?"

I turned and saw Cricket Hobson standing beside her desk.

"Mr. Johnson, down in Mingo County, in eighteen and ninety, they took my Granddaddy's farm from him—men in shiny suits carrying briefcases. They said the railroad owned all the minerals under his land. Then they took over everything above the ground to get to the coal."

Cricket stopped speaking and her lower lip quivered. When she spoke again her voice cracked. "My Daddy was a coal miner at Switchback. Sixty-seven men he knew died in that mine, but he lived to tell about it. After that he helped miners organize for safety and decent pay."

Mr. Johnson's mouth fell open. Then he sputtered, "I...I...That'll be quite enough out of you, Cricket." He raised himself to his full height and stomped the heel of his right foot hard against the floor. "Sit down and shut up!"

Cricket continued to stand. She said, "When the coal company found out what my Daddy was doing with the other miners, they threw him and his wife and little baby boy out of their house. Daddy moved his family into a tent camp along with other miners thrown out of their homes."

Mr. Johnson's eyes darted around the room, back to Cricket, then around the room again. His face turned a deep red and he spoke in a loud voice, just short of yelling. "I said, young lady, sit down." He began to walk towards her.

Cricket spoke faster and louder, "One night in the middle of the winter, when my Daddy was at a meeting, sheriff's deputies raided the tent camp." Then she screamed, "My Daddy's wife and baby boy were shot to death!"

Mr. Johnson stopped in his tracks.

Cricket paused and looked at Mr. Johnson who looked at her with his big eyes.

Then she spoke softly, "My Daddy stood with Sid Hatfield at Matewan. And he was on the other side of Blair Mountain from you, Mr. Johnson. He was shot in battle, and he killed the man who did it. He was proud of the red bandanna he wore around his neck." Cricket sat down.

The room had a silence that resembled the quiet that settles over Kettle after a hard thunderstorm—you knew something powerful had just happened. I gripped my desk top so tight my knuckles turned white.

Mr. Johnson flipped the toggle switch on his intercom and announced to Mr. Lawton that Cricket Hobson would be coming to the office. Then he yelled at Cricket, "Leave this room, now. Now! Go to the principal's office."

Cricket put her shoulders back and stood straight and tall. She walked towards the classroom door. Before she got to the door, the Cedar Creek Gang stood and joined her.

"You girls—back in your seats," Mr. Johnson yelled. They never looked at Mr. Johnson, and followed Cricket out the door.

Then Beverly Shade stood and walked to the door. She turned and looked at me. I wanted to join her but feared Mr. Johnson.

75

Cricket's lists flashed through my thoughts. I stood on wobbly knees, got my bearings and walked to her.

Mr. Johnson's mouth fell open as one by one our entire class stood and followed Beverly and the Cedar Creek Gang out of the classroom. Well, almost our entire class. Everybody arrived at Mr. Lawton's office except Ralph Persinger and Billy Swan Ronk.

Mr. Lawton took one look at the classroom full of students filing into his small office and told us all to go to the library. When we got there we started to laugh and slap each other and Cricket on the back. Beverly took my hand, beamed at me. With all the noise, you'd have thought we'd already won the Homecoming football game. Miss Mounts told us to be quiet, which we found hard to do.

At a fast clip Mr. Lawton headed down the hall towards Mr. Johnson's classroom. As he rounded the first corner in the hallway he nearly collided with Billy Swan Ronk, who joined us in the library. I wished I could have been a little mouse in the corner and listened to Mr. Johnson and Mr. Lawton. Right before noon Mr. Lawton called Cricket Hobson to his office.

Word of all that had happened spread during lunch hour. Before lunch hour ended, Cricket joined the Cedar Creek Gang in the cafeteria at their usual table. They wore big smiles. By the time we returned to class no one talked about anything else. Our afternoon class schedule continued as usual, but things had changed.

At three o'clock on a sunny but cold Friday afternoon a few days later, the Homecoming parade rolled down Main Street. A reviewing stand had been erected in front of the Bank of Kettle. Mr. Lawton and a few of the teachers, as well as Mayor Baumgartner, sat in folding metal chairs on the stand. The Kettle High marching band led the parade, although the majorettes marched without Ruthie Southworth. Ruthie wore a fur coat over her long blue dress and sat high on the junior class float as Queen's Attendant. The floats had been decorated with colorful crepe paper and carried large posters and banners that called for the Tops to win the Homecoming game. The football team stood on the bed of a blue Dodge flatbed truck and the players waved at the crowd. June Ann Morris sat atop the senior class float and looked regal in her flowing red gown, though in the chilly air she had put a heavy wool blue coat around her shoulders.

Our sophomore class float had fewer decorations than the other floats, for we had to decorate the gym along with our float. But the float had lots of colored crepe paper and a couple of large signs with bright red letters, "Go Tops!" Cricket sat on a riser in the center of the float. She wore a lacy light blue gown with crinolines that fluffed her skirt outwards at least a foot, maybe more. Cricket had bare shoulders—no coat. She beamed a radiant smile. Even William White said that Cricket looked kind of pretty.

Just as our sophomore class float approached the reviewing stand, Cricket's right hand pulled something from beneath her. Then she tied a red bandanna around her neck.

Chapter 4

THE POWER OF SIN

That Sunday morning service marked the end of the Kettle Methodist Church's nineteen and forty-six "Witness for Christ Week," a time to save souls, to bring folks to Jesus. The week-long revival stretched across two successive Sundays, with services on each of the six evenings between. Momma told me I had to attend each of the Sunday morning services and at least two of the weekday evening services, which I had done. William White's Momma had set up the same requirement. "Our Mommas are in cahoots," he observed.

When the "Witness for Christ Week" began I worried, as I had every February as far back as I could remember, that I'd be singled out by church elders to have my soul saved. Attending revival services with William White didn't reduce my fear any, for he had the annoying habit of remembering my past sins and reminding me of them. Like the time I fibbed to Momma when I told her I was helping out over at Grandpa's barn, when in fact William White and I had gone to the river for a swim. To make matters worse, he always seemed to have himself in a peck of trouble of one kind or another. "You're a sinner if ever there was one," I often told him, though I grinned when I said it.

The week of services featured a visiting revival preacher. At the end of each sermon he appealed to sinners to turn their lives over to Jesus, what we referred to as the altar call. That's when the elders of the church got organized and moved like a swarm of hornets chasing a dog that had disturbed their nest. Of one mind, single file they came after sinners.

William White once said, "God sends them church elders after sinners, Freddy. They're charged with divine energy and the sinner is powerless to resist once the guns of God are turned on him. And they may be gunning for you, Freddy."

"William White Wallace, though you are my best friend, if you say things like that, I hate to think what my enemies might say about me. Anyway, what about you? You fibbed that day when you told your Momma you had helped out over at Grandpa's barn. You went swimming in the river with me. Maybe God and those men are after you."

The final Sunday morning service of the Witness for Christ Week offered the elders their last chance to bring sinners into the fold. In past years the last service of revival meetings had produced large and special spiritual events. The presence of Jack P. Camm that Sunday, sitting quietly beside his wife and daughter in a rear pew, loomed large and special. Jack P's reputation as a man who lived what some folks called a sporting life made him a prime target for being saved. Jack P and his shiny light blue nineteen and forty Plymouth convertible with its white canvas top, white side-wall tires, chrome polished to a high shine and a spotlight mounted just in front of the driver's door. Later I said to William White, "If folks at church could've taken both that car and Jack P to God, they would've."

William White and I had voted Jack P's convertible the car in Kettle. Sometimes I imagined what it might be like if William White and I had a car like that and drove it around Kettle. Girls walking along the street would wave to us, sometimes joining us for a ride. Maybe, when we got a little older, we'd drive across the

Ohio River to a town where they had nightclubs. We'd listen to the swing sounds of big bands, jitterbug, drink beer.

On warm summer evenings Jack P would slowly drive up and down the streets of Kettle, the car's top lowered, nodding and waving to folks as his eyes scanned the sidewalks and front porches. William White said, "He looks like he's lost his puppy and figures it might be just about where I am."

Jack P always wore a freshly laundered shirt, had his crew cut trimmed, and grinned a slight smile that put a curve in his square-shaped face. I told William White, "When he grins like that I think Jack P knows something really nice about me but isn't going to tell what it is."

One morning on the street in front of the Post Office, I over-heard Albert Newcomb talking with two of his friends about Jack P. Albert wore his peg leg with the face of Jesus carved on it. "I know for a fact that Jack P. Camm drove the twenty-one miles down highway Route 42 to Huntington and visited the Dew Drop Inn in the early hours of this morning. Mr. Ludlow P. Word said he saw Jack P's Plymouth convertible parked there when he brought the United States mail from Huntington to Kettle."

The two fellows standing alongside Albert looked up from sharpening their pocket knives on the stone ledge of the Post Office window. One of them said, "I wouldn't mind taking a little trip to the Dew Drop myself."

When I told William White about the conversation, he said, "Not me, Freddy. The Dew Drop Inn is on Ninth Avenue where all the colored folks live. I read in the Huntington newspaper about a man getting killed, knifed, in the alley behind the Dew Drop. They'd probably go after me as soon as I put my foot inside the front door."

On a warm evening in June, William White and I, along with William White's Aunt Beatrice Gebhardt, sat in the green metal chairs on Miss Beatrice's front porch drinking cool glasses of lemonade. We enjoyed the twilight of the day and said hello to folks as they walked by. There had been a thunderstorm just before supper and the air had cleared, become fresh. Miss Beatrice told us that lightning added sweetness to the air.

Jack P's convertible rolled down the street towards us, its top down. Jack P, alone, drove with his left hand on the wheel and his right arm extended along the top of the front seat, looking like a picture you might see in a *Saturday Evening Post* magazine advertisement. He wore a light blue shirt that matched the color of his car, and had his crew cut neatly trimmed. William White said Jack P used pomade to make the front of his crew cut stand up. Jack P couldn't have been much over thirty, but he had gray around his temples. William White called it a distinguished look.

His eyes seemed like tiny dark pinpoints, too small for his head, darting one way then another. Jack P slowed the Plymouth as he passed Miss Beatrice's porch. He looked up at us and nodded. Politely and emphasizing each of our names as he said them, his tone of voice making me believe he'd been thinking of us all the way down the street, Jack P said, "Evening, folks. Miss Beatrice. William White. Freddy."

Miss Beatrice answered first, "Good evening, Jack P."

Then William White, "Jack P."

By the time I said my "Jack P" the streetlight reflected off the polished surface of the Plymouth's trunk. We kept our eyes on the back of the car until elm branches overhanging the street blocked our view. Then Miss Beatrice, as if she spoke to no one in particular, asked, "I wonder what will become of him? I do worry about Mabel and the children."

Mabel was Jack P's wife. Miss Beatrice used that same tone of voice when she discussed one of her tenth-grade English students who she liked but had just failed a test. Or when a member of her church lost a loved one. I didn't know why she should worry about Mabel Camm.

One evening in our kitchen, in a quiet voice Momma said to Daddy, "I'm sure Jack P gallivants in places he shouldn't when he's out in that car. Hester Kinder said she saw him driving towards Blue Sage with a young woman in the car. It wasn't Mabel."

Daddy sighed and said, "I hope Mabel and the children don't run into him when he's out on an escapade. Maybe they'd all have been better off if Jack P's heart murmur hadn't kept him out of the Army."

On a Saturday afternoon in late January, just a few weeks before the beginning of this year's Witness for Christ Week, William White and I had stopped at Gruber's Store to get some red licorice and RC Colas. Some men stood near the pot-belly stove in the front of the store. Hartford Wilson, wearing his black wool cardigan sweater, Wallace 'Wink' Winkler in his blue gabardine suit, his "good luck sales suit," Barney Brammer in his bib overalls, and two other fellows I didn't know who wore wide-brimmed hats and looked like they'd come in from field work on their farms.

I had just opened my RC Cola when the conversation turned to Jack P. Camm's car. Wink, who earned his living principally in the trading of horses and cars, although he sometimes dealt in wagons, trucks, tractors, and cattle, said, "I heard first-hand from my brother-in-law, William Boyd Shunt, and he heard it from his cousin who lives in Huntington, that Clifford Odell his self, of Odell Chrysler Plymouth in Huntington, said, 'That car'll bring folks in the door.' He offered Jack P nearly double what he had paid for that Plymouth in nineteen and forty. Clifford called it a real showpiece." Then he gave a wink of his right eye, what folks called his trademark. Wink often looked most serious when he winked, as if he had to confirm an important truth he had just shared. When I talked with Wink, his winks made me feel appreciated. Daddy told me he figured Wink's punctuation of his trading transactions with a serious wink had sealed many a deal.

Hartford Wilson asked, "Wink, if you was Jack P, would you take that deal?"

Wink's face took on a serious look. "Yes sir, I'd make that swap real fast. It ain't every day you can double your money." Wink.

Barney Brammer put his thumbs under the buckles of the front straps of his bib overalls, "Wink, that might not be such a good deal after all, everything considered." He paused, looked around the group and added, "That car brings Jack P such things as money can't buy." Another pause. "At least such things as none of us could afford to buy, though we sure would enjoy them."

Everybody laughed. One fellow punched Wink on the shoulder. Wink laughed even more as he rolled into Hartford Wilson who stood next to him. Then Wink looked around the group and gave everybody his trademark.

I wondered what a car might bring that money couldn't buy.

The final Sunday morning revival service had a packed house, with well over a hundred people in the sanctuary. More people than last Wednesday night when Arden Conner had been saved. At the end of that service at least half the congregation gathered in front of the altar around Arden, who stood tall, running his hands through his long gray hair, beaming, a new man. He laughed and wept. Folks around him laughed and wept too.

William White whispered to me, "How do you laugh and cry at the same time? What does it feel like? Are you happy or sad?"

At the Dixie Palace, William White and I had seen the actress Veronica Lake laugh and cry at the same time. In a movie, her boyfriend, Van Johnson, had been an Army Air Corps pilot. He flew back to the airbase just outside of London after all the characters in the movie, as well as me and William White, thought his P-38 fighter had been shot down over the English Channel on his very last mission. Veronica Lake didn't wail and wave her arms in the air and say things like "Oh Jesus, I'm with you!" the way Arden did. She didn't talk about the love she felt for everybody around her, for she loved Van Johnson. She laughed and cried when Van's plane landed.

A lot of people, including Mr. Bertram Billups, the Reverend Aubrey Pierce Price, guest evangelist from Purdue, Kentucky, and Dr. Y. Younts Yoder, the minister of the Kettle Methodist Church, laughed and cried with Arden, and slapped him on the back, then slapped each other on the back. They reached up in the air to grab and shake each of Arden's hands as he waved them at God. Arden yelled, "I love you folks. I love Jesus. I thank you. I'm a saved man with a clean soul. And I'm just bustin' with love."

84

As I entered the sanctuary as the choir sang the first verse of the opening hymn. I'd arrived a few minutes late. I scanned the congregation for Holbert Holcomb. I planned to sit beside him. Holbert represented a safe haven. Even though I didn't care much for him, by pairing up with Holbert during each revival service, I would closely associate myself with a boy who, hands down and no questions asked, had the reputation of a Christian—safe territory. Even better, Holbert looked for sinners that needed to be saved. One of the hunters, not the hunted. And I didn't think he would hunt me if I sat beside him. On Monday of the week before our Witness for Christ Week, I even sat beside Holbert at noon in the school cafeteria, something nobody ever did voluntarily.

Holbert still had lots of baby fat, sweated a lot, and had a squeaky voice. And I didn't like his habit in church of probing his ears with the little finger of each hand and, when enough time had passed and he thought nobody would see him, in turn placing each of his little fingers in his mouth. Then he would stare towards the stained glass window behind the choir loft as if he wanted to contemplate Jesus, and use his lower front teeth to chisel out the earwax from beneath his fingernail. He chewed with so little movement, if I hadn't been watching him I would hardly have known what he had done. Then he'd swallow. Nasty, but I could put up with it. I needed an insurance policy.

I thought about Van Johnson up there in his P-38 with German fighter planes somewhere nearby, a menace to his life. What would he do?

Make a decision to fly a course, and then fly it. I banked my plane in a wide turn.

I scanned the sanctuary for Holbert. Not there! My stomach cringed and filled with a sudden worry, the kind I got when with no warning, a teacher said in a serious voice, "Go to the principal's office." Then I scanned again. There he sat, behind the pulpit, alongside the Reverend Aubrey Pierce Price and Dr. Y. Younts Yoder, all dressed in black suits. I made a quick turn towards the rear of the sanctuary, spotted William White and dove for a seat beside him. Folks had to scoot over to make room for me. Fourth pew from the rear of the church, and possibly a safe place—out of the line of fire?

At age twelve Holbert Holcomb had been elected Teen Christian Leader by the members of the Kettle Methodist Youth Fellowship, the youngest, and first technically non-teen, person to hold the position. At the time Holbert fell short of his thirteenth birthday by a couple of months. William White told me that his Aunt Beatrice, a Sunday School teacher, had confided to him during a family dinner, "The election was rigged. The Sunday School teachers put heavy pressure on everybody to make sure no candidate ran against Holbert." She went on to tell William White she opposed Holbert's becoming Teen Christian Leader because she didn't think he had enough maturity to be respected by other young folks. "But," she said, "I was unable to swing enough votes to move things my way."

When I thought about my protection strategy and its central feature, Holbert, I worried that a few church elders might see through my plan. Or, that Holbert himself might turn on me. At one service in last year's Witness for Christ Week, Holbert had sat along side Billy Johnson, then a sixth-grader. During the altar call, Holbert got up and brought Mr. Nathaniel R. Lawton, our Kettle High School principal and well-known Christian leader, back to the pew to talk with Billy. Billy's father made no secret of drinking beer, and he swore and told jokes with four-letter words in them. Sometimes Billy told his Daddy's jokes to boys at school. Holbert knelt beside Billy and prayed. In his prayers Holbert loudly described what he called Billy Johnson's sins.

Mr. Lawton knelt along with Holbert, both of them dressed in suits, beside Billy, who wore blue jeans and a faded old orange shirt. They raised their voices and said, "Lord, we ask your blessing and grace on the soul of Billy Johnson."

I'll bet five minutes hadn't passed until Holbert and Mr. Lawton escorted Billy to the altar. Billy knelt and cried and put his head on the altar rail. Holbert and Mr. Lawton knelt on either side of him. Each of them put a hand on Billy's back, like enemy soldiers with their captured prisoner. "There, but for the grace of God…" I whispered.

After the service people grinned at Billy, shook hands and congratulated him. Saved! Everyone grinned and shook hands with Holbert and Mr. Lawton, who shook hands and grinned at each other. I said to William White, "Folks seem happier for Holbert and Mr. Lawton than for Billy Johnson." In the war, when a fighter pilot like Van Johnson shot down an enemy airplane, he put a small German flag on the nose of his plane. Maybe Billy became a little marker in the mental lists of people like Holbert and Mr. Lawton. Billy, red-faced, stood in the middle of all the congratulating. At first he grinned as he watched all the laughing and hand-shaking. Then his grin faded. Billy stared at the floor and rubbed the toe of his right shoe around a spot on the carpet.

The last day—the last service. Dampness spread under my armpits and my stomach felt like it had a flock of Monarch butterflies in it. Did Van Johnson feel this way before his plane lifted off the ground on his final combat mission? In the movie, just before he left the barracks for the airfield, Van wrote a letter to his best friend, wounded in action and taken to a hospital. "If I can get through this one, then for me it's all over, over there."

If I could get through today's service, then it would all be over for me too. I would be home, free for another year.

I settled into the plane's cockpit, revved the engine, and headed down the runway. My last mission.

Reverend Aubrey Pierce Price began his sermon. He stood tall behind the pulpit. The light of the chandelier reflected off his shiny bald head. In a soft voice he read a verse from Acts, "Men and brethren, what shall we do…." then boomed, "Repent and be saved in the name of Jesus Christ our Lord." Forty minutes later, in voice so powerful it must have been heard by God himself, Reverend Price told folks how to get right with God. He removed his suit jacket and hung it on the back of one of the tall oak chairs behind the pulpit. Sweat soaked his white shirt. Daddy called this kind of sermon a stem-winder.

From the congregation folks punctuated Reverend Price's sermon with calls of "A-men!" and "Yes, Lord!" They began to fidget and move back and forth in the pews.

The action would soon begin—the attack on sinners. The Altar Call. On Wednesday night Reverend Price had begun The Altar Call with a booming, "Find 'em! Pray 'em! Bring 'em home to Jesus!"

That Sunday morning Reverend Price began the attack on the sinners in a way I hadn't expected. While, ever so softly, the congregation sang "Lead Me Gently Home," he asked Christians in the congregation to please stand, walk around the sanctuary and locate sinners.

Surprise attack!

"Yes, go to your friends and loved ones who've sinned. Help 'em. Bring' em home to Jesus." Many Christian folks stood, walked through the church and dropped to their knees beside people. Aisle seats seemed to be a favorite spot for sinners. After a Christian knelt beside a sinner, others would swarm in, kneel, put their arms around the sinner and each other, and pray.

How did the Christians identify sinners? I knew most of the folks singled out, for example Mr. Harmon Wilcox, a mechanic at the Harley Mount's Texaco Station and Garage, who got identified as a sinner at a service earlier in the week. Whenever my Momma stopped at the Texaco Station for gas, if Mr. Wilcox filled our tank he'd politely ask my Momma if he could check the oil. And he smiled and talked like everybody else when he shopped at Wilson's Dry Goods or Gruber's Department Store. He seemed like a regular person, but he'd been targeted as a sinner.

If folks viewed Mr. Wilcox as a sinner, maybe they viewed me as one too. Once I had stolen two cigarette butts from an ashtray at a cousin's house, and William White and I had smoked them out behind the elementary school. That Sunday morning, right then and there, I asked for forgiveness—put my prayer on record with Jesus. I added a request that Jesus protect me from the attack of the Christians. Even before I finished my prayer I wondered if I should pray to Jesus for Christians not to come after me. The

Christians worked for Jesus, and I wanted to ask Jesus to call them off, protect me from his own people. My thoughts got all tangled up with themselves and I ended my prayer. I hoped that people seated on either side of my pew would give me some cover, some protection.

Follow Van Johnson's plane. Look for cloud cover.

Earlier in the service Holbert had led a prayer from the pulpit, and in it singled out the need for more young people in the Kettle Methodist Church to become witnesses for Christ. He looked directly at me when he said it. In his look, had he sent some kind of signal about me to others? Would I be one of the youth that Christians, led by Holbert himself, would descend on? A young sinner targeted to be a witness for Christ.

Enemy guns firing, but not yet on target.

Holbert's prayer led me to take evasive action—I nodded my head in agreement and slumped to a lowered position.

Roll my plane to the right. Dive, change altitude.

I waited on the final hymn and prepared myself for the full force of The Altar Call. I focused my gaze and total, prayerful, attention on the stained glass window behind the choir loft, the look of a Christian, I hoped.

In the middle of a sentence, Reverend Price stopped speaking, closed his eyes and bowed his head. The church remained silent for perhaps a full minute, though it seemed like an eternity. Sitting behind and on either side of Reverend Price, Holbert and Dr. Yoder quickly bowed their heads.

The sudden silence, the change in the rhythm of the service, surprised people. Folks whirled their heads this way and that trying to figure out what had happened. Then, as they caught on, they did a quick forward neck bend and jerky head duck into a prayerful position. Mrs. Wanda Burnside, after a series of rapid side-to-side twists of her head, jerked and ducked so fast she banged her forehead against the pew in front of her and her large red hat fell off. She didn't seem hurt by the blow, though her face turned a deep scarlet and many people, including Holbert and

Reverend Price, did another quick head jerk, this time upwards, to see what had happened.

Reverend Price ended the silence by asking in a soft voice, "Are there Christians out there who will stand and testify to the meaning of Jesus in their lives? Are you there? Will you speak?" In soft and quiet tones the choir began to sing, "On a hill far away, stood an old rugged cross, the emblem of suffering and shame..."

Mr. Ludlow P. Word, our local postmaster and long-time teacher of the men's Bible class at the Kettle Methodist Church, stood. He adjusted his wire-rimmed glasses and smoothed the lapels of his brown suit. In a voice loud enough to rise above the soft music he said, "Jesus has been my friend for over forty-five years. I found him and accepted him into my life as a young man. It happened one day while I worked in a field not far from this very church. I drove a wagon pulled by my horse John. Some of you may remember John. A snake appeared in John's path, coiled and ready to strike. It scared John and he bolted. The wagon was jerked off center. We'd been moving slowly, and I was standing in the wagon. The force of John's sudden move threw me out of the wagon. As I fell, in midair I heard the word, 'Jesus.' To this day I don't know where it came from. Well sir, I yelled that word. Jesus! A honeysuckle bush I had never before seen broke my fall. A divine power had entered my life. Lying safely in the soft branches of that bush I pledged to take Jesus as a partner in my life. Since then many of my life's falls have been softened by His help. He will soften your falls, too."

Mr. Word's face wore a concerned expression. I'd seen that look once before—at the Post Office after I mailed a letter without enough postage. Mr. Word found the letter and the next time I went into the Post Office he took me into a back room filled with mail bags. He sat me down, peered over the top of his glasses and said he knew I hadn't deliberately tried to cheat the government. But I needed to understand the importance of the rules of life, including the rules of the United States Post Office, and obey them. For a long time afterwards, I didn't do anything, not even turn on the radio, without wondering about the rules that covered my actions. One day when William White started to walk on the left side of the sidewalk on Main Street, I pulled his arm and told him I thought the rules said we had to walk on the right side.

After all the "Amen's" recognized the value of Mr. Word's testimonial, other people stood and testified about Jesus in their lives. Listening to them I wondered, could I gain protection from being singled out as a sinner by standing up and saying things like, "Jesus kept me from drowning when I went for a swim in the culvert where Cedar Creek goes under Route 42"? It would be tough to do without blushing and appearing to have made it all up, but it might work. In a movie Robert Ryan did something like that after his plane had been shot down over Germany—he put on a German Army uniform and walked past a whole bunch of German soldiers. They would have shot him dead if they'd recognized his trickery. I wondered what folks might do if they discovered me in an act of spiritual trickery. And some people in the congregation knew a lot about me, including my second-grade teacher, Miss Ball, who had caught William White and me smoking the cigarette butts behind the elementary school. I decided to keep my mouth shut.

Keep flying. Use cloud cover.

Reverend Price issued his final Altar Call—the all-out search to find sinners and bring them to the altar.

Guns firing. Explosions around me. The battle has begun.

Reverend Price boomed in a sincere voice, "Come forward and let Jesus enter your heart. Begin a new life, one filled with Christian love." The choir sang, "Softly and Tenderly Jesus Is Calling," in a way even I thought should be attractive to sinners. Nobody moved. Time passed. The choir sang two more hymns. Reverend Price gazed at the congregation, prayed aloud, gazed some more. I caught one gaze straight on.

Direct hit.

Reverend Price shifted his look to a side pew.

Direct hit but no major damage.

Reverend Price called in reinforcements. "Christians, you who have found friends and loved ones to bring to Jesus, walk with them to the altar. Help them build the foundation of a joyous hereafter in a wondrous eternity." Two members of the congregation walked friends to the altar. Then two more.

Mr. Word, Mr. Lawton, and other Christian leaders, including Holbert, massed in a group at the front of the church. They faced the congregation and scanned the pews. Then they turned and whispered among themselves.

I shut my eyes shut tight and scrunched my eyebrows towards each other. I hoped I looked prayerful. Light bursts appeared on the insides of my eyelids. My heart raced.

Anti-aircraft shells exploding around me. Hold the course. Steady.

I peeked through my eyelids and saw Holbert lead the knot of men with long and sober faces up the aisle, my aisle. They approached me.

Enemy aircraft at ten o'clock!

Holbert walked at the front of the group, moving with the familiar waddle that kids at Sunday School tried to imitate. The Teen Christian Leader stared straight at me, nodded, and held eye contact with me. The group moved ever closer.

I bowed my head, prayed.

Enemy planes, dead ahead.

Would the Teen Christian Leader open fire, shoot me down? One more sinner, gone?

Bullets from the German machine gun fire tore through my P-38. What to do? Bail out, parachute? Keep flying?

Teen Christian Leader Holcomb and the band of Christian men neared my pew. Then Holbert stopped and knelt beside me. The men stood behind him, their eyes on me.

"Dive, dive, dive!"

Holbert opened his mouth to speak.

"Roll!"

"Brother Freddy, do you want to join us to talk with a sinner?"

My eyes still closed in prayer, I shook my head, "No."

I pulled out of the dive, dipped each wing twice, the OK signal.

Holbert stood, he and the men moved on.

The rounds from the German planes streaked into the darkness. I flew on.

Holbert Holcomb and the pack of Christian men rounded the rear pew and massed on their target—Jack P. Camm.

The German planes had their target in sight. All guns firing.

"Wwhhoooo-aaaahhhhHHHH!" pierced the prayerful but tense silence of the Kettle Methodist Church sanctuary. The sound resembled a blast from the horn of a paddleboat pushing coal barges down the Kanawha River. It must have blammed shock waves into every bubble of air in every crack and cranny in the church.

I flinched, along with William White and most everybody else in the congregation. Goose bumps rose along the surfaces of my arms. William White said in a shushed voice, "Freddy, what was that?"

Everybody looked towards the source of the sound—Jack P. Camm. He knelt in front of his dark oak pew, his outstretched arms reaching towards the ceiling. Behind him bright sunlight passed through the large stained glass window in the rear wall of the church, spreading rays of deep red, blue and gold across Jack P and the men kneeling in a huddle around him. Folks who turned quickly enough saw the splintering of the huddle when Jack P sprang from his kneeling position and leaped into the aisle, much like the quarterback he'd been on the nineteen and thirty-four Kettle High football team. Jack P banged into and nearly knocked over Mr. Bertram Billips, who since nineteen and twenty had rung the church's bell to announce the beginning of Sunday morning services and such special occasions as the end of World War II.

Jack P wailed again, "Wwhhooo-aaaaAAAAHHHH!"

He waved his arms and ran full speed down the long green-carpeted aisle past rows of pews filled with worshipers. Jack P knelt at the center of the walnut altar, below the oak pulpit. Behind the pulpit the choir loft rose at an upwards angle. The choir, in their royal blue robes, sang the hymn, "Softly and Tenderly Jesus is Calling." Behind the choir maroon velvet drapes clothed the walls except for a small round stained glass window. Jack P bowed his head and spread his arms along the altar rail. Then he removed the coat of his dark blue suit, held it in his right hand and raised both arms towards the ornate silver chandelier above the pulpit.

William White whispered, "Jack P's handing his coat to Jesus."

Head back, his eyes looking upwards, Jack P's deep voice boomed, "Take me! Take me! Jesus, take me!"

"If not me, take my coat," William White said.

I leaned towards William White, "Shush. Jack P. Camm is being saved. It could have been you they came after. Or me."

The group of men and one teenager who, a few minutes ago had walked up the aisle and huddled around Jack P, now knelt around Jack P at the altar. Two of the men put their arms on his shoulders.

Warmth, even laughter, spread through me. Safe! A voice inside me said, "Thank you, Jesus."

I turned my plane, headed home. Soon the lights of the airbase dotted the ground below me. It was over, over there. For the first time that night I allowed myself to think ahead. The guys at the barracks. An evening at the officers club. Van Johnson. I wondered if Veronica Lake had a friend. Then I thought, one that looks like Beverly.

Early one Saturday morning a few weeks later William White barged into my bedroom. "Up, Freddy, get up! We've got to do this and you have to help."

I rubbed my eyes. "What's going on?"

"Jack P has put his car up for sale. We've got to scrape up the money and buy it. Let's figure out how to do it. I can see us, Freddy, moving through the streets of Kettle early in the evenings, top down, that light blue body all waxed to a high gloss, the chrome spotlight polished. Think about it, Freddy. We might even date cheerleaders. We got to buy that car, Freddy."

I became infected with William White's enthusiasm. I could see myself driving that sweet blue machine with the top down on a summer evening, Beverly sitting next to me. Maybe I'd get a crew cut and some pomade.

Momma yelled from downstairs, "Freddy, time to get up, chores to do."

I shook my head, "William White, we are sixteen years old. We earn a little money mowing lawns in the summertime. That is a serious car. Buying it will require serious money. And we don't even have our driver's licenses yet."

Wink Winkler bought Jack P's nineteen and forty Plymouth convertible. Not long afterwards, Clifford Odell Chrysler-Plymouth in Huntington had the car on display in their downtown showroom.

At Gruber's Department Store, Wink told everybody he had it first-hand from his brother-in-law, William Boyd Shunt, who heard it from his cousin who lives in Huntington, that people came to the Clifford Odell Chrysler-Plymouth showroom every day just to stand and look at that car.

One evening during supper our conversation drifted to the sale of Jack P's Plymouth convertible. I brought myself to the forward edge of telling my folks about how William White and I had admired that car, and how excited we got over William White's idea that the two of us might buy it.

Just then Daddy said in a quiet voice, "That car was no good, not for Jack P, not for anybody. And I don't mean mechanically. We're better off having it out of Kettle."

Momma nodded.

I drank my milk.

Chapter 5

THE GREAT KETTLE RIOT OF 1947

Summertime in Kettle drifted along at the pace of an old tree limb floating down the Sour Apple River. I would never have dreamed of a riot in our town, but it happened.

In late July, nineteen and forty-seven, Kettle had entered the third week of a heat wave with no rain. Each day the temperature neared eighty degrees shortly after sunrise and climbed into the high nineties by early afternoon. More than once the temperature had hit a hundred degrees. The Sour Apple River that snaked along the south side of Kettle, its water normally a rich shade of coffee with cream, in the three previous weeks had received so little runoff from the surrounding hills that it looked like a trickle of old thick coffee with only a little cream. Just six weeks earlier William White Wallace and I had taken a swim in the river, then got on inner tubes and let the current float us downstream.

That evening after I went to bed, I imagined I took a trip on the river. Below the covered bridge I put Daddy's old green Johnboat, full of supplies, into the Sour Apple and floated ten miles downstream to the Watoga River. I held my course another eight miles to the Ohio River, then hugged its downstream banks for days, until I reached Cairo, Illinois and the Mississippi. Then I floated down that great river to the Gulf of Mexico, like a modern-day Huck Finn. I kept going, right into the Atlantic Ocean. Then through the Panama Canal and on to points east. One day I stepped ashore in Hong Kong.

The *Kettle News Leader* reported that the last time our town had a heat wave this long, the summer of nineteen and thirty-one, there had been an outbreak of spinal meningitis. After three boys died the mayor had ordered the town's public gathering places—our churches and the theatre—closed. Now the paper said that Mayor Raymond T. Baumgartner had prepared a similar order and discussed it with town council. After the article appeared Momma told me I couldn't go to the movies until we had some rain and the weather cooled.

William White and I had our lawn-mowing business going full blast that summer. We had our eyes on a twenty-nine Chevy coupe and hoped to save enough to buy it at the end of the summer, in time for our senior year at Kettle High School. Until the drought got bad, we got up at dawn each morning and worked at a good clip in order to wrap up our day's work by the time the heavy heat settled in, early afternoon. When we cut the last blade of grass, we'd bike over to the river and take a swim. With the river dried up, we hunted for cool shady places, sat and rested.

Late one morning, about the time we sweated through mowing the Dickensheets' lawn, one of the few that had grown enough that week to be cut, the temperature hit ninety degrees. And the humidity hung on us like a steamy old blanket. As we finished the last, hillside, portion of the yard, heavy blue-black clouds rolled in from the west and a thunderstorm storm dropped a large amount of rain. We ducked into the Dickensheets' garage until the storm passed. William White speculated that the storm might signal an end to the dry spell and the heat. No such luck. When the sun came out after the storm, ninety-two degrees came with it, now even more humid than before. Small pools of water stood in the low spots in the yards up and down the street. I said,

"William White, let's call it a day. If it cools off, maybe we can get some of the guys together and play softball."

I went home and had just finished taking a shower down in the basement, washing off the sweat and grass, when Shufflehead Meadows, who hung around with William White and me that summer, poked his long face and unruly mop of blond hair through the door at the top of the steps and yelled, "Freddy, Freddy! A man pulled a gun on Miss Hattie McClintock. Tried to rob her. William White was there and saw it happen. He's down at Bertha's Place."

We ran the three blocks to Main Street then over to Bertha's Place. Along the way, Buster Bragg, one of the guys who played softball, joined us. We walked in the front door of Bertha's Place. A small group, their backs to us, faced William White, perched on a stool at the counter, like he used to do when Lorna C ran the restaurant as Miss Kettle's Place. Since Bertha bought the restaurant, little had changed other than a new sign above the front door. The RC Cola clock still hung behind the counter beside the doorway to the kitchen. Each of the red Formica tables had four chrome-plated chairs around them. Bertha had the same booths too, with their red Formica table tops and cracked black leather seats. Five round red stools sat in front of a long red counter top at the back of the large rectangular room. Bertha had scooted the Wurlitzer juke box, with its arched brown acrylic top and red and yellow front panels lit from behind, from beside the front door to a spot near the first booth. Tunes cost a nickel apiece, although Bertha had fixed the juke box so we could play six songs for a quarter.

Words flowed out of William White's mouth like the fast-moving water on Main Street's gutters during our storm. A small gathering of folks listened to him. Whit Saunders stood at the rear of the group wearing his wide-brimmed hat and, even in a heat wave, his khaki trousers tucked into his lace up boots. William White had his back against the counter, the elbow of his left arm on the counter top and an RC Cola in his right hand. When he spoke he gestured and the RC went up and down in front of him.

"You should have heard her scream. Yes sir, it was piercing," he said.

"William White, what happened?" I asked.

"You folks don't mind, do you? Let me tell these boys the story from the beginning."

People nodded their heads and Whit, a steady fixture at Bertha's Place, said, "OK." Everybody, even us kids, called him Whit, just like a member of the family. He inspected gas lines for Coal Valley Gas and did most of his work early morning. The remainder of most days he could be found at Bertha's Place, "Acting in my capacity," he said, "as a community resource to folks who have questions about the cost and value," he always emphasized the word value, "of converting their home heating to gas." Since most people in Kettle already heated their homes with gas, Whit got few questions. This provided him, as he described it, "more time to relax and consider other important questions about our Kettle community."

"Boys," William White said as if he had just met us for the first time, "here's what happened. I had my softball glove on the handlebar of my bike, riding over to the ball field, hoping we'd play a game or two." He paused, and then as if he'd just recognized us, and with a serious expression on his face, he spoke slowly, with concern. "I'm sorry I never made it to the field. You know how much I like softball. But when something like this happens, well…" His voice trailed off and he stared at us for a few seconds. William White's comment reminded me of a scene in the Western movie he and I had seen last Saturday night. After a cattle rustler shot a friend of Randolph Scott's, Randolph, who had the responsibility to drive a herd of cattle to Dodge City, knelt beside his wounded friend and said, "but when something like this happens…" then looked off into the distance.

Buster Bragg pushed his Cincinnati Reds cap back on his head and slammed a softball into his first baseman's mitt with a pop. William White flinched. "Come on, William White, tell what happened."

"Well," William White said, "I was riding my bike along the sidewalk on Maple Street, enjoying the shade of the overhanging tree branches. I approached Miss Hattie McClintock's place. About the time I passed the upper side her front yard there was a scream from her front porch—a most piercing scream. Another scream. Then," he made his voice high pitched, "'Help. Help! Robber!'

"I hit my brakes. In front of me a white man carrying a pistol leaped down the front porch steps and ran to the parked car. A Ford was parked on the street to my left—he paused and lowered his voice—with a colored man behind the wheel. He started up the car, revved the engine and before you could say 'gimme an RC' the white fellow jumped in the car, slammed the door and the car peeled rubber down Maple Street."

William White paused and took a long swallow of his RC Cola. His eyes watered. "Boys, this stuff is good. Sometimes I worry, you know, that I drink too much of it." Before he got shot, Randolph Scott's friend, standing at the bar in a saloon, had said the same thing and then wiped his mouth with the back of his hand. William White wiped his mouth with the back of his hand.

Shufflehead, who would enter the tenth grade for the second time in September, listened to William White with his eyes wide and his mouth in a fixed open position. Shufflehead blinked his eyes and asked, "And? And? Is that it?"

"Easy, Shuff, it's comin'," Whit said.

"I knew I had to make a command decision. I don't know how else to put it. A command decision. I could either go help Miss Hattie, or I could head downtown and find Chief Tackett. A split second, that's all I had." William White paused and looked from left to right across the faces of the group in front of him. "What would you have done?" he asked us.

Just as Shufflehead answered, "I would've..." William White said, "I could see Miss Hattie wasn't hurt. And out of the corner of my eye I saw Bernadine Blackwood, who lives next door, running across her yard towards Miss Hattie's porch. I had never before seen a colored man in Kettle. I got to admit that weighed more on

101

me than Miss Hattie, who at least was healthy enough to scream. So I hightailed it downtown to find the chief and report the crime."

He took another sip of the RC. "Oh, and here's a little detail that may prove to be important—the kind of detail that leads to convictions. That car was a two-door black nineteen and forty Ford coupe. I got the license number. Ohio plates, CC 742. Yes sir, CC 742. Nineteen and forty black two-door Ford coupe.

"I found Chief Tackett sitting on the front steps of the bank, drinking coffee and talking to some folks. I yelled—William White cupped his hands around his mouth—" "'Chief, Miss Hattie McClintock has been robbed at gunpoint. Terrorized by a nigger and a white man.' Chief Tackett sprung into action so fast he spilled coffee down the front of his shirt, though he didn't pay a bit of attention to the spill.

"'What happened, William White?' the Chief asked.

"I told him about riding my bike along Maple Street, hearing Miss Hattie's screams, seeing the man with the gun and the car with the colored driver. 'Describe the man with the gun,' he asked me. 'White, about six feet tall, wearing a gray suit, white shirt and necktie. And, I'm not sure about this, has black hair. Maybe brown. The driver was a colored man. I couldn't see him very well. But he was a nigger all right, I'll guarantee that.' I described the car and the Ohio plates, CC 742.

"About then the telephone bell on the outside of the police station rang. It was Bernadine Blackwood calling to report the crime I'd just told the chief about. If he had any doubts about what I said, her call removed them. The chief called the Sheriff's office in Huntington, then the State Police. He told them what had happened, including the details of my description of the offenders and their car. Offenders is police talk for the crooks. You know, them who does the deed.

"'Which way was they headed, William White?' the Chief asked me. I told him they took off down Maple Street at a fast clip and they turned right when they got to Main Street."

Shufflehead brushed his blond hair out of his eyes and spoke in a surprised voice, "William White, you cain't see Main Street from Miss Hattie's house."

William White rolled his eyes. "Don't need to, Shufflehead. I got a sense, I don't know how, but I got a sense about things like that." He turned and looked at me. "Remember last week, Freddy, when you said, 'Let's bet a nickel on which direction the next train will be heading' and I said, 'West.' By golly it was west and I was five cents richer." He looked at Shufflehead, "There you are."

Shufflehead shook his head sidewise and muttered, "Well, I'll be a monkey's uncle."

A siren sounded in the distance and got louder. We looked out the plate glass windows towards Main Street. Chief Tackett's nineteen and thirty-eight, two-tone blue Oldsmobile came barreling past, the red lights mounted on the front bumper and the single red light mounted on top of the car a-blazing. People sat in the back seat of the car—looked like two of them.

William White got excited and said, "Maybe the chief got 'em. Maybe the offenders have been apprehended. Come on, let's go find out." He jumped off his perch, pushed through our small group, and ran out the front door. We followed William White's lead and headed down Main Street, then the two blocks up Benson Street to the jail.

The chief had parked his car in the shade of the big elm tree just beyond the small porch-like roof on the front of the old white frame Town Hall. The building had two floors and a peaked roof, but the second floor got no use other than the storage of town records. The front door and a tall double window opened on to Benson Street. The large room inside the front door served mainly as a place for the town clerk to receive folks' payments for water, electricity, and taxes, though the office opened only on Mondays and Fridays. Town Council held meetings there the first Wednesday night of each month. The back part of the building housed the jail, a cell with two cots, a washbasin, and a toilet. The jail didn't get much use except for an occasional Saturday night when some fellow drank too much beer and Chief Tackett put him in the lock-up for a few hours.

Half our little crowd from Bertha's Place stood in the shade of the elm tree and the other half under Town Hall's front porch roof. In about five minutes Chief Tackett came out, shut the door and locked it.

When the chief turned towards us, William White approached him and said, "Chief, we were over at Bertha's Place. I had no sooner told these folks what happened, and how I gave you information about the offenders, when you drove by with your siren blowing and your red lights on. Did you catch 'em?"

The chief hitched up his gun belt, sucked in his belly and looked across our group. "Boys, I've apprehended the two men who terrorized and attempted to rob Miss Hattie McClintock." He paused then said, "Keep your eyes peeled for strangers in town. For all we know these two fellers may be part of a theft ring. They may have accomplices who've spread out through town." The chief took off his hat and rubbed a red bandanna across his bald head. "And one of 'em a nigger. Here in Kettle. Can you imagine that?"

"How'd you catch 'em, Chief?" Shufflehead asked.

"Well, first thing every police officer has to recognize is the help of alert citizens. William White here provided the details I needed to identify the men."

Shufflehead leaned forward, "Where was they, Chief?"

"William White said they turned right on Main Street, so I got in my car and did the same thing. I figured I'd just keep goin', the same way they probably did. But I only had to drive about a mile, to Buster's A&W Drive Inn. The building looked good as new after the fresh coat of orange paint Buster give it. The big gravel parking lot was empty except for one car. A black Ford coupe bearing an Ohio license plate, CC 742." William White's face lit up like a Christmas tree. He beamed a smile so big his mouth nearly connected his ears.

"I was eager to close in on the criminals, but I first studied the situation. Good practice in law enforcement. The building looked deserted, though Buster must have been in there. A tray was attached to the driver's side window of the Ford. I parked sidewise behind the car—that way they couldn't back up and make a getaway."

The chief paused and surveyed our group. "Now, boys, this here is the strange part of the story. They was sittin' there with a couple of root beers just like nothin' had happened. Ain't that somethin'? A nigger and a white man try to rob an old lady, and then they go to Buster's to drink root beer and eat hot dogs. I'll be honest with you, at first that puzzled me. Then I asked myself, what would criminals do to throw you off their trail?" Without breaking stride the chief answered his question. "Well, I'll tell you what they'd do. Act normal, that's what. Just set there like nothin' happened. Though I must admit I was surprised about Buster servin' a colored feller. Then, I suppose as long as he stayed in the car it would be all right. The Ohio plates may have swayed Buster a little. You know, his showing courtesy to out-of-state folks, even the colored. Buster had no way of knowin' they was criminals."

The chief paused and made eye contact with each of us. Then he spoke slowly, "I walked around to the Ford's passenger side, not the driver's side. I didn't want the colored boy, the driver, throwin' his door open and slammin' the tray into me and my gun. Boys, prior plannin' always pays off in law enforcement."

The chief squared his shoulders and hooked his thumbs into his gun belt. "I knew the element of surprise was with me. The passenger side window was down, so I eased around there and pulled ol' Roscoe out of my holster and poked him through the window—right next to the temple of the white man. I said, 'Now if you fellers will please open this door real slow like and quietly step out here, we won't have any trouble.'

"I took a couple of steps back from the door and the white man stepped out. Just like you said, William White, he was wearin' a white shirt and necktie. I could see his suit coat in the back seat. It was gray, as you reported. The nigger started to open the driver's door with the tray attached to it and get out on the other side of the car. I said, 'Whoa, boy, whoa. You just slide over here, real easy like, and step out on this side,' and that's what he done.

"I had 'em put their hands on the roof of the car and hold steady. With my right hand I kept my thirty-eight aimed at 'em, and with my left hand I frisked them. That' part of police training. I knew they had at least one pistol, but neither of 'em was carryin' it. I lifted their wallets and told 'em to get in the back seat of my Olds. After I locked the doors, I checked their wallets. They both had driver's licenses, so we got positive ID's on 'em.

"While they was gettin' into my car the white fellow said, 'Officer, we're salesmen. There's some kind of mistake.'

"I said, 'Yes sir, you're right.' I figured I could afford a little laugh and I gave 'em one. Then I said, 'There's been a mistake, all right, a big one. You thought you could come into a sleepy little town on a hot summer day and rob an old lady. I agree with you, sure enough there's been a mistake.'

"Then the colored feller started to say somethin'. He got out, 'But ossifer,' and I poked ol' Roscoe right up to the end of his nose. I said, 'Boy, I'd think twice before I said anything I might regret.' That nigger's eyes got as big as saucers. That was the end of that."

William White stepped forward and extended his hand. As he and Chief Tackett shook hands, William White said, "Chief, I'm proud to know you." Chief Tackett sucked in his belly, smiled and nodded his head.

Whit Saunders walked up and shook the chief's hand. "Good work, Chief." Then Buster Bragg did the same thing. Everybody followed suit and we had a long process of hand-shaking and congratulating Chief Tackett. By the time the chief shook Shufflehead's hand the whole thing seemed overdone, but once the hand-shaking and congratulations got rolling it seemed like we had to continue until everybody had a chance to do it. When Shufflehead said, "Chief, I'm proud to know you," Chief Tackett looked past Shufflehead and muttered, "OK, OK."

The crowd broke up and William White insisted we go back to Bertha's Place. He said he wanted to be near the Police Station in case the chief needed him. Shufflehead and I, along with Whit Saunders, walked back to Bertha's with him. Half way there we had ourselves drenched in sweat. As we turned the corner on to

Main Street, Whit said, "Boys, she's going to top a hundred again this afternoon. May've already hit it. And it feels like the humidity's as high as the temperature."

Shufflehead asked, "Whit, somebody told me a chicken will sweat on a day like this. Do you think that's true?"

"With all them feathers, Shufflehead, a chicken's heat has got to be dang near unbearable on a day like this. I'd say they sweat, though as a matter of fact I have never looked into it," A few steps later Whit added, "But you know, when it comes to sweatin' on a hot day, boys, the colored folks has got it all over us. They do it by the bucket. That ol' boy over in the jail is likely to drown his buddy before the afternoon is over."

When we got to Bertha's Place, there Bertha stood on the sidewalk in the hot sun outside the front door of her restaurant. She held a coffee can and a paint brush. Her curly black-and-gray hair had wilted down over her forehead. Bertha's blue skirt and blouse hung a little loose, for she'd been on a diet, and in places stuck to her sweaty body. Whit once told us that Bertha had a big-boned frame and a diet wouldn't make much difference in her size.

Bertha handed Shufflehead the can, about half-full of liquid bacon grease. "Shufflehead, hold this please." Then she dipped the brush into the can and painted a small square of bacon drippings, about one foot on each side, on the sidewalk.

"Why don't I just pour the stuff on the sidewalk, Bertha?" Shufflehead asked.

"Honey, you don't understand. This is a publicity event. Everything has to be done artfully."

Even though the sun was blistering hot, a few people passing by had stopped and gathered around to watch the goings on. I could see the tall frame of the *Kettle News Leader's* owner and editor, James Garfield Worthington, coming down the street. He carried his press camera and wore a white straw hat. James Garfield's white shirt was so wet it stuck to him.

Bertha put down her paint brush and ducked into the restaurant. In no time at all she came back with a tray full of ice-cold bottles of RC Cola. Everybody took one and smiled, except for

107

James Garfield. He needed his hands for his large press camera, though he smiled and thanked Bertha.

Bertha cleared her throat and spoke to everybody in a loud voice, "Folks, you've heard people say it's so hot you could fry an egg on the sidewalk, right? Well, we're going to try to do that. And by golly, today it's so hot that I believe this egg will fry."

"Shufflehead, step over here. Let's get one last dab of bacon grease on the sidewalk."

After a final pass with the brush, Bertha pulled a large brown egg out of her apron pocket, knelt down, cracked the egg on the concrete and poured its innards over the area she'd painted with Shufflehead's bacon grease. Then she stood up. Along with Bertha, we watched and waited to see what would happen. Even with the heat, everybody crowded in close, though we opened up one side of the group so James Garfield could take pictures.

At first nothing happened. That yellow yolk just laid there like one eye looking up at us. Then Shufflehead poked me in the side and yelled, "Look, Freddy. It's cookin'." I never I thought I'd see this, but the egg white had begun to turn from clear to white. Everybody gave a little cheer and some folks applauded. Bertha beamed proudly at the egg. Shufflehead stared at it, his mouth hanging open.

James Garfield took a picture of Bertha and Shufflehead squatted down smiling at the egg. Bertha held a spatula next to the egg like she would flip it over, though she didn't do that. Shufflehead grinned proudly and held his can of bacon grease in front of him.

I said, "Shufflehead, by this time next week you'll be famous."

His face got red. "I ain't eatin' that thing, I'll tell you that."

Everybody laughed.

After James Garfield took his pictures the crowd broke up. A few of us went into Bertha's Place. Bertha had three large electric fans going at top speed. The temperature inside the restaurant matched the heat on the street outside, but the breeze set up by the fans felt good. Outdoors not a sliver of air moved. Inside or outside, though, the air seemed to stick to you.

Bertha walked over to her old wooden Emerson radio sitting at the far end of the counter near the pop cooler. She tuned it to the Cincinnati Reds baseball game and then picked up her Reds baseball cap that she kept on top of the radio and put it on her head. Bertha had long been a big fan of the Reds. Each season she took a couple of trips to Crosley Field in Cincinnati to see the team play. The previous year William White and had I joined her and a group of folks from Kettle on a baseball excursion train from Huntington to Cincinnati. We bought Reds baseball caps at Crosley Field.

Bertha said, "Boys, we've been so caught up in the excitement around town, we doggone near missed the game. It's already the third inning. The Brooklyn Dodgers are in Cincinnati."

While we watched the egg cook on the sidewalk, OK Carlson had taken a seat at the counter. Bertha poured him a cup of hot coffee and he sipped it. I wondered how OK could drink hot coffee on a day like this, but he had a reputation as a different sort of fellow. OK's farm work gave his body the lean look of a younger man, though someone told me he had turned fifty. The muscles of his chest and shoulders bulged underneath his white t-shirt. OK's dark blue ball cap was pushed back on his head. His face and neck had a deep reddish-brown color, but his forehead remained white. OK looked up from his cup of coffee and said, "Maybe hit don't matter if we listen to the game."

Bertha smiled and said, "Maybe not to you, OK, but it does to me."

"They say Branch Rickey is goin' to be run out of baseball," OK replied.

Shufflehead stared at the pack of cigarettes OK had rolled up in the left sleeve of his t-shirt. "Who's Branch Rickey?"

"Get to know that name, Shufflehead. Branch Rickey owns the Brooklyn Dodgers. The nigras has got him in their hip pocket. He's the man what brought in Jackie Robinson to play baseball with white folks. Robinson's over there in Cincinnati today, at Crosley Field, playin' for the Dodgers. Just like he's a white man who belongs there."

"Well if he plays for the Dodgers, don't he belong there?" Shufflehead asked.

"You don't get it, Shufflehead. He's a nigra. The Cincinnati Reds and the Brooklyn Dodgers and all the other teams in baseball is white. He don't belong there."

Shufflehead's mouth inched itself open then hung in a near-gaped position, which usually meant he had to think hard about something. One time William White saw Shufflehead with his mouth gaped open and said "Shufflehead's setting a trap for flies."

Bertha jumped in, "OK, there ain't much we can do about it. Anyway, if Robinson can hit and field and hold his own in the game, I don't see why him or anybody else, even you, can't play ball."

"There is something can be done about it," OK replied. "And the Saint Louis players are threatenin' to do it."

"Whut?" Shufflehead asked.

"Very simple. When the Dodgers come to town, just don't play. Stay home. Don't take the field. A couple of times of a-doin' that and Mr. Branch Rickey'll think twice before he puts Robinson on the field."

Whit Saunders pushed his chair back from the table. "I read about that in the newspaper, OK," he said. "The Saint Louis players made a stink and talked about pullin' those shenanigans when Brooklyn came to play a series a couple of weeks ago."

"That's right."

"And," Whit continued in a matter-of-fact voice, "Branch Rickey said, 'Fine, don't play. We'll accept the forfeit and a score of nine to nothing.' Them's the rules, OK, like it or not. As soon as Mr. Rickey said that, the Saint Louis players shut up and the games was played."

"Well, I don't read no newspapers like you, Whit. But I know this. It's wrong for a nigger to be out there on the field with white players. The nigras have their own leagues. Robinson used to play for the Kansas City Monarchs."

Whit said, "Well, you got a point. They've had their own leagues for twenty years. Robinson played there. But even if he is a nigger, I don't fault him or anybody else for trying to get ahead and join a National League team."

"Well he is a nigger, and he ought to go back," OK said. "If'n I had my way we'd send him back. But first we'd deal teach him a lesson, real private-like, and set an example. One that'd cause Robinson and others like him to stay away from the Dodgers and all them other major league teams."

Bertha refilled OK's cup with hot coffee. "You don't mean that, OK."

"I never been more serious in my life, Bertha. You don't realize what's goin' on. I been there. I seen it happen. Baseball is just a small part of the nigras' plan. The next thing you know they'll be movin' into Kettle. Niggers takin' up with white women. I watched it happen in Tulsa when I was growin' up."

My Daddy and one of his friends had talked about OK one day at our house. Daddy said there'd been a rumor that years ago OK had killed a man out in Tulsa. In nineteen and thirty-five OK moved to Kettle from Tulsa. He bought a farm and grew tobacco and corn up on Burnt Church Road.

OK had been widowed the spring his boy Carl finished first grade. Most Sundays OK brought Carl to our Kettle Methodist Church Sunday school. Then he and Carl would attend the Sunday worship service together. They always sat by themselves in a side pew, but sang and joined in the services. Carl had coal black hair and stood about my height. Momma said he was nice-looking. He took classes with me at Kettle High, and had a hard time in most every subject. OK came to our school a lot and worked with Carl's teachers on his homework assignments. William White took a liking to Carl and helped him when he could. At the end of our eighth-grade year, OK brought William White a spiral notebook. "A little thank you gift," he said, "for helping Carl in math."

I'd never thought about the things OK described—Jackie Robinson playing baseball. Negroes taking up with white women. No Negroes lived in Kettle and as far as I knew none ever had. In our problems of democracy class at Kettle High we agreed that separate but equal had been a fair way to treat colored people. At the C&O Passenger Station in Huntington they had their own entrance and drinking fountains, just like white folks. Their fountains had the same water ours had. And their benches in the terminal had the same hard oak wood that folks sat on in the white section.

William White said he read that Negroes didn't have the intelligence of whites. From what I had seen among the colored folks in Huntington, mostly janitors and street sweepers, he had that right. In the movies, Steppin' Fetchit and Bill 'Bojangles' Robinson added a lot of fun, but I wouldn't want one of them to take Joan Crawford or Barbara Stanwick on a date.

Bertha gave a thin smile to OK. "Oh, you and Tulsa," she said. "That was a long time ago. Ancient history. These is modern times."

"Not so long ago, Bertha. Only twenty-six years. I was there." OK talked towards his coffee cup even though he'd directed his words to Bertha. "By nineteen and twenty-one the nigras in Tulsa had got it into their heads that they was as good as white folks. One of 'em helped his self to a white woman. Just had his way with her, people said. We got ourselves deputized by the law, and armed. Then we rolled through Greenwood, better known as Niggertown, fixin' things. First we took care of the men who might take a shine to our women. Then, just to drive it home, we tended to some of their women."

OK paused. He gazed at his cup of coffee. Everybody looked at him but nobody spoke a word. I didn't know which made the most noise, a horsefly beating its wings against the inside of the front window or the pounding of my heart.

OK looked up at Bertha and grinned. "Thirty-five city blocks. All of Niggertown, burned to the ground. Yessir, burned to the ground. Businesses. Homes. Hit didn't matter. Three hundred dead, they said later. I don't know, it could've been more. I'll tell you this, I did my part. Even got myself a little trophy, a ear off'n a dead nigger." He gave a little laugh. "After that night everybody in Niggertown was rounded up and put in tent camps behind tall wire fences till things settled down. After they was let out, all the nigras was required by law to carry ID tags the city issued to 'em. Anybody without one got arrested and locked up. Still seems like a good idea to me. Maybe Mr. Jackie Robinson should carry a nigra ID tag."

Willam White and I looked at each other. Shufflehead gaped and stared at OK. On the radio, the baritone voice of the Cincinnati Reds broadcaster, Waite Hoyt, described the Reds-Dodgers game. Whit and Bertha turned and stared at the radio, like it had a life of its own. Me too. So did Shufflehead and William White. OK stared at his coffee. Waite Hoyt's words had to take a back seat to the killing and burning OK talked about. My stomach had a sinking feeling. A trophy—a human ear? Waite Hoyt said the game had no score, but his words just bounced around in my brain—a human ear?

The screen door opened and Chief Tackett walked in. Whit Saunders greeted him. "Hi Chief, anything new on the crooks?"

"A little." Chief Tackett eased himself into his favorite seat, the kitchen side of the back booth, the one nearest the counter. Nobody ever sat in the chief's seat except Bertha, and she rarely ever sat down, so most of the time the seat stayed open for him. The chief's big belly pressed smack up against the table, even with his back flat against the booth. He took off his police cap with its shiny black bill and khaki top, and placed it on the table. Then with his red bandanna he wiped sweat off his face and the top of his head. The chief picked up last week's issue of the *Kettle News Leader* lying in the booth and looked at the front page just like it had fresh news.

Bertha handed the chief a cold bottle of RC Cola. "On me, Chief."

"Don't keep us in suspense, Chief," Whit said. "What's happenin'?"

The Chief looked up from his paper. "Well, the white feller is Edward Ralph Young. Driver's license says he's from Ironton, Ohio. He pronounced Ohio, "Uh-hi-uh." The colored boy is George Washington Walker. He's from Huntington. They're both twenty-seven years old. I impounded the car. It's over at Buckingham's Gulf Station."

OK jumped in. "Colored boy? Impounded car? What's goin' on, Chief?"

"We got us a couple of crooks, OK. May be part of a theft ring, though I don't as yet know for sure. Thought they could pull a fast one and rob Miss Hattie McClintock at gunpoint. But William White here," he nodded at William White, "was too quick for 'em. He reported the crime and gave me a description of the offenders and their car, includin' the license plates." The chief nodded again towards William White, who broke into a big grin. "I arrested 'em down at Buster's A&W Drive Inn and locked 'em up. Case closed."

OK rotated his counter stool until he faced the chief. "Gunpoint? Chief, them boys robbed Miss Hattie at gunpoint?"

"Well, they tried to rob her. But the joinin' of her screams with William White's passin' by caused them to take off. But they didn't get far. No sir, not far a-tall."

Everybody looked at the chief, then at each other, smiled and nodded their heads.

The loud smack of OK's hand against the counter caused everybody to jump. Bertha looked wide-eyed at OK.

OK's voice rose and his face turned a dark crimson, "By God, it ain't right. One nigra's playin' baseball at Crosley Field, and another one's is right here in Kettle, a one hundred percent all-white Christian town, aimin' to take a old lady's money."

"Easy, OK," the Chief said. "Hit's near a hundred degrees this afternoon. You're goin' to drive the temperature to one hundred and one."

Shufflehead laughed. "That's a good'n, Chief."

OK turned and stared at Shufflehead, who got red in the face, looked down at his shoes then muttered, "Sorry."

"Chief," OK said, "do you mean to tell me that them boys tried to rob Miss Hattie and now they're over in the hoosegow? Just a-sittin' there?"

"That's right, OK. We'll have a hearin' later today or maybe tomorrow. Anderson Burns went with his wife up to her sister's place in Hamlin. Soon as he gets back."

"Who's Anderson Burns? What's he got to do with it?"

"OK, Anderson Burns is the town's Justice of the Peace. He's deputized by Circuit Court Judge Orley Higgenbotham and under the judge's order to hear any local cases and settle 'em if possible before bringin' 'em down to the County Courthouse. The judge says they's been too many nuisance cases comin' in from Kettle and other little towns around the county. Cases that ain't needed to come into Circuit Court. They clog up the system, Judge Higgenbotham said. Them was his words. Clog up the system. And he's the judge."

A slight grin eased across OK's face, but not the kind of grin that comes after a joke. More like a grin that happens in a baseball game after you hit a fast curve ball thrown by a good pitcher. "Well, chief, I think you got the right idee," he said big and loud. "We should settle this case right here in Kettle. No need to drag them boys down to the courthouse in Huntington. No sir, no need a-tall." He sat erect on his counter stool. "Yes sir, settle things right here in Kettle." His voice rose, "The sooner the better. I think I know how we can do it, and do the judge a favor at the same time."

"Easy, OK. This is a matter for the law."

OK's grin widened and showed his pearly white teeth. "That's right, chief. And you're the law. You deputize me and I'll be the law too. If you have to take them fellers over to Anderson Burns's place for a hearin', they're likely to be more'n a match for you." He paused and his grin gave way to a most serious look. "I'm strong and I know how to handle a gun, if you git my drift."

"I'll study on it, OK. But I think I'll do just fine. Anyway, most likely Anderson Burns will come to Town Hall. We'll have our hearin' in the front office."

"You and that Burns is no match for them crooks."

The chief gave a big sigh, "It's a hearin', OK, not a prize fight. Now just let it be."

"Call it what you want, Chief." His voice rose and his face reddened. "But I call it a skirmish in a war over who's gonna control the U. S. of A. We fought a battle in Tulsa. Won that one."

OK jumped up from his counter stool. He looked at everybody and yelled, "Looks like we're goin' to fight another one right here in Kettle. What do you folks think? Will it be us or the niggers?"

Nobody said a word. OK walked to the front door. Then he turned and looked squarely at Chief Tackett. "I wonder about you, Chief. Just which side are you on?" He turned and pounded the heel of his right hand into the screen door so hard the door sprung open, went all the way around and banged against the front of the building. OK stepped out on to the street, then turned and gave one last look into Bertha's Place before pulling the bill of his ball cap low over his eyes. At a fast pace he headed down the street.

We all stared at the front door, like OK still stood there. The only sound was Waite Hoyt's voice on the radio. One by one we all turned and looked towards the radio, as if Waite himself stood at the end of the counter. He said the Dodgers had the bases loaded, and Jackie Robinson had come to bat. He faced Johnny Vander Meer, who had pitched two consecutive no-hit games for the Reds in nineteen and thirty-eight, but hadn't had a winning season since forty-two. Robinson worked the count to three balls and two strikes—then we heard the crack of the bat hitting the ball. Waite Hoyt could hardly raise his voice above the noise of the fans at Crosley Field. On a close play, Robinson slid into second base. Safe. His two-base hit had cleared the bases. Three runs had scored. The Dodgers led, four to one.

Chief Tackett took a long pull on his RC Cola, then stood up and placed the bottle on the counter. "Well, that hit by Robinson ain't goin' to help OK's attitude any. Thanks, for the RC, Bertha. Sure hit the spot. Nice to see you folks. Though, now that I think about it, I've had better conversation."

"Chief, is OK a-goin' to come after them crooks?" Shufflehead asked.

"Nothin' is goin' to happen, Shufflehead. You and everybody else, just go on about your business. And I'll go on about mine." He walked towards the front door, then turned and said, "William White, stay close. If'n we can hold the hearin' this evenin', I'll need you to testify." Then, talking more to himself than any of us, he said, "I better call Miss Hattie as well."

The chief put on his cap and pulled the shiny bill down until it was about even with his eyes. "I'll git over to the jail and check on them boys. Hit's hotter'n blue blazes in there. There ain't no windows in that cell. Maybe I could git a fan set it up in the doorway. I think Thelma Jean has one that we ain't usin' over at the house."

Bertha wiped a damp rag across the counter top where OK's cup had been, then paused. "Something ain't right. Just ain't right. I don't trust OK Carlson any further than I can see him. And right now I can't see him at all."

The clock in front of the Bank of Kettle struck three as we left Bertha's Place. William White and I each went home. I stretched out on the cool grass in the shade just behind our back porch. Momma said we'd have cold sandwiches for dinner and eat on the porch. Suited me fine.

Lying there I thought about all that had happened in the short space of this day. Mowing, a thunderstorm, robbery, William White, arrests. OK Carlson. Some days it seemed like nothing at all happened in Kettle. Then we'd have a day like this, when more things happened than occurred in a month.

I must have drifted off to sleep, for the next thing I knew Momma nudged my shoulder. "Freddy, William White is on the phone."

"I'm calling you from Bertha's Place. Get down here. OK Carlson is up on the platform at the railroad station giving a speech. And there's a crowd on the street, some of 'em people I've never seen before. They're getting all riled up."

I started towards the front door and Momma said, "Your Daddy will be home soon, then we'll eat. Don't go far or stay long."

Dark clouds gathered beyond the hills west of town. This time of year we sometimes got an early evening thunderstorm. With this heat wave and dry spell, we could use another rain like we had earlier today, only longer, wetter. Daddy once told me an evening thunderstorm cleansed the air of all the foul words of the day. When I thought of what OK said down at Bertha's, I figured today's air could use some cleansing.

OK stood on the loading platform at the railroad station. His voice carried up the street. He waved his arms and paced from one side of the platform to the other as he yelled his words. A crowd of maybe fifty or more men stood in the gravel parking lot between the platform and Main Street. I joined a small group that included William White and Shufflehead, standing across the street in front of Bertha's Place.

William White said, "Freddy, OK's been giving quite a speech. He said robbing old ladies at gunpoint is nothing compared to what those boys in jail have in mind. He talked about baseball teams filled with Jackie Robinsons, whole teams of colored players. That's just a start," he said, "and then he started naming names of women around town and some girls in high school, real slow like. He described each of them and asked the men to imagine those women and girls with colored men. Nigras who'd have their way with them."

"That ain't true, is it Freddy?" Shufflehead asked. "A colored man ain't goin' to take up with a girl like Beverly Shade, is he?"

"No, Shufflehead. That's just OK talking crazy. Beverly isn't going to take up with anybody she doesn't want to take up with."

Lots of what OK said troubled me, but I had to admit he made a good point. Negroes had their place, but not here in Kettle. And not with Beverly. Separate but equal.

In the hot and sweaty crowd standing below OK, one fellow held a long wooden axe handle. A short fat man had a shotgun. Some faces began to fall into place, men I sometimes saw in town on Saturday afternoons.

All of a sudden OK became silent. He wiped his forehead with a green rag and looked at the crowd. Then he yelled out, with an emphasis on each word, his voice rising, "Answer me this. Are we goin' to take it? Are we?"

Right away the crowd of men answered him, just like one person standing there, "No!"

OK yelled, "Are we gonna do somethin' about it?"

"Yes!"

"Are we gonna do it tomorrow?"

A tall man wearing a railroad cap and neckerchief yelled, "Hell no," then lots of men joined in with a chorus of "Hell no."

"Well, when are we gonna do it?"

"Now!" the voices said.

"Let's go." OK leaped off the platform and ran up Main Street. The crowd ran behind him.

We figured OK had headed for Town Hall, so we took a route through alleys to avoid the crowd. The light of late afternoon had shrunk noticeably as the clouds gathered. Thunder sounded off in the distance.

When we got to Town Hall, OK stood in front of the porch of the old white frame, two-story building. The gray slate on the roof had a few missing tiles, and the paint on the west side of the building needed a new coat. He faced the crowd gathering around him on the street. Behind him, Chief Tackett stood in the screen door of the front entrance to Town Hall. He had his thumbs hooked over the top of his leather gun belt. His light khaki shirt had turned dark brown with sweat.

OK yelled, "The chief here," he turned and pointed towards the screen door, "says those boys are gonna have a hearin'. Well, I say let's do it, let's have a hearin', right here and now. Are you ready?"

"Yes" the crowd yelled. One man said, "Let's hear the evidence, Chief." In the sky a long and deep rumble sounded. "Bring out the nigger. We ain't got all night. Looks like it's gonna rain." Some of the men laughed.

OK turned his back to the crowd and faced the chief. "How about it, Chief? We're a law-abiding group of assembled citizens, ain't we? Let's have a hearin'."

119

Chief Tackett opened the screen door and said, "OK, we'll have a lawful hearin' inside when Anderson Burns arrives."

A car approached with its horn lightly beeping. The crowd made way for a dust covered dark blue thirty-six Chevy sedan that pulled up to Town Hall. Mrs. Myrtle Mae Burns drove, though her head of blonde hair barely rose above the steering wheel. The car stopped and Justice of the Peace Anderson Burns opened the door on the passenger's side. He put his cane on the ground and steadied himself as he stepped out of the car.

Mr. Burns stood beside the car and looked at the crowd. OK and the men grew quiet as they turned and looked at Anderson Burns. Most folks knew Mr. Burns, though we looked at him like a new arrival to Kettle. He stood a good six inches above the height of the car. A few weeks earlier the *Kettle News Leader* had carried an article about a party to celebrate his fiftieth birthday. Mr. Burns wore a metal brace on his left leg. He'd had polio as a child. His thick red hair blew in the light breeze, the first air moved by nature that I'd felt all day.

Mr. Burns nodded his head towards the crowd then said in his deep but soft voice, "How'd do gentlemen." Then he turned and walked at a slow pace towards the Chief and the front door. Mrs. Burns drove away.

The chief held the screen door open and Mr. Burns walked into the front room of Town Hall. The double front window had been fully opened, and Shufflehead, William White, and I positioned ourselves on the other side of the window's screen. The crowd milled around the front door.

Anderson Burns removed his suit coat. "Hot outside, Chief. Worse in here." He walked over to the dark wooden desk at the rear of the room. The desk had been positioned to face the chairs in the room much like a teacher's desk in a classroom. He eased himself into the large oak swivel chair behind the desk.

"Are all the witnesses here, Chief?"

"Almost here, your honor. I called Miss Hattie McClintock and she's on her way. It's only a few blocks. She should be here direnkly." The chief said the word "directly" the way my Grandpa

Lemley said it and inside myself I smiled. "The other witness, William White Wallace, is here, your honor. He's yonder, just outside the winder."

Mr. Burns looked over our way and said, "Which one of you boys is William White Wallace?"

William White identified himself and Mr. Burns asked him to come in and sit near the desk. About then I heard a woman's voice say in a brisk manner, "Out, out of my way." The crowd parted and Miss Hattie McClintock walked by Shufflehead and me. The chief opened the screen door for her. Miss Hattie wore a black skirt and blouse. A small black hat with a small veil sat atop her gray hair and the veil came down in front of her eyes. The chief motioned for her to sit beside William White. Miss Hattie carefully lined up the front legs of her chair so their position matched those of the front legs of William White's chair on a crack separating two oiled oak boards of the floor.

Mr. Burns said, "Thank you for coming to the hearing, Miss Hattie."

She replied, "Anderson, I'm always ready to see that justice is done."

Mr. Burns studied some papers on the desk, and then looked up. "As you folks may know, I am Justice of the Peace Anderson Burns. This JP court is now officially in session, acting under the direction of the Cabell County Circuit Court, Judge Orley Higgenbotham presiding."

Shufflehead and I put our faces against the window screen so we could see and hear everything that happened.

Mr. Burns no sooner got the word "presiding" out of his mouth when OK banged open the screen door and yelled across the room, "Mr. Justice of the Peace, how long's this hearing a-gonna take?"

"I don't believe I know you, mister...."

"My name's OK Carlson, Mister Justice of the Peace Anderson Burns. Me and those men outside are here for the thing that's in your title, justice, Mr. Justice of the Peace. Yessir, and we mean to have it."

Chief Tackett's back stiffened.

"Mr. OK Carlson," Mr. Burns said quietly. He looked down at his note pad, took a fountain pen from his pocket, removed its cap and wrote something, then looked up. "Mr. OK Carlson I will politely ask you to remove yourself from this room. I'd advise you to do that now."

The chief's right hand moved to his holster and gripped the butt of his pistol.

The men in the crowd outside started yelling, "Bring 'em out Chief," and "Let's see the nigger, it's him we want. We done had our hearin', let's have some action."

OK took a couple of steps towards Mr. Burns's desk. Chief Tackett chief drew his pistol, held it by his side pointing at the floor and stepped in front of OK. Hardly a breath of air separated them.

OK glared at the chief. The screen door burst open and men spilled into the room. They yelled and pushed each other forward. One man fell into OK's backside, pushing him into the Chief's frontside.

Chief Tackett took one step backwards as OK lurched forwards, off balance. The chief slammed his left forearm against the side of OK's head, knocking him to the floor. The chief raised his pistol, pointed it at the ceiling. The sound of the pistol's firing exploded in the small room.

Miss Hattie screamed and covered her eyes. Along with everybody else, Mr. Burns and William White flinched, and then stared at the chief. William White sat ramrod straight in his chair, his face drained of color. The noise of the gunshot in the room stunned everybody. Like me, they must've had a ringing in their ears. Bits of plaster fell and a cloud of dust drifted from the ceiling. OK lay still on the floor and the men who had crowded into the room stood motionless. The men in the street backed away from the front door.

In a firm voice the chief said, "OK, you git up. Now you boys move out of here. Real quiet-like." He waved his pistol towards OK and the men in the room. OK picked himself up. He and the ten or fifteen men who had crowded into the room eased themselves backwards through the door, their eyes fixed on the barrel of the chief's pistol.

The chief followed the men into the street. Once outside, the men started to grouse among themselves. Chief Tackett yelled, "I said, out of here." He pointed his pistol in the air and fired another shot. The men ran down the street, rounded the corner and disappeared.

Shufflehead whispered to me, "Freddy, now he's only got four rounds in his gun."

The chief holstered his pistol and walked back into the room. "I don't believe we'll have any more trouble from them fellers, Your Honor."

"Thank you, Chief Tackett. Now, let's all settle down and get on with our business. Please take a seat, Chief." Mr. Burns gestured to the empty chair beside William White. "Tell this magistrate's court what happened. Then we'll examine the evidence."

The chief sat down and described William White's report of the crime, Bernadine Blackwood's phone call with a similar report, and William White's descriptions of the offenders and the license plate. He ended with an account of the arrest of the two men at Buster's A&W Drive Inn.

When Mr. Burns asked, "Miss Hattie, has the Chief correctly described the events of this morning, in so far as they involved you?" she immediately stood up. "You may remain seated," Mr. Burns said.

She sat down. "Oh yes, exactly correct." Miss Hattie spoke quickly and in a matter-of-fact and snippy manner. "A white man and a colored man in the same car. And now they're in there," she pointed towards the closed door behind Mr. Burns, "mixed races in the same cell. Can you imagine? Up to no good, I say." Miss Hattie had a way of pursing her lips when she spoke that Shufflehead once tried to imitate. But he couldn't purse his lips and speak clearly the same time. Miss Hattie continued, "Though in his account of the robbery attempt, the chief omitted the terror

I felt when the white man placed his gun right in front of my nose. But then the Chief would have no way of knowing that directly, would he? Nor would he know the even greater terror I felt when I saw a nigger waiting in the car to do God knows what to me. Makes me shudder to think about it. Those big strong men and tiny little me, an old lady. Terror was what I felt, all right. I screamed. Screamed again. Later I thanked God for the power of an old lady's scream."

"Thank you, Miss Hattie. I'm sure it's been difficult for you. And I don't like the lockup situation any better than you do. But, as you know, we have only one jail cell in Kettle."

Mr. Burns nodded at William White and said, "William White, this is an informal hearing about what happened today. Please stay seated and I'll ask you to answer a few questions truthfully and to the best of your ability. Will you do that?"

William White sat straight in his chair, his hands on his knees. "Yes sir, Mr. Justice. I mean Mr. Anderson…uh… Mr. Burns."

"William White, you heard the chief's description of this afternoon's events. Did the chief describe the events correctly, in so far as they involved you?"

"Oh, yes, sir. Very correctly."

"I understand that you heard Miss Hattie scream as you rode by on your bicycle. And you saw a man leap off the porch, get into a car, a black Ford coupe, and speed away. Is that correct?"

"Yes, sir."

"Did you see a gun? Was the white man carrying a pistol?"

"Oh, yes, sir. He had a pistol in his hand, left hand, when he jumped off the porch. No question about that."

"Thank you, William White."

The sky had grown darker while Miss Hattie and William White testified. The lights in the room and the darkness outside made it seem like a hearing in the dead of night, not six o'clock in the evening.

Mr. Burns made some notes, and then leaned back in his chair. He drew a pressed white handkerchief out of his pocket and wiped his brow, then passed the handkerchief around his neck.

"Chief, do you have the pistol the man carried?"

"No sir, I don't."

"Well, where is it?"

"Mr. Burns, I impounded the car and searched it. Searched it real good. The car's trunk was loaded with Bibles. Different sizes and types. Some of 'em looked pretty expensive. Lots of Bibles, but no gun. Door to door Bible sales—a good cover for what they was up to, if you ask me.

"After I searched the car, I drove along the highway down to Buster's A&W, real slow-like, and peered along the shoulder of the road as best I could, bein' alone and searchin' and drivin' at the same time. Then I give Buster's parking lot a good goin' over. Nothin' there. I thought, it's possible they threw the gun out the window at some spot well away from the highway, or even drove over to the covered bridge and dropped the gun into the Sour Apple River. I don't know. All I know is I don't have their pistol."

Anderson Burns curled the corners of his mouth downward as he listened to the chief's news. He looked at his notepad and remained silent for a minute.

"Mr. Burns," the chief said, "if you feel it is worth doin', tomorrow mornin' I could swear in a search party and have 'em walk along the highway down to Buster's place. It would take a little time and cost the town some money, but, yes sir, we could do it."

About the time Chief Tackett said, "Yes sir, we could do it," a bolt of lightening cracked. Bright blue light surrounded us and directly overhead a deafening boom of thunder exploded. Shufflehead jumped and banged his head against the windowsill. The lights dangling from the ceiling in town hall dimmed.

The lights came back to normal and Mr. Burns said, "Chief, would you bring the prisoners into the room?"

The chief opened the door to the back room. Miss Hattie unsnapped her purse, pulled out a handkerchief and placed it over her nose and mouth. The sweet smell of the perfume reached our window along with the sweaty stench.

Shufflehead whispered, "Pee-yew, Freddy. That stinks."

125

The chief followed the prisoners into the room. "Now you boys walk right slow-like and sit down in the two open chairs in front of Justice of the Peace Burns's desk. I'm puttin' you on notice that this here is an extension of the Cabell County Circuit Court. No funny business. You understand?"

"Uh-huh. We understand."

The two men walked, or you might say stumbled, into the room, handcuffed together. The white man had a short and muscular build, not six feet tall as William White had described him. The colored man stood tall and thin. They wore white shirts rumpled and wet with sweat, and blue gabardine trousers. The chief guided them to the two chairs and they sat down facing Anderson Burns.

Miss Hattie pointed at the white man and said, "That's him, the one with the nigger. He's the one that tried to rob me."

No sooner had the men sat down than the screen door opened and in walked Editor James Garfield Worthington, carrying his large press camera, and another man. Mr. Burns turned to them and James Garfield introduced the man with him, Nick Blasingame, a reporter for the *Huntington Herald Dispatch*. Mr. Blasingame stood about the chief's height, maybe five foot ten, and had a heavy five o'clock shadow beard and dark curly hair. He wore a white shirt and had his necktie loosened.

James Garfield approached Mr. Burns's desk and said, "Sorry we're late, Your Honor. May I interrupt to take a couple of photographs?"

Mr. Burns nodded and said, "We'll pause a moment for the gentlemen of the press." Then he smiled and said to James Garfield, "There may be a little bit of history here. It's not every day you get to photograph a colored man in Kettle's Town Hall."

James Garfield walked behind Mr. Burns's chair. When he took a photo of the two men seated in front of the desk, the flash bulb in his camera crackled and for an instant the room filled with white light. After he replaced the flashbulb and pointed the camera at the two witnesses, William White lit into a big grin. Miss Hattie straightened her veil, placed her purse on her lap, and clutched its top with both hands, grim-faced.

Mr. Blasingame walked to the back of the room, stood in front of the window, opened his notebook, and started writing. Shufflehead said in a loud whisper through the screen, "Hey, down in front." I poked Shufflehead in the ribs with my elbow. Mr. Blasingame moved to his right, towards the door.

For a moment Mr. Burns gazed at the two accused men seated in front of him. The colored fellow kept crossing and uncrossing his legs and twisting his head around to look towards the back of the room. The white man kept a steady look straight ahead at Mr. Burns.

"I am the local Justice of the Peace, Anderson Burns. This is a brief hearing to determine if you'll be sent to the Court House and charged with the crime of attempted robbery. Attempted armed robbery. Do you understand that?"

The white fellow answered, "Yes sir, we understand."

Mr. Burns looked at the two men and said, "I should add, in my years as this town's Justice of the Peace, we've never had an armed robbery in Kettle. Neither have we had any colored. Or trouble with them." He paused and looked at his note pad, then turned towards the white man. "You are Edward Ralph Young?"

"I am."

The colored fellow had turned again towards the back of the room when Mr. Burns said, "Boy, look at me. You are George Washington Walker?"

The darkie snapped his head around and said, "Yas-suh, your honor, I am." His raspy voice reminded me of Rochester on the Jack Benny radio show.

"Edward Ralph Young, you are accused of the attempted armed robbery of Miss Hattie McClintock. And you, George Washington Walker, are accused of being an accomplice to the crime. Do either of you wish to say anything?"

Edward Ralph Young sat to the left of his buddy, his right wrist handcuffed to George Washington Walker's left wrist. When Young began to speak, he raised his left arm and hand to gesture, emphasize his words, the way normal folks do. Miss Hattie let out a scream that like to burst my eardrums, followed by, "Don't shoot. Don't shoot!"

Although his long-sleeved shirt covered his arm, at the end of it instead of a hand he had a shiny steel thing that looked like a pincer. As he spoke his left hand, held about chest high, moved back and forth.

William White's chair fell with a bang as he dove to the floor and covered his head with his arms. Chief Tackett pulled his pistol, stood and looked around but didn't seem to know where to point it.

Anderson Burns spoke calmly, "Miss Hattie, there's no weapon and no cause for alarm." He paused then added in the tone of voice a parent uses with a child, "Chief, you can put your gun away. William White, please pick up your chair and sit down."

After everybody got themselves resettled, Mr. Burns continued. "Now, Mr. Young, you were saying?"

"Your honor, we was discharged from the Army about a year ago. We come home and had a hard time finding work. I might as well tell you, you'll find out anyway, we was arrested in Huntington a few months ago for drunk and disorderly. We'd been hired to do day work at Tri-State Tobacco Warehouse, you may know the place, down by the Ohio River. The first morning, when we showed up for work the supervisor took one look at George and said, 'No colored is working for me,' and fired him. I quit right on the spot. That day we drank too much beer and went back to the warehouse. After the supervisor got off work, we raised a ruckus with him, had a fight. That's when we got arrested.

"In spite of drinking beer, which we admit to, we're Christians, which led us to get jobs selling Bibles door to door. For the most part, we been selling 'em in Huntington, where George grew up. While we was working there, George's uncle told us we ought to try selling Bibles in Kettle. He said folks in Kettle was God-fearing Christians. Today was our first day in town."

Mr. Burns looked at the white fellow real serious like and asked him, "Did you and your colored friend attempt to rob Miss Hattie McClintock at gunpoint."

"No, sir."

"Then tell me, why did Miss Hattie McClintock believe you were attempting to rob her?"

"Well, Your Honor, you seen what just happened. I'd say it was this device, my metal hand, what made her think that." He extended his arm and moved his artificial hand towards Mr. Burns. "My metal hand, a prosthetic they call it, sometimes startles people. Scares 'em. It's made of steel and it's shiny. I can under-stand why at first somebody might think it's a pistol."

Young glanced to his right, towards Miss Hattie, and said, "At her front door, when the lady started to scream I tried to show her what it was. Held up my hand in front of her. But that just made things worse. She screamed louder. Yelled for help. Said I was a robber."

"That's right," Miss Hattie said. "I screamed all right. You'd scream too if you had one of those things pointed at you. And a colored boy sitting in a car in front of your house. I watched them drive up and park. I knew they were up to no good. What's the world coming to?"

Young continued, "I got scared and run off her porch. Jumped in the car and told George to hit the gas. We hightailed it out of there."

No one spoke for a moment. A strong gust of wind blew dust and leaves around Shufflehead and me. Mr. Burns made some notes, and then asked, "I'm curious, Mr. Young, would you tell me how you came to have an artificial hand?"

"It happened overseas, Your Honor." Young said he had been in the Army, a sergeant in an infantry division that landed at Normandy. A couple of days later his unit got into a firefight and a German soldier threw a grenade that got him. Took off his right hand and killed his buddy. The Army sent him to the USA and a hospital where they attach artificial hands and teach wounded veterans how to use them. While he talked, another strong, this time longer-lasting, blast of wind hit us. The wind had a slight chill to it and carried the moist smell of rain.

Young looked at the floor, then at Mr. Burns. "My steel hand can do most things a regular hand does, Your Honor, though it's not much good for petting a dog or nothin' like that. Once I danced with a girl at a canteen, but soon after we started dancin' she walked back to her chair and set down."

Mr. Burns turned to the colored man. "Did you see combat, Walker?"

"Yes, suh." Walker said he belonged to a Negro tank battalion in Europe and got shot up pretty bad in both his legs. He met Young when they were in a rehab unit. Walker pointed at Young, "He helped me learn to walk again."

"Do you men have any proof of your service in the Army?"

The two men looked at each other, and then Young spoke. "Yes, sir. Maybe you'd call it proof. We both got our old dog tags. Still wear 'em. They got our names and serial numbers. You could check the serial numbers with Army records. Wearing the dog tags is a habit, I suppose. Until now I thought they brought me good luck. Now that I think about it, we got wounded wearing those tags and we been arrested twice wearing them. Maybe we ought to quit."

Each man reached under his shirt and pulled a chain with Army dog tags on it over his head and handed the tags to Mr. Burns. Young did this using his artificial hand, which got everybody's attention. Shufflehead elbowed me, "Look at that, Freddy."

Anderson Burns inspected the tags, made some notes, and handed them back to the men. He studied the notes on the pad in front of him, and then looked up.

"Kettle has never been the kind of town that cottoned to coloreds. I see no reason for us to start now. Under the law, separate but equal means what it says." He paused and then said, "Separate. And in Kettle we obey the law. Nothing personal, Walker, that's just the way things are. You boys shouldn't have been riding around town together."

Mr. Burns pushed his chair back from the desk and sat erect. "But the law also says equal, and in my court that means an impartial application of the evidence. Miss Hattie and William White had reasonable cause to be frightened. To believe there was a robbery in progress. But the absence of a pistol and the presence of what could easily be mistaken for a pistol, Mr. Young's artificial steel hand, tells me there was no robbery attempt. Just understandable mistakes in judgment by Miss Hattie and William White. Of course, you, Mr. Young, made your own mistake in judgment, coming to Kettle with a colored. But that's all we have here. Understandable mistakes in judgment."

Miss Hattie interrupted, "But Anderson, that man..."

In the gentle tone of voice a teacher might use in explaining something to a child in school, Mr. Burns said, "Miss Hattie, please. I appreciate your concern. But based on the evidence, I believe this hearing has gone about as far as it needs to go. I thank you and William White for your time and your testimony. Do either of you have anything to add?"

William White shook his head sidewise. Miss Hattie pursed her lips and said, "A colored man in Kettle. I wonder what the world's coming to."

"Chief Tackett—anything to add?"

The chief looked at the floor and shook his head, no.

Then in an official-sounding voice, Mr. Burns said, "I have heard the testimony of everyone involved in this incident. As Justice of the Peace I see no reason to remand these men to the Circuit Court. I hereby release these men, and ask you, Chief Tackett, to take them to their automobile at Buckingham's Gulf Station."

Everybody stood up. Edward Ralph Young and George Washington Walker both grinned and said, "Thank you, Your Honor."

The chief's mouth turned down at the corners as he said, "Now you fellers has suffered some inconvenience, I know. We're real sorry about that, but I'll get you to your car, and..."

Suddenly the room filled with OK's voice, loud and strong. He stood on the street side of the screen door. "Hey Judge, we'll get 'em out of town for you." Behind OK stood a large crowd of men. With the wind kicking up and everybody so intent on the proceedings, nobody had heard them sneak back. The short fat man bearing a shotgun stood beside OK.

"Me and the boys, we had our own hearin', Mr. Justice of the Peace, but we didn't come to the same conclusion as you. We ain't exactly a bunch of nigger lovers."

A second later lightning struck not far from Town Hall. Right on its heels, thunder exploded.

Chief Tackett turned and handcuffed himself to Young, and then Young to Walker. They walked single file to the screen door. The chief had his pistol in his right hand. The wire spring on the old wooden screen door stretched and squeaked as the door opened wide and the three men passed into the dark street and the wind, the chief's pistol in front of them. The crowd moved towards them and then backed away from the pistol, opening a path in front of Chief Tackett. To the side, behind the chief and the two men, the crowd closed in, moving along at the chief's pace, like the water of a stream curling behind a log as it floated in the current.

OK and the short fat man with the shotgun planted themselves in the chief's path, and everything came to a halt. Chief Tackett and OK stared at each other. The man with the shotgun raised his gun and pointed it towards Walker's head. Nobody moved.

A sudden burst of light and then an ear-bursting crack and blast of an explosion hit us. The light nearly blinded me. The ground shook. In an instant the tall elm tree beside Town Hall split down the middle and most of the old tree's canopy fell in two large chunks. One section fell across the roof of Town Hall. The other deposited itself directly on the crowd in Benson Street, burying us in its branches. Buckets of rain mixed with hail began to fall. A gale force wind kicked in and whipped the hail and rain around the fallen tree and the crowd. The few men who remained standing ran for shelter under the porch of Town Hall.

Chief Tackett and the two former prisoners, along with most everybody else not under the porch, fell to the street. Later the chief said he dove, pulling Young and Walker to the street with him. He said he thought the man had fired his shotgun, "Maybe blowed Walker's head off."

Above the roar of the wind and rain, OK Carlson yelled, "Harley, git your damn shotgun. Them boys is goin' to escape."

"Git it yourself. And git this tree off'n me."

I pulled myself up and pushed my way through the wet leaves and branches. Shufflehead grabbed my shirttail and followed me. I could see Chief Tackett and the two men, the three of them still handcuffed to each other, making their way out of the thicket of branches and leaves.

Beep beep beep—the car's horn penetrated the wind and rain. Mrs. Myrtle Mae Burns slowed her Chevy to a stop in the center of Benson Street alongside the wide swath of the fallen tree. Mr. Burns walked through the door of the white frame building and paused under its hand-lettered sign, Town Hall, Kettle, W.Va. Then he walked forward into the rain. His left leg, the one with a metal brace on it, dragged behind him like it could barely keep up with the pace of his right leg. The wind first tousled his long red hair, then the driving rain plastered his hair to his head. With his wooden cane in his left hand, Mr. Burns steadied his chunky body against the wind. He made his way to Chief Tackett and put his right hand on the chief's arm. He walked with the chief and the two former prisoners, the three of them handcuffed links in a human chain, around the tree's wet branches to the Chevy. Mr. Burns opened the car's rear door. The chief and the men trailing him climbed into the car's back seat.

Mr. Burns turned towards the car's front, passenger side, door. OK Carlson had planted himself squarely in his path, his white t-shirt soaking wet against his muscular body. One of OK's hands supported the barrel of the twelve-gauge shotgun and the other tightly gripped the lower gun stock, his finger against the gun's trigger, knuckles white.

"That nigra is comin' with me." OK pushed the business end of the barrel against Anderson Burns's chest, his voice deep and raspy. "Mr. Justice of the Peace, out in my barn I got me a ear that I took off'n a dead nigra. Leastways they said he was dead, I don't know. Step aside or I might soon have one of yourn."

Mr. Burns's deep voice penetrated the wind. It was no longer the soft voice I had heard inside Town Hall. "Mr. Carlson, we will now leave. Peacefully. If there's any trouble, I'll order the chief to arrest you."

"Dead men don't prosecute nobody." OK pointed the gun at Mr. Burns's chest.

The two men stared at each other. Water streamed down their faces. OK's face reddened. Anderson Burns' face paled, his cane trembled.

Mr. Burns spoke in a quiet voice, barely loud enough to rise above the wind. "Kettle is not like Tulsa, Mr. Carlson. We're not your kind of town."

OK glared at Mr. Burns, poked the business end of the shotgun barrel into Mr. Burns' shirt buttons.

William White gripped one of my arms, Shufflehead had both hands around the other one. We edged closer to Mr. Burns and OK.

"Pull the trigger, Mr. Carlson," Mr. Burns said in an earnest tone of voice, much like a parent instructing a child to do a chore.

OK stood motionless, glaring at Mr. Burns.

"Pull the trigger!" Mr. Burns' deep voice commanded.

I started to speak to William White, but at the last second I turned to OK, "Too bad Carl's not here, Mr. Carlson."

OK's glance grazed my face. A second later he backed one small step away from Mr. Burns.

Mr. Burns slowly raised his cane, placed it against the shotgun and nudged the barrel aside, then downwards towards the street's wet bricks.

With its last passenger on board, the Chevy drove away at a speed so slow it seemed uncertain of itself. The short fat man grabbed the shotgun from OK and pointed it at the rear end of the Chevy. "Want me to shoot?" He yelled. "Whut you want me to do, OK?"

"Take that shotgun and stick it up yore ass, Harley."

The rain ended as suddenly as it began. The crowd broke up. We looked like old dishrags, soaking wet, waiting to be wrung out.

William White said to Shufflehead and me, "Boys, let's head down to Bertha's Place. We need a cool drink."

When we walked in Bertha smiled and said, "Set down, boys. RCs comin' up. Good storm. Dampened the heat of the day. Cooled off some hot tempers."

"It'll take more than a storm to do that, Bertha," I said.

Beverly and Mary Sue sat at the counter drinking iced tea. Beverly wore an armless light blue cotton dress, Mary Sue a yellow skirt and blouse. They smiled at us. "What's been going on?" Beverly asked.

William White jumped in. "You girls should've been there. Nearly had a riot over at Town Hall." He described all that happened and wrapped it up with OK holding the shotgun on Mr. Burns. "White knuckles, his finger on the trigger—the end of the barrel against Mr. Burns' chest. Mr. Burns dared him to pull the trigger, 'Pull it!' he yelled." William White paused and looked at me. "Then our boy here stood up to OK and said, 'Too bad Carl's not here.' OK took a step back, and then lowered his gun. That's all she wrote."

Beverly's blue eyes flashed at me, a smile spread over her face. Heat flushed across my face, probably turned red too.

We had each drunk about half of our RC Colas when Chief Tackett and Whit Saunders walked in. The chief's khaki shirt and trousers had turned dark brown, soaked with rain. Whit looked as he always did, dry as a bone.

"Well, Chief," Whit said, "Them boys and their Ohio plates CC 742 is on the road."

"Good idea you had, Whit, takin' up a little collection for gas. Never occurred to me. I expected Anderson Burns to give a little money, but when Miss Hattie took fifty cents from her purse, I got to admit I was surprised," the Chief said. "The money from James Garfield helped too. I don't know why that Nick Blasingame feller wouldn't donate anything. I heard him say something to James Garfield about reporters not gettin' involved in their stories. Strange if you ask me."

"Uh-oh," I said. "Momma asked me not to be late for supper." I jumped up and ran home, hoping my news about what had happened would offset Momma's upset about my tardiness.

Two days later, Thursday, the weekly edition of the *Kettle News Leader* carried an item in the section titled "Kettle Stirrings," the editor's personal column about small items of interest to folks in Kettle.

"On Tuesday Edward Ralph Young of Ironton, Ohio, and George Washington Walker of Huntington visited Kettle on business. Mr. Young and Mr. Walker are decorated veterans who served in Europe with the US Army's 90th Infantry Division and 761st Tank Battalion, respectively. While in town they spent time with Chief Arthur R. Tackett, Miss Hattie McClintock, Mr. and Mrs. Anderson Burns and yours truly, Editor J.G. Worthington.

The morning after the wild evening at Town Hall the *Huntington Herald Dispatch* had carried an article in the lower right corner of its front-page. The article, written by Nick Blasingame, bore the title, "Riot in Kettle."

Momma read the article at our breakfast table, put down the paper and said, "This article speaks of Kettle in what I'd call unflattering terms. And there is no mention of the voluntary offering to help those men buy gasoline."

Daddy nodded, then added, "Maybe Mr. Blasingame's professional ethics prevented him from including it."

For months folks speculated about the causes of what everybody had started to call the Great Kettle Riot of nineteen and forty-seven.

At the dinner table one evening in September, Daddy said, "A riot doesn't occur in a vacuum. Folks have got to look at Kettle, and the kind of town we are. And where we fall short. We all bear responsibility for it."

Not long afterwards, from the pulpit of the Kettle Methodist Church, Reverend Y. Younts Yoder spoke to the congregation about the causes of the riot, "The devil did it," he said.

And late one evening at Bertha's Place, William White and I talked about the riot. He stared into the tiny dark brown bubbles of his RC Cola and said, "Freddy, I think I did it."

Chapter 6

UNDER A DEATH SENTENCE

Most everybody knew that Pappy Roosevelt brewed corn liquor in a shed behind the hog pen furthest from the two-lane black-top county road that ran by his place. But the smells of the still and its corn liquor got lost in the powerful odors of the hog wallows' mud and manure.

One summer afternoon in nineteen and forty-seven I stopped at Bertha's Place for an RC Cola. Whit Saunders and I talked for a while and the topic of Pappy Roosevelt's illegal brewing came up. I asked Whit, "Do you figure the sheriff knows about Pappy Roosevelt's corn liquor?"

Whit nodded and grinned. "Wink Winkler's brother-in-law, William Boyd Shunt, has a cousin who's a friend of Deputy Sheriff Truitt Crabtree. According to Wink, Truitt said, and I quote, 'We figure it's better to have Pappy Roosevelt half-drunk in his hog wallow than stone sober in the streets of Kettle.'"

The Roosevelts, Harlan McKinley Roosevelt and Ovieta Blankenship Roosevelt, lived on the family's hog farm with their son, George Boy. George Boy and I had been in school together since first grade. He earned mostly "S's," satisfactory, in grade school, and in high school he got C's, except for A's in shop and vocational agriculture. By the tenth grade George Boy towered above the rest of us, over six feet tall.

At school George Boy would walk up to you, smile, and stick out his hand like he wanted to shake your hand. Then just after starting a good hand shake, he would begin to squeeze your hand and knurl your knuckles until you yelled whatever word he told you to yell. One time in the school cafeteria George Boy got hold of William White's hand, squeezed and knurled his knuckles and said, "Say 'damn,' William White, say 'damn.'"

William White scrunched up his face in pain and held back as long as he could then yelled, "Damn!" George Boy laughed and released his grip but our principal, Mr. Lawton, heard what William White yelled and told him to go to the office. After a while you'd think nobody would fall for the false promise of George Boy's outstretched hand. But there's a compelling feature to a fellow grinning and sticking out his hand for a shake, even George Boy.

Sometimes George Boy would sneak up from behind, put his thumb and forefinger on either side of one of the muscles connecting the back side of a boy's neck to the top of his shoulder, and then pinch and squeeze real hard. Always a surprise, and it hurt like the devil. Once in eighth grade George Boy did it to a girl. She let out a piercing scream then fell to the ground and laid there kicking her legs in the air, screaming and crying. To the best of my knowledge George Boy never again pinched a girl's neck.

Even though I often looked over my shoulder to make sure George Boy wasn't sneaking up behind me, sure enough, sooner or later I'd feel his pincer bear down on me. The last time it took my breath away. I winced and dropped my shoulder down low hoping he would let go. "Ahhhhh." George Boy laughed and said, "What's a matter Freddy, cat gotcher tongue?"

Just to compound things, George Boy sometimes had a bad case of the uglies. Not the kind of ugliness that's inherited from parents. The kind that got put on and worn by choice. He had coal black hair that he often didn't comb, and it was common for him to have a pimple or two on his face that needed to be popped.

When George Boy had a cold he'd go a long time without blowing his nose, and then when snot started to drip towards his upper lip and he saw somebody look at him, he'd shoot his tongue up and lick away the snot. He'd stand there and laugh with strands of boogers hanging between his lips.

William White once said George Boy had twice the strength and half the intelligence of an ox.

To be fair, George Boy sometimes washed and combed his hair, and popped his pimples. Momma said, "When George Boy fixes himself up, he can be right nice looking." And George Boy had grown into a powerful halfback on the Kettle High football team. Kids in school, as well as the coaches and folks in town, admired his accomplishments on the athletic field. In the tenth grade George Boy earned a starting position on the Kettle Tops. At times he could be a nice guy. Maybe that's why we fell for his tricks. Sometimes George Boy and I would talk and laugh together at Sunday school. One day in the summer after fourth grade a lot of us kids had gathered at the Sour Apple River beach in Riverfront Park. While we played a softball game, Missy Witherspoon, who couldn't swim, fell into the river. She screamed for help. George Boy threw aside his softball glove, jumped in the river and pulled her out. Later his Momma beamed when she said, "George Boy didn't know how to swim. I don't know how he did it, but he saved Missy."

George Boy's given name, George Boyd, got changed to George Boy long before he entered first grade. Whenever Pappy Roosevelt asked him his name, George Boy would insist that his name was "George Boy!" Pappy Roosevelt would laugh and George Boy would laugh, and before anybody knew it, "George Boy" got stuck on him like a bug on flypaper.

The Roosevelts' hog farm sat about two miles beyond what folks called "the other end of town." Most folks lived in "this end of town." The other end often had a lingering and unpleasant odor, mostly due to the nearby swamp. Starting with the spring thaw, continuing through the summer and until a hard freeze in winter, the swamp oozed a smell that resembled a mixture of swamp slime and rotten eggs. The rotten eggs portion of the odor came from an underground spring that fed the swamp with sulfur water. In addition, the swamp's aroma got a powerful boost from Pappy Roosevelt's hog farm, particularly on warm days. When a breeze passed over the farm and swamp and then blew into Kettle, many a lady would walk around town holding a perfumed handkerchief over her nose.

George Boy's Momma, Ovieta Blankenship Roosevelt, always made a point of identifying herself to strangers as "Not of the New York Roosevelts." William White said he doubted anybody would make that mistake. Most folks knew her husband had grown up on Mud Fork, about ten miles from Kettle. She also insisted that her full three names be used when ever she got singled out for having done something special at a club meeting or a church social. Mrs. Roosevelt took special pride in her Blankenship family's history for it included a colonel in the Confederate Army and a cousin who in nineteen and twenty-two ran for election as a Republican candidate for Congress.

She had powerful arms with large biceps, and stood tall. When she fluffed up her brown hair she seemed even taller. Whenever she came to town she wore a nice dress and hat, and when only running an errand she looked like most women did when they dressed for Sunday church services. Mrs. Roosevelt sometimes did volunteer work in the schools and belonged to the Kettle Women's Preparedness Club, an organization that emphasized keeping up with the times. One year she chaired the club's committee on modern cooking and stood strong for cooking complete meals from canned foods.

People often shook their heads in wonderment at the fact that Ovieta Blankenship had married Pappy Roosevelt. When I asked Momma about it, she said, "Harlan"—she always called Pappy Roosevelt by his given name—"was in the same class at Kettle High School as your father and me. He was a nice-looking young man. People often said he had considerable promise, even though he had a difficult time in his academic subjects." Then she laughed, more to herself than towards me, a quiet little laugh that caused the dimples in her cheeks to dent in. She looked pretty when she did that. "Harlan once told me that for a tall girl I was right pretty, and then asked me out on a date. I told him I appreciated his asking me, but I said no, for I already had my eye on your Daddy. Not long after that he and Ovieta started dating. She was in the class two years behind us." Mamma smiled and said, "I guess he liked tall girls, for she was taller than me. They had quite a courtship. Seemed like once it got started they were never apart."

Although my Momma called him Harlan, folks around town knew him as Pappy Roosevelt. I asked Momma where his nickname came from. She said she didn't know for sure, but guessed that everybody's hearing George Boy call him Pappy Roosevelt might have done it. Or maybe it happened because of the combination of Pappy Roosevelt's large size and the fact that he looked older than his age. Sometimes he looked sixty, if a day, but he graduated from Kettle High with Momma and Daddy. Other than when he went to church, Pappy Roosevelt always wore his dirty bib overalls, brogans, and wide-brimmed straw hat. Due to his mouth continually carrying a large wad of tobacco and an oversupply of tobacco juice, two brown lines ran from each corner of his mouth to his chin. Even after he cleaned up for church.

Pappy Roosevelt took pride in his hogs' blue ribbons at county fair, often winning over hog farmers from Kentucky and Ohio. "But," Whit Saunders commented, "he can't take full credit for it. Pappy Roosevelt married into the Blankenships, who first developed that hog farm and its prize-winning stock."

At Gruber's Department Store one day when some fellows discussed hog farming, Hartford Wilson said, "After Pappy Roosevelt got into the Blankenships' hog business, he took to hog raising like a duck takes to water. And on the side, he developed a profitable little hobby." Pappy Roosevelt began to produce corn liquor about the time George Boyd began to insist he had the name of George Boy.

Pappy Roosevelt attended Marshall College in Huntington while Ovieta Blankenship finished high school, and the summer after she graduated they married. He studied to be a high school chemistry teacher. After failing freshman English for the fourth straight semester he quit college. Pappy Roosevelt told some fellows at the Post Office, "It were the verbs what sunk me."

Soon after the wedding Pappy Roosevelt got a job as an assistant in a research lab at the Union Chemical plant near Charleston. The elder Mr. Roosevelt said, "We're just dirt farmers from Mud Fork, but my boy Harlan's smart—he's got what it takes. He's gonna do well at Union Chemical."

Momma told me that at the wedding reception Mr. Blankenship gave a toast to the couple and talked about his new son-in-law's chemistry background. How it might lead to the invention of new formula-based hog diets, and even greater improvements in the Blankenship family's line of hogs. She said, "You'd have thought he just got a new prize boar, not a son-in-law."

Pappy Roosevelt's career at Union Chemical started and ended the summer he married Ovieta Blankenship. Officials at the plant blamed Pappy Roosevelt for an explosion in the lab where he worked, one that took out most of the building's plumbing.

One summer day when all of Kettle smelled like a hog pen, I walked by the Post Office. Barney Brammer and another fellow, both of them wearing a railroad engineers' hats, stood there sharpening the blades on their pocketknives on the smooth stone of the Post Office's front window ledge. They talked about Pappy Roosevelt. Just as Barney mentioned the lab explosion, Pappy Roosevelt walked by. He stopped and stared at Barney for a couple of seconds, and then said in a loud voice, "Barney Brammer, it warn't my job to warsh out all their danged test tubes."

The elder Mr. Blankenship passed away not long after Pappy Roosevelt became a full-time hog farmer. Folks said that once Pappy Roosevelt began to run the farm, he devoted considerable time to what he proudly called "Research on secret hog food recipes. Fine-tuned mixes of chemicals and exactly right portions of meats and vegetables."

Barney Brammer and his friends smirked when they talked about Pappy Roosevelt's "research." But I had a different view of it and said so to Barney. "I figure that's how new ideas get tried and take hold in life. Pappy Roosevelt may be a little different, but he's trying new things. Experimenting."

Barney said, "Well, now, Freddy, maybe you're right. I sure like his experiments out in the shed beyond the hog pen."

I found it difficult to bring together the rough-looking man who had a hard time smiling with Momma's description of Harlan Roosevelt when they attended Kettle High School. How could a man age so fast? Then I'd remember the blow that fell on him, the loss of his little girl, Opal. The way it happened would age anybody. Opal had been born about two years ahead of George Boy and lived only about a year and a half. One day while Pappy Roosevelt took care of Opal, Mrs. Roosevelt went to the store. He mixed up feed and chemicals for the hogs while Opal played and toddled around the back yard. Pappy Roosevelt walked down to the hog pens to put the mixture in the troughs. "I kept lookin' over my shoulder, and she was right there," he said later. "I only turned away once, when I poured the mix in the troughs."

When Pappy Roosevelt returned to the back yard, he couldn't find Opal. He looked everywhere, called some neighbors, then called Chief Tackett, thinking somebody might have snatched her. The chief alerted the Kettle Volunteer Fire Department. The men came out to the farm and looked high and low. One of the firemen noticed that the cover on the underground cistern next to the house had been pushed ajar. "Well," Momma said, "you can guess the rest. He directed the beam of his flashlight down into the dark of the cistern. There in the water was little Opal. She was floating face down, not moving.

"Harlan changed after that," Momma told me. "Before his little girl died he got up early and went out to work in the barn or the hog pens. He looked for ways to improve the stock, win the hog competition at fairs around the region. After Opal's death he stopped." Momma described how, since then, on warm mornings, Pappy Roosevelt would dump his special mixes into the hog troughs, and then sit for hours in one of the old wooden Adirondack chairs he'd placed beside each of the hog pens. He'd

145

spend his mornings watching the hogs wallow in the mud. Near each chair he kept a garden hose, and from time to time he'd grab it, twist the nozzle and spray water into the hog pen to increase the mud supply. Then he'd reach into his hip pocket, pull out a small flask of corn liquor and take a sip.

Momma said, "I've often wondered what life might have been like for Harlan and his family if Opal hadn't fallen into that cistern." What if I'd had a sister and the same thing that happened to Opal had happened to her and my Daddy? Would he spend his days sitting in our back yard drinking corn liquor? What if, years from now, I had a little girl and it happened to me—what would I do?

George Boy worked around the farm and helped out with what he called "Pappy Roosevelt's scientific work." On warm mornings, as soon as he got his chores done, George Boy would join his father in one of the Adirondack chairs, grab a hose, and add water to a hog pen's mud supply. The two of them sometimes made bets on whether either of them could lift some or all of a particular hog.

Barney Brammer told folks at Bertha's Place that one day he delivered some feed grain to Pappy Roosevelt's farm, and while he unloaded it Pappy Roosevelt pointed to the largest boar in the hog pen and asked, "George Boy, do you think you can lift his hind end?"

"You bet, Pappy Roosevelt!"

"Twenty-five cents says you cain't do it."

Barney said George Boy jumped up out of his chair, climbed into the pen and sloshed through the mud to that hog. He grabbed the hog's hind legs a couple of times, but the slime on the hog caused him to lose his grip. When he finally got a firm hold on both hind legs the hog commenced to squeal and thrash about in the mud. The hog kicked loose from George Boy, ran a few yards away and then turned and launched a surprise attack—hit George Boy right about the knees and flattened him. George Boy got up, now as muddy as the hog, and ran head first into the critter. The two of them rolled and grunted in the mud like two men in a wrestling match. Pappy Roosevelt jumped into the pen and helped George Boy bring the hog down. Pretty soon George Boy had himself seated on the hog's back and the hog's legs had splayed out underneath him. Pappy Roosevelt stood beside George Boy and the hog.

Pappy Roosevelt broke into a dark brown grin and put his hand on George Boy's shoulder. Barney said he yelled to them, "Congratulations, boys."

Pappy Roosevelt raised George Boy's right hand, like a referee does after a boxer wins a prize fight. George Boy hopped off the hog and Pappy Roosevelt hosed the mud and hog slime off the two of them. After they sat down in their chairs, Pappy Roosevelt smiled, took a nip of corn liquor and said, 'Ornery booger, warn't he, George Boy?'"

"Yep, Pappy Roosevelt, he were."

"Let's mark 'im."

From the barn Pappy Roosevelt brought clippers that resembled a pair of pliers. George Boy threw a rope over the hog's neck, looped it around his front legs, pulled the big boar to the ground and wrapped a couple of turns of rope around his snout. The hog squealed and bit at the rope as Pappy Roosevelt clipped two bloody notches in the lower section of his right ear.

"He don't seem none too happy, Pappy Roosevelt."

"Well, son, cain't say I blame him. As good as we treat them hogs, the truth is they's all livin' under a death sentence. But when you think about it, ain't we all?"

Chapter 7

A Day of Beauty and the Beast

That morning early in September, nineteen and forty-seven, the sky seemed unusually blue. An autumn sky, even though the morning's warm air signaled that summer still had a few weeks before its run would end. Here and there a maple tree wore a touch of gold. The downtown stores got ready to close at noon, customary on Wednesdays. At Kettle High School we neared the end of fourth period and began to close our books to go to lunch. Most everybody, teachers and students alike, had something to say about the football game coming up on Friday night, the Kettle Tops against Tipple High's Hornets. I walked Beverly to the cafeteria. Just an ordinary day in Kettle—until noon.

Shortly before noon a long black four-door Lincoln passed down Main Street and parked in front of Bertha's Place. Whit Saunders, later quoted in the *Kettle News Leader*, gave an eyewitness account of what happened. "I was sitting at the counter of the restaurant and got a surprise when I turned to look out the front window. It's not often we see a Lincoln parked on Main Street in Kettle. Two men and two women got out and walked into the Bertha's Place. They seated themselves at the front table and acted real comfortable, not at all like they were in a strange place, which they were. One of the women laughed as she told the others a story. Her laugh sounded familiar. Her face and blonde hair reminded me of somebody—I could have sworn I knew her. Bein' a friendly sort, I walked over and said, 'Excuse me maam, don't I know you from somewhere?' She looked at me and smiled. 'It's possible,' she said. 'Maybe you do.' She stood up and stuck out her right hand, 'I'm Ginger Rogers.' I did a double take and shook her hand. I felt dumbstruck and stood there shaking her hand with my mouth hanging open. She must have figured me for an a-number-one-country rube. Imagine that, Whit Saunders shaking the hand of Ginger Rogers. I finally blurted out, 'Pleased to meet you, Miss Rogers, welcome to Kettle, to Bertha's Place,' then walked back to the counter and set down.

"She looked exactly like she does in the movies, except she wore a blouse and slacks—not one of them flowing gowns she wears when she dances with Fred Astaire." Further on in the article Whit added, "Bertha heard Miss Rogers introduce herself to me and got all excited. Without them even orderin' anything, she carried cups of coffee to Miss Rogers her friends. Bertha ended up with more coffee in the saucers than in the cups."

Right away Bertha got on the phone to her sister, who called two cousins who then called friends. When we walked into American history class right after lunch William White Wallace ran up to me and yelled, even though he stood no more than two feet from me, "Freddy, Ginger Rogers is at Bertha's Place!" He put his hands on my shoulders, poked his face right up next to mine and added in a voice turned serious, like he wanted to warn me of an outbreak of chicken pox, "She's there, at this very moment."

Ginger Rogers having lunch in our town—I couldn't believe it! I imagined her putting food in her beautiful mouth, chewing and swallowing and beaming looks around Bertha's Place, while the rest of us around town just went on about our business. I wished I could sit at the counter and gaze across the room at Ginger Rogers. Who knows, maybe she'd gaze back at me, then we'd stand and walk towards each other. Music from the juke-box would begin to play "The Continental." Ginger would extend her arms, I'd stand, place my arms around her, and we'd dance.

After school that day William White and I went to Bertha's Place. Whit Saunders sat at the counter. Ginger Rogers had seen him in his customary work clothes, his tall leather boots with his pants tucked into them, his red and black flannel shirt, and his wide-brimmed hat which he wore both outdoors and in. He pushed his hat back on his head and told William White and me that during the ninety-three minutes the "Ginger Rogers party," he called them, had lunch at the center table in the restaurant, the sidewalk in front of the restaurant filled with folks from Kettle. He paused and took a deep breath, and then gave the kind of sigh a parent gives when describing something silly a child has done. "Some of them pressed their noses to the plate glass window to watch her eat." Whit paused again, then said, "I walked outside and asked 'em, 'What're you people doing? Can't you see our guests just want a quiet lunch? Now please step back and give 'em some privacy.' When I walked back to my seat, Miss Rogers smiled at me. Imagine that, Ginger Rogers smiling at me."

Whit frowned and looked down. Then he looked at William White and me and in an exasperated voice said, "But wouldn't you know, when Miss Rogers and her friends walked out the front door, folks was maybe three or four deep along the sidewalk. They opened a path for her and her party to get to their car. Then they began to applaud. One fellow give a big whistle." Whit smiled, "And here's the good part. Miss Rogers, ever a lady, looked at them, smiled, and gave a little wave. The folks with her didn't seem too happy. They hustled her into the back seat of the car and drove off at a pretty fast clip. I wasn't sure what to make of Miss Rogers' friends, but I could see she was in touch with people like us. Maybe that's what makes her a star, a real star. In touch with common folks, understands us."

Bertha pointed out Ginger Rogers' chair to William White and me. We took turns sitting in it, on the very spot where she sat when she had lunch. After he sat in the chair William White stood up and said, "Hey, Freddy, watch. This is me and Ginger Rogers."

Then he turned his back to us, wrapped his long arms around himself in a hug so we could see his hands on his back, turned his head sidewise, shut his eyes and puckered up his lips like he was kissing somebody. He whispered, loud enough for me and Whit and Bertha to hear, "I love you too, Ginger. Hold me." Whit and Bertha rolled their eyes.

Ginger Rogers holding William White? He'd probably pass out from the thrill of it. When I thought about her holding me I could feel my whole body tingle, though I didn't think I'd pass out.

You'd think an event like Ginger Rogers coming to Kettle would be enough excitement in one day to put Kettle on a map of the world. But one more event had yet to happen in a day we'd remember for years to come.

The second event began about eight-thirty in the evening, not long after sunset. The western sky had orange and pink hues that faded to a robin's egg blue overhead and then to a darker blue in the east. In the dusk of that Wednesday evening, out at Pappy Roosevelt's hog farm, Pappy Roosevelt's son, George Boy, and Junior Don Kincaid, both seniors on the Kettle High football team, passed a football in the yard behind the Roosevelts' old white farm house. A feature story in the *Kettle News Leader* the following week that reported the events of that night quoted George Boy, "Junior Don had just throwed a high pass towards me. I looked up to catch it when that strange thing appeared in the sky. I yelled, 'Look, Junior Don,' and pointed at a bright saucer-shaped red and yellow something in the sky just above the hills. It moved northeast to southwest, real steady, and seemed to come to rest just on the other side of Broke Hill. Daddy had stretched out on the back porch glider and I yelled to him, 'Pappy Roosevelt, a flyin' saucer's landed on the other side of Broke Hill!'

"He jumped up and yelled through the kitchen door, 'Momma, call Chief Tackett. Tell him we got a flyin' saucer out here. Hit the ground on the far side of Broke Hill.' Daddy, who thinks way ahead of most folks, said, 'Momma, keep your eyes on the hogs, they may be in on this. Take a shotgun down to the hog pen and guard 'em.'"

Then Junior Don, Pappy Roosevelt, and George Boy ran across the field towards Broke Hill. It's called Broke Hill because of a ridgeline with a steep cliff and ravine right at the center of its crest.

At the time of all the excitement out at Pappy Roosevelt's hog farm, William White and I, along with five or six fellows, sat on the front steps of the Bank of Kettle. Early evening had to be my favorite time of day in Kettle. In warm weather, homework and chores done, boys from school and men from around town gathered on the Bank of Kettle's wide front steps to watch traffic on Main Street pass by and talk about whatever happened around Kettle that day. That evening we talked about Ginger Rogers's visit. Wink Winkler, wearing a khaki shirt and trousers rather than his blue gabardine "make a sale" suit, described her lunch order. His large eyes and long face took on a serious look as he said, "I got the whole story from a neighbor who heard it from Whit Saunders, a eye-witness." He bit off a piece of plug tobacco, chewed, and continued, "Ginger ordered a BLT with mayonnaise and a small tossed salad, French dressing. And iced tea. Bertha asked her, 'Do you want sweet tea or regular?' Well, Ginger looked at her and said, 'Sweet tea? I've never had sweet tea. I'll try that.' Then Bertha said, 'Honey, you won't be sorry. It's real good.'" Wink looked at us with his mouth half open for a few seconds—I could see the wad of tobacco lying on his tongue—and then said, "Can you imagine that? 'Honey', she called Ginger Rogers. 'Honey, you won't be sorry. It's real good.' That's what Bertha said to Ginger Rogers. Now ain't that something?" Then he smiled and punctuated his remarks with his customary big wink.

Across the street the large silver outdoor telephone bell on the wall of the Police Station rang. Chief Tackett, who had been sitting on the top step listening to Wink's story, walked across the street. He hung up the phone and yelled across the street to us, "Boys, we got us a flyin' saucer. Hit's on the ground out at Pappy Roosevelt's place. Come down just over Broke Hill." Then he hightailed it towards his blue Oldsmobile. He revved the engine and tore down Main Street, siren screaming and red lights flashing.

Wink looked at William White and me and said, "Come on, boys, let's go," then ran towards his red nineteen and forty Ford pickup truck. William White and I ran to the truck and jumped into the front seat. Wink gunned the engine and we took off for Pappy Roosevelt's place.

Wink's old truck bounced over the hog gate that Pappy Roosevelt had put at the entrance to the farm. Most farmers called it a cattle gate, a little bridge made of pipes laid sidewise with enough space between them that the hoof of a steer or heifer would slip off the surface of the round pipes and into the crevices. Pappy Roosevelt built his gate sized for hogs' feet.

Chief Tackett had parked his Olds by the barn, left the driver's door wide open and the red lights on top the car flashing. Wink pulled his truck in behind the chief's car. The chief stood just beyond his car looking towards Mrs. Roosevelt, standing with a shotgun near the large hog pen beyond the far side of the barn.

Chief Tackett yelled to her, "Whar'd they go?"

"Broke Hill."

The chief looked at Wink then at William White and me. He said with excitement in his voice, "I'm goin' in after 'em. If you boys want to come along, let's go."

We ran across the field towards the woods at the base of Broke Hill. When we reached the edge of the woods we heard voices and a thrashing of branches. Pappy Roosevelt, George Boy and Junior Don Kincaid came running out of the woods towards us.

Pappy Roosevelt took off his straw hat, wiped his brow and his bald head with a red bandanna. "Boys, they's somethin' in there. And whoever or whatever it is ain't here on a social call. I figgered it was goin' to attack us, Chief. Didn't give it a chance. We ducked and run. Right now, at this very minute, Kettle West Virginia may be under attack. I say let's arm ourselfs and go in there shootin'."

"Now Pappy Roosevelt, I recognize it's your farm and this thing, whatever it is, is trespassin' on your land. But I'm the law, and I'm in charge. I'm also armed." Chief Tackett said in a calm voice.

"So's Momma," Pappy Roosevelt replied.

"I know that. I mean if anybody's goin' to start shootin', it'll be me. At least at first."

William White said, "George Boy, what's going on? What did you see?"

"Yeah," Wink said, "tell us."

George Boy told his story about passing football and seeing a red and yellow object pass west to east in the sky. His eyes beamed and his cheeks got red. "The thing was near as bright as a full moon in October, but not round like the moon. More oval-shaped. And it had other colors in it, not just yellow. Red and blue. Went down on the other side of Broke Hill." He paused and took a deep breath. "Me and Junior Don and Pappy Roosevelt run into the woods, up Broke Hill then through the center ravine. We headed towards the clearin' on the far side of the hill. But before we got out of the woods we heard somethin'. Well, I should say first we smelt somethin'. A sour smell, acid-like. My Pappy put his arms out and stopped us and we sniffed."

Pappy Roosevelt extended his arms.

"Then we listened, heard somethin' movin' around, over towards the edge of the clearin'. Dusk was fadin' fast and it was near dark in them woods. We didn't have no flashlight. We moved forward real slow-like, and then I saw a huge creature of some kind. It skeert the beJesus out of me. I yelled, 'It's a monster. Let's go!' And here we are."

Chief Tackett sucked in his belly, raised himself to his full height, and spoke with authority, "If'n that creature shows its face again, things'll be different." He pulled his thirty-eight revolver out of its holster. "Ol' Roscoe will be right in the palm of my hand." He waved his pistol towards us and William White ducked.

"Easy, Chief," Wink said softly, then winked.

"Sorry boys. Sometimes law enforcement gets to me."

I thought to myself, "Might get us, too."

Junior Don picked up a rock and threw it deep into the woods. "Let's go. This time we'll be ready."

Chief Tackett asked us to gather close around him. "Now I want you boys to understand somethin' before we start. I don't know what we may be facin' in there. They said in July one of these boogers crashed in Roswell, New Mexico. It was in the Huntington papers. One story said they was four creatures from outer space. Two was dead and two was taken prisoner by the Army. I don't know what we got here. It may be Martians or God knows…and we don't know what they're up to. But it's likely they're up to no good. No good a-tall. So, before we start I want you to know you can bow out. Right now. No hard feelin's. I'll understand, and if need be I'll go in alone. The truth is those of us who goes in there could be puttin' our lives at risk. And we all have friends and families to think about. So, if'n you don't want to come along, now's the time to step aside."

Nobody spoke or moved. I thought about stepping aside, but couldn't do it. The chief's offer made me feel like a man, somebody who could make a decision to help out his community. Less than an hour earlier I had jumped into Wink's truck without much thought—something exciting was going on and I didn't want to miss it. But now we faced what could be a threat to ourselves, maybe to our town. Our little group might be all that stood between the creatures in that flying saucer and Momma, Daddy, Beverly, and our way of life. I couldn't turn away.

"All right, boys, here's the plan. We're goin' in two abreast. Got that?" The chief looked around and we nodded.

William White said, "Count on me, Chief. Got it."

"Me and George Boy and my Roscoe here will take the lead. Then Freddy and Willam White. Next is Pappy Roosevelt and Wink. Junior Don, you guard the rear." He looked up at six-foot three Junior Don. "This is important, Junior Don. I want you to walk backwards and prevent that thing from sneakin' up behind us."

"Chief, I can't walk backwards in the woods. I'll fall for sure. How about if I watch over my shoulder?"

The chief pondered Junior Don's question for a moment. "OK. Watch real careful-like."

Darkness had nearly replaced the dim light of dusk. Chief Tackett unclipped his flashlight from his belt, switched it on, and pointed it at the ground. We looked at each other in the reflected light.

"OK," the chief said, "now there's one more thing. Who's got a white handkerchief?

Everybody searched their pockets. Pappy Roosevelt and Junior Don pulled out red bandannas. Wink had a blue one. Junior Don held his up. "Will this work, Chief?"

"Junior Don, is that white?"

Junior Don, Pappy Roosevelt, and Wink looked at each other then stuffed their bandannas in their pockets.

William White held out a white handkerchief. "Here's mine, Chief." I remembered that William White always carried a hankie. His Momma insisted on it.

The chief took it. "Thanks, William White." He handed it to Junior Don.

"Carry this in your right hand," Chief Tackett told Junior Don. "It's possible we'll be attacked. And, God forbid, I, possibly along with others of you, may go down. If that happens, you wave the white handkerchief, Junior Don, the sign of surrender. If them creatures is halfway intelligent, if they have any sense of human decency, they'll know what a white flag means. Those of you still alive give yourselves up to the creatures. What they may do to you I don't know. They don't teach this kind of stuff in law enforcement courses. But you'll be alive, at least for a while. Maybe you'll live to tell the story of what happened out here tonight."

He looked around the group, then at Junior Don. "Got that, Junior Don?"

Junior Don's voice cracked when he said, "Yep, Chief, I got it." After a pause he asked, "Chief?"

"Yeah, Junior Don."

"Are we gonna die?"

"Junior Don, what I'm sayin' to you is known in law enforcement as a contingency plan." The chief spoke in the same tone of voice he used when, years ago, he visited our third-grade classroom. "It's what you are to do if, I repeat, if, somethin' bad happens. Like if the monster does me in. Me, Junior Don, not you."

"Okay, Chief."

"Everybody understand?" the Chief asked.

We nodded and muttered that we understood. Suddenly I wondered about being on the other side of Broke Hill in the dark of night, maybe facing a bunch of Martians. I wondered what Beverly would say about my being here.

"All right, everybody, line up," the chief said. We took our places in the order the chief set up. The chief passed the beam of his flashlight across us and gave our group a once-over, like a sergeant inspecting his squad. He took his place at the front of our lineup, waved the pistol in his right hand in a wide overhead arc, and said, "Come on, boys, we're headin' in."

We followed the chief's beam of light into the dark woods and up the hill to the ravine. I had hiked on Broke Hill many times in the daylight, but never at night. Twice I tripped over tree limbs. Up ahead I saw the chief's flashlight bobble then bounce along the ground when he tripped and fell. After he picked up himself and the flashlight, the beam dimmed. We had to wait for him to find his gun.

William White whispered, "Freddy, Roscoe's lost." I told him to shush.

When we came to the far edge of the ravine the chief spoke in a raspy whisper, "Everybody stop." He turned off his flashlight.

The woods around us filled with silence. Then in the distance I heard the soft flute-like call of a whip-poor-will.

George Boy said, "Take a deep breath."

Right away I smelled an odd, acid-like smell. Not a bad smell, just an odd one. Out of place.

Pappy Roosevelt said, "That's what we smelt a while ago. Just before we seen the monster. That thing is near, boys."

Where would I be in the morning—lying wounded or dead in these woods? Looking at Earth through the porthole of a flying saucer? When I left home after dinner, I hadn't said goodbye to Momma and Daddy.

The chief switched on his flashlight and whispered, "All right, slow and steady now. When we git to the far edge of the woods we'll stop before goin' into the open field. Out there we'll be exposed, and that may be where the saucer ship landed. For all we know them creatures may be able to see in the dark. Could be watchin' us right now, though I don't think even they can see through trees. Not unless they have X-ray vision. Come to think of it…"

At a slow pace we moved forward. Near the edge of the woods we heard a shuffling noise in the branches of the trees ahead of us. "Stop," the chief ordered. He directed the beam of flashlight into the woods surrounding us.

William White grabbed my arm. "Holy cow!"

Up in the branches of a maple tree, at the other end of the chief's dim and now trembling beam of light a face looked down at us, the face of a creature that had to be at least ten feet tall. He had large round eyes and a long gray face. Something resembling a wide nose spread down the middle of his face. The tree branches partially hid his massive body.

With a quiver in his voice the chief yelled, "Who's there? Who are you?"

No answer, though the monster blinked his eyes.

"What do you want?"

Blink.

William White pulled on the chief's shirtsleeve and said, "Chief, maybe they don't speak English on Mars. Maybe the thing communicates by blinking. I know Morse code. Put the light on my face. I'll blink your words to him."

Chief Tackett shined the beam of the light on William White's face. "Tell him we come in peace, William White."

William White looked towards the creature and began long and short Morse code blinks of his eyes. The chief spoke loud and slow, the way somebody might talk to old person who is half deaf, "We—come—in—peace."

Pappy Roosevelt said, "Boys, blink at him about the hogs. Ask him, are the hogs in cahoots with him and his buddies?"

William White began to blink and the chief started to speak when in the branches of the maple a great stirring began.

The chief made a quick turn and swung his beam of light from William White's face towards the monster. But he turned so fast the flashlight slipped out of his hand. At that moment George Boy burst into a run into the darkness towards the creature, yelling, "Come on, big man, just me and you!"

"Look out!" Pappy Roosevelt boomed.

The thing flew right at us.

In a heartbeat the chief commanded, "Hit the ground." Lying on his stomach, Chief Tackett got off two shots at the approaching creature. Then as the monster flew beyond us into the dark woods, the chief rotated his body and fired four more times.

We lay still for maybe a full minute. I raised my head up and looked behind us, in the direction where the monster had flown. In the darkness I could only see Junior Don's long arm up in the air waving the white handkerchief back and forth.

"Stay down," the chief yelled. "There may be another attack. That thing flies like Superman."

Lying beside me, William White whispered, "Where's our Kryptonite when we need it?"

The chief stood and passed the weak beam of his flashlight around our group. "Everybody still here? Everybody OK?"

We stood up and brushed the leaves off our clothes. I asked, "Where's George Boy?"

Then we saw George Boy lying face down, not moving. We ran to him. Pappy Roosevelt knelt, turned him over and lifted George Boy's shoulders. He held his son's head and patted his cheeks lightly. "George Boy, do you hear me?"

George Boy's eye's flickered, and then opened wide. "What happened?"

"Easy, son. Just take it easy." Pappy Roosevelt motioned towards Chief Tackett, then pointed at George Boy's forehead. "Shine your light here, Chief." George Boy had a knot in the center of his forehead.

"Looks like he clipped you a good 'un, George Boy," Pappy Roosevelt said.

The chief turned his light towards Junior Don. "Junior Don, step over here and hold George Boy's feet up. 'Bout a foot off the ground. Lie still, George Boy. Pappy Roosevelt, lower his shoulders to the ground. Son, this'll git the blood back up towards your head."

Junior Don started to lift George Boy's brogans, but George Boy kicked his feet and stood up. "Gimme one more shot at that dang monster." He cupped his hands around his mouth and yelled into the woods, "Hey, if'n you're out there, come on back. Let's do it again. Just me and you."

The chief put his hand on George Boy's arm and in a calm voice said, "OK, George Boy, hold on. Let's take a look around. There may be others of 'em. And somewhere out there," he pointed his flashlight towards the edge of the woods and the field beyond, "they may be a flyin' saucer. A space ship, parked and waitin'. Waitin' for what I don't know. Maybe they're a-takin' specimens back to Mars, or where ever. Human specimens."

"Chief, do you think it might be somethin' else?" Pappy Roosevelt had a slight quiver in his voice. He spoke slowly and it seemed hard for him to get each word out. "Maybe they's a-bringin' somethin' or somebody to us." His voice cracked. "Maybe little Opal's spirit is on board."

Nobody spoke. George Boy wiped his eyes and put his hand on Pappy Roosevelt's shoulder. Little Opal's spirit on board the flying saucer? If she appeared to us, would she look like the toddler who died? Or would she look older? She'd now be nearly twenty. Would Pappy Roosevelt recognize her?

Chief Tackett turned to William White, handed him the flashlight, and broke the silence. "William White, point the light at my belt." The chief removed cartridges from his gun belt and reloaded his pistol. "OK boys, let's walk over to the field. George Boy, I'm a-givin' you a order. Whatever happens, you are not, repeat not, to charge that monster."

161

George Boy was silent. When we started walking he turned towards Pappy Roosevelt and whispered, "He cain't stop me."

It was only twenty yards or so to the edge of the woods. The night sky had no moon but bright stars. Out in the field we had enough light that at least we wouldn't trip and fall as we moved around. We stood under a large oak tree at the edge of the clearing and the chief flashed his beam across the field. Slowly, left to right. Then right to left. He did this a couple of times. In the weak beam of his light we didn't see anything out of the ordinary.

We walked about ten yards into the field. Pappy Roosevelt, on the right of the chief, yelled, "Chief, lookee here."

The Chief pointed his light at the ground in front of Pappy Roosevelt. "Dang, boys, looks like they done been here and gone."

There on the ground we saw weeds pushed down in the same direction, forming two long and parallel marks about a foot wide, maybe four feet apart, and about ten feet in length. "Skid marks," William White said. In between them lay a trail of large dark spots that resembled oil drippings, and at the end of the trail a small pool of oily liquid. Beyond the oily liquid a circular section of weeds had been burnt.

The Chief pointed his beam of light to the small burnt circle. "Well boys, it looks like we found their landing spot. Possibly their takeoff point as well, though for all we know they may be peekin' at us from just around the other side of the hill. Junior Don, give me William White's handkerchief. We'll put it here to mark this spot, then we won't have no trouble findin' it when we come back in daylight."

Junior Don handed the chief the handkerchief.

"Chief, my Mom keeps a count of my hankies. She'll kill me if I lose one."

"William White, this here is law enforcement. Tell your Mom to call me."

The chief cast his light around the area. "Boys, I don't think we're goin' to find anything else. There's nothin' more to be done out here. That thing, whatever it is, landed, launched a surprise attack on us, and has done took off. Hit and run, you might say."

Chief Tackett took off his cap and wiped his forehead with a blue bandanna. "Let's head back to your place, Pappy Roosevelt." Then the chief's voice took on a most serious tone. "Now boys, we're goin' to walk back through them woods. Hit's dark in there and for all I know one or more of them creatures may be waitin' for us, just like before. Then again, maybe not—possibly they got a taste of lead, I don't know. We'll go back through the woods lined up like before, except this time Junior Don won't have his white handkerchief. So, listen carefully, I'm goin' to give you a new contingency plan. Ready?"

We nodded.

"Here it is. I figure by now the creature probably knows I'm the law. So, if'n he's still here, he's likely to aim his attack at me. If and when that happens and I go down, I want you to take off runnin', each of you goin' in a different direction. Now there's four directions, north, south, east, and west, and six of you." The chief asked each of the four of us standing next to him say one of the directions and told us we should run in that direction. I got "south." He assigned Wink northeast and Junior Don southwest.

Then the chief said, "That thing, no matter if he can fly, cain't follow everybody all at once. At least one of you is likely to live. Go to Pappy Roosevelt's place and call the sheriff. Tell him to call the National Guard. Have 'em bring tanks."

Everyone looked at the chief and nodded. William White gave me a light tap on the shoulder. I did the same to him.

The chief continued, "For all we know, Pappy Roosevelt was right and the hogs is in on this thing. At this very moment them Martians may be over at Pappy Roosevelt's place with the hogs doin' God knows what to Mrs... Maybe them creatures and the hogs is going to reverse the tables on us and pack up human specimens for a slaughterhouse in space. Who knows? I don't want to upset you, Pappy Roosevelt, and I pray I'm wrong, but your wife may have gone down already. On the other hand, we ain't heard Mrs. Roosevelt firin' her shotgun, so let's assume things is OK."

"I'll kill them sons of bitches," Pappy Roosevelt said, slamming his right fist into his left hand.

"You'll have to git in line behind me," George Boy added.

"Everybody ready?" The chief looked around the group. "OK, let's move out."

We walked back through the woods in our column of twos following the chief's light, now flickering and ever dimmer. In the dark of the woods William White leaned towards me and made a ghost-like sound, "Whhooooo, whhooooo."

Chief Tackett stopped everybody, then walked back and put his light right in William White's face. "Son, there may be lives at stake here. It's possible Mrs. Ovieta Blankenship Roosevelt is already done in. This ain't funny."

"Sorry chief, Pappy Roosevelt."

After that nobody spoke. I walked behind the chief. A couple of times he pushed through low-hanging tree limbs and they came thrashing back into my face. I imagined Beverly walked along beside me, wondered what she'd be thinking about all this. I told her William White and George Boy had showed courage, so had Chief Tackett. She nodded. "Do you think we've been foolish to come into the woods?" She nodded again.

When we entered the field behind the barn Chief Tackett ran over to his car. He switched on the two-way radio and called the sheriff's office. Then the State Police. He talked fast and described what happened, and then added, "In my opinion we are under attack."

Pappy Roosevelt took off running towards the hog pens and we followed him. Before we got to the hog pens a shotgun blasted.

George Boy yelled, "Momma, you OK?"

"Yes, your Pappy startled me. I thought he was Martians."

Pappy Roosevelt told the Chief, "Hogs's a lot smarter'n most folks give 'em credit for. I figured they might a-worked out a plan to escape.

Chief Tackett nodded.

"Cain't say that I blame 'em. Even though some of 'em is show hogs and seems to take pride in their work, they all face the same end. I'd be lookin' for a ride outta here too."

Then everybody walked over to the back porch of the Roosevelt house. About the time Mrs. Roosevelt brought out glasses of cold sweet tea we heard sirens in the distance. Soon two cars pulled into the yard beside the house. One was a brown Chevy from the Sheriff's Department, and the other a blue Plymouth with "W.Va. State Police" painted on each front door. Deputy Sheriff Truitt Crabtree walked up to the porch. Most everybody knew Truitt, for he grew up in Kettle. He'd graduated from Kettle High about five years ago. A State Police officer joined Truitt on the porch.

"Evenin' boys," Truitt said. He looked good in his brown uniform, all starched and crisp. His wide shoulders, narrow waist, and height, just over six feet, gave Truitt a powerful look. Girls liked the way he combed his dark hair with a Marcel wave in the front. William White told me he heard that Truitt had worked on some important cases and built himself quite a reputation around the County Courthouse.

"Hey, Truitt," everybody said.

"Gentlemen," the State Police officer said. "I'm Trooper Bill Persinger. What's going on?"

Trooper Persinger had a short and muscular build, like a center on a football team, and his dark green uniform was all rumpled. He looked to be about my Daddy's age. His Smokey the Bear official State Police hat added some height to him but I whispered to William White that he'd need more than his hat to get in the big leagues of law enforcement with the likes Deputy Truitt Crabtree.

When Trooper Persinger looked towards William White and me, we lowered our heads. Trooper Persinger had stopped us one night when we drove his Daddy's car too fast, just west of town on U.S. Highway 42. He gave us a good talking to, but no ticket.

Chief Tackett stepped forward, "Truitt, Trooper Persinger. I been the officer in charge here. But I'm really outta my jurisdiction. Still, we faced an emergency and somebody had to step in and take charge."

Pappy Roosevelt interrupted, "The chief here's a brave man. So's my George Boy."

Trooper Persinger said, "I'm sure you did the right thing, Chief Tackett. Why don't you describe what happened."

"Yeah, chief, tell us about it," Truitt added.

The chief took the two men through the events in the woods and our discovery of the landing spot. Then he said, "George Boy, tell 'em what you first saw when you and Junior Don was passin' football and you looked up and saw a red and yellow saucer-like object bright as a full moon comin' west to east low in the sky appearing to come down just beyond Broke Hill. And, yes, how you pointed and yelled for Junior Don to look up and he seen it too."

"Well," George Boy said, "it was like this," then he went through what the chief had just said and in about the same words. William White looked at me and rolled his eyes. At the end, George Boy said, "Pappy Roosevelt told Momma to watch the hogs. Guard 'em. It's possible they was in on the whole thing. Plannin' a escape."

"That's right," Chief Tackett said. He snapped his fingers and added, "I forgot about them hogs. Still not sure about 'em. This is one strange case."

Deputy Crabtree nodded. Trooper Persinger pulled out a notepad and studied it.

A black two-door Mercury drove up alongside Pappy Roosevelt's house and parked. James Garfield Worthington, editor of the *Kettle News Leader*, stepped out of the driver's side. Nick Blasingame of the *Huntington Herald Dispatch* got out of the passenger side of the front seat. Both men wore white shirts and neckties pulled loose from their collars. James Garfield's height and gray hair gave him a distinguished look. Mr. Blasingame, shorter than James Garfield, had short curly black hair. They walked over to the porch. Mr. Blasingame's unfavorable article about The Great Kettle Riot of last summer came to mind.

After all the back and forth greetings, the chief asked James Garfield, "How'd you fellers come to know about this?"

"Well, I got a call from Truitt, Chief, and thought I'd better get out here," James Garfield said. "Nick was already in town, covering the Ginger Rogers story. I figured he wouldn't want to miss out on this, so I invited him along."

Chief Tackett squinted his eyes and frowned at Nick Blasingame. "I hope you do a little better with this story than you done coverin' that little incident last summer with them Bible salesmen."

"I hope you do too, chief," Nick Blasingame replied in a surly tone of voice.

Truitt spoke up. "Now, men, I'll want to get statements from each of you. I heard what George Boy said, and I took a few notes. But it's important to get personal accounts of what happened from each witness. I'll start with you, chief, if it's OK. Then let's just follow the order you walked in in the woods. George Boy, then William White, Pappy Roosevelt, and so on. Chief, let's me and you start by settin' down over there in the porch glider." After they sat down, Truitt took his notebook and pencil out of his shirt pocket and the chief began to talk. Later the chief said, "Truitt flipped that notebook's cover open just the way Nelson Eddy done it in that movie about the Northwest Mounted Police."

William White turned to me and commented, "The only difference is that Nelson Eddy didn't drop his."

Trooper Persinger said in a firm voice, "If it's OK with you Deputy Crabtree, I'd like for these boys to lead me into the woods to where things happened. And maybe they could show me that spot in the field where the thing landed. You could take everybody else's statements, and then get theirs when we come back."

Truitt nodded.

Trooper Persinger turned towards William White and me. "Will you boys lead me to where it happened?"

I looked at William White and he looked at me. "I don't know, Trooper Persinger. We been through a pretty scary time," I said.

"Boys, no harm will come to you. Guarantee it. I'll be armed." His spoke in a voice low and firm.

William White didn't look any too happy about going back into the woods. Maybe he didn't want to be alone with Trooper Persinger. Me either. But I figured we could help the trooper, or we could sit here like knots on a log listening to Truit talk with everybody about what we already knew.

"William White, let's help Trooper Persinger," I said, emphasizing the word "help." I added, "We'll take an old feed sack with us. We can leave it in place of your handkerchief."

After a few seconds William White said, "OK, I'll go," though he sounded uncertain.

"Trooper Persinger, Nick Blasingame and I would like to tag along, if it's all right," James Garfield said.

"No problem. Just stay behind us."

I found an empty feed sack in the barn and we headed into the woods. "Just follow your path from before," Trooper Persinger said.

Trooper Persinger carried a flashlight with a bright beam and he, William White, and I walked three abreast. He asked, "Can you boys tell me some more about what happened in the woods? What did the monster look like?" After we answered him, he asked us a couple of more times in different ways to describe the creature's face. Then, "What about the nose?" he asked. "Tell me about his nose."

I wondered why the trooper had such an interest in the monster's nose, and described it as best I could. Then William White took a turn at it. We'd described the monster's nose for what must have been the third time when Trooper Persinger asked, "Now what about the eyes? Tell me about his eyes."

Before we finished our description of the monster's eyes, William White got all excited and told the trooper how he figured the monster communicated by blinking. "I experienced it firsthand, Trooper Persinger. So did Chief Tackett. After the monster blinked at us, Chief Tackett put the light on my face and I blinked back at the monster in Morse code while Chief Tackett said, loud and slow, 'We—come—in—peace,' though we don't know for sure that the monster understood English or Morse code. But if he did, well, yes sir, you might say that me and the monster was face to face, communicating with one another. I'll never forget it. It's not every night you talk with a creature from outer space."

Trooper Persinger said, "Now that's a fact. Yes, sir, that's a fact."

James Garfield and Nick Blasingame had little penlights they shined on their notebooks. They wrote as we talked.

When we arrived at the tree where the monster had hidden, William White pointed up into the branches. "That's where he hid just before he attacked us."

Trooper Persinger handed William White his flashlight. "Shine the beam on the place where he was." William White placed the beam up in the tree. The Trooper asked, "Where was his face?" and William White rolled the light beam around branches about ten feet above the ground.

"Then he charged you? Came running at you?"

William White, his mouth moving like a car in high gear, told the trooper how the monster flew at us like Superman, and about George Boy's bravery in charging at the monster. "Over there, towards that rock. That's where the monster conked George Boy. Knocked him out."

Trooper Persinger flashed his light on the ground. William White poked me in the side and whispered, "He's looking for clues." He turned to James Garfield and Nick Blasingame. "Police work going on."

Then the trooper headed for the field beyond the woods. "Where are the tracks of the landing and take off?"

Right away we spotted William White's handkerchief. William White picked it up and tucked it into his hip pocket. He sounded relieved. "I'm glad to get this back. Momma's touchy about me losing hankies." I spread the feed sack on the ground.

Trooper Persinger put his light on the skid marks, and then pulled a small tape measure out of his pocket. He measured their length and width, then the separation between them. He made some notes in a small black notebook. He examined the oil drippings between the skid marks, and the small pool of oil at the end of the marks. He knelt down and put his finger in the oil and then sniffed it. Trooper Persinger pulled out his handkerchief and wiped it through the pool of oil, then folded the handkerchief and put it back in his pocket. He picked up some ashes from the burnt spot.

"Well, boys, I think that's about it. Let's head back."

Nick Blasingame spoke up. "What do you think about all this, Trooper Persinger? Is there evidence of a flying saucer? A monster?"

"We can talk later, fellows. There's a lot to think about."

When we got back to the back porch Truitt had just finished up with Wink. "Glad you're back, boys. William White, it's your turn."

William White joined Truitt on the glider. Everybody else sat in the metal chairs spread around the porch. The chief pulled his chair up close to listen. So did James Garfield and Nick Blasingame. Mrs. Roosevelt refilled our glasses with ice-cold sweet tea. Trooper Persinger headed towards the barn.

Pappy Roosevelt watched him pass out of the yard and said in a matter-of-fact way, "I'll betcha Trooper Persinger's goin' to get to the bottom of things with them hogs. If they had a escape plan, he'll find it out."

After Truitt finished making notes on the eyewitness testimony of William White and myself, he put his pencil behind his right ear and with a smooth move of his right hand flipped his notebook so the cover came over the top and closed.

James Garfield asked, "Well, Truitt, what do you think about all this?"

Nick Blasingame immediately followed with, "Do you confirm that there was a monster from outer space, Deputy Crabtree?"

Truitt slowly stood, stretched, and rose to his full height. He walked to the banister this side of the screen around the porch. He hitched up his trousers, then put one foot up on the banister and spoke softly, "Well, boys, there's little doubt. Little doubt in my mind. Something strange went on, all right. Out there. In those woods and in that field. Tonight. You could call it otherworldly. Yes sir. Otherworldly. We have eyewitnesses. And there's no question that a young man got conked on the head. Conked a good one. Whoever or whatever hit George Boy was not from around here."

A couple of weeks earlier, Whit Saunders had said over at Bertha's Place. "Boys, there's two classes of people in the world. Class One is those that's from here. Class Two is those that's not from around here." He got a serious look on his face and said, "Watch out for Class Two." He grinned real big and added, "And some of Class One," then gave a big laugh.

Deputy Crabtree looked around the porch at us. "As an officer of the law I'm ready to render an opinion. Subject to review, you understand. By the sheriff. He always reviews our findings. But I don't think there'll be much question about this one."

Nick Blasingame spoke up, sounding a little exasperated. "Deputy Crabtree, it's getting late. What's your finding?"

"Boys, hear me out. Hear me out. This is from the point of view of the law. Not Deputy Sheriff Truitt Crabtree. The law sometimes moves slowly. In my view what we have here is a simple case of trespassing and assault. Trespassing and assault by person or persons unknown. Probably from outer space."

Pappy Roosevelt lit into a big grin. "Well I'll be... Imagine that, Momma, a creature from outer space. Right here on our farm."

Truitt continued. "It appears there's no harm done. No permanent harm I mean. Everybody had a scare thrown into them. George Boy's got a knot on his head. That'll go away. We have a case of simple trespassing and assault. And the offenders has fled the scene, fled into parts unknown."

Chief Tackett stood up and shook Truit's hand. "Good work, Deputy Crabtree." He turned to James Garfield and Nick Blasingame. "One day this boy'll be widely known in law enforcement."

Pappy Roosevelt asked in a hesitant way, "Truitt, do you and the chief think them creatures is a comin' back tonight? I mean, do you think maybe they was lookin' for somethin'? Or maybe bringin' somethin' or somebody?"

There was a long silence. Pappy Roosevelt's words in the dark of the woods about little Opal rang though my thoughts. How had he learned to live with what had happened? Maybe he hadn't. Maybe I couldn't either.

The chief's voice brought us back to the present. "Pappy Roosevelt, nobody knows what might happen when you're dealin' with creatures from outer space. But my guess is them visitors found out what six slugs from a thirty-eight pistol can do. I don't think you'll be seein' any more of 'em."

Trooper Persinger stepped on to the porch. Nick Blasingame told him that Deputy Crabtree had concluded that a creature from outer space visited here tonight. He asked, "Do you concur with his finding?"

Trooper Persinger said he'd file a report in the morning. After the captain approved it, Mr. Blasingame could read it.

"Do you agree with Deputy Crabtree?" Nick Blasingame asked again.

"Read my report. Good night, men, Mrs. Roosevelt. Thanks for your cooperation."

"Well, boys, it's late," Pappy Roosevelt said. "George Boy has a goose egg on his forehead and a big game on Friday night. We got to get him rested and healed. Let's call it a night."

Wink looked at William White and me. "Come on, boys, the truck's a-loadin' up."

"I'll lead the way back to town," the chief announced. He got in his Olds and turned on the flashing red lights. Junior Don's car followed Wink's truck and our little caravan headed back to Kettle.

I asked, "Why do you think he has his red lights on, Wink?"

"Boys, this has been official business. Still is, till he turns those lights off." Then he winked.

The next morning when I came downstairs to breakfast Daddy handed me the *Huntington Herald Dispatch*. He had folded it in half and circled a story in the lower portion of the front page. "A Saucer for Kettle?" Nick Blasingame's name was beneath the title. I muttered "Uh oh." The story had three long paragraphs of eyewitness descriptions of events out at Pappy Roosevelt's hog farm, including George Boy's sighting of the flying saucer, a monster purported to be ten feet tall and "... the attempt by Chief

Tackett and William White Wallace to talk with the creature, who they believed communicated with eye blinks. Their message was transmitted by Mr. Wallace's blinking at the creature in Morse code while Chief Tackett held the beam of a flashlight on Mr. Wallace's face and slowly and loudly spoke the words 'We—come—in—peace'." The story went on to describe the attack on George Boy, and the chief's emptying his revolver, and ended with the discovery of the skid marks, the oil droppings, and the burnt spot in the field.

The article then turned to the report on the incident written by Trooper Persinger. I did a sharp intake of breath. The story said, "Trooper Bill Persinger noted that the marks in the field were approximately the same dimensions as the rear tires on a tractor. The spilled oil at the site is currently undergoing testing. Trooper Persinger stated in his report that early indications suggest it is well-used 30-grade motor oil.

"When this reporter asked Trooper Persinger about the monster itself, its height, large eyes, and massive nose, he said, 'Anyone interested in following up on this incident might first check with an ornithologist. The face of a barn owl dimly seen through the leaves of tree branches at night could bear a strong resemblance to the description of the face of the alleged creature. And tree branches below the owl might resemble a large body.' When asked about the blow to the head of George Boyd Roosevelt, Trooper Persinger answered, 'If you tripped and hit your head on a rock you might incur about the same injury.'

"Commenting on the acid-like smell, deep in the woods, Trooper Persinger said, 'I understand that Mr. Roosevelt's farm produces many strange smells. The wind may do odd things with them.'"

I paused to catch my breath. I thought about Chief Tackett and William White. Pappy Roosevelt and George Boy. Wink Winkler, Junior Don, and Truitt Crabtree. And how they would feel when they read all this. Nick Blasingame's article ended with these words. "But what about the sighting of the object in the sky? From Charleston and as far away as Baltimore, there were reports of what appeared to be a meteor in the sky about the time the object was seen above the Roosevelt farm. Was it a meteor? Or, did the town of Kettle get a saucer?"

I dropped the paper on the kitchen table and sat down. Beverly would read this, then she'd ask me about it. I put my elbows on the table. My head felt so heavy it took both hands to support it. I wanted to cry, but held back.

"It all seemed so real," I said to Daddy. "I was proud of George Boy and Chief Tackett. Of everybody out there. Even Junior Don."

Daddy sipped his coffee and his dark eyes took on a most serious look. "Freddy, the light of day is sometimes cold and harsh. But that doesn't take away from what happened. Bravery is bravery. Out there in the dark of the woods you all believed you were in danger. George Boy and the chief had the courage to put themselves in harm's way, between you and what they honestly thought was a monster. They and everybody else who was out there can take pride in that, no matter what is learned with hindsight."

"I'm going to tell George Boy and the chief I'm proud of them."

"I hope you do," Daddy said. "And I'm proud of you." He put his hand on my shoulder and gave me a couple of pats. Then I cried. I loved my Daddy.

Late that afternoon the weekly publication of the *Kettle News Leader* arrived in our town's homes and businesses. James Garfield ran a major headline. "Flying Saucer Lands Near Kettle." Then, right below it, just above the beginning of the story of the night's events, a smaller headline, "George Boy Roosevelt attacked by monster. Injury believed not serious."

Also on page one there was a second, smaller, story about Ginger Rogers' lunch at Bertha's Place, "Screen Star Visits Kettle." Whit Saunders's eyewitness description of the lunchtime events, including Miss Rogers's order of a BLT, salad, and sweet tea, made up most of the story. The story ended with Miss Rogers's wave to the crowd on the street as she left the restaurant, along with a comment "Kettle was privileged to play host to such a great star. Editor J.G. Worthington joins with Miss Rogers's local fans in the fond hope that she will again join us for lunch. Maybe dinner too."

I hoped Beverly had read the story, couldn't wait to tell her what happened out there on Broke Hill.

William White came running in the front door of our house right before we sat down to dinner. "Look at this, Freddy. Look at this." He waved a copy of the *Kettle News Leader* and pointed to the story about the Kettle monster. "There is a detailed description of my talking with the monster by blinking. And read this, how the chief unloaded six shots at the creature. Probably at least winged him, the story says."

Right after dinner William White and I went downtown. When we got to the front steps of the Bank of Kettle we could see that nearly everybody there had a copy of the *Kettle News Leader*.

Wink Winkler held up his *News Leader*. "Boys, fergit all about all that yeller journalism in the Huntington paper. James Garfield wrote the truth. Hit's right here, word for word. Listen to what the chief said." Wink read, "In over forty years of law enforcement, I'd never faced this kind of situation. There was no way of knowing what was out there. Or what that thing was going to do. I'll be frank, I was scared. I wondered if Kettle might be marked for destruction by forces far beyond our understanding. Far, far beyond. My job was to stop them.'" He looked around the group seated on the steps. Wink.

William White said, "Listen to this." He read aloud in a slow and prideful voice, "In the dark of night deep in the woods, with a single beam of light shining on his face, Kettle High School Senior William White Wallace," he paused and smiled, "William White Wallace faced the monster and courageously attempted to communicate with him using the apparent language of this visitor from another world, Morse code eye blinks. 'We—come—in—peace,' William White blinked as Chief Tackett spoke the words in a firm voice. William White's gaze did not falter in the face of danger."

Junior Don looked at William White and asked, "Wasn't you skeered, William White?"

"Well, Junior Don, you were there. It had to be done. I knew I had to do it. At the time I felt there was a chance I might build the monster's trust in us. If I was successful we might get a look inside that flying saucer. Maybe later teach him about our town and the American way of life."

Across the street Chief Tackett parked his Olds beside the Police Station. He climbed out and walked over to our group. William White said, "Chief, listen to this. 'The hulking creature, looming ten feet in height, suddenly became airborne and launched a frontal attack on the small group of brave Kettle men, led by Police Chief Arthur R. Tackett. Kettle High's star halfback George Boy Roosevelt attempted to tackle the monster and was knocked unconscious by a blow to the head from the creature.' Then, get this, 'Chief Tackett faced the flight path of the oncoming monster, raised his revolver and fired, probably saving George Boy from the monster's clutches. The chief dove to the ground, quickly rotated his body and continued to fire as the airborne creature passed over the group. The fired his pistol until the only sounds were the hollow thuds of the pistol's hammer falling on empty chambers.'"

The chief's face beamed. "That's what I done, I reckon."

"That's right, Chief. By God, that's what you done. You saved George Boy's life. Probably our'n too," Wink Winkler spoke with pride. He looked around. "You fellers shoulda seen him," then he gave a big wink.

"Boys, I just done my duty. You'da done the same thing." The chief sighed as he sat down on the top step. "Feels good to take a load off my feet. Today was quite a day. Ginger Rogers comes to Kettle in the mornin' and a monster from outer space comes to Kettle in the evenin'. Quite a day. Yes sir, a day of beauty and the beast."

Chapter 8

LOVE LESSONS

Phil took over the ownership and management of Buckingham's Gulf Station in the late nineteen thirties, after his Daddy, Ezra Buckingham, retired. I started working for him on Saturdays as the winter of nineteen and forty-eight turned to spring. Momma and Daddy encouraged me to take up what Daddy called serious part-time work. William White liked the idea too, "Gives me a good place to hang out on Saturday afternoons," he said.

My first Saturday on the job I even beat Phil to work. In a bright early morning sun I walked across what Phil called the apron, an expanse of concrete in front of the old two-story brick building and its two gas pumps, high test and regular, and peered through the plate glass window. The large room had a wood and glass counter and on a shelf on the wall behind it sat a cash register with a crank on its side. Beyond the counter stood tall metal bins of small parts for cars and trucks. Oil filters, windshield wiper blades, spark plugs, that sort of thing. Beneath the glass counter were Hershey and Clark Bars, air fresheners shaped like fir trees, pipe tobacco in tins. But no cigarettes. Phil had already told me that cigarettes would bring in every kid in town. "Pipe tobacco is for a different kind of smoker, such as me and Hartford Wilson," he said. Hartford owned Wilson's Dry Goods.

On the left front side of Buckingham's a tunnel-like driveway with the public restrooms passed through the building into the garage in the large rear section of the building. My duties included pumping gas, sweeping the tunnel, as well as the apron, and keeping the restrooms clean.

Just beyond the apron stood a large old oak tree that shaded a small patch of lawn and one side of the building. In warm weather Phil and his friends would take chairs from the front end, put them under the tree, and sit and talk.

A few weeks later we had a spell of warm weather and that Saturday everybody in town seemed to be out driving around. Phil had gone to Huntington to pick up some truck parts. Shortly after noon cars had lined up on both sides of the gas pumps. The horn on a muddy old Chevy truck began blowing, at first short beeps, then they got longer and longer.

A man leaned his head out the drivers window of the truck and a familiar, good-natured voice said, "Git them cars movin', Freddy. We got business to do." It was Ferlin R. Kintzmiller, a.k.a. Froud R. Kaltenborn. A woman sat alongside him in the cab of the truck. The sunlight reflected off the windshield and I couldn't see her face.

Phil Buckingham once told me that Ferlin R had to be about fifty-five years old, for he'd attended Kettle High School with him. But Ferlin R dropped out of school the day he reached age sixteen. "Got to admit, he looks good for a man his age," Phil said.

Ferlin R had the build of a basketball player, tall and athletically trim. He lived on his family's farm up on the Sour Apple River Road. Although he had a mop of gray hair, his face remained unlined, and his smile had the look of a younger man. When he walked, Ferlin R dragged his heels, slumped his shoulders and rolled with each step, a distinctive shuffle, some people said. William White called it a drag-ass way of walking. Other folks said he learned to walk like that while in jail. A substantial chunk of

Ferlin R's adult life had been spent off and on in the county lockup along with one brief stint in the state prison up at Moundsville.

The first Saturday I worked at Buckingham's, Phil asked Ferlin R about having two names. Ferlin R's face lit up with a smile and he said, "I took me a second name in nineteen and twenty-nine, and to this day I keep two delivery boxes at the Post Office. I don't git me a lot of mail, but what I do git is about equally divided between Ferlin R. Kintzmiller and Froud R. Kaltenborn. My second name, and I always say to folks you can guess which one it is, I took after an unfortunate misunderstandin' between me and the government about the makin' of alcoholic beverages. I got to say, though, that women seems to like me havin' two names. They often have fun guessin' which feller they're with. To tell you the truth, sometimes I ain't so sure myself."

After the customer in front of Ferlin R's truck pulled away I motioned for Ferlin R to drive forward. In the bed of the truck stood Chappie Goodman, a man Ferlin R called, "My quick-movin' friend." A woman stood beside Chappie but had her back towards me. Kettle folks knew Chappie well, for he made a living doing chores around town. Other than his ever-present khaki shirt and matching ball cap, the speed with which Chappie did everything distinguished him from normal-moving folks. When Chappie mowed somebody's yard he pushed the mower so fast that he ran behind it. When he talked he spoke so fast people often had to ask him to repeat what he said. His high-pitched and squeaky voice didn't help any. And Chappie could slip his hand into a fellow's hip pocket, lift his wallet, and be halfway to Kentucky before anybody knew what happened, a skill that led him to attend every parade in Huntington. Folks who knew Chappie gave him a wide berth or put their wallets in their front pockets when he approached them. Chappie's lifting habit landed him in the county jail from time to time, "where," Chappie squeaked, "fate placed me and Ferlin R in the lockup at the same time. We became close friends and business partners, yessir, that's what fate done for us."

One time when Chappie came in to buy some candy, he said to Phil, "Other than my speed, I'm about average in most anything

179

you can measure, except for two outward adornments, and one of 'em is my nose," then he laughed his high-pitched laugh that sounded like an old screen door blowing back and forth in a strong wind. He got it right about his long nose. I didn't know about his other outward adornment.

When Ferlin R's truck pulled up to the pumps I took a closer look at the women, maybe I should say girls, with Ferlin R and Chappie, and recognized the Posey twins, Lovey and True. They lived up on the Sour Apple River near Ferlin R and had been members of my class at Kettle High School. They dropped out our sophomore year. Shortly after they turned sixteen, their Daddy died after his truck got hit by a train at a grade crossing. Not long afterwards their younger brother, Horace, woke up one morning with his legs paralyzed, polio. The girls had to go to work to help support the family. They first got jobs at Gruber's Department Store, though they didn't last long. William White told me they talked to customers so much that nobody got waited on. After that they began waiting tables in the coffee shop at the Daniel Boone Hotel in Charleston. William White said they made a lot of money in tips from the politicians that hung out in the coffee shop. William White figured that the politicians valued talking more than they valued eating—and the Posey twins fit right in.

Although I had a hard time telling the girls apart, it looked like Lovey sat with Ferlin R and True stood in the truck bed with Chappie. Their faces looked so much alike, and both of them had blond hair and they usually dressed in identical outfits. Today they had on light blue blouses and dark blue skirts.

At school I once asked the Lovey and True how I could tell the difference between them. One of them took a half-step towards me and said, "I'm Lovey. You'll always know it's me once you connect my face to my special mole. It's in a secret spot that I only show to people I want to know me real well. That might include you, Freddy." She paused and batted her eyes. "Maybe me and you could get together and share my secret. Then you'd know the difference between me and my sister." She looked into my eyes and added, "From now on and forever."

About then William White walked up and poked his face in between us with raised eyebrows and a big smile. Lovey and True walked away. I told William White what Lovey said and added, "If you hadn't showed up I might've learned about Lovey's secret mole."

"You might've learned more than that," he laughed.

By the time I started filling the tank of Ferlin R's truck with gas I couldn't see Chappie and True. They'd disappeared below the sideboards around the bed of the truck. In the cab of the truck Lovey sat with her arms around Ferlin R. When I asked, "Fill 'er up, Ferlin R?" she unbuttoned a middle button on his shirt, put her hand inside it and pulled the hair on his chest.

"Cut that out, Lovey, and yes, Freddy, fill 'er up."

When I walked over to take the gas cap off the neck of the tank, Lovey said, "What about me, Ferlin R? You want me to fill 'er up? I'm not sure I can. Do you think maybe you could fill me up?"

I put the nozzle into the neck of the truck's gas tank. Chappie's voice came from inside the wooden slats around the bed of the truck. "Oh, do that. Do it again."

True giggled and said, "Chappie, you're a-tirin' me out. Do it yourself," then they both laughed, or maybe I should say, Chappie squeaked and True laughed.

I squeezed the handle of the gas pump as hard as I could and blasted gasoline into Ferlin R's tank at top speed. The unprivate sounds of Chappie and True's private activities, no more than three feet away, got to me. Part of me wanted to get Ferlin R's truck out of here, right away. Another part of me wanted to jump up into the bed of the truck. I imagined what True might look like undressed, and felt myself getting aroused. That's when gasoline sloshed out of the top of the gas tank on to my pants' cuffs and shoes.

May arrived, and with it came the nineteen and forty-eight Kettle High School Prom—I would go with Beverly Shade. I couldn't believe it. We'd been dating off and on since tenth grade, but I'd admired her since long before that. Beverly's family had moved to Kettle when I entered fifth grade. During that summer her parents bought the old Cavendish place, a white frame three-story home with gables. It had a wide porch that extended across the front of the house then wrapped half-way around each side.

The first day Beverly came to school William White put a thumbtack on her seat, but she saw it before she sat down. When she picked it up William White waved at her. Even though he was my best friend, I thought he did a dumb trick. After I got to know her better, Beverly told me she thought the same thing.

The next day during lunch hour we chose up sides for a soft-ball game, William White's team against mine. While we picked players, Susie Mac walked up and asked, "Can I play?" On his very next choice William White said, "Susie Mac." Susan MacLendon, had been the first girl to develop a chest, a bust. Sometimes William White and I would stare at her. Well not at her, at her front. One day she wore a tight-fitting t-shirt to school and all day long William White kept elbowing me in the side saying, "Hey, look at that."

A boy on William White's team said, "If we got to have a girl on our team, you got to have a girl play for you, Freddy. Make it even."

Beverly Shade had watched us choose up sides. She stepped forward and said, "I'll play."

No other girls stood nearby, so I said, "OK, Beverly's on our team."

Right away she picked up the softball and tossed it to a member of our team. I noticed her height and long arms, as well as her dark brown curly hair and sky-blue eyes. I had no idea if she could hit or catch. In part because of her height and reach, I asked her to play first base. I'm a little ashamed to admit the other part, but I figured if she couldn't catch the ball and we lost the game, we could always blame her. I needn't have worried; she caught the ball. Every time.

Near the end of noon hour we had a tie game, nineteen to nineteen, and our team came to bat. We got a couple of singles and a walk, and then Beverly Shade stood at the plate, bat in her hand, bases loaded. On William White's first pitch she swung hard and connected, driving the ball past the outfielders. It rolled all the way up to the school just as the bell rang to end noon hour. Everybody on our team jumped up and down and cheered as base runners crossed the plate and scored.

With the school bell ringing and the ball still rolling, William White waved his arms and yelled real loud, "Game over, game over. According to the rules, the school bell ends the game. This is officially a tie game, nineteen to nineteen."

Everybody on our team started yelling at William White. Beverly Shade stood nose to nose with him, her face all red, and she said in a challenging way, "What rules? Show me. I hit a home run just before the bell rang, William White Wallace, and you know it."

William White stubbornly held his ground. "Sorry, Miss Shade, you probably don't yet understand the official rules of elementary school softball. Game called on account of the school bell."

Most of William White's players had begun to walk towards the school, but he gathered three of them around him and spoke in a voice that reminded me of a teacher talking to upset kids, "Tie game. Tie game. School bell rule." They looked at him and then put their heads down and started walking towards the school building. Junior Don Kincaid, who played in center field and had watched Beverly Shade's hit whiz past him, threw his softball glove on the ground and kicked it along in front of him all the way to the school building.

Beverly turned to our team, smiled, and started shaking our hands. "Good game, good game, nice to win," she said. We all smiled back at her and did the same thing. I liked Beverly Shade.

In the summer before our freshman year, during our town picnic at the Kettle Fourth of July Celebration of nineteen and forty-four, Beverly's Mom had baked a raspberry cobbler pie. Beverly saw me walking by their picnic table and invited me stop to eat a piece of cobbler, which I did. In the process I promptly spilled raspberry juice down the front of my shirt. When Beverly stepped up with a wet cloth to help me remove the red stain she stood very close to me. I found myself looking straight on and deep into her eyes, pools of blue. Her dark brown hair and suntanned face made her eyes seem even brighter. I ate two more pieces of her Mom's pie while Beverly and I laughed and talked. I thought about inviting her to go to a movie, but decided against it. At the time William White and I still had feelings for Lorna C.

Since then, most Saturday nights William White and I've gone to a movie at the Dixie Palace and later hung out at Bertha's Place. On occasion I've asked Beverly to go to a movie. Maybe the reason I didn't ask her more often grew out of a fear she'd say no, though she never did. One Saturday night during our junior year, halfway through the feature film, I put my arm around the top of her seat, and then slowly let it slide onto her shoulders. William White told me how to do it. He called it "A good move. Smart."

Beverly didn't think so. She reached up and pulled my arm down on to the armrest between us. "That's not nice in public," she whispered, but she then reached over and held my hand. That started us holding hands in the movies. Maybe William White got it right after all.

One afternoon at the beginning of our senior year, William White and I stopped at Bertha's Place for RC Colas. He gave me an odd look and then said, "This may sound a little weird, but I've been thinking about it, and believe it's true."

I never knew what would come next when he started out like that. "Believe what is true?"

"About you and Beverly Shade."

"What about me and Beverly Shade?"

"Well, strange as this may sound, when I think of the two of you I think of Humphrey Bogart and Ingrid Bergman in the movie, *Casablanca.*" William White often cast himself as something of an authority on Hollywood. After Ginger Rogers's visit to Kettle, he often talked of moving to Hollywood. One time he said, "If I do move there I plan to go out with Ingrid. It's possible that in time I may propose to her. Of course a lot depends on Ginger."

We stood near the mirror behind the back booth at Bertha's Place. I looked at my reflection—tall, skinny, still some freckles, brownish-red curly hair, no Humphrey Bogart. I said, "You must know something I don't," and then I rolled my eyes.

But I had to admit that Beverly did bear a resemblance to Ingrid Bergman—those high cheekbones, beautiful eyes and an inviting trace of a smile that suggested something more to come. Her face carried a beauty that positively radiated. When we talked I felt like the only person in her world. At that moment she became my world too. When Beverly laughed, her eyes, her whole face, seemed to dance. We laughed a lot, too, not always at jokes, just at little things, often when nobody else understood our humor. We ended our dates with a kiss, a light peck on the lips. When we said goodnight after we had seen the movie *Gone with the Wind*, I tried to kiss her the way I saw Clark Gable kiss Vivian Leigh. Beverly jumped back away from me.

"Did I do something wrong?"

A sheepish little grin spread across her face and she replied, "I thought you were going to bite me."

Late on a warm Saturday afternoon at the end of March, Phil and I sat under the oak tree. He asked, "Freddy, what do you plan to do after graduation?"

"I don't know. Momma and Daddy talked with me about going to Marshall College. I'd like to do that. My grades are good, mostly A's and B's. Daddy said if I decided to go to college he and Momma could help some, but they couldn't afford to pay my way. I'd need to earn some money first."

Phil said in a soft voice, "Well, I never went to college."

That surprised me, though I'd not thought about Phil's education after Kettle High. "And even if I went to college this fall," I said, "I wouldn't know what to study. College is supposed to prepare you for something, and I don't know what that something is."

Phil said, "I began working here at the gas station for my Dad, and took some correspondence courses to learn things like book-keeping that would help me in the business."

I had begun to wonder if maybe that's what I should do when Phil popped a big question on me. "Freddy, after you graduate, how would you like to come to work here full time?"

That day Phil wore his blue and gray striped coveralls with the orange Gulf insignia stitched over the left front pocket and "Buckingham's" stitched just below it. With his wide shoulders, coal-black hair, and big grin he looked impressive. I imagined myself dressed like Phil and working here with him every day. I enjoyed my work on Saturdays and, in my mind's eye, I liked the future I could see for myself working for Phil. At the same time, I wondered if by not going to college I might be avoiding something important, not stepping up to a challenge. Beverly planned to go to the West Virginia University in the fall and study to be a teacher. Would I risk losing her if I kept working and didn't go to college?

Phil went on, "Here's what I've been thinking, Freddy. You could be in charge of the front end. I'd offer you a salary of thirty-five dollars a week. That divides out to just under a dollar an hour, though when you're on salary you really don't figure things by the hour. Still, if you did, it would be almost double what I'm now paying you on Saturdays." My heart skipped a beat. "You'd be in charge of the gas pumps and products in the front end, consumable products, items from behind the counter, candy, air fresheners, fan belts, generator belts, oil filters. Things like that. Now if a customer wanted to order a new fender, that would be a durable product and fall under my area of responsibility."

Down at the bottom of my mind I recognized that I'd never heard things like candy and fan belts called "consumable products" and fenders called "durable products." In the rest of my mind I didn't know what to say to Phil. Life after Kettle High seemed like an unknown road, and Phil had just put fork in the road. If I turned at the fork and took the path that had now opened up, working at Buckingham's, I knew I'd enjoy the work. If I turned down the fork's other path, I couldn't see far ahead. It appeared dark.

"I appreciate your offer, Phil," I said. "I'd be real proud to work here, but I'll need a little time to think about it. And I'll want to talk to Momma and Daddy."

Phil wrinkled his forehead and a real serious look came over his face. "Well, that's the right thing to do." He paused. "Now there's one more thing, Freddy." Then he hit me with the first real honest-to-God business deal of my life. "As part of your pay, in addition to your salary I'll give you a commission of five cents on every quart of oil you sell. The commission is for oil sold at the gas pumps, and doesn't include oil changes done back in the garage, or bulk sales of oil across the counter. Some folks, for example a farmer like Pappy Roosevelt, will come in and buy oil a case at a time. It's a commission on oil sold at the pumps and poured into an engine." I did a quick mental calculation. Every twenty quarts sold meant I'd earn an additional dollar. Not bad.

"Think about it. I don't need to know right away," Phil said. "Like you said, talk to your Mom and Dad. I can wait until graduation. After that, if you decide you don't want the job, I'll need to start looking for somebody."

I thought of a plan to boost oil sales and told William White about it. "I'll keep a little tally sheet in my pocket and count the number of cars and trucks that come in for gas. I'll tally up the number of customers that ask to have their oil checked, and the number of customers that buy a quart or two of oil. Then I'll calculate the percentage who actually buy oil."

William White canted his head sidewise, "Is that it?"

"No. After a couple of weeks of counting, every time I put gas in a car or truck I'll check the oil without the driver's asking me. Just pop the hood and check it. I'll wager that oil sales will jump up. And I'll know how much they've increased."

"Sounds like too much work to me. What about this? Does Phil care if you read magazines when there are no cars at the gas pumps?"

In the weeks that followed I tested my plan to boost oil sales, did what I described to William White. People often thanked me for the quality of service I gave them. I always returned their thanks but never mentioned the possibility of a commission on my oil sales, that stayed private, a business arrangement between Phil and me.

From time to time I wondered if my attention to oil sales took me away from thinking about my choice of paths at the fork in the road. One evening I spoke with Momma and Daddy about Phil's offer and whether or not I should go to college. They told me I had good health and a long life ahead of me. If I wanted to, I could take another year to two to decide about college. Daddy reminded me that if I wanted to enroll at Marshall College next fall, they could help me some financially but I'd still need to work part-time.

The Saturdays rolled by and graduation came ever closer. We prepared for the junior-senior prom at Kettle High. During the week of the prom we decorated the gym with crepe paper and banners, and the day of the prom kids brought in lilacs, tulips and six dozen white roses. We placed them around the gym. Lots of kids brought in their favorite records, mostly for dancing but some just for listening.

The night of the prom the girls in the junior and senior classes dressed up in gowns that billowed and flowed with layers and layers of something I heard them call crinolines, beneath the skirts. Each girl had done something special to give her hair a distinctive look—some of them had their hair curled, others flattened out their curls. Some fluffed their hair and piled it on top of their heads. They all wore makeup and different shades of pink and red lipstick. At moments I imagined I'd been transported to a land filled with beautiful women.

The guys wore white shirts, ties and suits. My suit was dark blue. I wore it to church sometimes. Daddy said, "Freddy, with your white shirt and a red and blue striped tie, you look right smart." I agreed with him, though I didn't say that out loud, except to myself when I looked into my bedroom mirror.

William White wore a blue suit too. And a white shirt. He liked my tie so much he bought one identical to it. I didn't much care for his doing that, since we planned to double date at the prom. "We'll look like a couple of bookends," I whined.

He broke into that little grin he always got when he thought he had pulled a good one. "Best-looking bookends in Kettle."

William White and I decided not to drive the old twenty-nine Chevy we bought at the beginning of the school year with the income from our yard-mowing business. With its torn seat covers and moldy flooring the old car didn't meet the standards of an event like the prom. Daddy said I could borrow our family's nineteen and forty-one black Dodge sedan for the evening. It had four doors and a large back seat with plenty of room. William White and I had the car as clean and shiny as the day it came out of the factory.

On prom night, William White and Susie Mac sat in the back seat while I went in to get Beverly. They'd had two earlier dates this spring, and William White had admired Susie Mac since fifth grade.

I handed Beverly a white orchid corsage and helped her pin it to the front of her gown. Her Mom told us how nice we both looked. Beverly wore a gown of pink and the bottom of her skirt extended wider than her shoulders. Her tan skin complemented the light pink of the dress. Beverly's blue eyes sparkled and her dark brown hair curled around her face like a soft picture frame.

Beverly's Mom said, "Well, Freddy, I suppose you know about Beverly's plans to go to the university in September."

I nodded my head. Beverly had mentioned that she'd been accepted to attend the university up in Morgantown, but until that moment I didn't know for certain that she would go.

"We're very proud of her," Mrs. Shade said. Then I thought I heard her voice harden just a bit as she asked, "And what about you, Freddy, what are your plans?"

I felt like a teacher had just announced a pop quiz and I hadn't studied. I stiffened. Somebody turned on a garden hose in my armpits.

"Well, Mrs. Shade, I'm not sure what I'm going to do." I thought about the fork in the road. My heart picked up a faster beat. I cleared my throat but my voice sounded squeaky. "I've talked with my parents about going to Marshall College, but money's a little tight right now." I paused and Phil's offer popped into my mind. I gave her a big smile. "And Phil Buckingham has made me a very attractive offer to work full-time for him."

Mrs. Shade looked at me for a few seconds. Then she squeezed out a little half-smile, the kind I'd seen people at church put on when they talked about some guy who just got out of jail for the fourth time and told everybody he'd stay on a straight and narrow path. "Isn't that nice. Phil seems to have a very good business."

"Oh yes maam. Only last Saturday one hundred and thirty-seven cars came in for gas." I paused and thought for a second. "Actually that number includes both cars and trucks." She held her half-smile and nodded.

Before we walked out the front door, Beverly's Mom said, "Don't forget, honey, tomorrow morning you're going with me to the meeting in Huntington."

When I opened the car door for Beverly, I glanced towards the back seat. William White sat with his back towards the front seat and Susie Mac had wrapped her arms around him. I yelled, "Hello!" probably louder than I should have, for they both jumped. William White popped around, face forward. Susie Mac too. Her lipstick extended in wide bands around her lips and William White wore quite a bit of it. On the drive over to Kettle High, Beverly sat near the passenger side door and didn't say much.

That night the Kettle High gym looked like a make-believe ballroom. Soft dim lights, along with the mums and roses among the crepe paper decorations, gave the old gymnasium a warm and festive, yet soft, atmosphere. A special place that would last for only a few hours, then disappear. When we walked in the door, a Glenn Miller record, "Sunrise Serenade," played. William White took Susie Mac in his arms, swept her up might be a better way of describing it, and they danced across the gym floor.

I asked Beverly, "Would you like to dance?"

"Just a minute, Freddy, I need to tell Mary Sue something," and then she walked over to a group of girls. Mary Sue had been

Beverly's best friend since grade school. They always seemed to have something private to share.

A bunch of the guys stood on the other side of the room. I walked over and said, "Hey." George Boy Roosevelt answered, "Hey, Freddy," and punched me on the shoulder.

William White and Susie Mac danced and held each other so close it looked more like one person dancing, not two. I wondered if they practiced, then remembered they'd only had two dates.

Susie Mac looked pretty in her blue gown. She had her curly blonde hair cut short in what William White said her Mom called her "summer style." William White, always thinking ahead, told me, "I really like Susie Mac's new haircut. If we neck and make out, her hair will look the same afterwards as it did before we started."

"Lucky you," I replied with some sarcasm in my voice.

"Seriously, though, there's something about her. I don't know what it is. It's like I've been waiting and waiting for somebody, and I just found out that it's Susie Mac."

Beverly looked my way, and I walked over to her. "Ready to dance?"

I put my arm around her and right away could feel her pull back, enough to put a few inches of distance between us. I arched my arm around her to allow for the space between us and we danced through Bing Crosby singing, "Now is the Hour." I thought about the words, "Now is the hour, when we must say goodbye…" Our class would soon graduate and say goodbye to each other. From the way things had been going, I wondered if Beverly applied the words of the song to me. After the music ended everybody walked over to the punch bowl, except for William White and Susie Mac who stood motionless near the center of the dance floor. They nuzzled their faces into each other's necks, their eyes closed.

During the last dance I held Beverly close, but I could feel stiffness in the way she held me, and the mechanical movement of her dancing. When the music ended everybody began to leave. We met up with William White and Susie Mac. "Hey," I said, hoping

I sounded surprised by the wonder of what I would say, "I got an idea. Let's go to the East End Diner in Huntington." Actually, the idea hadn't just occurred to me, though I had tried to make it sound that way by rehearsing how I would say it. William White and I had planned this move for quite some time. First to the East End Diner, then to Gobbler's Knob, a place on a hilltop in Ritter Park in Huntington where late at night kids went to park and neck.

"Sounds good to me," William White said. Also rehearsed.

"Me too," Susie Mac added. Purely spontaneous.

Beverly got a most serious look on her face and said, "I don't know. It's now nearly ten-thirty. By the time we go there, eat, and then drive back, it's likely to be well after midnight."

Inside me, a little voice said, "She got that right."

"My Mom told me I'd have to be home between eleven-thirty and twelve. Mom said she'd be waiting up for me."

We drove up Main Street and parked in front of Bertha's Place. Bertha had kept the restaurant open late because of it being prom night. She even put a sign in the front window, 'After-Prom Party Tonight.' Bertha wore a black lacy dress, though her large size stretched the dress. I had never seen Bertha out of her blue uniform.

Lots of the kids from the prom had already arrived. Bertha put a small bowl full of nickels on the table beside the jukebox, so we had continuous music. Somebody kept selecting Hank Williams's "Your Cheatin' Heart." Some of the kids moved the tables away from the center of the restaurant and danced.

Whit Saunders sat in the back booth. He said, "This is a first—dancin' at Bertha's Place." He laughed, "Better pull down the shades, Bertha."

Whit had no sooner said, "Pull down the shades," than the front door opened and in walked Ferlin R, Lovey, Chappie, and True. They looked around the room at everybody all dressed up in suits and gowns, and then Chappie squeaked, "Ferlin R, we didn't git ourselfs dressed up proper."

The little group turned to leave, but True pulled on the back of Chappie's shirt and said, "Chappie, I want to dance."

"I ain't no dancer, True."

I had walked over to the counter to order two RC Colas. "Your chea-ea-tin heart, will tell on you-ou..." Suddenly True stood at the counter in front of me with her arms extended. The next thing I knew we had begun slow dancing. She pressed against me, laid her cheek against my chest, and I inhaled the sweet scent of her. Her legs touched mine as we moved to the music.

True turned her face upwards to me and her lips parted ever so slightly. I stared into her blue eyes and at that moment the world contained only True and me slow-dancing in Bertha's Place.

True's body jerked away from me as Chappie pulled her left arm. Lovey stepped in between us and put her back to me.

"Quit your lollygaggin' with Freddy," Lovey yelled. "He ain't got time for you."

Ferlin R grabbed Lovey's hand and yanked her towards the door. She pulled Chappie, who pulled True, and the little group went out the door.

William White, Susie Mac and Beverly sat in the booth laughing. My face felt red-hot. "Let's...let's order some food," I sputtered. We ordered hamburgers, French fries, and RC Colas. When I placed my order I asked Bertha to hold the onions.

About the time I finished my hamburger Beverly looked at the round "Drink RC Cola" clock on the wall beside the door to the kitchen. Eleven-thirty. She said, "I should be getting home."

Beverly and I climbed the steps to her porch and stood by the front door. Beverly said, speaking slowly, almost as if she wanted to hear herself say the words, "Thank you for the corsage, Freddy. And for a nice evening. It was very special."

"You're welcome," though I wondered if in truth she'd had a nice evening. I'd felt uncomfortable through most of it.

Beverly stared at a spot on the floor of the porch for a few seconds, and then looked into my eyes. In a voice that broke and sounded like she might cry, she said, "I know I wasn't much fun tonight Freddy, and I'm sorry."

"No, you were fine. I enjoyed our dancing and talking," I lied.

"It's OK." Her voice took on a soft, sad tone. "You don't have to be nice about it." She had tears in her eyes. I wondered if I had said something to make her cry.

"Remember when you picked me up this evening and my Mom asked you about your plans after graduation?"

"Sure."

"Well, she talked to me about all that before you arrived. She had heard from one of her friends that Phil made you a job offer and it was likely you wouldn't to go to college. I guess she just wanted to hear it from you. All afternoon today she talked to me about how important it is to get an education, and how Daddy missed the boat by not going to college. I said, 'But Mom, Dad has done well working at Union Chemical.' She told me, 'It could have been different, and better. Don't let that happen to you.' All that talk with her kind of derailed my thoughts this evening. I'm sorry Freddy."

I didn't know what to say. During the prom I knew something had been wrong, but didn't know what. All of a sudden it felt like somebody had loaded heavy weights on to my body.

Beverly stood there with a long sad face, but even when long and sad her face carried grace. She looked again at the porch floor, and then turned her face towards me. "This is hard for me to say, Freddy, but I don't think we should see each other on dates any more." Suddenly Bing Crosby sang, "Now is the hour…" Tears ran down Beverly's cheeks.

"I'm sorry, Freddy."

"I don't want you to have a bad time with your Mom, Beverly. But, don't you think…I mean, couldn't we date some this summer? You know, go to the movies just like we have."

"I'd like to do that, Freddy. But I know if we date, I'll not be able to live with Mom. She'll make my life miserable. I like you a lot, maybe too much. I enjoy our time together." She gave me a little half smile. A tear rolled down her left cheek. "I'm sure we'll see each other once in a while at Bertha's Place or around town."

Her half-smile disappeared. "Anyway, come September everything will end. I'll be gone."

End? I couldn't believe it. Not just the prom, everything—softball, raspberry pie, holding hands in the movies.

Beverly looked at me ever so softly and we held each other's gaze for a long time. Then she said, "Good night, Freddy."

"Night, Beverly, I muttered." An enemy torpedo had struck my heart.

I began to turn to walk off the porch, I mean I got ready to turn but had not actually turned, when Beverly's hand touched my cheek, "Freddy?"

I would have said, "Yes?" but her long arms wound themselves around me and she pulled us close together. I put my arms around her, though I hadn't figured out what I should do. Then her lips touched mine. So soft. Through her gown and crinolines, she pressed her body against me. I returned her kiss. It became a slow and long kiss. Her lips moved ever so gently, and then parted just a little, something new to me. I did the same but wondered how far I should open my mouth. Her tongue played along my lips and then moved lightly inside them. My heart raced and my breath came in short gasps. I pulled her towards me as tightly as I could. She pulled me towards her. I'd never held anybody like that. And I had never been held or kissed that way. Her body moved back forth, rubbing and exciting me. Her hands slipped under my jacket and moved gently up and down my back. Our kiss went on so long I wondered if I would be able to breathe.

Though I didn't want that kiss ever to end, it did. As I touched my lips to Beverly's neck she whispered, "You'll have to go now," and gently pushed away from me.

"Are you sure? But..." She placed her fingers against my lips.

Then Beverly put one hand on each side of my face and looked at me. "I've wanted to hold you like that for a long time, Freddy."

We looked into each other's eyes. Tears rolled down her cheeks. Mine too.

Beverly said, "I care about you so much, and I think of you every day. But I live with Mom and Dad. And I'm going to the university in the fall. That's my life." She gave me a quick hug. "Good night, Freddy."

I turned away, confused. This time she didn't stop me. What had happened? As I walked down the porch steps I felt filled with love, yet empty.

When I pressed the starter on the Dodge I looked in the rear-view mirror. I couldn't see William White and Susie Mac, though I could hear the rustle of crinolines and giggling. I wanted to go somewhere and be alone.

Susie Mac giggled after William White said, "Oh, chauffeur, to Miss MacLendon's house, please. By the way," he added, "this is one wild lady."

A light thump of a hand against a body sounded and Susie Mac said in a low voice, "If you want another one of those just keep talking like that."

At Susie Mac's house the place looked dark except for a light on the front porch and a table lamp shining through the living room window.

"Looks like everybody's gone to bed," I said to the rear-view mirror.

Two heads slowly rose up in the back seat. Susie Mac said, "Mmmm, William White stop it." She looked out the window. "My parents go to bed early."

William White laughed, "Well, I guess it's just us and a dark house."

"Dream on, William White. Come on, let's go in."

William White told me he would walk home. He and Susie Mac strolled up the sidewalk to Susie Mac's house with their arms around each other. On my drive home I lightly touched my tongue to my lips and tasted Beverly's lipstick. I pretended that she sat in the car beside me. "I love you," I whispered.

After I went to bed I thought about the prom and our good-night kiss—then her words that put an end to everything. I wanted to hold Beverly. I felt an empty place inside me, one only she could fill. My stomach gave a little jerk, then another one that rippled up through my chest. And another, this time a big one.

Then tears came and I cried a deep cry that rolled down into my guts and pulled my stomach muscles tight. I turned face down and pulled the covers over my head.

Two weeks later in the auditorium at Kettle High School our senior class had its graduation ceremony. Seventy-two of us graduated, many of us in school together since first grade. Families and friends filled the auditorium. Before the ceremony we lined up for our procession, wearing our black gowns and flat square mortarboard caps with one corner pointed forward just above the forehead. The orange tassels on our caps were all on the left side of the cap's forward point. My heart jumped a beat when I looked at Beverly, smiled, and she returned my look then broke into a smile.

Our principal, Mr. Lawton, gave a speech about citizenship. I only half-listened for I had my attention on Beverly, seated a couple of rows in front of me. Mr. Lawton lowered his voice to a serious tone and said, "Above all else, as you enter the world you should commit yourselves to the struggle against Communism, at home and around the world." The only commitment I had involved keeping my gaze focused on the back of Beverly's beautiful shoulders.

Holbert Holcomb, class valedictorian, spoke next. Holbert may have been the smartest kid in our class, but he couldn't hit a baseball if his life depended on it. His round shape and triple chin said to me he should drop some weight. I half-listened to his speech. It was just a matter of time until Holbert got around to the question he had talked so much about in our problems of democracy class. Sure enough, once again he asked, "Is it right for there to be Negro players in major league baseball? Last season there we had the first one in the National League. Now they're in the American League. Soon they'll infiltrate every team, both leagues."

About the time Holbert asked if the Communists put the Negroes up to playing in the National League, Beverly turned to talk with Mary Sue, sitting beside her. Mary Sue planned to go to the university in the fall. She and Beverly would be roommates. I had a clear view of Beverly's profile. I imagined her cheek against mine and remembered how, after the prom, our lips, our bodies, had touched, pressed. And our kiss. When people felt the kind of longing I felt at that moment, how could they go on with their lives without fulfilling their love? Would I live my life without Beverly? Could I live my life without her?

When Holbert finished his speech everybody gave polite applause until George Boy Roosevelt, sitting right behind William White and me, stood, put his hands in the air and clapped and whistled like he did in Kettle High assemblies after somebody made a boring speech. George Boy's actions prompted others folks to do the same thing, and the next thing I knew Holbert received a standing ovation.

Then came the time to give awards to graduating seniors. Even though my grades put me near Holbert in the academic ranking of our class, I hadn't excelled in anything. I had no reason to expect an award and didn't receive one. William White received the award for creative writing. When he returned to his seat I shook his hand and we shared big grins. The Daughters of the American Revolution history award went to Beverly. She'd often told me how much she liked history, particularly American history in the period of the Civil War. Beverly knew the names of all the generals and units that fought at the battle of Gettysburg. As she walked across the stage to receive her award she held her head high and walked with grace.

Finally we came to the awarding of diplomas. William White punched me in the ribs with his elbow, "We're gonna be out of here," he whispered all too loud.

One by one Mr. Lawton read our names and each member of our class walked across the stage to be handed a diploma. Mr. Lawton wore a sober look on his face, and in a deep voice said, "Congratulations" to each of us. The quiet of the ceremony got disrupted when I walked across the stage and William White cut loose with a loud whistle, the kind you get when you put your fingers in the corners of your mouth pull down and blow hard. Everybody jumped, and then laughed. Mr. Lawton's head snapped around and he gave William White a dark stare. Later, William White asked, "What's he going to do, expel me?"

After the ceremony, outside on the lawn I walked towards Beverly but before I reached her a large bunch of relatives surrounded her, shaking her hand and talking with her. I got close enough make eye contact and we smiled at each other.

Two weeks before graduation I had again talked with Momma and Daddy about the fork in my road, and whether I should go to college or go to work. Daddy took out a pad of paper and showed me a method he said Ben Franklin used to weigh decisions. "For each alternative in a choice," Daddy said, "Mr. Franklin would create a list of positive and negative features. He'd study and weigh them, and then select his alternative." Daddy and Momma helped me list the positives and negatives of going to college or accepting Phil's offer, and then told me they knew I'd make the right decision. By the time I went to bed my uncertainty about what to study in college, along with limited finances, led me towards full-time work for Phil.

On Wednesday of the week before graduation I told Phil I would accept his offer. Phil gave me a big grin and we shook hands. He pumped my arm up and down with enthusiasm. It felt good to know he wanted me to work for him. Phil gave me three sets of what he called our warm weather uniforms, light blue cotton trousers and short-sleeved light blue shirts. The round orange Gulf insignia with the word Buckingham's stitched just underneath it had been sewn above the left pocket of each shirt.

The Monday after graduation, my first day of full-time work, I got to Buckingham's bright and early. I jumped right into my program of cleaning each customer's windshield and popping the hood to check the oil. That day eighteen percent of all gas customers made oil purchases. Easy extra money, I figured, and good for Phil too. I decided I'd put my oil commission earnings into a little fund I'd use for college. Or maybe I'd use the money to set up an apartment of my own.

That evening I called Beverly. I told myself I wanted to tell her about my first day of full-time work. In truth, we hadn't spoken since the prom and I wanted so much to hear her voice. Her Mom answered and in a polite but matter-of-fact way said, "Beverly's out. I'll tell her you called, Freddy." A couple of days later, when I hadn't heard from Beverly, I called again and her Mom said the same thing.

I went through this a couple more times before I began to get the picture. Beverly Shade's house had been sealed off, at least for me. It made me think of the Russians sealing off part of Berlin. Her Mom might as well have put a big sign, "Freddy Lemley— keep out" in the front yard, or maybe posted some armed guards around the place. Maybe the Russians could send over some sentries to help her out. With my work each day at Buckingham's I couldn't go places during the day where Beverly might be, like Bertha's Place or the Kettle Public Library. One night I dreamed that Beverly drove her family's car to Buckingham's for a tank of gas. I jumped in the car and we drove off together. We just drove on and on. The dream seemed so real, but when I woke up the car and Beverly had disappeared. I tried to go back to sleep, hoping another dream would bring her back, but it didn't work. I tried to fix the images of the dream in my memory, but by the end of the day they had faded.

Every once in a while William White brought me news about Beverly. One day he approached me with some hesitation, started to speak then stopped a couple of times. Finally he said, "I don't want to tell you this, but you ought to know.

"Beverly went with Holbert Holcomb to a band concert in Ritter Park. Susie Mac told me Beverly's Mom thought she should go. Pushed her into it."

I had to sit down. "Damn him," I said. My face flushed. From what I'd learned about Mrs. Shade, William White's report made sense. I took a couple of deep breaths. Although I felt jealous, I had to admit I felt a little relief that Beverly had a date with fat boring Holbert, one guy I doubted she'd ever fall for.

Once in a while Mrs. Shade drove their family car to Buckingham's for a tank of gas. When I saw her coming I would start stocking the shelves and Phil would wait on her. On a couple of occasions when I had to wait on her she surprised me with her pleasant manner.

200

One morning I told William White about how Mrs. Shade acted towards me.

He said, "Mrs. Shade reminds me of a picture I saw in the newspaper of a Russian soldier guarding the border of West Berlin. The soldier held a rifle and at the same time smiled at a little German kid. Sure, Mrs. Shade smiles and acts nice, but you can't cross the border." Then William White looked at me most seriously and added, "Maybe God is teaching you a lesson. About how folks can seem nice on the surface and all the while work against you."

"I may seem to be a little slow in these things, William White, but I got it. He can end the lesson."

After lunch our business slowed down. Phil left to make a couple of service calls—a fellow had a dead battery and Miss Hattie McClintock had a flat right rear tire. Mid-afternoon I put a lawn chair under the old oak tree and sat for a spell. What might I have done differently towards Beverly? I suppose if I told her Mom I intended to go to college this fall we might still be dating. I thought about Beverly preparing to go to college. Did she continue to think about me each day?

How do people come to care about each other so powerfully that they share their lives? Get married? I again imagined our passionate kiss after the prom, and how I wanted that moment to last forever. I wanted to feel her, every part of her, next to me.

What's it like for a couple to love each other so powerfully that they shed their clothes and fall into bed, and then do it? In the movies after a couple kisses with passion the screen fades to black. Then it's the next day. Will I ever get to point with Beverly that the screen will fade to black? And if did, would I know what to do?

About then Ferlin R's old truck rolled up to the gas pumps. Lovey sat in the front seat beside Ferlin R. He smiled and said, "Gimme two dollars worth of regular, Freddy."

I put the nozzle in the neck of the truck's gas tank and squeezed its handle. In the bed of the truck Chappie began squeaking and True laughed, and then the bed of the truck gently rose and fell as they bounced around. I squeezed the handle to speed the flow of gasoline.

By the time I finished putting two dollars' worth of gas in the truck, Ferlin R and Lovey stood alongside me. Ferlin R opened his wallet. Lovey placed one hand inside the right front pocket of Ferlin R's pants and ran her other hand through his hair. Then she nuzzled her lips against his neck and whispered, "You remind me of Froud R. Kaltenborn. Ain't it time to go, Froud R? Ain't it?"

In a whisper Ferlin R said, "Just hold on, darlin'. We'll be done here in a minute. Then we'll head up Sour Apple River and git down to business."

A trail of blue exhaust drifted behind the old truck as it drove away. The people in the truck never finished high school. But I knew that they knew what happened when, in the movies, a couple kissed with so much passion the screen faded to black.

Chapter 9

FADE TO BLACK

William White Wallace gave me a sharp poke in the ribs with his elbow. I jerked awake. "Fried chicken," I blurted out, like a balloon suddenly losing its air.

Hartford and Iretta Wilson, dressed in their solemn Sunday best and seated in the pew in front of us, jerked their heads around as fast as two old weathervanes hit with a gust of wind. Iretta pursed her mouth and shook her head sidewise. My face turned red.

That Sunday in August, nineteen and forty-eight, known as Communion Sunday, William White and I sat in the sanctuary of the Kettle Methodist Church. But I couldn't get my thoughts on the spiritual food of communion—I had a powerful hunger for another kind of food, Grandma Lemley's Sunday dinner. Half-runner green beans with liberal quantities of bacon and onions that would cook slow all morning. Mashed potatoes and gravy. Fried chicken so crisp it crackled when I bit into it. My thoughts had just settled over the fried chicken when it came time for us to go to the altar and take communion. That's the moment when William White poked me in the ribs.

Junior Don Kincaid and Lucy Vittitoe sat to the right of William White and me. They looked over and started giggling. Lucy placed one hand over her mouth and her other hand on Junior Don's lips. Junior Don's giggles stopped but he kept laughing on the inside, for his body shook and he wore a big grin.

After communion I returned to my seat and made an effort to pray and reflect on the body and blood of Jesus. But my thoughts kept veering over to Grandma Lemley's biscuits, so tender and delicious they must have been inspired by God. It's possible that God had a hand in Grandma Lemley's desserts, too: fruit and berry pies in the summer, pecan and chocolate pies in the winter, all with crisp flaky crusts that held rich sweet mixtures. Grandma had told me that today she'd serve one of my favorite desserts, peach cobbler with vanilla ice cream.

Outside after the service ended, Junior Don and Lucy walked over to me and William White, just beyond the white rose bushes beside the front door of the church. Lucy wore a matching light blue skirt and blouse. William White once told me he liked for Lucy to wear pastel blue, for the color complemented her light brown hair, matched her blue eyes. Junior Don towered over Lucy's small frame. He wore what he called his Sunday-go-to-meetin' suit, one of blue gabardine that he'd bought for last year's junior prom. Junior Don had grown so much since then that it barely fit. And beneath his necktie, he had to leave the top button of his shirt unbuttoned.

"Freddy, I wish you and Beverly was still dating. I've got Dad's car. Lucy and I are going to a movie in Huntington tonight. We could double date."

A pang slammed through my heart. I smiled and mumbled something like, "Thanks, Junior Don, me too." Since the night of the prom I'd not heard from Beverly. Around town I only occasionally got a glimpse of her, and then at a distance. Did she feel right about her decision for us not to date this summer? I sure didn't.

William White popped into the conversation with a big grin, "I'm not doing anything this evening, Junior Don. Be happy to join you."

Junior Don and Lucy laughed. Junior Don gave William White a friendly punch on the shoulder, "No offense, William White, but third wheels only work on wheelbarrows."

After dinner Grandpa Lemley pushed his chair back from the head of the table, stretched his long legs, and suggested we leave the dishes and go set a spell on the porch. "Let our food settle," he said. At the other end of the table Grandma jumped up so fast that by the time I put down my fork I saw only the back of her green dress and her gray hair as she skedaddled out the front door. I took the final bite of my peach cobbler, then, along with Momma and Daddy, got up from the table.

Sitting on the front porch we had a view across the valley to the hills on the far side of the river. Dark gray clouds spread across the horizon beyond the hills. The newspaper had said that we might get some rain. The distant hills had a dark green cast dappled with purplish-blue where the clouds shaded them. The valley, spreading out below Grandma and Grandpa's place, reminded me of a patchwork quilt. Old fence lines outlined the gray and brown shapes of farm fields and pastures. White houses and red barns dotted the quilt, and Route 42 threaded its way among them like a thin gray ribbon.

We sat quietly in the still and humid afternoon air. Momma, after commenting, "The day is positively torpid"—she was always testing me with new words—tried to stir up some conversation about an article she'd read in *Time* magazine about Whitaker Chambers, Alger Hiss, and the Communists in government. But Daddy and Grandpa Lemley seemed more interested in quiet porch sitting and food settling, a process that required them to close their eyes for extended periods. The only movement of air came from Grandma's and Momma's slow movement of their paper fans from the Smith Sisters' Funeral Home. The fans moved like two clock pendulums, back and forth, over and over. The Smith Sisters had distributed the scallop-shaped fans to all the ladies' Sunday school classes in Kettle's churches. One side of the fan had a reproduction of the painting, "The Last Supper," and the other side held an advertisement for the Smith Sisters' Funeral Home, "Your family's counsel and support in a time of need." As I watched Jesus and the Disciples move left to right, right to left, my eyelids began feel heavy, to close.

About the time my eyelids drooped shut, a strong and cool breeze kicked up. Grandpa Lemley walked to the front porch railing and peered across the valley. "Looks like we're gonna get that rain you promised us, Freddy." One of my contributions to the dinner conversation had been a detailed rendering of the weather report I'd read in the Sunday edition of the *Huntington Herald Dispatch.*

Within fifteen minutes the sky turned gray and a light rain began to fall. Before long the sky darkened and the rain got heavier. When the wind began to blow rain into the porch we decided to move indoors. Everybody went into the kitchen to start on the dishes.

I picked up a plate and began to scrape its chicken bones into the garbage. Maybe I looked like I didn't enjoy my job, for Grandma Lemley placed her hand on mine and suggested, "Freddy, on Wednesday I put a few boxes of old clothes in the attic. At the far end, near the bookshelves. I wonder if you would take a look and straighten them up? You know, stack them properly."

Grandma used one of her little tricks to get me out of the kitchen and into something she knew I enjoyed, like poking around in the attic. I once found some toy cars and trucks in the bottom of an attic trunk, "Those were your Daddy's favorite toys when he was a boy," Grandma told me. I found *Saturday Evening Post* magazines going back to nineteen and thirty, and a whole set of Tom Swift books describing his adventures as a young inventor. "Your Daddy's," Grandma said in a voice touched with the sadness of long-ago memories. The summer I turned eleven I went to Grandma's attic almost every morning, sat on the old couch near one of the attic windows and read a Tom Swift book. Before that summer ended, I'd read them all.

When I opened the attic door at the top of the stairs, I spotted some boxes at the far end of the attic that looked out of place. I moved them to an area just beyond the bookshelves and placed them in an orderly stack.

The rain produced a steady drumming on the old farmhouse's tin roof. The dark sky beyond the two small gable windows didn't produce much light. I turned on a couple of old lamps and their soft yellow light spread a warm glow across the large room. The room had a high ceiling, the crest of the roofline, and a shape that followed the L-shaped footprint of the house. With the soft light falling over the trunks, boxes and old furniture, and the gentle sound of the rain on the roof, the attic seemed to envelop me like a cocoon—a small world with its own life.

I had just put the last of Grandma's boxes in neat order when I noticed a hatbox on the top bookshelf, above the Tom Swift books. I brought it down and opened it. The box contained tissue paper, all fluffed up, the way tissue paper would be poofed up around a new hat. I separated the layers of tissue and found a bottle opener with the words "Coney Island" printed on its round red handle. Beside the bottle opener a small square of folded tissue contained a lock of light brown hair. And at the bottom of the box lay a small book with a scratched and well-worn dark green canvas cover.

I opened the little book. It appeared to be a diary, written in pencil. At the top of the first page the printed date said, "January 1, 1863."

My thoughts flashed to a Movietone newsreel at the Dixie Palace. Some men in what they called pith helmets explored man-made tunnels deep in the ground beneath the Egyptian Pyramids. They had discovered some ancient treasures.

I needed more light to read the diary's small and faded writing. I walked to the couch and sat down under a lamp. When fully opened, each page measured about two inches wide and six inches in length—three days on the left page, three days on the right.

"January 1. Returned from reconnaissance."

"January 2. The Army tried to move but stuck in the mud."

A soldier's diary! If the year was eighteen and sixty-three, it had to be the Civil War. But whose diary? A relative? Union or Confederate?

I skipped ahead, looking for words or phrases that would give me clues about the writer and his Army life. Even in a hurry I had to go slowly, for I had difficulty reading the cramped and tiny writing.

At July first I stopped. One word practically leaped off the page: Gettysburg. I took a sharp intake of breath. My arms tingled and goose bumps rose up on each of them. I didn't have Beverly's knowledge of the Civil War, but I knew about Gettysburg. What some folks called "the high water mark" for Robert E. Lee and the Army of Virginia. The little book in my hands had been there.

I put my head back on the couch's soft cushions, rested the diary on my lap, and thought about the little book. The experiences recorded on its pages, its unknown journey from Gettysburg to Grandma's attic. I listened to the patter of the rain on the roof and thought about troops going to battle in the rain. .

A gentle touch fell on my shoulder and I opened my eyes. Grandma Lemley stood beside me. She laughed, "Time to get up, Freddy."

"Look at this, Grandma." I showed her the diary and the hatbox. "This diary was written in the Civil War," I said excitedly. "The soldier who wrote it fought at Gettysburg." I handed her the little book.

"You know, Freddy, I remember the hatbox but never got around to looking inside it. I figured it had one of Momma's old hats in it."

She studied a few pages of the diary then said, "Well, this is surely something. Let's go tell the others."

I ran down the stairs two steps at a time with Grandma close behind me. We gathered everybody around to look at the diary. We gently and carefully passed the little book from one of us to another, much like folks might do with a newborn baby.

I described the hatbox, along with the lock of hair and the Coney Island bottle opener. Grandma Lemley said, "There were some things of Mother's in that part of the attic. She put them there not long before she passed away."

We talked for a while about the Civil War, Kettle families whose men had fought in the two armies, then Grandma asked me to take the diary and study it, "See what you can find out," she said.

Grandpa Lemley went upstairs and brought back a long-handled magnifying glass. He smiled and handed it to me. "That's small writing. This might help."

Before I went to bed that night I cleared off the old maple desk in my room where I used to do homework. Since graduation I had been piling stuff on it. I gave the diary a special place in the center of the desktop. I placed Grandpa Lemley's magnifying glass beside it, along with the Sheaffer pen Grandma and Grandpa Lemley bought me for graduation, and a spiral notebook, one I bought for classes during my senior year but never used. Tomorrow I had a full day of work ahead of me at Buckingham's, but in the evening I could begin to study the little book.

When I turned off the light I intended to clear my thoughts before going to sleep. I usually did that by saying a prayer. But the next thing I knew Beverly and her blue eyes looked deep into me. We stood on her front porch after the prom and held each other. As Beverly placed her lips against mine, I lightly touched my tongue to my lips. I felt an excitement, not a readiness for sleep, passing through my body. I puffed up my pillow and turned over. I shifted my thoughts to the movie William White and I saw last night, but it didn't help. Lana Turner gave John Garfield a kiss so long and passionate that the screen faded to black.

Monday morning I walked to Buckingham's Gulf Station. I wanted to arrive at work a few minutes early, just before seven o'clock. Walking along I thought about my usual routine: unlock the front door and flip the switch to turn on the orange neon "Open" sign just above the door. Seven cases of oil had come in late on Saturday afternoon. Before we got busy I wanted to get them into the racks in the storage room. When I crossed Main Street and walked on to Buckingham's concrete apron, the station's wide-open front door surprised me. As I got closer voices came from the tunnel, the passageway to the garage in the back where all the repair work is done.

I met Phil Buckingham and Peyton Gruber on their way out. Back in the garage I could see Hiram and Blaine, our two mechanics, pushing a wrecked car to one side of the grease rack. Police Chief Arthur R. Tackett walked just behind Peyton and Phil. Peyton said something to Phil, but he spoke so softly that I couldn't hear him.

"Morning, Phil, Peyton. Morning, chief."

Phil's eyes, bloodshot, had dark circles beneath them. Grease and oil stained his white t-shirt. "Freddy, I'll have to ask you to run things by yourself in the front end this morning."

"What's going on, Phil?"

"Uh, Freddy, last night there was a terrible car accident. George Boy Roosevelt crashed into Junior Don Kincaid. I brought the cars in on our wrecker. Junior Don's Buick is back in the shop and George Boy's Plymouth is behind the building."

My shoes stuck to the floor. My heart raced. I wanted to know what happened, but dreaded finding out. Whatever happened had been so bad it kept Phil up all night. Junior Don and George Boy? My thoughts seemed paralyzed, but every fiber of my body felt ready to leap—towards what? What had happened?

Peyton put his arm on Phil's shoulder. "Go on home, Phil. Get some sleep. This'll all wait. Come back after you've rested."

Chief Tackett said, "I'll stick around for a few hours, Phil. There's likely to be a crowd of people here this mornin'. I'll keep things a movin' so you fellers can do business."

Peyton walked Phil to his car. After he returned, he walked over to me, pushed his Cincinnati Reds baseball cap back on his head, and spoke softly. "Freddy, you haven't heard about the accident, have you?"

I shook my head, "No."

"This isn't easy to say. I know George Boy and Junior Don

were your classmates and friends. But the truth is this." He paused, took a deep breath, then said, "Last night, just before midnight, George Boy was driving home from his summer job up at Union Chemical in Charleston. He came west on Route 42 towards Kettle. Junior Don was driving in the other direction with Lucy Vittitoe and Mary Sue Robbins…."

Peyton's mouth moved and I could hear his words, but his voice sounded distant, like it came from the other side of a valley. My thoughts became as slow and thick as molasses. Peyton said that the accident occurred just this side of the county line. Nobody knew why, but Junior Don's car had turned sideways across the highway and George Boy's car hit it, at full highway speed, smack in the middle of the passenger side door. The impact threw Junior Don and Lucy out the other side of the car—Junior Don went fifty feet down the highway. Mary Sue was left in the car.

My stomach felt like it fell to the ground. I stared at Peyton. I stammered, "Were they….I mean, are they going to be…"

Peyton reached over and gently grasped my arms just above the elbows, and then looked at me with a long face. "Freddy, I know they were your friends. And I'm awful sorry to tell you this," his chin quivered, "but Junior Don, Lucy and Mary Sue all died. Doc Simonton said they were killed instantly. George Boy is in the hospital."

My friends. And Mary Sue and Beverly had been best friends, like Junior Don and George Boy. At church yesterday morning, Lucy and Junior Don sat in our pew. My God, after church Junior Don said, "Freddy, I wish you and Beverly were still dating, we could…."

Peyton's voice seemed to come from the furthest part of tunnel. "George Boy got banged up pretty bad, but they say he'll live."

Small white dots began to dance between Peyton and me. Darkness crept in around the outer edges of my vision. I put my right arm against the wall of the building and steadied myself.

Peyton put one arm around my shoulders and with a firm grip guided me into the front end of Buckingham's. I sat down in one of the metal chairs, put my elbows on my knees, rested my head on my hands and closed my eyes. Peyton sat beside me in the other chair. Tears came to my eyes and waves of sadness rolled from my stomach to my chest. At first I tried to hold back my feelings, I didn't want to fall apart at work, in a public place. But the waves rolled over me and I let go and cried. In between the waves I could hear myself breathing in what sounded like gasps.

After a few minutes the waves stopped and I sat quietly with Peyton. Then Peyton reached over and placed his hand on my back. "Things like this never make sense, Freddy. Never. We try to find reasons for them. We hope and pray that maybe God has a plan. That's what we say. But the truth is we don't know. Can't know."

Peyton sat back in his chair. He took off his cap and rubbed his hand across his bald head. "After we lost our boy Bubby in that car wreck, I kept trying to figure it out, you know, figure out God's plan. But I couldn't. I still wake up at night remembering things I wanted to tell Bubby. One night I dreamed he stood beside the bed, wearing the blue suit he had on the day he got his medical degree."

Then Peyton and I sat without talking for twenty minutes. About seven thirty a car pulled up beside the gas pumps, our first customer of the day. I went out to wait on them and when I came back Peyton had gone and Daddy had seated himself in Peyton's chair. He stood and gave me a bear hug, held me in it for a long time. He stayed with me through the morning while I worked.

During a lull in business traffic Daddy said, "Freddy, life takes its toll. In the twenty-one years since my class graduated from Kettle High, at least eight of my classmates have died. Maybe more that I don't know about. Three of the fellows died in the war. A couple of people contracted TB and lost the struggle. Two died of polio. Childbirth took one. Sometimes it seems like life is a sad roll of the dice. We're lucky to be here."

Daddy's words, though sad, had a calming effect. Maybe I needed to learn a little of what life had taught Daddy, what life had to teach each of us lucky enough to be alive.

An hour after Daddy arrived a crowd gathered at Buckingham's. Chief Tackett stood near the outer edge of the apron, where it joined U.S. Route 42, our Main Street. He waved his arms and asked people to stay clear of the front of the station so business traffic could move through. Once in a while he gently blew his whistle to make sure folks stepped back to let a car through. Odd to see so many people at Buckingham's, all of them with long faces. In a town where everybody had something to say most all the time, it seemed even stranger that they said so little. When folks talked they spoke in a somber whisper, like at church or a funeral. Most folks would first walk around to the back of the building to see George Boy's forty-seven Plymouth coupe with its front end smashed so badly it resembled a shut accordion. Then they'd walk through the tunnel to the shop and look at Junior Don's Daddy's big four-door nineteen and forty Buick, now folded into a V-shape.

Phil hadn't turned on the ceiling lights near Junior Don's car and I left them off. Blood covered the car's front seat. It must have been Mary Sue's. In the seventh grade, on Valentine's Day, William White and I had sneaked up on either side of Mary Sue and planted a big kiss on each of her cheeks. Mary Sue's blood had rushed to redden her cheeks as she laughed. Now it colored the front seat of Junior Don's car.

About ten o'clock William White came to Buckingham's. He visited each of the two cars, and then he took one of the metal chairs and placed it on the grass under the big oak tree beside the station. He sat there until noon, most of the time slumped forward with his elbows on his knees, his head in his hands. Once in a while he sat erect, watching folks come and go. I had never known William White to be silent for so long. A couple of times he wiped his eyes with a white handkerchief—maybe the one he carried the night we looked for the UFO with George Boy and Junior Don.

About noon William White left his chair and walked into the station. "Freddy, you know, don't you, that Junior Don, Lucy, and Mary Sue went to a movie in Huntington." I nodded that I did.

"Then they stopped at Bertha's Place for about an hour before they drove up Route 42. Right?" I nodded again.

He smacked his right fist into the palm of his left hand, his eyes widened. "If they had just ordered one more round of RC Colas, or another bag of potato chips, something, anything, it all might have been different."

"What do you mean?"

"Well, think about it." William White described how George Boy's car hit Junior Don's car squarely in the center of the passenger side door. "What if the point of impact had been forward or rearward of that spot just a bit, or even two or three feet?" Then William White, talking more to himself than to me, wondered aloud, "Why did Junior Don's car jump broadside across the highway? Was it because he had his right arm around Lucy and just a loose grip on the steering wheel with his left hand? Maybe he leaned forward to say something to Mary Sue and the right front tire of the Buick dropped off the edge of the pavement. Did the car then twist itself to the left and swerve across the road?" He paused.

"Now here's my point," William White said slow and thoughtful-like, much the way a teacher would speak to a class at Kettle High. "The accident required perfect timing in order to happen the way it did. If Junior Don's timing had been just a tiny bit different, his Buick would not have been perfectly positioned sidewise across Route 42 with the passenger's side door the point of impact at precisely the moment George Boy's Plymouth arrived at that spot in the road." He went on to talk about how George Boy might have clipped the front or back end of Junior Don's Buick, or there might have been no accident at all. "A second, or even a half-second, that's all they would have needed, and Junior Don, Lucy, and Mary Sue would be alive right now. We'd joke about how Junior Don's car jumped across the highway last night."

William White paused and looked towards Main Street through Buckingham's plate glass windows. He spoke towards the windows, "If they'd ordered one more RC Cola, another bag of potato chips. Anything that might have changed the time they got in the car." William White's voice rose and his lips quivered, he turned to me, "Anything at all, and they'd be here. Anything. That's all it would have taken."

William White's eyes filled with tears. "Freddy, after church Junior Don told me he and Lucy didn't want a third wheel on their date. But they got one, Mary Sue. That could have been me. I wanted to go with them." He sat down, put his head in his hands and cried. I put my hand on his shoulder.

I again heard Junior Don's voice say, "Freddy, I wish you and Beverly were still dating…." A cold chill moved deep in my body.

About two o'clock the phone on the front counter rang. "Buckingham's Service Station. This is Freddy."

A deep voice said, "Hello, Freddy. This is Mr. Lawton."

Mr. Nathaniel R. Lawton, the principal of Kettle High School. I first thought a teacher had reported me for something and Mr. Lawton called to tell me to get over to his office. Then I remembered that I graduated in May.

"Hello, Mr. Lawton. What can I do for you?"

"Freddy, I know you've heard the sad news of the tragedy in our town. I'm sorry about your friends. Are you doing all right?"

"Thanks, I guess I'm doing OK." Not the truth, but I didn't feel like getting into a discussion with him.

"Freddy, this morning Junior Don's parents asked if I would make arrangements for two young people to be pallbearers for Junior Don."

"Yes, sir."

"I'm calling to ask, would you be one of Junior Don's pallbearers? The funeral will be on Wednesday, two PM at the Kettle Methodist Church. I've also asked William White Wallace. The family will provide the other four pallbearers."

I wanted to hang up and run. But I took a deep breath and said, "Yes, sir, I'd be honored to do it, though I'll have to ask Phil Buckingham about taking time off."

"I've already talked with Phil, Freddy. He said it was all right."

Some things never change. I surprised myself with a small inward smile. Mr. Lawton always stayed one step ahead.

Late that afternoon Phil came back to work, looking a little better but washed out and tired. Hiram and Blaine, the mechanics who worked in Buckingham's garage, had sat down with me just before Phil walked in.

After he poured himself a cup of coffee, Phil told us how it took him until about three AM to haul both of the cars to the station. "Bringing in George Boy's Plymouth got a little complicated," he said. "I had the front end hooked to the wrecker and raised up properly, but on the way to Kettle somehow George Boy's car dropped into low gear. The sudden drag nearly pulled the car, my wrecker too, off the road. I was just this side of the culvert over Cedar Creek. Good thing there wasn't any traffic on Route 42 or we might have had another accident to tend to."

Blaine pushed his greasy leather ball cap back on his head and said in his soft voice, "Got to watch low gear on them Plymouths, Phil. Seems like a Plymouth's low gear just pulls into itself. I seen it happen many times, though never when being pulled by a wrecker. That's a first for me, how about you Hiram?"

Hiram looked out the window, nodded, and wiped his hands on his coveralls.

Phil continued, "After I got both cars here and put in their places, Pappy Roosevelt showed up. Said he wanted to look at George Boy's car. He'd just come from the hospital. George Boy was doing OK. He told me the force of the accident caused George Boy's knees to get banged up pretty bad, and his chest got boogered when it hit the steering wheel. Ovieta, George Boy's Mom, stayed at the hospital, but Pappy Roosevelt said he had to get back look after the hogs. I think he just wanted somebody to listen to him, for he started talking ninety miles an hour about all the things George Boy and Junior Don had done together— working on the farm, swimming down at the river, playing football at Kettle High. He said, 'I never in a million years would have figured George Boy to be the agent of Junior Don's death, but that's what he was.' I put on the coffee pot.

"About the time I handed him a cup of coffee, Pappy Roosevelt said, very quiet-like, 'I reckon George Boy will have to learn to live with what happened, the same as I done. I never would've figured me to be the agent of our little girl Opal's death. But I was.' Then he talked about Opal, and how cute she was when she puttered around the yard while he mowed the grass and did chores. And how she fell into the cistern that day. "He said, 'I'll never forgive myself for Opal's death, though my wife and folks around town seems to have forgive me. I hope and pray folks'll now do the same for George Boy.' Me and George Boy, we're killers."

Along with the other businesses in Kettle, on Wednesday morning Phil put a "Closed" sign in the front window of Buckingham's. All three funerals would be held that day. Mary Sue's at ten o'clock in the morning at the Kettle Baptist Church. Lucy's at noon, Upper Creek Church of Apostolic Faith. Junior Don's at two o'clock, Kettle Methodist Church. William White and I tried to figure out a way to attend both of the girls' funerals before being pallbearers for Junior Don, but couldn't do it. Mary Sue's funeral didn't present a problem, but Lucy's funeral at noon on Upper Creek, about five miles from town, did. We might have been able to attend if Lucy's funeral had been in a Methodist or Baptist church. But the Apostolic Church of Faith had a reputation for funeral services that lasted at least two hours, usually longer. We decided to stay in town and miss Lucy's funeral, though we felt bad about it.

William White and I arrived at the Baptist Church ten minutes before the service for Mary Sue began and got the last open seats in the back row of the sanctuary. William White had said, "Oh, we'll be there in plenty of time," and I made the mistake of believing him. The front of the church had eight-foot-high racks of flowers extending from either end of Mary Sue's casket to the walls of the sanctuary. In the warm air the scents of the flowers blended into a sweet aroma that thickened the air of the large room, made it hang heavy. I took a deep breath and whispered to William White, "It's like breathing honey."

Momma and Daddy walked in and nodded at me. Some folks in a center pew scooted over and they sat down. The Roosevelts sat just behind them. Pappy Roosevelt looked hot and uncomfortable in his dark gray wool suit. Mrs. Roosevelt, like Momma, wore a black dress and hat. Momma turned and said something to them. She and Pappy Roosevelt hugged each other, and then Momma and Mrs. Roosevelt hugged one another. Daddy and Pappy Roosevelt shook hands.

The service leaflet listed Beverly's name as one of the speakers for the service. After the first hymn and a prayer, she walked to the front of the church and stood beside Mary Sue's closed bronze casket. Beverly wore a pink dress that complemented her tan skin and blue eyes. Before she spoke our eyes met and her face reddened. Then Beverly placed her left hand on top of the casket and read a poem she had written. She spoke about her friendship with Mary Sue, and her love for her. Beverly's face looked drawn and sad, with small lines across her forehead I had never seen before. Grief wrinkles, William White later told me, he had read about them in *Reader's Digest.* I wanted to walk to the front of the church, take her hand and comfort her.   After Beverly read the first verse of her tribute to Mary Sue, her lower lip began to quiver. Shortly afterwards she stopped speaking and closed her eyes. Tears ran down her cheeks. Beverly's Mom walked down the aisle and put her arms around her.   In less than a minute Beverly recovered and finished her remarks while her Mom stood beside her.

On her way back to her seat she paused and looked at me. I held her gaze and hoped my expression reflected the love I felt for her. Then I wiped tears from my eyes.

After the service William White and I rode with Momma and Daddy to the cemetery. We stood on the outer edges of the crowd gathered around Mary Sue's gravesite. Her Mom and Dad, along with her brother and grandparents, sat on metal chairs placed on artificial grass beneath a canopy. The canopy also sheltered the casket, resting on straps above the open grave. Mary Sue's family sat there crying. I realized that I couldn't bring myself to cry any more. I even tried by scrunching up my stomach, shutting and tightly squeezing my eyes. I just hadn't anything left. Later William White told me scientists had discovered that the tear glands dried out after periods of heavy tear production.

William White and I stayed at the gravesite after the service had ended and everybody left. Four men filled the grave with fresh dirt. Mary Sue in the darkness beneath the earth? The image caused me to shiver.

Beverly had once mentioned that Mary Sue loved yellow roses. William White and I each brought a yellow rose with us. We placed the flowers at the head of her grave.

We walked to my house. Momma served us fresh lemonade and ham sandwiches, and then she and Daddy sat with us on the front porch. We chatted some about Lucy, Junior Don and Mary Sue, then sat silently until time for Junior Don's funeral.

The Kettle Methodist Church had filled when William White and I arrived. Beverly sat near the front of the church. We walked down the aisle to our seats, a front pew bearing a small sign that said, "Reserved for Pallbearers." As I walked past Beverly, she looked up and I held her gaze for a few seconds.

Junior Don's open casket had been placed in front of the altar. His face looked like him, yet it didn't. Reconstructed, I guessed. Chief Tackett had said that Junior Don had been thrown quite a distance from his car.

I had learned that Miss June Boone Smith did the work to reconstruct Junior Don's face. Miss June, along with her sister April Boone Smith, owned the Smith Sisters' Funeral Home. Miss June had a reputation throughout our region for her artistry in giving the dead a look of life. But Junior Don may have been more than even she could do. The right half of Junior Don's face looked like a mask made of putty and makeup. His right eyebrow had been painted on.

During the service each person who spoke looked at Junior Don, talked to him. Nell Kincaid, a cousin of Junior Don's who had a powerful soprano voice, sang a solo, the first two verses of "Nearer My God to Thee." By the end of the first verse most folks in the sanctuary were tears.

Reverend Y. Younts Yoder led the service and in his deep bass voice spoke of the Youth for Christ Revival two years ago when Junior Don had been saved. He paused and looked at Junior Don, and then said in a soft voice, "Junior Don, I know there's a foot-ball team in heaven, with Jesus playing quarterback and he's passing to you, the right end." His voice became louder. "And I can hear a chorus of angels cheering as you catch that pass and run into the end zone for a touchdown." He held his gaze on Junior Don and was silent for a moment. He looked across the congregation and boomed, "Halleluiah!"

William White and I flinched.

When the service ended, Miss June closed the lid of the casket and directed our group of pallbearers to lift the casket off its stand. The six of us, one pallbearer on each corner and two in the middle, picked up the casket, heavy with its own weight plus the hundred and eighty pounds of Junior Don. We walked slowly up the aisle. William White and I supported each of the casket's two rear corners. A procession formed behind us, with Junior Don's Mom and Dad walking immediately behind William White and me, followed by the rest of the family. We walked at the front of a parade of tears and sadness.

We passed through the front door of the church and carefully carried the casket way down the church's four front steps. William White and I had just stepped from the bottom step to the flat concrete sidewalk when from behind us we heard a loud moan. Then Junior Don's Mom's body landed with a thump on top of the casket. She had jumped from the top step.

Inside the casket Junior Don's body bounced. William White dropped his corner and fell to the sidewalk. I hung on and kept our end from falling to the pavement.

Mrs. Kincaid wept in loud spasms and moans, her feet by then on the sidewalk but the upper half of her large body still spread across the end of the casket. She pounded her fists on the casket's silver top, thump, thump, thump! Her black hat and veil fell to the ground. "No, noooo. Don't take my baby. Don't leave me, Junior Don. Don't leave me. No! Noooo!"

Miss June and Junior Don's Dad gently lifted and nudged Mrs. Kincaid off the casket. When they got her upright her knees buckled. Miss June and Mr. Kincaid had to hold her up.

By then William White had picked up the weight of the other rear corner of the casket. We carried Junior Don to the hearse. Miss June opened the wide rear door across the rear end of the hearse, and we slid Junior Don's casket into the rear of the old black Cadillac. The Kincaids got in the back seat of what the Smith Sisters called "the family car," a black four-door nineteen and forty Chrysler.

At the cemetery we carried Junior Don's casket from the hearse to the gravesite and placed it, him, on the straps connected to the chromium posts at each corner of the open grave. Risers covered with flowers surrounded the gravesite. The pallbearers stood together at one end of the gravesite's canopy. The Kincaids— Junior Don's parents, grandparents, brother and cousins—sat in the chairs beneath the canopy.

Reverend Yoder conducted the brief service. Later I realized I hadn't heard a word of it. I couldn't take my eyes off the pit, the open grave, below the casket, its dark mouth waiting to swallow Junior Don.

William White pulled on my arm and said, "Hey, Freddy, it's over. Let's go home."

Everybody had left except William White and me, and the fellows who placed the cover on the vault at the bottom of Junior Don's grave. The first shovelful of dirt made a hollow thump as it hit the top of the underground vault containing the casket.

William White asked, "Are you OK?"

"I think so." I pointed towards the grave. "I got lost in there."

"Come on. Let's go to Bertha's Place. You need a cold RC."

In the days after the funerals we started to adjust ourselves to life without Junior Don, Lucy, and Mary Sue. The stream of people coming to Buckingham's to view the smashed cars dropped to a trickle. Phil caught up on his sleep. George Boy got out of the hospital, though he faced a long period of recuperation at home.

The Saturday morning after the funerals Peyton Gruber and Hartford Wilson walked into Buckingham's with a dozen dough-nuts for everyone. I had just finished my second glazed doughnut when a familiar dark blue nineteen and forty-eight Chrysler pulled up to the gas pumps. My heart took a swift little jump, for Beverly sat behind the wheel. Then my heart took a jump in the opposite direction—her Mom sat beside her. I muttered to myself, "A Russian soldier guarding West Berlin."

I walked to the car wondering how best to approach Beverly. Act happy? Surprised? Casual? By the time I stood beside the driver's window it didn't matter. I lit into a big smile and wished her a good morning.

She grinned and said, "Hey, Freddy."

"Hey, Beverly."

Her Mom leaned over, smiled and said, "Good morning, Freddy." She had always spoken politely to me, but this morning she sounded like she meant it.

I smiled. "Hello, Mrs. Shade."

"Mom and I are going to Huntington to get some clothes for college. So, fill 'er up, Freddy."

I filled the tank and got lost in my thoughts about how good Beverly looked this morning in her white blouse and pink skirt. I thought about Beverly's tribute to Mary Sue at the funeral on Wednesday, one hand on the coffin. Then I had the memory I liked so much—our holding each other on her front porch after the prom, and the most wonderful kiss of my life. All of a sudden a loud gurgle came from the neck of the gas tank and gasoline popped out on to the fender of the car and my shoes.

"That'll be two dollars and ninety-three cents," I said to Beverly.

Her Mom leaned over and handed me three dollars. Beverly had her Mom's height, dark hair, blue eyes.

I handed Beverly seven cents change. In a few weeks she would be on her way to the university. Until now, at least for me, her phone had been disconnected and the house sealed off. Would I see her again this summer? Ever?

"An interesting thing happened," I said louder than I should've. I told Beverly and her Mom about discovering the old Civil War diary. When I mentioned the word Gettysburg Beverly's eyes lit up.

She broke into a big grin. "Mom, Freddy has something really exciting."

Her Mom, still known in my thoughts as "The Guard," whispered something to Beverly, who whispered something back to her. Then they drove away.

A couple of hours later I answered the phone, expecting a call about some spark plugs I'd ordered. On the other end of the call, I heard the last person I'd have thought would call me, Beverly's Dad. After a couple of comments about the weather he said, "I heard about your civil war diary, Freddy, and it sounds interesting."

In the pause I knew I should say something, but what? My brain seemed out of control. "Th... Thanks, Mr. Shade."

"I wonder if you'd bring your diary and join us for dinner on Sunday night?"

It took me a few seconds to catch my breath and say, "Sure, I'd like that." Then I nearly yelled, "Thanks."

Saturday night and most of Sunday I studied the diary. I talked with Grandma and Grandpa Lemley and we pieced together information about the soldier who kept the diary, Quentin Keppler, from family Bibles and a half-done genealogy Grandpa had started years ago. Grandma called Quentin "the diarist." We found an old book with a picture of Quentin and his family. Quentin had two brothers who became college presidents. In the picture, Quentin wore his Union Army uniform, that of a sergeant. He served in the Eighty-third Pennsylvania Volunteers and his unit fought at Gettysburg. The Eighty-third also fought at the second battle of Bull Run, where Quentin had been wounded. He recovered and later fought and died in the in the Wilderness Campaign, at the battle of Laurel Hill, in Maryland, on May eighth, eighteen and sixty four. One history book described the Wilderness Campaign as the bloodiest engagement of the Civil War.

Had Quentin been carrying the diary the day he died? How did the little book get returned to his family? Had I discovered a lock of his hair in the box in Grandma's attic?

On the last pages of the diary, the end of December, eighteen and sixty three, Quentin wrote about re-enlistment and how much he looked forward to it. He had no way of knowing that re-enlistment would start him on the road to Laurel Hill and his death.

When I thought about Quentin's death, my memory returned to the deaths of Junior Don, Lucy and Mary Sue. Just like Quentin felt when he re-enlisted, I'm sure they shared an excitement, joy in being together, when they got in Junior Don's car and started up the highway.

During the Civil War, did every family, every community, North and South, go through the heartache we felt in Kettle when three young people died? Our *Compton's Encyclopedia* reported that over three hundred and fifty-nine thousand Union soldiers died in the war. Over two hundred and fifty thousand Confederate soldiers died. On both sides most of them had been young men. I tried to imagine Junior Don's death repeated six hundred thousand times but I couldn't get my thoughts around the size of it. Neither could I imagine the pain those deaths must have produced.

Mr. Shade met me at the door with a warm handshake and a big smile. Mrs. Shade stood right behind him and handed me an ice-cold glass of RC Cola. "I heard this is your favorite, Freddy," she said.

The Shades' living room had soft chairs and oriental rugs with rich red, orange, and blue tones. Artwork hung on the walls, prints mostly of mountain and seacoast scenes. The dining room opened into the large kitchen and had a fireplace. Above the fireplace hung a large oil painting of young girls in ballet costumes dancing.

Mrs. Shade's dinner, stuffed pork chops, mashed potatoes and spinach, hit the spot. Mrs. Shade insisted that I have seconds. Beverly giggled when my seconds became thirds.

During the first part of dinner we talked of the accident and funerals. Beverly's eyes filled with tears, so did her Mom's. I didn't want to burst into tears the first time I sat at the Shades' dinner table, and stayed calm, eyes dry. Mr. Shade remained quiet.

Later Mrs. Shade said, "Freddy, Beverly told me how you plan to work and save your money, maybe go to college later."

"Yes maam. College is what I plan to do, but I'll have to pay my way, at least most of it."

Mr. Shade jumped in, "Good idea, Freddy. Figure out what direction you want to take. College is important. Prepares you for more advanced kinds of work. I'm sorry I missed it."

Mrs. Shade placed her knife and fork alongside each other across her plate. She looked at me with a serious expression, "I'll be honest with you, Freddy. When I learned you decided not to go to college this year, I was very concerned, even disappointed. You're a bright young man and I know you and Beverly care about each other. But I felt that Beverly should date boys who take their future more seriously. To me that meant boys who were going college. Boys like Holbert Holcomb."

"I know what you're saying, Mrs. Shade. Please know I'm serious about building a future for myself, and for a family."

Mr. Shade beamed a big grin at me and said, "I know you will Freddy. I have confidence in you."

Beverly put her hand on my arm.

I looked at Beverly. "Your daughter means more to me than I can tell you."

"Thank you Freddy," Mrs. Shade said. "You know, the terrible accident we experienced only a week ago has reminded about the unexpected turns life takes, some of them tragic. It also reminds me that Beverly's life belongs to her, not me."

As Mrs. Shade served dessert, Mr. Shade said, "Freddy, I hope you've brought that diary with you. Let's have a look."

We spent the next hour passing the little book around and talking about Quentin's life in the Union Army. They read the July entries about the fighting at Gettysburg with great interest. Mr. Shade recollected a time when he was a boy and visited the Gettysburg battlefield with his Dad. When we came to December in the diary I told them about Quentin's death the next year in the Wilderness Campaign. Afterwards nobody spoke for a little while.

Mr. and Mrs. Shade shooed Beverly and me out of the kitchen so they could do the dishes. We went out on the front porch and sat in the glider. I don't remember reaching over to hold her hand, but we sat there holding hands. It seemed so natural.

Beverly's Mom and Dad came out on the porch and sat with us for a few minutes. I started to pull my hand away from Beverly, but she grasped it tightly. Mr. Shade said, "We're turning in early. I have to leave on a business trip early in the morning. Glad you could join us for dinner, Freddy. Thanks for bringing the diary. It was interesting. And it brought back lots of memories of my trip with my Dad."

I thanked Mrs. Shade for a delicious dinner.

She gave Beverly a hug and we said goodnight. Mrs. Shade went inside, then came back out on the porch and gave me a hug.

We listened to the songs of a chorus of cicadas and crickets. Lightening bugs placed a thousand jewels of light around the yard. One landed on Beverly's arm. She gently pushed her index finger beneath the tiny creature then gently lifted him. We watched the little fellow's luminous alternating pulse, light to dark, dark to light, as he crawled the length of her finger. Then he flew away.

We sat quietly for a few minutes. Then I turned to Beverly, "I've missed you."

"I've missed you too."

Our arms wound around each other and I felt her lips on mine. Our kiss became deeper and more exciting than our kiss the night of the prom. We held each other tightly. Soon Beverly began to take short and rapid breaths—my heart raced and my breath came in gulps. Beverly put her hands under my shirt and slowly unbuttoned it. I unbuttoned her blouse. Moments later I felt her warm smooth body against mine. My next to last thought—how much I loved Beverly. My last thought—fade to black.

Chapter 10

PEYTON

Peyton Gruber had decided he would die that day. But I didn't know it when he drove his old Chrysler into Buckingham's Gulf Station that Saturday morning in October, nineteen and forty-eight. He parked beside the gas pumps, just like he did every Saturday.

And just like I always did, I walked over to the window on the driver's side and asked, "What can I do you for, Peyton?"

Peyton pushed back the bill of his Cincinnati Reds ball cap and gave me a little smile that raised both ends of his mustache ever so slightly. "Fill 'er up with regular, Freddy."

I'll bet we'd had that small exchange thirty times. I thought later that if somebody had asked me at the time I filled Peyton's gas tank, "How's it going, Freddy? What's your day like?" I would have said, "It's a beautiful fall day. The air is crisp and the leaves on the old oak tree behind the station are turning yellow and gold. There's a bright blue sky and a warm sun. It's much like yesterday, probably similar to tomorrow." Nobody asked, so I didn't say all that. But later I thought about it, and how wrong I had been about the day. Well, not exactly wrong. A day can be beautiful but it's not the whole truth about the day.

Peyton got out of his car and stretched, put his hands in his pockets and walked with his shoulders slouched to the oak tree where Phil Buckingham and Hartford Wilson sat in lawn chairs. As I filled Peyton's gas tank, my thoughts centered on my new dark blue corduroy ball cap. It had the words "Gulf Oil" in light gold letters stitched on the front of the cap on top of the dark gold outline of Gulf's round company insignia. The nicest ball cap I'd ever owned. I thought about different ways to position it—down over my eyes, pushed back on my head, small tilt to the right, major tilt to the left, depending on how I felt at the moment. When I walked out to Peyton's car I wore the cap level, about half way down my forehead. In my reflection from the front window I looked right businesslike. Eighteen years old and Buckingham's assistant manager of front end services.

Before Peyton had retired from his job the previous year at the insurance agency, every Tuesday afternoon after work he and his wife Hanna Mae would drive their Chrysler to Buckingham's for a tank of gas—week in, week out, twelve point five gallons.

Phil Buckingham said, "Uncle Peyton and Aunt Hanna Mae are folks of routine."

Each week after I filled the tank I cleaned the windshield under the watchful eye of Hanna Mae. Before I finished wiping the water off the glass, her wiry frame would scoot across the front seat, and her white head would move back and forth while her eyes moved slowly, left right, up down and around every inch of the windshield. Then she would point her right index finger at the spots she felt needed more attention. She never failed to find one or two of them. I took pride in my work and always winced when she began begin her inspection.

Hanna Mae would smile and say in an encouraging way, "Freddy, you're getting better at cleaning, but you've got to sharpen up just a tad."

Sometimes I couldn't see any dirt where she pointed. But I smiled back at her and cleaned the glass beyond the end of her finger. "Thank you, Hanna Mae," I'd say, though inside of me I didn't feel like smiling.

One day I said to Phil, "I think the woman has twenty-ten vision. She sees dirt where no normal person's eyes can see it."

Phil counseled me, "Remember, Aunt Hanna Mae is first of all a teacher. She takes pride in pointing out things the rest of us need to learn."

During Hanna Mae's windshield inspections Peyton would sit behind the wheel with a serious expression on his face and look straight ahead. Sometimes he would take off his Cincinnati Reds cap and run his hand over his bald head, or he might twist the ends of his mustache and rotate the rear view mirror in order to take a peek at it. His mustache didn't quite qualify as a handlebar mustache, for Hanna Mae insisted that he keep it trimmed, but it came close. When Hanna Mae visited her family over in Parkersburg, he'd let the mustache grow, even start waxing it if she stayed away long enough. But the day before she returned he always trimmed it. Phil and I used to tease Peyton about it. He'd smile, and say, "Well, boys, I live with her, not with you."

After Peyton retired from the insurance agency he drove in every couple of days. "Fill 'er up," he'd say, but Peyton came in so often it turned out to be only a few gallons. I figured he didn't have much else to do. At least Peyton didn't care about a spot here or there on the windshield. He would hang around and visit with Phil and me and whoever had brought their car in for a lube job or oil change, or the folks who walked in to sit a spell.

Phil kept three old dark green metal lawn chairs in the front end of the station and encouraged folks to sit and talk, share a cup of coffee. Kettle always had something going on worth talking about—tobacco crops, hogs, weather, and new babies. In good weather we moved the chairs outdoors under the oak tree beside the station. More than once Daddy joked, "If Phil Buckingham got paid by the word instead of by the gallon he'd be a rich man."

While I pumped Gulf regular into the Chrysler's tank, Peyton went to the pop cooler and got himself a Dr. Pepper. Then he joined Phil and Hartford under the oak tree, seated himself in the third lawn chair and sipped his drink.

After I filled Peyton's tank with gas I parked his car in the area on the far side of the station where we put vehicles after we finish working on them. Phil called it the playpen, the place where kids wait on their parents to pick them up.

Hartford, too, had a reputation around town as quite a talker. He and his wife, Iretta, had owned and operated Wilson's Dry Goods for over thirty years. People often visited the store to talk with Hartford, not to buy fabric or factory-made goods. I could see him and Phil laughing about something, though Peyton had a serious expression on his face. Hartford's big belly laugh boomed so loud that I heard it over by the gas pumps. He had gained weight in recent years and I thought his laugh had gotten louder too.

I walked over to collect for the gas, a dollar twenty-two, just as Peyton said, "Wasn't that the Christmas pageant of nineteen and forty-two?" He handed me two dollars.

Hartford replied, "Was it that long ago? Dang, Peyton, I think you're right. It was forty-two."

After I returned with Peyton's change I sat down in the grass and leaned against the oak tree. Hartford, Peyton and I, along with Doc Simonton and William White Wallace, had been in the Christmas Pageant of forty-two. Hartford, Doc, and Peyton, being much older, had the roles of the Three Wise Men. William White and I, twelve years old, had been shepherds. The story of the nineteen and forty-two Christmas Pageant varies a bit, depending on whether you hear it from Peyton, Doc, Hartford, or William White. I'll tell it my way, the only way I can tell it.

During the summer of forty-two, William White took me and Shufflehead Meadows into the living room at his house, placed his right hand on a stack of four Bibles, his left hand on a New Testament and then swore to us that that he would not be in the Christmas pageant that year. We couldn't figure out why in the heat of the summer William White would be so concerned about an event of next winter. I later learned that it had to do with a private dispute between William White and his Mom over William White's middle name, and his recent discovery of the fact that there nobody on either side of his family who had the first or last name of White.

His Mom had told him in a tone of voice William White described as ending any and all debate, "William White, your Dad and I chose the word 'White' with careful thought and delibera- tion. The name has the quality of cleanliness, even stainlessness, one that will help steer you towards a life of sinless purity."

One evening at supper I mentioned what William White's Mom had told him about his name. Momma laughed lightly and said to Daddy and me, "Anybody can see that even at age twelve, a path of sinless purity seems hopeless for William White."

I laughed too and added, "It wouldn't be no fun, neither."

Momma smiled and said, "You mean 'any fun, either' and you don't know until you try it."

William White's threat made sense when I thought about the importance of his Mom to the Kettle Methodist Church Christmas Pageant. Each year the pageant's printed program listed the people in it and the roles they played, as well as the Christmas carols sung and who sang which solos. At the bottom of the last page, year after year, the program had the words, "The Christmas Pageant was produced and directed by Junetta Teague Wallace." William White viewed his threat as a major weapon his battles with his Mom. But his weapon turned out to be a dud. For the second year in a row he appeared in his shepherd's outfit.

Junetta Teague Wallace had become known around Kettle as a leader in The Three Names Movement, a local effort to encourage people to call each other by their three given names, including, of course, herself and William White Wallace. When the Women's Club or a church social needed a speaker, Mrs. Wallace would put other things aside and speak about what she called "the dignity achieved when using three names." The founder of the movement, Ovieta Blankenship Roosevelt, often introduced her.

In her talks, Junetta Teague Wallace mentioned famous people like Louisa Mae Alcott and Ralph Waldo Emerson, along with

Henry David Thoreau, William Jennings Bryan and Franklin Delano Roosevelt. That year she added Claire Booth Luce to her list. One time William White attended a meeting where his Mom spoke, and at the end of her talk added with a big smile, "Mom, don't forget John Wilkes Booth." The next day his Mom made him do extra chores as punishment. She said that in addition to being a smart-aleck, he'd damaged the Three Names Movement.

On the evening of December twentieth, nineteen and forty-two, a large congregation filled the dimly lit sanctuary of the Kettle Methodist Church. The air carried the aroma of the fresh-cut evergreens that had been hung along the molding next to the ceiling on all four sides of the sanctuary. On either end of the altar six red candles burned in each of the two silver candelabra. Two small spotlights had been set up in the last pew. The beam of one lit the Christ Child in the manger along with Joseph and Mary standing beside side him. The other light beamed on the shepherds, William White and me, on the opposite side of the altar from the manger. William White discovered that if he carefully positioned his arm he could get the spotlight to reflect off the crystal on the face of his wristwatch. And then, with a sober look on his face, just a poor shepherd tending his flock, he could throw his own beam back into the darkened congregation. Miss Hattie McClintock flinched as William White's beam of light penetrated the veil of her hat and hit her smack in the left eye.

The spotlight turned from William White and me to the Three Wise Men, dressed in robes and turbans of rich colors. They walked down the aisle led by the first Wise Man, Peyton Gruber in a bright red robe and matching turban. Hartford Wilson, in a blue robe and turban, followed right behind him, then Dr. S.I. Simonton, our town's physician, wearing gold. All three men sang in the Kettle Methodist Church choir, though Hartford had become known as a high-risk singer after his solo performance during a Thanksgiving special music presentation. When he reached and held one of the higher notes in his solo, the upper plate of his dentures fell onto his tongue and caused him to crack the note. Then Hartford garbled the words of the verse as he attempted to continue his solo and, while holding his hymnal in his left hand, put the fingers of his right hand in his mouth and restored his upper plate to its correct location. Hartford later blamed the whole incident on what he called, "The danged poor quality of the sticky stuff that held my dentures in place."

When the Three Wise Men had walked about halfway to the altar, they paused while the organist, Mrs. Hazel Dickensheets, rendered one verse and chorus of the hymn, "We Three Kings." Then they resumed their deliberate walk forward, each step coordinated with the slow movement of the hymn. In unison the Three Wise Men sang the chorus of the hymn.

Peyton's solo, describing his gift of gold for the Christ Child, would be sung as the Wise Men approached the manger. After the chorus ended, Peyton took a deep breath and then, a second before he began to sing the first word of his solo, his red turban slipped and dropped over his eyes. Peyton's head became mouth, moustache, nose and turban. Mouth and moustache stopped moving and Peyton didn't sing. He stood motionless, as if transformed into a zombie by an unknown power. Mrs. R.R. Whitcomb later commented, "Peyton's suddenly frozen position made me think of the poor people of Pompeii, trapped forever in all those strange positions when Mount Vesuvius erupted." She paused and gave an ever so slight smile, then added, "including some who were in bed."

Peyton's quick stop caused Hartford to plow into Peyton's back, and Doc Simonton in turn to crash into Hartford's back, knocking Hartford's gift of frankincense for the Christ Child out of his hands. It clattered across the sanctuary floor underneath the first pew. Hearing the noise, and not hearing Peyton's voice, Mrs. Hazel Dickensheets stopped playing the organ. The sight of her standing and craning her neck towards the manger caused people seated in the sanctuary to stand up and crane their necks to get a good look at whatever had happened. Only the squeaks and shuffles of standing and neck craning sounded across the sanctuary.

Peyton stood motionless, rooted to the spot where he had ceased all forward movement, his red turban resting on the bridge of his nose. Then he extended his arms straight in front of himself, still holding his gift of gold for the Christ Child in his left hand. He rotated his body towards the choir, like a slow-moving fixture in an amusement park. Then he rotated in the opposite direction towards the congregation and during his turn began a low but rising moan, "Ohhhhhhhhhhh," that continued unbroken sound for at least ten seconds.

Later Peyton said that suddenly seeing nothing but the red of his turban, he believed he'd had a heart attack. Then, when he turned towards the congregation, the beams of the spotlights caused a brightening of the field of red before him. "I expected to be dead within seconds." We laughed when he told us, but at that moment, in the middle of the Christmas pageant, everybody stared at Peyton and listened to his low and rising moan.

Doc Simonton handed his gift of myrrh to Hartford and walked forward to Peyton. Doc pushed Peyton's turban up on his forehead and gave him a couple of gentle pats on his back.

Peyton's ceased his moan, opened his eyes wide and blinked. He looked first at Doc Simonton, then across the congregation and exclaimed big and loud in his deep baritone voice, "I'm alive—thank God, I'm alive!"

Hartford commented that while this may have been an important discovery for Peyton, to those of us in the pageant and, he imagined, most folks in the sanctuary, it seemed that Peyton had interrupted the Kettle Methodist Church Christmas Pageant to make an announcement about something that everybody knew anyway.

In the silence of the moment that followed Peyton's announcement, William White yelled, "Praise the Lord."

Jimmy Lunceford and Harley Bill Cremeans, at the time about six years old and seated in the front pew of the church, broke up laughing. Harley, a tow-headed kid, had a high-pitched squeaky laugh that infected people and made them want to laugh along with him. In a few seconds laughter passed through the congregation like a wave, rolling from the front to the rear pews of the sanctuary.

After folks recovered from their laughter, the Three Wise Men reassembled themselves and Mrs. Dickensheets struck up "We Three Kings" again. Peyton, followed by Hartford and Doc, sang their solo verses, then one final chorus in unison.

A car pulled up to the gas pumps and I walked over to wait on the folks. When I returned to the little group, Hartford had moved his chair a foot to the right to position himself in sunlight. I sat down in the grass.

Hartford said, "Peyton, you were in rare form the night of the pageant."

Peyton removed his Cincinnati Reds cap with his left hand, and rubbed his right hand across his bald head. He smiled. "Well, Hanna Mae reminds me of my brief career as an actor every once in a while."

Then Peyton's face became very somber. "Hart, do you think I could have been an actor?"

Hartford looked up into the branches of the old oak tree. So did I. Towards the ends of many branches the leaves had turned a bright golden orange. Sunlight fell through the tree's limbs, lingering on the gold leaves and transforming the green patches into dark blue. Then Hartford looked at Peyton and in a serious voice said, "Peyton, I think you could have been anything you wanted to." He paused then smiled and added, "That is, if Hanna Mae would approve it."

Hartford cut loose with his big belly laugh. Phil and I laughed too. Peyton didn't, though he smiled and nodded. Then he smoothed the ends of his moustache.

"What's Hanna Mae up to these days, Peyton?" Hartford asked.

"Oh, the usual. Running the house and all. Now that I'm retired, each day she makes sure I get my chores done." Peyton paused and a smile washed over his face. "But we find time to enjoy things together. Little things. We work in the garden. And on rainy days we read or listen to the radio. Yesterday afternoon Hanna Mae baked cookies and we had tea on the side porch. As we sat there I wished Bubby had lived longer and married. Maybe a grandchild would have been there to have cookies with us." Bubby, Peyton and Hanna Mae's son, Peyton Gruber, Jr., died in an auto accident not long after he finished medical school.

"Most of the time, though, it's chores." His smile disappeared. "I swear, sometimes I think retirement is like a new job. Only there's often more demands than at what I used to call work."

Hartford chuckled and said, "Well, Peyton, maybe you could find a quiet little place where you could escape all that." Then he really hoo-hawed and slapped his knee.

I laughed too. Phil had told me about what happened the summer Peyton figured out how to escape the never-ending list of chores that Hanna Mae handed him each Saturday morning. Any chores that didn't get done that day would float forward into the evenings after work during the following week. And it seemed like Peyton could never get all his chores done, even though Hanna Mae added new chores at a slow rate. He once told Phil, "I feel like I'm bailing chores out of a leaky boat that takes them on faster than I can bail."

Hanna Mae told her friends, "Those chores just hang out there like a wet wash on a rainy day." She went on to say that Peyton always seemed to be working on them, though sometimes she couldn't find him.

In the heat of the summer Peyton had found an escape. He would crawl through an opening in the house's foundation and relax in the cool darkness under the house. He'd lie on that sweet black earth and snooze away an hour or two.

One hot and humid Saturday in July—the temperature must have been ninety-five degrees—Peyton went outside to complete his list of yard chores while Hanna Mae did her weekly house cleaning. Along about three-thirty Hanna Mae began to polish the maple table that had belonged to her Mother. She dropped her can of furniture polish when she heard the screams of a man's voice coming from beneath the floor in the back section of the house. She ran through the house, out the kitchen door and into the back yard.

Hanna Mae exclaimed to her friends, "I thought the noises

were coming from under the rear section of the house. Just as I started to poke my head through the opening in the back section of the house's foundation, Peyton's Cincinnati Reds cap appeared and he came right behind it, scrambling out of there."

Peyton flopped to the ground and laid on his back, panting and wheezing.

Hanna Mae looked down at Peyton, her arms akimbo and her mouth gaping. After she regained sufficient control to speak, Hanna Mae asked, "Peyton, just what the devil is going on?"

Peyton just laid there looking up at her. Then he raised himself to a sitting position and said, "I guess I'll have to tell you. Truth is, I felt tired and went under the house to take a little snooze."

Hanna Mae learned that after Peyton stretched out on his favorite sleeping spot, an area where he had scooped out indentations in the earth to form body contours that matched his shape, he found an unexpected guest in his makeshift bedroom.

Peyton's voice took on a small quiver as he described to Hanna Mae what happened. "A few minutes ago, in the darkness under the house I stretched out in my spot and my right hand brushed something unusual. I grasped it, something round, long, wet and slick. Then I grabbed the other end of whatever it was with my left hand. 'Oh my God!'"

Phil said he figured that at an intersection in Peyton's brain the sensations from his right hand met the sensations from his left hand and registered the presence of a recently shed snakeskin, one of significant size. That's when Peyton began to scream and jump and bump his way out of there.

Phil ended the story by saying, "From that Saturday forward there was a remarkable increase in Uncle Peyton's productivity."

After the snakeskin incident a slight change seemed to take place in Peyton. He had always been fun to be around, though never what anyone might call the life of the party. But after the incident Peyton didn't seem to smile as much as he used to. I asked Phil, "What's happened to Peyton? He seems a little under the weather these days."

Phil replied in a thoughtful voice, "Well, Uncle Peyton got

himself into a pickle with Aunt Hanna Mae because of his little hideaway under the house. She's on him these days. Now when she gives him a list of chores to do, beside each chore she puts an estimate of the time she figures it should take him to complete each one."

I guess I must have looked dumbstruck. Phil laughed and put his hand on my shoulder, "Maybe I should hire Aunt Hanna Mae and have her run this place. She'd get some real work out of you, Freddy."

I laughed at Phil's joke, but the thought of Hanna Mae Gruber bossing me around didn't seem all that funny. I looked across the room we called "the front end" and thought of all the things she could find to be cleaned up. Just for openers the display stack of oilcans hadn't been lined up properly and the windows could use a good washing. Today's *Huntington Herald Dispatch* and *Charleston Gazette* lay on the floor near the stove. The guys who came in and read the newspapers left their disposable coffee cups on the floor beside the stove. And the floor needed to be swept. Hanna Mae would have a field day with this place. And me.

Peyton's life in retirement seemed to be a mixed blessing for him. He would come to Buckingham's a lot, then I'd see him over at Bertha's Place, or over at the Post Office. At the bank. Just hanging around. You might say moping around, like an old beagle looking for somebody to pet him, or a place to lie down.

During a slow period one morning in August, Phil and I had just poured ourselves some coffee when Peyton came in and said, more to Phil than to me, "I can't believe it. I just stopped by the insurance office. The place where I spent thirty years of my life. Nobody had the time of day for me. What's the world coming to?"

Phil said, "Sit down, Uncle Peyton. Have a cup of coffee."

Peyton sat down and as he took his first sip of coffee Phil asked, "So, other than a stop over at the agency where those folks were so thoughtless as to do their work, what's been happening this morning?"

Phil had no sooner got the word "morning" out of his mouth when four cars suddenly drove in. Two of them stopped at the gas pumps. The driver of one car blew his horn and yelled, "Please hurry, I have to go to Beckley," like he had to complete some kind of mission. A fellow driving a Buick told Phil he wanted a lube job and oil change right quick, he had to get to Huntington by noon. Miss Hattie McClintock parked her Ford squarely before the front door where it blocked everybody's movement and said, "Phil Buckingham, there is a strange noise coming from under the hood of my car. I want you to please have somebody fix it."

In the hustle and bustle of taking care of all the customers, Phil and I forgot about Peyton. When things finally settled down again Peyton had gone, though before he left he'd washed his coffee cup and put it back in the cupboard.

The following week Peyton came into Buckingham's looking concerned and serious. "Where's Phil?"

"Phil's out on a run to Myrza Jane Bixby's house, Peyton. Her Chevy's battery is dead, needs a jump-start." I paused, then added, "Peyton, I hope you don't mind my asking, but you look like you just lost your last friend. Anything wrong?"

Peyton poured himself a cup of coffee then walked over to a chair and dropped into it with a sigh. "Freddy, I just came from Doc Simonton's office. Recently I've had a shortness of breath when I do chores or walk for a spell. Doc looked me over and told me I've got a heart problem. 'Nothing to get all upset about,' he said. Easy for him to say. It's my heart, not his."

Then, the day before Labor Day our local ambulance, a black Cadillac hearse from the Smith Sisters Funeral Home with its flashing red lights turned on and a cot instead of a casket in the back, sounded its siren big and loud as it left Kettle. The ambulance didn't slow down for our town's only stoplight. About an hour later Phil called to tell me he had driven his Aunt Hanna Mae to the hospital in Huntington. Peyton had suffered a heart attack. The Christmas pageant came to mind, and how we laughed when Peyton looked into the red of his turban and thought he'd been hit with a heart attack. At the hospital Doc Simonton counseled Peyton that his heart attack could've been a lot worse; he'd be back to normal in a month or two.

After he got out of the hospital, Peyton often came into Buckingham's and reflected on Doc's counsel. One day he said to Phil and me, "You know, normal is a funny word. Normal after a heart attack just isn't the same as normal before a heart attack. And now they got me on a strict diet. No more grits and butter. No more breakfast with sausage and gravy." After a long pause he said, "No more ice cream."

Ice cream may be something most folks can enjoy or not enjoy; take it or leave it. But for Peyton ice cream had special qualities. One warm summer afternoon he and I sat under the oak tree at Buckingham's while he slowly ate a cone of chocolate coconut ice cream. Peyton licked the ice cream and described the many taste sensations of chocolate coconut. "Freddy, it makes a difference if you eat chocolate coconut fast or slow. Fast will dull the taste of it. No sir, slow is the way to do it, and with two rolls of the tongue, one on the cream and one when you bring the cream inside of your mouth. That's the best method in order to appreciate the full flavor of chocolate coconut ice cream. The nuttiness of the coconut alters the impact of the chocolate on your taste buds.

"You may not realize it," Peyton went on, "but the differences between chocolate and chocolate coconut are greater than you might at first think." Once Peyton started to compare different flavors of ice cream it typically set off a lengthy lecture about the large and small shadings that separated the flavors of ice cream. I excused myself to go finish a chore Phil had asked me to do.

Now, on that beautiful day, Peyton, Phil, and Hartford had been sitting and talking under the oak tree for well over an hour. A few cars had come in for gas and I had taken care of them. I did some inside work, swept the floor under the lube rack and straightened up the tools on the workbench beside the rack. Every now and then I walked over to the oak tree for a little more of the conversation.

The talk turned to gardening and Peyton complained, "This season the birds seemed to get more enjoyment out of my sunflowers than Hanna Mae and I did."

Hartford smiled and replied, "I had the same problem. I rigged up a scarecrow with bottle caps attached to long pieces of twine I hung from the scarecrow's arms. The bottle caps swang in the breeze and spooked the birds out of the garden." Phil and Peyton nodded thoughtfully.

"I should've thought of that," Peyton commented. "Anyway, seemed like I scared the birds away myself. We had so much rain, every time the sun came out I had to hoe the weeds out of the sunflowers. Out of the bean patch too."

When Peyton said the word "hoe," I knew what would come, I just didn't know how long it would take. Peyton must've had the same thought. The moment he said the word his face resembled a scared rabbit, or at least a rabbit who thought he might be scared but had to wait to find out what would happen.

Hartford extended his legs in front of his chair, put his hands behind his neck, and arched his back. He exhaled the word "Well," stretching it out as he stretched himself, then continued, "a hoe is a marvelous little tool. It can do many things. Though, of course, it has its limits. Sometimes a rake works better." He turned to me and winked.

Peyton had a slight smile on his lips but it didn't extend as far as his eyes. Along with Phil, I grinned, though with some sadness in my heart as I remembered what happened the night of the hoe and the rake.

Hartford spoke in a speculative manner and said, "Yes sir, I suppose a fellow could even use a rake to fight a raging house fire," then he looked at Peyton and whooped a good belly laugh.

Peyton snorted a small laugh, "Hart, we've been through that a hundred times."

One evening in November, nineteen and forty-six. Momma, Daddy, and I had been invited to dinner at the Gerlachs'. On the other side of the hollow from Peyton and Hanna Mae's place, below the Gerlachs', Mr. Gerlach had built a large log cabin as a summer getaway. He hadn't used it much. Most folks couldn't figure out why he had built it, only a hundred yards or so down the hill below his home. In nineteen and forty-four Mr. Gerlach sold the log cabin and a couple of acres to Phil Buckingham's newly married sister, Audrey, and her husband, Prescott Ben Blevins, their first home.

We had just set down to Mrs. Gerlach's roast beef dinner when the phone rang. After Mr. Gerlach said, "Hello" he listened for a short time, then turned to all of us at the table and announced, "It's Albert Higginbotham." Albert and his brood of little Higginbothams lived further up the hill. Mr. Gerlach listened for a few seconds then replied with concern, "We'll look into it Albert, thanks," and hung up. "Albert said there's a bright orange glow that appears to come from behind Audrey and Prescott Ben's place."

I jumped up from the table and ran to the front window and looked down the hill. "Holy cow!"

Daddy and Mr. Gerlach rushed to the window. Mr. Gerlach yelled, "There's orange light all right. Could be a fire!"

Daddy told Momma to call the Kettle Fire Department, and then Daddy, Mr. Gerlach, and I headed out the door. We ran down the hill to Audrey and Prescott Ben's place. Mr. Gerlach tripped and fell over a branch in the yard but Daddy and I kept on going.

The log cabin had no lights on and no cars in the driveway. Flames had crawled up the back wall of the house. Daddy spotted an outdoor water faucet near the far corner of the rear of the house. We searched for a garden hose but couldn't find one.

Daddy told me go back to the Gerlachs' and get a garden hose. As I ran up the hill Daddy yelled into the darkness and across the ravine towards Peyton and Hanna Mae's home. We had seen Peyton working in his garage when we drove to the Gerlach's. Daddy made his voice real deep and stretched out his words. "Pey-ton, Pey-ton," then again, "Pey-ton, Pey-ton." I wondered if Peyton would hear him. He might have gone inside the house; could be listening to the radio.

Peyton's voice returned Daddy's call, crossing the darkness of the hollow, "Yes, Gas-ton, Wha-at? Wha-at, Gas-ton? Wha-at is it?"

"Pey-ton, bring a hose, bring a hose."

No reply.

"Pey-ton, bring a hose, bring a hose."

"O-K. I'm com-ing."

I continued up the hill and ran into Mr. Gerlach. He said his hose had sprung bad leak at the end of the summer and he hadn't replaced it.

I ran back to the log cabin and reported to Daddy what Mr. Gerlach said. The flames grew larger. I wanted to do something, but had no way to fight the flames. I felt helpless.

But Peyton's hose would change things. Daddy stood near the outdoor faucet ready to go into action. I stood near Daddy and prayed with all my might for Peyton to bring that hose. "Come on, Peyton, come on, come on."

In the distance the fire siren on top the Kettle Police Station sounded long wails. Momma had made her call. But the firemen had to drive from their homes to the fire station, and then drive the fire truck the two miles from town to Audrey and Prescott Ben's place. That could take another ten minutes, and the flames kept growing larger and hotter.

After what must have been no more than two minutes but seemed like an hour, footsteps clopped across the small footbridge in the darkness of the ravine between Peyton's home and the Blevins's log cabin. I closed my eyes and prayed it for it to be Peyton with his hose. Sure enough, in the light of the flames Peyton appeared out of the darkness and ran up the hill towards Daddy with something long in his hands. Daddy stood at the faucet ready to connect the hose, like a runner at the start of a footrace waiting for the starter's gun.

Out of breath, Peyton gulped for air, cheeks red. He extended the object in his hands towards Daddy. "Gaston," he said, "I couldn't find a hoe, but here's a rake."

Daddy and I stared at the rake now in Daddy's hands. Daddy tossed the rake aside, yelled, "Come on," and the three of us ran to the cabin's front door. Daddy put his shoulder to it, but the heavy oak door wouldn't budge. He moved to the window beside the front door and raised his foot to stomp through the screen and break the window. A boom sounded inside the log cabin and flames shot through the room behind the front door. The inside of the house first glowed blue, then bright orange as furnishings burst into flame. "Propane," Daddy yelled. Flames licked at nearly every window, like big angry dogs wanting to break out of their pen. We backed off the porch and watched the house glow an ever brighter red-orange. Then the flames broke through a window, then another and another.

Peyton looked at his shoes and spoke sadly, "Sorry, Gaston. Freddy."

Daddy put his hand on Peyton's shoulder. "Well, Peyton, hose, rake, or hoe, it wouldn't have mattered one stitch. In fact we might have got ourselves in a peck of trouble. We could have been in there when that propane blew."

The distant siren of the Kettle Volunteer Fire Department's bright red truck became louder. The engine in the old truck, a nineteen and twenty-eight Ford, strained in second gear as it climbed the hill to Audrey and Prescott Ben's place. Behind the truck came a long column of cars with sirens and flashing red lights, volunteer firemen. Phil Buckingham once warned me, "Never step into the street when the fire siren is blowing. Those boys come at top speed, fixed on fighting flames."

The fire truck and cars roared into Audrey and Prescott Ben's driveway and spread across the front yard. The fellows hooked up a three-inch hose to the tank on the truck and began to pump water into the flames. Daddy walked away and said, "We might as well fight a brush fire with a water pistol."

The fire truck's water supply didn't last long. Ten years ago the town of Kettle had bought the truck, fully outfitted, at an auction. The old Ford had once been part of the fire department on Henry Ford's estate in Dearborn, Michigan. Folks in Kettle took pride in their fire truck, but it had been outfitted to fight fires where firemen had access to water hydrants, as they did in Kettle. Not country fires like this.

About the time the roof caved in, sending flames and a shower of sparks into the surrounding trees, Audrey Blevins arrived. She stood in the front yard, crying. Peyton walked over and put his arms around her.

Hartford stretched again and said, "Well, boys, I been sittin' under this ol' tree and jawin' with you far too long. It's noontime and my stomach's startin' to rumble. Iretta gave me some chores to do. I better get home and do 'em."

Phil snapped his fingers and said he forgot to put a bushing in a truck. He went into the shop.

When Hartford stood up Peyton looked at him with a sad expression on his face, and in a voice to match said, "Hart we've been friends a long time. Done a lot of things together."

"Yep, Peyton, we have."

Then Peyton stood and gave his friend a bear hug and patted him on the back. Hartford's eyes got big and a look of surprise passed over his face. He returned Peyton's hug, patted him on the back and grinned. "See you ol' buddy." Peyton had tears in his eyes.

A car pulled up to the gas pumps and I left the shade of the oak tree to wait on the driver. When I finished Peyton and Hartford had gone.

That afternoon, shortly after the clock at the bank chimed three, the phone rang. Hanna Mae asked, "Freddy, is Phil there?" Phil spoke with her. Right before hanging up, he said, "Freddy will be there shortly."

Then he said, "Freddy, I'd like to finish the bushings job on that truck. Would you take the pickup and drive to Aunt Hanna Mae and Uncle Peyton's place? She hasn't seen Uncle Peyton for a couple of hours. With his heart problems and all, she's worried about him. It's a nice afternoon. He's probably taking a walk in the woods. Take a look around. If you can't find him, stay with her until he comes back. I'll take care of things here."

I said, "Hey, it beats pumping gas." Phil laughed.

The station's old Dodge truck stayed in second gear all the way up the hill to Peyton and Hanna Mae's place. Then I nudged her into neutral and coasted down their driveway, past the brick outdoor grill Peyton built. The driveway looped around the garage, a separate building from the house. I parked between the garage and the back of the house.

I started to knock on the back door but before my knuckles touched the wood Hanna Mae had the door open.

"Freddy, I'm worried about Peyton."

"Phil told me, Hanna Mae."

"He seemed to be in such an odd mood this morning. He asked, no, he insisted, that I fix grits, sausage, gravy, and eggs for breakfast. With his heart condition, I didn't want to do it. But he seemed fixed on it, so I did. I told him not to ask for this every day. He said I needn't worry about it. A couple of hours ago, he came back from town eating a cone of coconut chocolate ice cream. Then he told me he had some outside things to do, gave me a hug and went out the door. He never gives me a hug before he goes outside."

"He's probably just taking a walk. I'll take a look around."

I walked up the driveway to the path across the front of the garden. Maybe I'd find some scuffed dirt or some other sign that Peyton had passed this way. I meandered along the Gruber side of the ravine, the one Peyton crossed the night the log cabin burned. Then I turned and walked along the edge of the woods below the house.

"Peyton? Peyton?" I called towards the woods, loud enough for him to hear me, but not so loud as to disturb Hanna Mae. I continued around the lower edge of the front yard, then past the woods towards the small yard that trails over the hillside.

I had a cold RC Cola in the pickup truck, and walked back to get it. I opened the bottle and took a long pull on the RC. The carbonation made my eyes water.

The truck sat next to the single-car garage. Peyton might be in there—maybe his heart had acted up and he'd sat down. Even fallen asleep. It's possible he could've passed out.

The double doors on the front of the garage had been left partly open. I walked in and looked around. The Chrysler took up most of the space. A heavy workbench extended across the far end of the garage, beyond the front of the car. Some shelves extended along each side of the garage and boxes had been stored in the overhead rafters.

I walked past the left side of the Chrysler towards the workbench, glanced inside the empty car. Then as I approached the workbench, two scuffed old brogans dangled in front of me. My knees buckled and I fell to the dirt floor. My chest constricted and my vision blurred.

Peyton hung with his feet dangling above the hood of the Chrysler. His head lay against his left shoulder. Just flopped over. His face had turned reddish blue. Until now, outside of a church or the Smith Sisters' Funeral Home, I had never seen a dead man.

I ran into the yard and threw up. My stomach continued to heave long after it had emptied. I sat down with my back against the wall of the garage. My breathing finally came back to something close to normal, but I couldn't stop my hands from trembling. Every time I shut my eyes I saw Peyton's dangling shoes and then his reddish blue face.

I walked back into the garage, steadying myself by placing my hand on the car. I looked up at Peyton and had thoughts of the morning, of Peyton, Hartford, and Phil, stories under the oak tree. Then I wept. In my crying, my stomach contracted over and over. I knelt and breathed in gasps. After a short time the gasps stopped, but when I looked up at Peyton they started again.

After I got myself under control I wondered what I should do. It seemed wrong to leave Peyton hanging there, and at the same time it seemed wrong to move him. I had to do something. Hanna Mae shouldn't have to see this.

I leaned my head forward against the wall of the garage and closed my eyes. "God, help me get through this. Give me strength to do what I have to do." I remained in that position for a full minute after my little prayer.

I climbed up on the workbench and spread my feet and braced myself. I pulled Peyton towards me then lifted him until I supported his weight with my left arm. In right hand I had my

Barlow pocketknife, the one Daddy gave me when I finished tenth grade. I reached up and cut the rope from the rafter, gently lowered Peyton until his brogans touched the workbench, guided his body as it slowly sank to the surface of the bench. I laid Peyton on his back then jumped down and poked around the shelves in the garage. I found an old blanket and spread it over him. My knees felt like old screen doors that'd come unhooked and moved back and forth in a strong wind.

I sat down, and leaned against the left front tire of the Chrysler, took deep breaths, and cried again. Afterwards I stared at the rounded blanket on the workbench and thought about Peyton. Kidding him about his mustache, chores for Hanna Mae. His friendship with Hartford. Ice cream. Heart problems, then retirement.

My thoughts turned to Junior Don, Mary Sue, and Lucy—they didn't have a choice in their deaths. Why had Peyton done this? How would I tell Hanna Mae?

I dragged my heels as I walked to the house. The moment I stepped on the back porch Hanna Mae opened the kitchen door.

She looked at me then brought her hands up in front of her face and began to weep. Her body shook.

I put my arms around her. "I'm sorry, Hanna Mae."

She rested her head on my shoulder. Her sobs shook her body and mine. In between breaths she kept repeating, "I knew it. I knew it."

Then Hanna Mae took a step back, "Where is he, where is Peyton?"

"He's in the garage. I put a blanket over him."

"Was it a heart attack?"

In a shaky voice I said, "No, Hanna Mae, he did it himself."

Her knees gave way and she fell into a kneeling position. I gently lifted her up and led her to a chair. I placed a glass of water in front of her. "I'll call Doc Simonton."

After my call Hanna Mae said, "Freddy, I'd like to be alone for a few minutes."

I sat in the yard, leaned my back against the side of the garage. Hanna Mae once told Phil that she and Peyton had fallen in love as children, the first time they saw each other. There'd never been anyone else for either of them. I thought of Beverly, how we'd met in fifth grade. How much we loved each other. If we had a life together would it end this way?

I took off my Gulf Oil cap, shut my eyes, and wished for Beverly to be sitting beside me, holding my hand. I turned my face skywards. The warmth of the late afternoon sun soothed me—the same sun that had lit the morning's blue sky and the gold leaves of the old oak tree beside Buckingham's. "What can I do you for, Peyton?"

A day can be beautiful, but it's not the whole truth about the day.

Chapter 11

DOMINOES

Most days I felt like a bunch of rhubarb that had been cut and left out in the sun. September of nineteen and forty-nine had to be the hottest in many years, and to top it off Boomer had us doing team work-outs at Art's Place until two in the morning—drinking beer, playing dominoes and doing ciphering drills. He'd yell at me, "Hey, Freddy, quick, what's 5 plus 3 plus 6? Quick, 6 plus 2 plus 4 plus 5?"

I liked the game and enjoyed drinking beer with the guys, but sometimes Boomer went too far. First, we had to drink three beers, part of the drill. Then, Boomer would hit us with word problems. "Your opponent opens with a double six. You're holding three bones"—that's what we called dominoes—"three bones with sixes, 6 and 2, 6 and 1, 6 and 3. Quick, what's the best play? Come on, quick!" He called it getting in shape. At that hour of the night, I called it brain busting.

Beverly had returned to Morgantown in early September, her sophomore year at the University. Her absence wilted me more than the heat. We'd dated a lot through the summer, and then in August her parents left for a weekend to visit friends in Louisville.

That Saturday evening we went to a movie, and came back to her house. We sat in the front porch glider until midnight, holding each other close. The joy of her touch, her kisses, stirred me. Her too. I unbuttoned her blouse and she unbuttoned my shirt, then we went indoors, holding each other tightly and walking sidewise like our lips and front sides had been welded together. For the first time we had an entire night to lie next to each other. Touching, talking. I didn't know anything could be so wonderful. Her warmth and her scent—I wanted them, and her, in my life. Always. But she had gone to Morgantown.

One night the combination of Boomer's long drills and Beverly's absence got to me. Shortly after midnight I had had enough. "Boomer, I got to get up at six in the morning, open Buckingham's Gulf Station and pump gas all day. These midnight practices are killing me." Boomer gave us a couple of nights off.

Boomer, Boomer Cremeans, had eased in to Art's Place about a year earlier, hanging out in the afternoons, buying a few rounds now and then, and sitting in on the dominoes games. I didn't know him, but Art gave Boomer an OK. He said, "Boomer's family had a farm up on Tinker's Creek, a few miles north of town. His Daddy came here to start a vineyard, but he could only get Concord grapes to grow. Used them mostly for jelly and juice, though he produced a fair-to-middlin' sweet wine."

Boomer told me he'd graduated from Kettle High the year I had been born, nineteen and thirty. "I been living at a boarding house in Charleston for nigh on to ten years, working at the bottling plant in Kanawha City." He beamed when he said, "I worked my way up to supervisor. Of the evenings I picked up a little money playing dominoes. Not a bad life. But I got laid off from my job when my company hit hard times. You may've heard about it. They lost that big Mason Jars contract and had to go out of business." Over at Bertha's Place somebody said that Boomer's company tried to expand, diversify they called it, to make lids as well as jars, and couldn't pull it off. Art recognized Boomer's talent and signed him on as manager of what Art called the pool department, a poolroom downstairs below the bar. Art weighed about

280, a man of limited movement. He needed somebody to watch over things downstairs.

"Real proud to be back in management," Boomer said. He had some glossy business cards printed up: "Boomer Cremeans, Manager, Pool Department, Art's Place, Rt. 42 West, Kettle, West Virginia. Phone 3210." The pool department had just two pool tables, but somebody needed to collect the nickel per game, take orders for beer, and most of all, to make sure that nobody stole the balls or ripped the felt on the tables. Art had a conniption fit when one kid showed off with a fancy shot and ran the tip of his cue stick through the felt.

Art's appointment of Boomer didn't surprise me. Boomer looked like a manager –always wearing a white shirt and necktie, his shoes polished, even when just hanging around. Boomer seemed thoughtful about things going on around him, as if he wanted to reflect on the full meaning of what somebody had said or done. He wore horn-rimmed glasses and slicked his hair straight back. Boomer always carried a small bottle of Wildroot Cream Oil for his hair. It made a bulge in his left front pocket. But Boomer's pride and joy had to be his pencil mustache. It started as a small block just under that little bridge that separated his nostrils, and split into two neatly trimmed lines of black hair above each side of his upper lip, with each line getting thinner then ending in a point.

And he had smooth moves. One of the guys said, "Boomer don't walk so much as he glides. It's like he wears magic shoes." I tried to imitate his walk, in fact each of us tried to do it, but no one could get it right. With his classy style, Boomer could have been over at the funeral home, a mortician escorting a widow during a service, or a teller taking your deposit at the bank, rather than a fellow racking up a new game of pool.

When Boomer talked to you he looked you right in the eye and spoke in a soft but firm voice. I should add that when he did this you couldn't be sure which of his eyes looked at you. His eyes didn't cross, but they seemed off center. Almost cross-eyed.

People seemed to take to Boomer. Art called him a natural leader. "Why do you think they made him a supervisor up at the bottling plant?" he asked.

Pearl Chapman followed Boomer around like a little puppy. Pearl dropped out of Kettle High the year Boomer graduated. Like Boomer, Pearl had been raised on a farm up on Tinker's Creek. Pearl had a skinny body and white hair, though he often said, "I ain't no albino."

One afternoon earlier that summer, Boomer, wearing a white shirt and tie, no jacket, drove his '46 Hudson into Buckingham's. He had the Hudson all shined up. Pearl sat alongside him in the front seat wearing a fresh white painter's cap and a clean white t-shirt, a pack of Camels rolled into the right sleeve. I walked to the driver's window and we exchanged some chit-chat, then Boomer said in a matter of fact way, "Freddy, I have been retained by Pearl to help him get his driver's license."

Retained?

He continued, "We're on our way to the courthouse in Huntington to get Pearl a learner's permit, the first step"—he beamed at Pearl, then me—"towards becoming a licensed driver." When Boomer paid for his gas, he told me in a firm, almost smug, voice, like he expected me to be checking on Pearl, "Pearl has all his papers in order to make the application." Pearl smiled at me and held up a cardboard folder. I could see documents sticking out of it. When I got my learner's permit I just went to the courthouse, took a blank application from the stack of forms on the counter in the County Clerk's office, and filled it out.

About the time Art hired Boomer as manager of the pool room, Boomer began to talk about organizing a domino league here in Kettle, similar to the leagues in the Huntington and Charleston taverns. One evening at Art's Place, Boomer asked if he could speak to me, private and confidential. I nodded OK, wondering if I'd done something wrong. We walked over to the corner furthest from the bar. Then in a quiet and respectful way Boomer said he'd been observing me. He wanted me to consider taking an important step in my life. "Freddy, with your experience in making change for customers at Buckingham's, all the adding and subtracting, you'd be a natural for the Art's Place Dominoes Team."

Just to myself I said, "I'm over eighteen. I can go to Art's Place and order a beer. Maybe I could make the grade and be on the dominoes team." Then I reflected for a second, and added, "That is, if we had a team."

Boomer set up some card tables in the rear of Art's Place, beyond the bar and customer area. Most evenings Boomer would pull some of the guys together and we'd play a few games. Up until then I had only played dominoes at home with William White. He always laughed big and loud when he scored—got the end dominoes to total the number five or a multiple of five. At Art's Place we played a different kind of game, faster-paced, and the players didn't laugh when they scored. The first player to score one hundred points won the game. The loser paid the difference between the scores of the winner and the loser, a penny a point. With a run of bad luck you could rack up some financial losses over the course of an evening. Of course you could win, too, which I did from time to time. One Wednesday night I cleared big money, $4.60.

With Beverly up at the university, other than going to church and the movies, I didn't have a lot to do in the evenings. The Jack Benny and Fred Allen radio shows occupied me on Tuesday evenings. Other weekday nights I listened to "This is Your FBI" and "Mr. District Attorney." It took a year or more for higher grade movies like *Easter Parade* and *Road to Rio* to get to Kettle. Most of the time we had movies that starred actors like Randolph Scott and Sonny Tufts. William White liked Ginger Rogers movies.

One evening after a few games of dominoes, Boomer looked around the tables, gave us a confident smile and in a loud voice said, "I believe you boys may be ready for competitive play. An Art's Place Dominoes Team might do OK in league play." He walked over to the bar, "Set these boys up with a round of beers, Art."

Benny Porter got a serious look on his chubby face and said, "Boomer is taking our money pretty regularly. If he thinks we're good, could be that we are."

Pearl replied, "Right, Benny. Anyway, they roll up the streets after dark. We might as well give it a shot."

The team tryouts took place at Art's Place on a Sunday afternoon. Boomer put a hand-lettered sign in the front window. "Dominoes Team tryouts today, 2PM. All are welcome. Must be able to cipher."

In the tryouts, each guy played a game of one-on-one dominoes with Boomer. To keep things even, Boomer set it up so that at the start of a game each of his opponents had the same seven dominoes in front of him, and he started the each game by placing a double six in the center of the table. The games varied with the plays we made and the luck of the draw from the bones pile. Pearl flashed a grin and winked at me when he played his seventh domino, ending the round, and left Boomer holding dominoes totaling over twenty points.

Even though nobody else tried out, Pearl, Benny, Scooter, Buster, and I congratulated each other when Boomer told us we'd made the team. Boomer shook my hand and welcomed me as the team's youngest member.

"Hey, we did it," Scooter said, then asked Boomer, "When's our first game?"

Boomer gave us a big smile, "Boys, congratulations to you! Be proud you're on the team. Practice your addition and subtraction while I get a few things going." Over the next week he made phone calls and visited some local bars. The next thing we knew Boomer had set up The Domino League of Kettle, West Virginia. Boomer appointed himself league commissioner, and—what else?—had business cards printed. That was Boomer.

The league had five teams, three from bars in Kettle and two from taverns out on Route 42. Boomer required that teams be sponsored by bars or taverns. At the time I didn't understand why, but like everything Boomer did, he had a reason for it. In this case it had to do with bonus points, something I'll explain later.

Not long after Boomer set up the league, he started dating Fanny. She had been runner-up in the "Miss Kettle of 1940 Contest." Fanny worked four to midnight for Art waiting tables and tending bar. Benny liked to stare at her while she worked. He had longing in his voice when he said, "Her long dark hair and cute rear end is a treat to watch. And I love those v-neck t-shirts she wears." Every time Fanny wore one of those t-shirts and leaned over to get a couple of beers out of the cooler, Benny would elbow me in the ribs and in a voice too loud for a whisper, say, "Look."

One time Fanny heard him, turned, shot him a frown at him and yelled, "Look at what, Benny? Tell me so I can look too." After that, Benny whispered.

When Art's Place had no customers Fanny would play the jukebox, sit in Art's big green leather chair, and listen to the music. Before she and Boomer became a couple, she'd put six or seven nickels in the jukebox and play only one song, Vaughn Monroe's "Red Roses for A Blue Lady." Afterwards she played Doris Day's hit, "It's Magic."

When guys tried to flirt with Fanny, she'd ignore them. Once Benny whispered something in her ear and Fanny slowly turned towards him. He lit up with a big smile, licked his lips and opened his arms wide just as Fanny's knee nearly rearranged his family jewels a light tap but she had a serious look on her face.

But Boomer? He just asked Fanny out, and after that nobody else could get close to her. Sometimes Boomer would look at Fanny, wiggle his eyebrows up and down, and then slowly move his tongue from left to right under his upper lip. This caused his pencil mustache to bulge in a wave, sort of like a snake crawling. Fanny would break into an embarrassed giggle and say, "Boomer, don't do that." Boomer would laugh, which told me that he had a sense of humor, something I wondered about when he drove us so hard during what he called "bones practice."

Boomer talked to Art about the responsibility of being a team sponsor, and to everybody's surprise got Art to spring for t-shirts, two per guy. That way we always had a clean shirt for league competition, except for Benny, a little slow on the wash cycle. The shirts represented a big investment for Art. Even at Christmastime, we felt proud if Art gave us, "regulars," as he called us, a free beer. The mere suggestion of money moving from Art's cash register to someone else's pocket would bring a look of concern to his face that would drive a teetotaling Methodist to drink. Fanny designed the lettering on the dark brown shirts, putting a big yellow double six domino on the back and "Art's Place" in yellow letters above the domino. On the front, left side, each guy had his first name printed, same shade of yellow as on the back of our shirts. Customized, not cheap. Boomer's shirts had "Coach" printed below his name. Scooter loved the color of our shirts. "Good for putting my tobacco crop in the barn," he said. Scooter always looked for an angle, a little habit that came in handy in competitive dominoes.

In a league match, four guys played one-on-one with four members of the opposing team, rotating to a new table and opponent after each game. Each team held one player in reserve. Boomer would watch the action and move from player to player, quietly whispering coaching tips to us. We used hand signals, too, just like a manager's signs to players in professional baseball. Boomer's right hand on the front of his left shoulder meant slow down the speed of play. Left hand on the right shoulder meant drink up, go for the bonus points, part of his overall plan. If one guy overloaded on beer and started playing kind of wacky, Boomer made the call and brought our reserve player into the game. Once a player had been pulled out, he couldn't return to match play that evening. Boomer described that rule to us in a voice that sounded very official, "Same rule as baseball when a manager inserts a new player into the game."

Since league rules gave each team only one reserve player, Boomer absolutely insisted that the reserve player not drink any beer until he entered the game. By watching the other team carefully, and inserting a dry player against a very wet opponent, a timely call by a manager could make a big difference. Boomer became a master at making those calls.

I'm not bragging when I say we had a strong team. We rode along in first place and the competition didn't seem all that tough. The other teams came from places like Harry's Bar and The Back Porch, and their guys didn't have great ciphering skills. Our guys could cipher well, Boomer made sure of that. Not all our players had finished high school, but they didn't flunk out. Life had given them some rough jolts.

Take Benny, for example. During the war, on a morning in one of the rainiest and darkest Februarys ever, Benny's Daddy went out behind the barn on their farm, put a loaded shotgun in his mouth and pulled the trigger. Benny dropped out of Kettle High to run the farm for his Mom.

Buster Whitington hit some major potholes in his life, too. In nineteen and twenty-five, right after he was born, his parents took off for Roanoke, Virginia. His aunt and uncle raised him. Buster's uncle worked at Gruber's Department Store unloading produce and stocking the bins and shelves in the grocery department. Everybody called him "produce man." In the store people would sometimes poke their heads through the door into the back room where the store received shipments, and yell, friendly-like, "Hey, where's the produce man?" Buster's uncle would wave and smile. Lot's of folks didn't even know his name. If they met Buster's uncle on the street they'd call out, "Hey, produce man," and he'd always answer "Hey."

One night in nineteen and forty-four, after Buster went to bed his uncle and aunt packed up and left town. Buster had just started tenth grade. He woke up the next morning all alone. Never saw his aunt or uncle again. Across the front of their house, one they rented, his uncle painted in big black letters, "I ain't no produce man—not no more!" A family in town took Buster in, but he had to go to work to support himself. He got a job at Gruber's Department Store, unloading and stocking produce, just like his Daddy. But nobody called him "produce man."

One evening after practice Boomer called our team together. In a voice that sounded like the Kettle High football coach at the start of the season, he said, "Whatever you guys might have been through in life, I believe you've got what it takes." He paused, lowered his head and looked at us over the top of his glasses. "To do well in dominoes, you have to be smart enough to cipher correctly and fast under the pressure of competition. You've shown me you can do it."

Boomer's confidence in our team meant a lot to me—to all of us.

He gave us a slight smile and wrapped up his talk with, "We've still got work to do—our play has to get sharper and faster. But I know you'll do it, and we'll rise above the other teams."

One evening I arrived early for practice. Art's wife sat at the bar drinking a cup of coffee. She told me she'd never played dominoes and asked me about the basics of the game. I gave it to her as simply as I could. "Each player picks seven dominoes, bones we call 'em. The player with the highest double goes first, lays his double on the table. His opponent then has to lay down a domino whose spots match the domino on the board. As play continues, in turn each player lays down a domino matching the end of a branch, what we call a 'leg,' Four next to a four. Three next to a three, and so on. When it's your turn, you study your bones and the board, figure all the possible ways of connecting one of your bones to the outer dots of each leg. And, here's where it gets tough, you mentally calculate whether or not you can score, get a point total of five, or a multiple of five –that's where the division comes in. You total the spots on the ends of legs, and then divide by five. If it comes out even, you've scored. It's important to keep asking yourself, what's been played? What's in your hand that you might use next turn, so you won't have to draw from the bone pile?"

Scooter walked over and listened to my description. He smiled, shook his head and said, "Going to the bone pile reminds me of putting your hand in a den of snakes. The best that can happen is you get away without getting bit."

I added, "Yes, but sometimes a trip to the bone pile just can't be avoided."

By then Boomer had joined us and he jumped into the conversation. "That's right, but at other times it's bad planning." When

Boomer saw one of us make a second trip to the bone pile he'd give us what we called "the ray"—his face would turn red and he'd scowl, then he'd lower his head and look over the top of his glasses. His almost crossed eyes would bore into us, like an angry parent after a kid had done something wrong. I told Benny, "The first time he hit me with the ray I felt like I was in second grade, standing in front of the class, and peed my pants."

Art's wife raised her hands like she'd had enough, said she'd be happy to be a dominoes spectator.

League play took place in the rear of the taverns. Boomer told us, "Each player is expected to have a beer in front of him at all times, and to keep the old elbow action going. That means drink up. League rules."

For league matches, each player paid three dollars. The money covered a small league fee and all the beer you wanted to drink. Bottles, though no draft, because each team's empties made up the bonus point calculations. Here's how Boomer described it to us— his big plan. "At the end of the evening there will be a grand counting." Pearl dreamed up the term, "grand counting," and it took hold. "First, each team's total points for the games will be calculated. Then each team's empty bottles will be counted." Boomer continued, "The difference between the two teams' total empties will be calculated," he paused and looked over his glasses, "using subtraction. Then the difference will be multiplied by five. That number of points will be added to the total match points of the team with the most empties."

Scooter spoke like he had made a discovery, "Boomer, if the games are close, bonus points could make the difference between winnin' or losin' the match."

"You got it, Scooter. Any questions about this?"

Pearl, not the brightest bulb on the tree, asked, "Now, Boomer, how does it work? I got to get it straight."

With Job-like patience, Boomer went through the whole thing all over again.

So, in league play we drank up.

The Abacus, a tavern located near a couple of small insurance agencies in Kettle, began to pull together a dominoes team. The insurance guys would go to the Abacus after work for a few beers and play some dominoes. No surprise to us, their ciphering skills would put them at the top of any arithmetic class. Before long the Abacus owner applied for admission of his team into the league.

I voted against the Abacus being admitted into the league. It seemed too much like bringing in a professional baseball team to play in a local league. Scooter voted against them too, and added, "I'm always on the losin' end of a vote. I voted for Albert Akers for mayor of Kettle, and he took the biggest whippin' since nineteen and thirty-two, when Wilfred Howell ran for office on the slogan, 'Hold true to Hoover.'"

One evening after the Abacus entered the league, Boomer asked me to mosey over there for a few beers and come back with a scouting report, for our first match with The Abacus would come up soon. I knew a few of the guys who hung out at the Abacus. After we said hello I made my way to the back of the room to watch the action.

I gulped—they had games with six legs moving at high rates of speed. And they played double nines dominoes! I knew double nines existed, and stores sold sets, but I had never seen double nines played. And fast.

I couldn't take my eyes off Marley Farcus. He handled the paperwork for the insurance on my car. A quiet fellow, about Scooter's age, medium height, balding, with thick lenses in his wire-rimmed glasses. And I don't quite know how to say this except to say it, he had a hump in his back. It gave him the posture of a question mark. Around town most folks referred to Marley as Humpy, Humpy Farcus, though nobody said Humpy to his face. Just behind his back, no pun intended. Some folks said Humpy's stoop had been caused by his bending over accounting books for long periods of time. Others said it came from his habit of bending forward when he smoked a cigarette. And he smoked a lot of them.

Humpy lived with his Mom and had never married. Most Sunday mornings Humpy walked his Mom to services at the

262

Baptist Church. No one could remember ever seeing Humpy go out with a woman other than his Mom, except for one time. Humpy had a date with Meredith Quisenberry and they went to see a Mickey Rooney and Judy Garland movie at the Dixie Palace. About the time Mickey fell in love with Judy, Meredith Q reached over to hold Humpy's hand. He began breathing hard, wheezing and stood up. Then Humpy fell across the people sitting in the row in front of him. Benny and Scooter sat near Humpy and Meredith Q. Benny yelled "Help!" He and Scooter carried Humpy to the aisle and stretched him out flat on his back. Everyone stood up and craned their necks to see Humpy lying there. Finally the manager of the theatre ran down the aisle with an empty popcorn bag and put it over Humpy's face. Pretty soon Humpy started to move. To the best of my knowledge, he never had another date.

Humpy had a reputation for being good with numbers, but I couldn't believe how fast he played dominoes. The moment his turn came, Humpy's right hand shot a domino onto the board like a rattlesnake striking a mouse, a move that put pressure on his opponent. Humpy didn't laugh much or make chit-chat. In match play he spoke only to criticize the other player and he did that a lot. He'd look across the table at the other guy, aim his magnified eyes through those thick lenses in a stare, then tell the fellow what he'd done wrong. While he waited on his opponent to make a play, Humpy would drum his fingers against the table.

Humpy loved to smoke cigarettes. Pearl, himself a smoker, said admiringly, "Humpy is very involved with tobacco and has become an accomplished smoker." Humpy often used the butt of the cigarette he'd finished to light the fresh one placed between his lips. Benny said, "Humpy smokes like a steam engine coming up Blair Mountain." Lucky Strikes. After a while, with Humpy's speed, his relentless criticism, and an endless cloud of smoke, opponents often caved in, particularly if they'd had a few beers. Later, when the Abacus played against Art's Place, it happened to me more than once.

After two beers I hustled out of the Abacus to give my scouting report to Boomer. "You're not going to believe what I saw." I described the six-legged games, the double nines and the speed of play.

Boomer listened to my report, nodded, and looked over my shoulder, staring into the dark area towards the men's room at the back of Art's Place. After I finished my report Boomer didn't move a muscle and continued his stare.

"Boomer, I hope you're dreaming up a game plan, because we're going to need a good one." Boomer turned and looked at me, slowly blinked his eyes and nodded. Then he walked away.

With the entry of the Abacus into the league the competition got a lot tougher. Before long their team climbed into first place. We occupied second place, though close on the heels of the Abacus. Boomer told us in an upbeat voice, "We can still win the league, boys. Hang in there. Practice your ciphering."

As much as I wanted our team to win the championship, I have to admit I didn't know if we could do it. Our team play seemed a little awry and I couldn't put my finger on why. Boomer hadn't thrown the ray for a couple of nights, not like him. He spent a lot of time coaching Pearl, and less time with Buster, who really needed the help. In his work with Pearl, Boomer threw word problems at him. "What do you do when you hold a bone with a five spot and you can play it but not score—play now or keep it till later?"

During practices Pearl and Boomer sometimes talked in whispers. While they talked each of them would look around the room like they wanted to make sure nobody heard what they said. At first I didn't much care. One night when Buster mentioned Boomer and Pearl's whispering, I said like it didn't matter to me, "Who wants to know?" Buster—working on his third beer and feeling the frustration of going to the bone pile for the second time in two turns—looked over at Boomer and Pearl and blurted out real loud, "Right, who the hell cares what they're saying?"

Pearl and Boomer both turned and stared at Buster and me. I thought Boomer might give us the ray but he held back. That made me wonder even more what he and Pearl had been talking about.

Pearl had been a strong offensive player, frequently getting big multiples of five. But he had hit a slump, slowed down, scored less often. I wondered if something else had fired up in his life. I later found I had it right, but I would never have guessed why. In April we neared the end of the Domino League's season, October first through April thirtieth. Art's Place had pulled into a near dead heat with the Abacus, neck and neck. Then came our last match of the season against the Abacus. Even Art said, "Well, boys, this is it. Tonight will likely decide if you got a shot at winning the league."

About the middle of the afternoon before the big match, Boomer's Hudson, looking like it had just been Simonized, pulled up to the Gulf pumps at Buckingham's then rolled slightly forward to high test. Boomer always bought regular gas. Boomer sat in the front seat, Pearl in the back, and beside each of them sat one of the Posey twins, Lovey and True, from up on Sour Apple River. As usual I had a hard time telling the twins apart, but it looked like Lovey sat beside Boomer and True beside Pearl. The twins had their blonde hair piled high on their heads. Lovey always told people, "I think I bear a resemblance to Lana Turner, the movie star. She has a cousin in Beckley, you know, and it's possible True and I are related to her." Her voice always trailed off when she got to the related part, causing the other person to lean forward to hear her. Then Lovey would say no more, smile and stare at them. A few weeks earlier I had heard Boomer and Pearl gossiping about Lovey and True ditching Chappie and Ferlin R.

While the tank filled I cleaned the windshield, even though it already sparkled. Boomer had polished every inch of that car. Wouldn't you know, Lovey leaned forward and from inside the car pointed her finger to a couple of areas of the glass, saying "I swan, Boomer, I think he missed those places." Boomer looked at me with raised eyebrows—not the ray or anything. I put the wipe rag on the areas she pointed to and did a little extra cleaning. I didn't mind doing that, but Lovey knew better. She just showed off for Boomer. When Boomer paid for the gas he thanked me for, as he put it, "attending to the problems pointed out by Miss Lovey Posey." He said it most seriously, but I could see True and Pearl in the back seat about to bust a gut holding in their giggles. And Boomer had alcohol on his breath—at only three in the afternoon.

All day my mind stayed fixed on the match against the Abacus. I played imaginary games against each of their players. The winner would take over first place in the league standings and be seen by the other teams as the best. That kind of thing can mean a lot coming down the last stretch of a season's schedule. As they say in baseball, we'd play a game that would decide who'd most likely win the pennant. I wondered what Boomer and Pearl had their minds on, and then thought maybe I knew.

That night we had the advantage of playing in our home territory, Art's Place. At eight-thirty, the time to begin scheduled play, everybody sat at the domino tables, ready to play, except for Boomer and Pearl. The Abacus guys, all but Humpy, more interested in smoking, kept saying, "Hey, we're thirsty, let's get started."

I joined Buster, Benny, and Scooter for a team huddle. We decided to begin the match. Pearl could be the reserve player if and when he and Boomer arrived.

I said to Benny, "I can't believe this. Boomer has never missed a match. Never ever." Fanny kept calling Boomer's place. No answer. Shortly after eight-thirty Art got out of his big green leather chair and walked to the front door and looked up and down the street for Boomer's car. To make matters worse, a fellow at the bar laughed and said he had seen Boomer, Pearl, and "some ladies who shall remain nameless," as he put it, "over at The Hat Rack Bar and Grille about six o'clock." He lowered his voice when Fanny served beers near him. Thank God for small favors. Though as things turned out, he might just as well have yelled out his news.

Fanny collected three dollars from everybody and served up the first round of beers. We started the match. The Abacus guys downed their beers down so fast they must have chug-a-lugged them. One of them said, "Hey, Fanny, bring us another round."

Scooter elbowed me and whispered, "They're going after grand counting, bonus points."

The Abacus guys seemed so smart-ass sure of themselves, like they could put away both the beer and us at the same time. They knew we didn't have a reserve player, and of course they did, in Lysander Preston. By day Lysander kept the books at one of the insurance agencies, and by night he became a human adding machine. Lysander remained stone sober, eager to get into the game.

Scooter called a team huddle and whispered, "We ain't got a shot at the bonus points if we don't drink up," so we sped up our pace of drinking. This seemed to spur on the Abacus team. By ten-thirty each of our guys had drunk three or four beers, and I don't know how many the Abacus team had put away. Art and most of the regulars gathered around the tables to watch the match.

With us trailing slightly in the point totals, the coach of the Abacus made his move and put Lysander Preston in to play against me. I choked as I took a sip of my beer, but I didn't choke in my play. If I just concentrated on the game, not Lysander's reputation, I could stay with him.

The only sounds in the bar came from the hum of the beer cooler and the alternating buzzing sounds made by the red "Art's" and green "Place" neon lights in the front window. And Humpy Farcus criticizing his opponent, Buster, who he had on the ropes.

A car drove into the parking lot. Car doors slammed and men and women laughed. Art's front door opened and everyone looked up as Boomer and Pearl entered, working hard to stop laughing, shut down their smiles and appear serious. Boomer pulled it off OK, but Pearl kept smirking and poking Boomer in the side and giggling. He stuck his head out the front door and yelled towards the parking lot, "Hey, stop that laughing, get serious." I figured I knew who came with Boomer and Pearl, but hoped I got it wrong.

Boomer glided forward, surveyed the action and the scores posted on the blackboard. Pearl stopped at the bar and grabbed a hot dog. He munched on it as he hustled to catch up with Boomer, dancing that little two-step he often did after winning a game. When Pearl two-stepped into the back area where we sat, he stubbed the toe of his shoe on that little riser Art had painted white to prevent anybody from tripping over it. He stumbled head first towards the tables and swore like a sailor as he hit the floor, though we had trouble understanding him for he had filled his mouth with the half of the hot dog that hadn't been squashed between his hand and the floor. The Abacus guys laughed and pointed at Pearl.

Our team tried to keep straight faces but Buster started howling and Benny joined in, then Scooter along with me. That made Pearl cuss even more. Still lying face down on the floor he yelled, "You wouldn't think it was so damn funny if it was your hot dog." We laughed harder. Later Scooter said, "I thought my sides was going to split."

Boomer stepped towards the playing tables, staggered slightly to his right, then said in a voice a little too high-pitched, "Players, please restrain yourselfs." That's what he said, "yourselfs." I muttered to myself, "Oh my God, we're sunk."

Play resumed. Boomer took his coaching position. He kept his eyes on Buster, as Humpy continued to clobber him. Buster had slowed his calculations and kept interrupting play to tell jokes everybody had heard a thousand times. Humpy criticized Buster almost non-stop. "You could have scored if you'd…." Or, "Not too smart a play, with what's likely to be in the bone pile." I got to admit, Buster gave Humpy a lot to work with. We needed a fresh player to go in for Buster, and only had Pearl, half or three-quarters drunk, sitting in a chair propped against the back wall and looking like he'd fallen sleep.

In the parking lot car doors slammed again. The front door of Art's Place swung open and in walked Lovey and True, giggling and pointing towards Boomer and Pearl. Their high-rise hair do's had toppled a bit, and their lipstick had smeared. Everybody stopped playing for a few seconds and watched Lovey sidle up to Boomer, even though he stood in his coaching position.

True pulled a chair up beside Pearl, who by then had started snoring, though he stopped and opened his eyes when she put her hand on his thigh. Speaking in a soft voice True asked, "Was you asleep, Pearl, honey?"

He answered, "No, darlin,' I was just checkin' my eyelids for cracks." The room had been so quiet that everybody heard what they said. Except for Boomer and Lovey, we all busted out laughing again.

Boomer gave the right hand on left shoulder signal to Buster, meaning to slow down, and motioned with his left hand for Pearl to warm up, prepare to come into the game against Humpy. Pearl, with True's help, got himself to a standing position. Boomer stood behind Buster, across the table from Humpy. Pearl walked towards them.

Fanny came out of the kitchen with a tray full of sandwiches and at least six long-necked bottles of Burger Beer. Perfect timing, I thought. Fanny's gaze fixed on Boomer at the instant Lovey's hand stroked the Wildroot Cream Oil bulge in the left front pocket of his trousers. Fanny looked at Lovey's well-placed hand and screamed, "You phi-landerer!" With that she threw the tray over Humpy's head. The sandwiches and beers spewed and sprayed all over Boomer, Lovey, Buster, Pearl, and True. Humpy, already stooped forward, had the presence of mind to lean further across the top of the table to protect the arrangement of dominoes.

Art jumped into the middle of everything and said firmly, "OK, Fanny, I think you'd better go home. Now!" She threw her apron on the floor and stormed out the front door. Art raised his arms like a teacher quieting kids in a classroom and said in a loud voice, "Everybody settle down and get on with the match."

Boomer chased after Fanny, but came back in two shakes. Her car peeled rubber as it sped out of the parking lot. After we cleaned up the mess, Boomer called a huddle and tried to get us back to normal. But he slurred his words.

Except for one, the Abacus guys walked around laughing and talking. Humpy sat quiet as a church mouse. His hands trembled as he lit another Lucky Strike. Maybe he'd had too much male-female craziness.

Boomer pulled Buster out of the game and put Pearl in against Humpy. Pearl never once looked at Humpy. He stared at the board and started making his plays. Humpy kept looking around, first towards the front door, then over his shoulder as if he expected something else to happen. And then, surprising everybody,

Humpy made a couple of real bonehead plays. Pearl, not sounding drunk at all, started criticizing him and really poured it on. Nonstop. The next thing I knew Humpy had to go to the bone pile and draw, three times. Pearl played like a demon and, I could hardly believe it, he soon built a big lead over Humpy. Pearl?

Yep, we won. Usually both teams hung around after league play, had another round of beers and discussed the games. That night the Abacus players slid out of Art's Place like a bunch of slugs on a rainy sidewalk.

Shortly after they left a car pulled into the parking lot. Art's front door opened and in came Fanny. She walked up to Boomer like nothing had happened. I wondered how she could put everything behind her so quickly. Boomer gave her a little grin, wiggled his eyebrows and put his tongue under his lip and rolled his moustache. When Fanny moved her tongue in and out between her lips real slow-like, then reached over and patted his Wildroot Cream Oil bulge, it hit me that she'd been in on the whole thing.

Pearl held True's hand and said, "Let's go," to Boomer. Lovey took Buster's arm and the two of them walked out with Pearl and True. Boomer told Pearl he'd ride with Fanny, and gave him the keys to the Hudson. Pearl had become a licensed driver. The six of them left.

Later I told William White that the Abacus boys had received a brain-splitting knuckle-knocking load of trickery worthy of an Academy Award. The Great Houdini couldn't have done it any better.

In the league competition, the Abacus guys lost it after that night—still good but their edge had disappeared. At the end of the season they wound up in third place. You could look it up.

At the beginning of the summer Beverly returned from the University. Even though league play had ended, Boomer wanted to hold practices a couple of times a week, sometimes more. I began to miss them to be with Beverly.

In early July the Tennessee Gas Pipeline came through Kettle, a 24-inch-diameter pipe running from Knoxville to Toledo. Lots of jobs opened up. Buster and Benny signed on and kept going north with the project. Boomer brought in a couple of new players. One of them didn't cipher well and the other one enjoyed drinking beer more than playing dominoes.

The next thing I knew Boomer had left town. Not long afterwards, our team called it quits. We raised a toast to our championship and to Boomer. Soon the league disbanded. Fanny said Boomer had found a good job in Huntington, but he'd asked that it be kept confidential.

Late on a warm night near the end of that summer, Beverly and I sat in the glider on her front porch. We rocked slowly, held hands and didn't talk. But inside me I had a lively conversation going on—about how much I loved Beverly, how I wanted to live my life with her—and then I thought, "Why don't you tell her that?"

When I began to speak the words jumped out so fast they surprised me more than they did her. I said at a rapid clip, "I love you, Beverly. Will you marry me?" I had hardly finished my question before she whispered, "Yes," and then wrapped her wonderful long arms around me.

I called Phil early the next morning to tell him the good news and ask for the day off. Beverly and I drove to Huntington and picked out her diamond engagement ring. Standing in front of the glass counter in the jewelry shop, I took her left hand in mine and gently placed a diamond ring on the third finger of her left hand. It slid on easily, looked like it belonged there. Then we gave each other a kiss that lasted so long the clerk began to clear his throat. When we looked up at him he smiled. That night we took a blanket to a remote section of the park along the Sour Apple River, undressed and touched the diamond over every part of both our bodies.

The last I heard, Pearl and True had a home up on Sour Apple River. Lovey moved to Charleston. Fanny worked for Art a couple more years, and then moved to her sister's place in Paintsville, Kentucky. Humpy contracted lung cancer and passed away. Art died of a heart attack one evening while sitting in his green chair. Not long afterwards his wife sold the building. Talk about sacrilege, Art's Place became a storefront church. A hand-lettered sign in the front window said, "The Apostolic Church of Faith." When I saw that sign I thought Art must be turning over in his grave.

One day I had some business in Huntington and stopped at the Eighth Street Drug Store to pick up some Band-Aids, mercurochrome, shaving cream, that sort of thing. I walked in and stopped, frozen in my tracks. Behind the prescriptions counter, decked out in a white pharmacist-like uniform stood a man who looked exactly like Boomer. I never heard that Boomer had a twin—it had to be him.

I said, "Boomer?"

He looked at me in that calm and expressionless way of his, glided a few feet in my direction and said, "Yes, can I help you?"

"Boomer, it's me, Freddy." He gave me a blank look. "Art's Place," I added.

He said, very pleasantly, "Yes, Freddy. Can I help you with anything?"

I got the articles I came to buy, paid for them and walked towards the door. I put one hand on the doorknob, and then turned to take a last look at Boomer.

He looked up at me from the prescriptions counter. Then he wiggled his eyebrows, rolled his tongue from left to right under his moustache and gave me a mischievous smile.

That was Boomer.

Chapter 12

THE END OF WHAT WE KNEW

All day Hartford Wilson's question to Senator Humphrey had nagged at me. Even as I sat down to dinner with Beverly and Jack, I again heard Hartford ask it. And once again, I waited on the Senator's answer, one that never came.

Jack sat in his high chair, stirring the tiny pieces of roast beef and mashed potatoes on his plate. I could have filled up, satisfied my hunger, just breathing in the rich aroma of Beverly's roast beef and gravy. She knew more ways than I could count to satisfy my multitude of hungers. After we finished dinner, I picked up our plates to carry them into the kitchen. Beverly put her hand on my arm, smiled and said, "It's a beautiful evening. You two take a walk. I'll do the dishes."

I gave Jack a piggyback ride to the end of the driveway and then across the narrow black-top road that marked the edge of our front yard. As we entered the open field beyond the road, the sun dropped below the horizon and the color of the sky began to shift from bright red to dark orange. Steep hillsides that extended to the horizon bound both sides of the wide field. Their middle sections had dark green thickets of rhododendrons dotted with balls of pink and white blooms. In the April twilight the blooms took on a golden cast. So did the pale blossoms of three crabapple trees along an old fence line to our right. Wild green onions and nubs of daisies, still a month from their first flowers, dotted the field.

I put Jack down. He laughed and his black curly hair bounced as he burst into a run towards a killdeer poking its beak into the fresh green growth of alfalfa. Jack's little footprints dropped behind him on the still damp earth—for a two year-old, he moved fast. The air carried the sharp scent of fresh earth, of spring and new life. I called, "Hey Jack, take a deep breath." He turned, waved to me and looked away. Jack had jumped into his own adventure.

While I watched Jack playing in the field, my thoughts returned to this morning at Bertha's Place, to the fellows who gathered for coffee and our unexpected visitor. You'd have thought a man who wanted to be President of the United States would've had an answer for Hartford. Since the moment Hartford asked his question the Earth had rotated less than half a turn. But when I thought about all that had happened in our little town to give rise to Hartford's question, it seemed like the Earth and I had traveled ten thousand turns, maybe even gone to Mars and back. How had it all happened? Right in front of everybody's eyes? One day everything seemed to be here. So certain. Kettle as we knew it, old trees lining its brick streets, a good high school, well-cared for churches. A community. Then, puff, puff—poof! Like somebody struck a match to an old brush pile, the town we knew disappeared.

As Phil Buckingham and I had walked along Main Street this morning to meet the fellows for coffee, we passed the bronze plaque attached to the old brick building occupied by Bertha's Place. Once again I stopped and stared at it. I liked the way the plaque's polished letters raised above its tarnished green base and reflected the morning sun. I told Phil the plaque looked like a two-tone jewel, added character to the building's weathered old red bricks. He nodded, but I could tell he felt he had to humor me. I knew the words on the plaque by heart, but couldn't keep from reading them for what must have been the thousandth time.

This plaque marks the site of the town's first building,
The Kettle Trading Post,
erected in 1809.
Incorporated as Kettle, Virginia, April 1, 1859.
This memorial dedicated
by Mayor Asa T. Baumgartner, April 1, 1909.

"Not the plaque again," Phil complained as he pulled at my sleeve. "For God's sake, Freddy," he said, though he smiled when he spoke.

Just beyond the plaque the plate glass window of Bertha's Place wore a light coat of fog on the inside due to last night's sudden temperature drop. When we opened the old front door it creaked, as always, but Bertha refused to oil its hinges. She said the creaks helped her keep track of everyone's comings and goings.

Hartford Wilson sat at a back table waving *Time* magazine at us. Pappy Roosevelt and Police Chief Arthur R. Tackett stood behind him. "By God, boys," Hartford yelled at us, "read this. Kettle is on the map! Yessir. On the map. We're famous throughout the U.S. of A.!"

William White Wallace walked into the restaurant right behind us, looked around and once again popped the question he always asked when he arrived, "What're you boys doing here?" Phil, Hartford, and some friends had been meeting on weekday mornings at the restaurant for over thirty years. William White and I had the honor of being the group's newest and youngest members. We joined the group only twelve years ago.

Phil, William White, and I seated ourselves in the chrome-plated chairs around Hartford's table. We leaned back, folded our arms, and settled in to watch the action. Hartford kept halfway standing and then plopping himself back into his chair as if somebody had shoved him down, like a slow-moving old Jack-in-the-box, his bald head all shiny, his eyes beaming and his face so full of a grin I thought it might split in two. He wore what he called his favorite sweater, the old blue one with leather patches on the elbows, and one of the faded red shirts he'd worn ever since

275

I'd known him. His smile made his face look younger than his seventy-plus years. Hartford lowered the magazine to the table, open to the article, and flattened its pages with his hand. Behind him Pappy Roosevelt and Chief Tackett stood and peered over his shoulder trying to read the article while Hartford kept distracting them with his arm-waving and bursts of comments.

"Dang it, Hartford, hold still!" Pappy Roosevelt said several times, but Hartford continued on his own path. Pappy Roosevelt's unruly hair stood on end and his coveralls had a generous covering of grass stains and mud, probably from his early morning slopping of his hogs. Pappy Roosevelt's lips silently formed the words of the article when he could see past Hartford long enough to read as much as a sentence. Chief Tackett stood to Hartford's right, his billed cap tilted forward, reading without lip movements but moving his head left and right, straining to keep his gaze on the page. The chief's bulging belly hung over his pistol belt and pulled against the buttons down the front of his shirt.

The aroma of fried bacon from Bertha's kitchen tempted me to order breakfast, even though Beverly, Jack, and I had just finished eggs, bacon, and toast. I told myself that if I got into a two-breakfast habit, I'd have the chief's belly in no time. No breakfast, I decided.

Phil slung his blue jacket on the back of his chair and dropped his maroon golfer's cap on the table. As usual, he'd parted his thinning gray hair on the left and combed it over in a failed attempt to cover the ever-growing bald spot on the top of his head. Bertha Benson, holding that damp rag that smelled of chlorine she always seemed to carry, stretched her large body across the entire width of the table as she wiped it. William White had said more than once that in her uniform, Bertha looked more like a great blue whale than a woman who might try to have her way with one of us. He always laughed when he said it. Others had when they heard it the first time, long ago. Bertha's right hand moved across the surface of the table while her left hand pushed her curly salt-and-pepper hair away from her face.

William White leaned towards me and said in a half whisper—almost low enough to keep the others from hearing him, but not quite, "What's going on, Freddy? You look different this morning." He put on that sly, smart-aleck grin he knew bothered me to no end, and then he said loud enough for everyone within twenty feet to hear him, "What were you and Beverly up to last night?"

William White's blonde hair had its little raised wave in front, just as it had ever since I'd known him, nearly twenty-five years. In the first grade, I used to tease him about that cowlick, among other things. I could make him cry in less than a minute. Could I still do it? Once William White became the owner of our local hardware and appliance store he took pride in wearing a necktie to work every day, but he never gave up his windbreaker for a suit jacket.

I gave him a sickly sweet grin and said, "So, stand up and comb your hair, Mr. Hardware Man. And when do you plan to start wearing a suit coat instead of that warm up jacket?" As soon as I said it, I wished I hadn't. After all, I wasn't exactly dressed up. I might be the owner and operator of Buckingham's Gulf Station and Garage, but with my same old blue work shirt and trousers starched to the nines I left myself wide open for one of William White's comebacks.

"About the time you learn your name." He peered at the front of my shirt, "Let's see," he leaned towards the front of my shirt, peered at it, "Freddy, isn't it?" William White grinned like he'd pulled a good one, but he'd used that line so many times before, I didn't even bother answering. He enjoyed poking fun at the letters of my name, stitched in white thread above the left pocket of my shirt.

William White's dumb and worn-out question hadn't registered with me anyway. My thoughts lingered on the brass plaque and the Kettle Trading Post.

The summer before our freshman year at Kettle High School, William White and I had worked in a crew that dug up and replaced the sidewalk in front of Bertha's Place, at the time named Miss Kettle's Place. Some fellows with a jackhammer removed the old sidewalk. Then William White and I dug about a foot below it in order for some workmen to install proper drainage. During our digging, we unearthed two crusty silver spoons and three small flint arrowheads. William White yelled, "Holy moly! These things are important! Yessir, they bear witness to peaceful dealings between the Indians and the settlers around the Trading Post."

During the fall term, for our ninth-grade social-science projects, we both wrote papers about our discovery. In early November, our discovered objects, "artifacts," our teacher called them, and our theory about their meaning got some unexpected recognition in the *Kettle News Leader* during Kettle's Annual Brotherhood Day, a local celebration of neighborliness towards Indians. In truth, the last of the Shawnee Indians left the area well over a hundred years ago. But still, the town enjoyed the yearly celebration and it seemed to get everybody started down the road to Thanksgiving. Some folks even started buying Christmas presents.

William White sat back in his chair while Bertha wiped the table in front of him. "Thanks, Bertha," he said, as if he owned the place. "Please serve these gentlemen and yours truly some of your delicious coffee. I'm buying today." Bertha grinned at William White like he'd offered to buy the whole restaurant and make her a very wealthy woman.

About then the front door swung open and Whit Saunders, ramrod straight, head high, came in at a brisk pace with a copy of *Time* in his hand. He got only a couple of steps inside when he stopped, pushed his wide-brimmed hat back on his head and boomed, "OK, Bertha's Place, wake up!" He held up the magazine. "Have a look at this, the April 5th nineteen and sixty edition of *Time* magazine." William White held up his hand and Whit handed him the magazine.

Bertha made one more pass with her damp cloth across our table, "We know, Whit, we know. Hartford showed us." Then she gave Whit a big smile. "And don't you look just dandy in that photograph."

Phil and I had already read the article—Phil had brought in his copy of *Time* with him earlier that morning when he stopped at the station to buy gas for his old work truck. I had to admit, the photo was pretty good. In it, Whit—dressed just like today, wide-brimmed hat, leather jacket, flannel shirt, and britches stuffed into his lace-up boots—stood on the front steps of the Bank of Kettle, shaking hands with Senator John F. Kennedy. The caption under the photo read, "On Kettle's Main Street."

Kennedy had come to Kettle ten days earlier on a sunny but windy and cool day in March. Two vans and three cars, one of them a big black Cadillac, with the senator and his campaign people rolled into town about nine forty-five that morning. The speech's time and date had been advertised in the *Kettle News Leader*, and for a few days Main Street stores had signs in their windows announcing the senator's speech. Each sign had a hand-lettered note along its top, "JFK at 10 AM—Please come!"

Shortly before ten o'clock a crowd of maybe a hundred folks, including William White and me, milled around in front of the wide front steps of the red brick Bank of Kettle. People working for Senator Kennedy handed out buttons, "JFK in '60", and white straw hats with red, white, and blue hat-bands and "Kennedy" printed in bold blue letters around the front of each hat. The clock hanging above the front steps of the bank chimed ten o'clock, and at the ring of the tenth chime Senator Kennedy's brother, Robert, bounded to the top step. He held up his hands to get everybody's attention, thanked us for coming and introduced his brother, who by then stood beside him. The brothers wore identical navy blue suits, white shirts, and neckties, yellow for Robert, bright red for Jack. During his introduction, Robert talked about the senator's WWII service as commander of a torpedo boat, PT-109, and his heroism after a Japanese destroyer rammed and sank the smaller boat. He ended with, "Jack Kennedy will bring new leadership to America," a phrase we heard a lot in later weeks. And every time we did, Whit would blurt out, "You heard it first, boys, right here in Kettle."

The wind tousled Senator Kennedy's thick head of brown hair while he spoke about "new frontiers" for our country. He kept his hands in the side pockets of his suit jacket during his speech, though a couple of times when he wanted to emphasize something he took his right hand out of his coat pocket and pointed with his index finger. His speech couldn't have lasted more than fifteen minutes, but he left a mark on Kettle in that short time. We'd never heard "West Virginia" pronounced with an "r" on the end of it.

After his speech the senator shook hands with a few people and posed for photos, including one with Whit. Then he and his brother hopped into the back seat of the black Cadillac. At the moment the car door slammed shut, the Bank of Kettle clock chimed ten thirty AM.

William White and I watched the Cadillac enter the four-lane, pick up speed, and head towards the Interstate. The other campaign cars and vans trailed along behind it. William White gave a half-hearted wave at the tail end of the caravan. "Wham, bam, thank you ma'am," he said and we laughed.

Whit pulled up a chair and sat down at our table. "Boys, I got to tell you, I may vote for that Senator Kennedy, even if he is a Catholic."

"I have always maintained you're a fair-minded man, Whit," William White said. Then he got a little grin on his face and added, "Those rumors of Kennedy installing a direct phone line between the White House and the Vatican are probably false."

The front door opened and Shufflehead Meadows, tall and skinny—lanky, folks called him—walked in. He stopped just inside the front door. His blond hair flopped into his eyes as he took off his Cincinnati Reds baseball cap and threw it across the room with a spin towards the chrome coat rack attached to the first booth, next to the counter. His cap spun around and secured itself to the top of the rack.

"Never miss," Shufflehead said with pride. "Hey, Whit, somebody told me you was famous. Howdja do that? Whut happened?"

Whit showed Shufflehead the photo. Shufflehead asked Bertha for a RC Cola, then sat down with us.

We talked about Senator Kennedy and Senator Humphrey, how much each of them wanted to win the West Virginia presidential primary, and the article in *Time*. Whit Saunders sounded a little awestruck when he said, "Boys, that *Time* article may be just the beginning of big things for West Virginia this year. I heard from my sister, who got it from a cousin who works at the public library in Huntington, that the *New York Times* is coverin' our Democratic primary. Can you imagine that, the *New York Times*? She told my sister that before it's all over, she wouldn't be surprised if our election was reported by Walter Cronkite on the CBS News!"

"The way I figure it," Phil commented, "the big-wig Democrats in New York and Chicago believe that if they can get West Virginia Democrats to vote for a Catholic like Kennedy, then they can get most anybody in the country to do it. There's a game being played here and it goes far beyond us."

Chief Tackett muttered, "That may be so, Phil. But game or no game, I got to tell you, that Kennedy's too slick fer me." Then his voice got louder, stronger. "Reminds me of that state road commissioner, the one what come here in fifty-two to speak at the ground-breaking cuttin' ceremony for the four-lane. All decked out in his fancy white Sunday-go-to-meetin' suit. Remember how he told us Kettle was entering a new era, and the four-lane would take us there? Now this Kennedy is sayin' we're headin' into a new era, "new frontiers" he calls 'em, and he'll take us there. The four-lane ain't done nothin' fer Kettle 'cept tear up the patch. I ain't so sure Kennedy will do any better. Though I must admit, Kennedy's better lookin' than the Commissioner."

Chief Tackett's mention of the ground-breaking ceremony for construction of the four-lane started a run of comments about the wide highway built through the center of Kettle in the early nineteen-fifties. Everybody called the road "the state's victory trophy." And then, right on the heels of the four-lane, came the Interstate highway—a one-two punch that sent our town reeling.

That's when Bertha's front door opened and a fellow I hadn't seen before came in. He appeared to be about thirty and had neatly trimmed blonde hair. He wore khaki pants and a maroon nylon windbreaker with University of Minnesota in gold letters across its front. He walked over to Chief Tackett and held out his hand, "I'm Ralph Swenson, from Minneapolis. I'm looking for a place where Senator Humphrey could meet with some local folks and talk with them."

The chief shook his hand. "I'm Chief Tackett, Ralph, and you done found the place you're lookin' for. Matter of fact, you're standin' in it," the chief replied as he shook Ralph's hand. "Ain't no place better than here. Bertha's Place is the heart of Kettle."

Hartford looked up at Ralph, "Sit down, son. Have a cup of coffee." Ralph pulled up a chair and shook hands with each of us as he introduced himself.

Ralph asked, "Is there a public phone nearby?" Bertha put a hot cup of coffee in front of him and pointed at the phone on the back wall beyond the end of the counter. Ralph said, "I'll be right back."

When he returned Ralph took a sip from the steaming cup of coffee Bertha placed in front of him, then asked, "Kettle, now that's an odd name for a town. Where'd it come from?"

William White jumped in before anyone could speak. "Right off the bat, Ralph, everybody asks about the name of our town. Well, in the early days there was a trading post here, built of virgin timber, right on this spot—Bertha's Place. You're the same as sitting in it. The old trading post was said to "always have the kettle on." The owner, Cletus Ramsay, kept an iron kettle full of hot cider hanging in the fireplace. In time the trading post and the area around it came to be called Kettle. Daniel Boone used to come here, at least we think he did. In our town hall there is a painting of the trading post with ol' Daniel standing in front of it. A sign above the front door says, 'There are no strangers here.' We still take pride in our hospitality."

"Well, you've sure showed it to me," Ralph said. "Thanks."

Pappy Roosevelt said, "Ralph, we was just a talkin' about how the West Virginia State Road Commission declared war on the town of Kettle and all the upset that followed. Maybe you, maybe even Senator Humphrey, would hanker to know of it."

"That's certainly the sort of thing the senator wants to learn about," Ralph said eagerly. "Me too."

Hartford took a sip of coffee, looked at Ralph, then puckered his lips and looked at the ceiling for a few seconds before he began to speak. "Nobody's sure when the long struggle between the State Road Commission and the town of Kettle started, Ralph, though I once heard our former mayor, Raymond T. Baumgartner, say, 'It was the date we got that first letter, June fourth, nineteen and forty-seven—the first shot in the West Virginia State Road Commission's war on the town of Kettle.' In the letter, the State Road Commission asked the town of Kettle to change the angle parking along Main Street, also U.S. Highway 42, to parallel parking."

"I was there," I said, "when Mayor Baumgartner read the letter out loud to Town Council. I'll never forget how the mayor read it, real slow, and when he got to the end he had a twinge of sarcasm in his voice. 'This change,' the letter said, 'will reduce the periodic impediments to smooth egress and flow of commerce caused by angle parking adjacent to a major highway,' and bore the signature of the State Road Commissioner. Well, the mayor placed his thumbs under his suspenders, pushed his double chin forward and added, 'To the best of my knowledge nobody in Kettle has complained of temporary impediments to smooth egress and flow of commerce caused by angle parking.'"

Hartford gave a big belly laugh and slapped his right hand against his thigh. Everybody around the table joined in the laughter.

I continued, "I joined in the applause, along with others at the meeting, when Town Council voted down rejected the request. Unanimous vote."

"Remember the mayor's annual Fourth of July Celebration speech that year?" William White asked. "Mayor Baumgartner grinned from ear to ear when he told everybody how he and town council took on the State Road Commission. 'An example of democracy in action,' he said, 'us little fellows fighting against the powerful interests of big government, doing what's right for our town. And winning.'"

"You shoulda heard 'im, Ralph. It was downright inspirational," Pappy Roosevelt commented. He took a sip of his coffee. I always wondered how Pappy Roosevelt could keep a wad of chewing tobacco in his mouth and at the same time drink coffee without swallowing the tobacco juice, but he did. Years of practice I guess.

"I wish I'd been there," Ralph said.

Pappy Roosevelt wiped his lips with the back of his hand and then spoke in a firm voice, "Well, if it hadn't been for ol' Bill, Hiram Anderson's horse, that new four-lane might never've happened. Maybe we'd still have Kettle the way it was."

"Whut'd Bill do?" Shufflehead asked. "Whut happened?"

"You remember, Shuff," Phil said with a small laugh, "It was late in the summer of forty-seven. There came ol' Bill pulling Hiram's wagon with crates of pigs stacked eight feet above the wagon's bed, ropes cinching down the crates to the wagon, heading to the railroad station. Planned to ship the pigs to the market in Huntington. Hiram, Bill, and the load of pigs were on Maple Street, sitting at the stoplight. Miss Hattie McClintock sat directly behind them in her pride and joy, her nineteen and forty blue Ford sedan. When the light turned green and Hiram's wagon didn't move right away, Miss Hattie laid on her horn. That model Ford had a deep, hard-sounding horn. Well, it scared Bill and he burst forward into the intersection, then jerked a hard left turn on to Main Street, also U.S. Highway 42—so hard the wagon went up on two wheels. Those big hogs rolled hard against the far side of their crates, shifting the wagon's center of gravity, and the whole shebang toppled over, busting most of the crates. There was pigs running everywhere."

"Don't fergit that Mack truck," Chief Tackett threw in.

Phil nodded his head and continued, "Ralph, right at that very moment a three-axle Mack truck pulling a big Pacific Intermountain Express trailer, a sixteen-wheeler, came barreling down Highway 42. The truck headed into the intersection where

Hiram had tipped over. The driver slammed on his brakes, the wheels locked and the rig jackknifed—then flipped over on its side. The P.I.E. trailer came down on top of Ol' Blue, Hiram's prize boar."

Chief Tackett pushed the bill of his cap back on his forehead and said, in a fed up tone of voice, "What a mess. A shame, too. Hiram told me Ol' Blue was the smartest hog he ever raised. That's sayin' a lot. Hogs are pretty dad-gummed intelligent."

"I ain't so sure that's true about Ol' Blue," Pappy Roosevelt said with a twinkle in his eye. "I know a thing or two about hogs. And a hog what couldn't figure out he should clear a path for a Mack truck ain't likely to be at the head of his class."

Everybody looked at Ralph for a second or two. When he broke into a big grin we laughed at Pappy Roosevelt's joke.

Phil continued, "I drove our wrecker over to the accident and pulled the tractor and trailer out of the intersection. Took nearly an hour." He put his hand on my shoulder. "Freddy here helped Hiram round up his pigs. The chief shoveled Ol' Blue off Main Street then began directing traffic. By the time we got everything moving again, traffic on Highway 42 had backed up outside of town for two miles in both directions."

Memories of the squealing pigs and what seemed to be two endless strings of cars and trucks had stuck with me. "Remember that big black Lincoln limousine at the end of the line of traffic?" I asked. "West Virginia license plate number one on the outside and the governor's wife on the inside. She glared out the rear window, her face all red and steamy."

"Yeah, she was late for a meeting in Huntington," Phil commented.

Ralph said, "Did that produce some fireworks?"

Harford jumped in. "You bet, Ralph. Less than a week later town council got a right testy letter from the State Road Commission. It said, 'The accident demonstrated the urgent need for changes in the flow of traffic through Kettle.' Then there was another letter, and another."

William White laughed, "The mayor told town council he wished to God both Hiram Anderson and the governor's wife had stayed home that day."

"Town Council said no to each of the letters, and then the requests turned to demands," I said. "You would've enjoyed Town Council's replies, Ralph. Each one matched the ever stronger words of the State Road Commission." Ralph nodded. "I wondered how far they could ratchet up this thing. Our local paper, the *Kettle News Leader*, printed the State Road's letters and town council's replies side by side. I sent them to Beverly, who's now my wife. She was studying at the university up in Morgantown."

Hartford grinned, "Things heated up, all right. The very next week the paper carried an editorial praising Kettle's elected officials for taking a hard line, standing up to the state." Hartford paused and looked around the table, then added, "At the time I worried that members of town council might suffer shoulder sprains from all the self-administered back patting." We laughed. Then Hartford got a mock serious expression on his face and added, "You boys try patting yourselves hard on the back. It's not easy to do." We laughed some more.

Pappy Roosevelt banged his fist on the table. "Laugh if you want. But them snakes in Charleston was up to no good. That long lull in the letters shoulda signaled that somethin' was afoot. Next thing we knew the State Road snuck in and tore down our covered bridge." His voice rose, "Couldn't believe it. Ralph, one August morning in the summer of fifty-one they just come in with a wrecking crew and pulled down the old bridge over on Sour Apple River Road. Dang good covered bridge. Beams of virgin chestnut. Built in the eighteen and thirties. Told us we was better off with a steel bridge."

"You'd have thought they'd talk with you about what they were going to do," Ralph commented.

"Shoulda taught us those boys in Charleston couldn't be trusted," Whit observed.

"No," Phil added quietly, "it took a lawyer to teach us that."

"I was there," I said to Phil. "January of nineteen and fifty-two. Remember, you sent me to the meeting to ask town council for an extra garbage pickup?"

Phil nodded and I continued. "Ralph, there was a lawyer from the State Road Commission at the meeting. He was dressed all snappy in his dark blue suit, starched white shirt, and striped necktie. A far cry from our mayor and town council in their old sweaters and wrinkled gabardine pants." Phil and Hartford chuckled.

Hartford interrupted, "I was there, too, Freddy. That lawyer's briefcase was crammed with legal papers. He set it on the chair beside him and smiled at it like the briefcase was a child at a piano recital. When he did that I figured we were in for trouble."

"Well, Ralph," I continued, "when Mayor Baumgartner gave the lawyer a turn to speak, he held up some of the papers, then passed them over to the Mayor. Told everyone he came to the meeting to officially inform the town that the C&O Railroad had deeded the railroad tracks and the old railroad station in the center of Kettle, as well as the right of way, to the state of West Virginia. 'Further,' he said, holding up a different bunch of papers, 'the State Road Commission is prepared to purchase, or use eminent domain legal proceedings to acquire as needed any and all property abutting U.S. Highway 42 through Kettle in order to upgrade the road to a four-lane highway.'

"The four-lane highway. That's when they done us in," Bertha said under her breath.

Ralph pointed out the front window towards the street. "The one that's out there now?"

"You got it," I said. "Then the lawyer spoke with an emphasis on each word. He read from a single sheet of paper that looked like an old letter." I quoted him as best I could remember his words. "'This change will reduce the periodic impediments to smooth egress and flow of commerce caused by angle parking adjacent to a major highway.'"

The lawyer went on to describe a new one-mile stretch of four-lane highway that would replace most of U.S. Highway 42, Main

Street, through Kettle and well beyond each end of town. "I couldn't believe what I heard, Ralph—a four-lane highway, smack through the middle of town." He told town council that the three blocks of Main Street in the business district would be protected, but separated from the new four-lane highway. Each end of Main Street would be connected to the new four-lane by short access streets.

"He smiled like a daddy giving a kid a piece of candy and added, 'Of course, Main Street will continue to be connected to the old streets leading into the residential part of Kettle.' But he told us the railroad tracks through the center of town, the old railroad station, fire station, flagpole and World War Two memorial, as well as the wide grassy mall on either side of the tracks, would go. Homes along Main Street on both ends of town would lose most of their front yards and shade trees."

Hartford said in a loud voice, "If I'd been a younger man, I think I would've punched him in the nose."

"After the meeting, when I got home my wife, Beverly, said, 'Freddy, you look like you're in shock. What happened?'

"The next issue of the *Kettle News Leader* ran the headline, 'Kettle under attack,' Hartford said. "Each week the paper carried follow-up stories on our attempts to stop the four-lane. But the war was over."

"I'll never forget the ground-breaking ceremony for the four-lane," Bertha said. Her face got red as she spoke. "There was that commissioner in his white suit, words pouring out of his mouth like oil on troubled water. Reminded me of the snake oil salesman that came to town when I was a kid. 'A new era for Kettle,' he said in his speech. Then Mayor Raymond T. Baumgartner walked up to the microphone. Remember what he said?"

We nodded our heads, except for Shufflehead, who asked, "Whut'd he say, Bertha?"

"Honey, it was short and sweet. Words to remember. The mayor put his right hand around the microphone's stand and stood there real quiet-like. He had shed his suit jacket and wore bright green suspenders over his white shirt. Raymond's face drooped. Maybe he just wanted to take a good look at folks. Or maybe he wanted us to take a good look at him and remember he'd decided not to run for re-election, I don't know. Between him, his dad and his granddad, a Baumgartner had been mayor of Kettle for nearly fifty years. Everybody got quiet, expecting a Fourth of July-type of speech. The mayor slowly said these words, 'God works in unseen ways.' He stopped and stared at the crowd. Just stared at us. We stared back at him. Then the mayor spoke five words I'll carry with me to my grave, 'So too does the devil.' Then he turned and walked away from the microphone." Bertha paused and looked around the table.

She continued, "The commissioner shook the mayor's hand and gave him a big smile, 'Truer words were never spoken, Mr. Mayor. None truer, indeed.'" Bertha looked down at her coffee cup, and then at us, "'None truer, indeed,' can you imagine that?"

With a twinge of admiration in his voice, Pappy Roosevelt said, "Ralph, it warn't two hours 'til them boys from the State Road was puttin' scaffolding up around the building." The admiration disappeared. "Then the next mornin', bright and early, they started tearin' the shingles off'n the roof."

I said, "A crowd lined up along the sidewalk in front of Gruber's Department Store and watched the wrecking crew begin to work on the old railroad station. I stood beside Mrs. Gertrude Gruber, leaning on her cane. She must have been about seventy-five then, not long before she passed away. Her eyes held a steady gaze on the old station and tears ran down her cheeks. 'It was always our center,' she said, 'I wonder what will go next.'"

Memories from earlier times, images of life on our old brick Main Street, different than the one that's outside Bertha's front door today, passed through my thoughts—walking along, meeting and talking with folks like Albert Newcomb; the Kettle High homecoming parade in forty-seven when Cricket Hobson put the red bandanna around her neck; hard goods unloaded from freight cars, and then tobacco, hogs and cattle loaded into the cars; Western Union telegrams about men wounded or killed in the war.

Hartford spoke quietly, "Gertrude Gruber was born here not long after the railroad station was built. Her daddy had deeded the right of way to the C&O Railroad for the tracks, then divided his farm into lots for the home sites and businesses that became Kettle. Didn't surprise me none that she died not long after they tore the old station down. Maybe she had a premonition of what the four-lane would do to our town. Didn't want to stick around for it. Sometimes I wonder if I should."

"Ralph, that was the summer town council give away the store," Whit said, anger rising in his voice.

"Sorry to hear it," Ralph replied.

Phil added, "Seemed like once Raymond decided to step down as mayor, everything began to fall apart. Can't blame him for stepping down, he'd done the job for nearly fifteen years. I didn't always agree with him, but by golly he kept town council on track."

"Ralph, here's something about government doing harm you can pass along to Senator Humphrey," Hartford said excitedly. "Early in July of fifty-four, the Kettle town council surprised everybody by voting to adopt a program set up by the governor to widen streets in small towns around the state. 'Good for commerce,' the governor said in a newspaper article. Town council voted to widen three of Kettle's oldest and prettiest, not to mention shadiest, streets. Mayor Baumgartner was the only 'no' vote."

Hartford said in an intense, but sad voice, "One of the councilmen said to the Mayor, 'Raymond, it's like the commissioner told us at the groundbreaking ceremony, we're entering a new era. The wider streets will be a blessing to Kettle—they'll give us smooth and speedy driving through town.'

The mayor asked, "Does town council understand that most of the maple and elm trees along those streets will be removed?"

Another councilman answered, "We'll grow new trees, Raymond, they'll just be set back a ways." Around the table the other councilmen nodded.

One added, "While they're growing, Kettle's commerce and trade will grow too. New era, Raymond. We're goin' places."

No one spoke. Then Ralph said in a soft voice, "I'll pass all this along to Senator Humphrey. I know he'll be interested."

After another period of silence, Hartford looked over at Bertha and raised his cup.

Bertha nodded. "OK, Hartford. Anybody else want refills? How about you, Ralph?"

We held our cups a couple of inches above the table, Ralph too. Shufflehead raised his RC bottle higher than our cups and gave Bertha a big grin. Bertha brought fresh coffee and an RC to the table. After she had served everybody she good-naturedly tousled Shufflehead's hair then sat down again.

A lull settled over the table. Maybe, like me, everybody's thoughts had returned to what the town used to be compared to today. I tried not to think about the old days too much. Each time I did Beverly told me I looked like I had the hang-dog blues. She said I should spend my time thinking about positive things, like our new home and our little boy, Jack—about the future. But sometimes I couldn't do it.

Hartford put two spoonfuls of sugar in his fresh cup of steaming black coffee and said, "We didn't know it at the time, Ralph, but the worst was yet to come."

Everybody nodded.

"What happened?" Ralph asked.

Phil answered him. "I'll never forget the morning I opened my *Herald Dispatch*, that's a Huntington newspaper, and read the story." Phil's voice reflected the surprise he must have felt then. "September of fifty-four, just when I thought things had settled down, they announced the Interstate highway was coming to town."

William White spoke up. "I'd read about the Interstate. President Eisenhower said it was to move troops and all of us, if necessary, to defend our country. Never occurred to me an Interstate would come right through Kettle. Anyway, if we needed to defend ourselves we'd take to the woods, not the highways."

Phil continued, "The newspaper told us exactly what would happen, and today it's history. Just like they said, that big highway swings in a wide arc on the north side of Kettle following the ridgeline of Tucker's Point."

"Another government program to do good. Lots of nice homes near Tucker's Point was tore down to clear the right of way," Chief Tackett added. "Damn shame. Tell Senator Humphrey that, Ralph. Damn shame."

"I'm sorry," Ralph said.

Momma had called Grandma and Grandpa Lemley the morning the story about the Interstate appeared in the newspaper. Grandpa told her that as soon as Grandma read the paper she began to cry and went out for a walk across the hill. He said he remembered a survey team coming through his alfalfa field nearly a year earlier. After he saw the map of the new road in the paper he figured their home would be squarely in the Interstate's path. Momma burst into tears and handed the phone to Daddy.

When Momma told me about her conversation with Grandpa I couldn't believe it—Grandma and Grandpa's place, with its view across the valley, gone? Even as I thought about it I could smell the sweet aroma of the fields of clover, just beyond the alfalfa. My Daddy had grown up there, played, then worked, in those fields. Me too. I felt like my insides had gone into a free fall. My times at the old place flashed through my thoughts. Climbing in the barn. Picking apples. Sitting on the porch and looking across the valley. The attic I loved to explore. All gone.

"Then a few weeks later they told us the rest of the story, Ralph," Whit added. "The new four-lane would be extended in order to serve as an access road from Kettle to the Interstate. Whole neighborhoods between the two roads would have to go in order to complete the connection."

Hartford Wilson stared at his cup of coffee and spoke softly, as if he was talking to it, not us. "They had it planned all the time—the four-lane and the Interstate. But they never told us. Raymond Baumgartner had it right, the Devil works in unseen ways. When them State Road people just up and demolished the old covered bridge, we should have figured they couldn't be trusted. We loved that bridge." Hartford sipped his coffee and then looked around the table, "Yessir, we got us a new bridge, new roads and wide streets. These days a fellow can get to and through Kettle in a snap. But I wonder, is there any reason to stop?"

Pappy Roosevelt said, "Henry Ford. It was him what started it—him and his infernal assembly lines."

Phil said quietly, "Maybe so. It's easy to point the finger of blame, Pappy Roosevelt. It is for me too." Then his eyes darkened and he raised his voice a couple of notches, "What's hard is to look in the mirror and wonder, 'Did I have a hand in it?' Most everybody has a car, some families have two of 'em. You drive a truck, Pappy Roosevelt. Me too. And nobody wants to get slowed down by traffic. Sure, I had a hand in it. We all did."

Hartford piped in, "You wouldn't know this, Ralph, but my Pop owned the first automobile in Kettle, a Ford, in nineteen aught nine," Hartford had a touch of pride in his voice. "I remember the day he brought it home. Mom and Pop liked the car so much that when my baby brother was born they named him Ford."

Hartford continued with enthusiasm, "Cars took Kettle by storm, Ralph. Folks sold property to get money to buy 'em. In nineteen and fourteen dealers right here in Kettle sold Fords, Maxwells, and Overlands. The ads in the *Kettle News Leader* made everybody want a car. Maxwell claimed to be 'The car that laughs at hills.' Ford said you could operate their car for two cents a mile. A Ford cost around four hundred dollars, Overlands a thousand—probably why they went out of business."

"In nineteen and twenty my Daddy built a gasoline station and garage," Phil said. "It wasn't the first one in Kettle, but it's lasted the longest." Phil put his hand on my shoulder, "Now with my retirement, Freddy here has got all the headaches of an owner."

The day Phil announced his retirement, a Tuesday in the spring of nineteen and fifty-six, two big events had happened. Late in the morning Beverly returned from a visit to Doc Simonton's office and phoned me all excited "I'm pregnant!" I nearly dropped the phone. Doc told Beverly that she and our little child looked healthy. That evening we drove to Charleston for a special celebration dinner. Beverly's blue eyes sparkled with radiance from deep within her.

After we went to bed we held each other so tight I didn't know which would happen first—my arms would break or my heart would burst with love. Later I put my ear against Beverly's stomach and rested my head there. I laughed and told her I thought I heard a voice say "Mom." As her tummy warmed my cheek I thought about our baby forming in there. Later I woke up in that position.

The second event came after lunch. Phil said he'd decided to retire, and offered me a way to buy the business out of its earnings. Phil's announcement and offer surprised me, but then I recalled how over the past couple of years he'd asked me to take on more and more responsibility—to the point that sometimes he didn't come in for a day or two. Beverly and I talked about Phil's offer every evening for a week. The opportunity excited us, but the financial risk caused us to hold back.

We decided to do it. I talked with Phil and folks at the bank. Once we had the paperwork finished, at age twenty-six I became the new owner of Buckingham's. Though calling me the owner had to be an overstatement. I had a mortgage on the business and hoped to someday own it. The day I signed the papers Momma and Daddy drove into Buckingham's and filled their car with gas. Daddy shook my hand and Momma gave me a big hug. Before they left I cleaned their windshield and checked the oil. One quart low.

Now, sitting in Bertha's Place with Ralph and the boys, I turned to Phil and said, "Once I became the owner of a business, I must have become a good credit risk. Not long afterwards, Beverly and I bought the old Poindexter home on Elm Street."

Hartford said, "I always liked that place. White frame, two stories. Big yard and shade trees. Nice. At least it was back then."

I turned to Ralph. "We looked forward to raising our children there, Ralph, but in no time I wondered if we'd made a good decision. After town council's new program of what amounted to exchanging our shady streets for wider thoroughfares, lots of folks around town began to put their homes up for sale, move out. The people who bought their homes often came from out of town."

"That must have been hard for you, for everyone," Ralph said.

Whit chimed in, "Wasn't long before town council had to hire a full-time night policeman, what with all the noise and rowdiness around Kettle after dark. How's that for a government program, Ralph?"

Many nights Beverly and I lay awake wondering what all the changes in Kettle would hold for our kids, us too. Sometimes one of us would touch the other in the special way that signaled we wanted to make love. One morning we talked about it and realized we made love just to settle ourselves enough to be able to sleep— different than the passion that'd been part of our lovemaking in the past. It troubled us.

Suddenly the front door of Bertha's Place swung open. A tall fellow in a bright red windbreaker stuck his head in and yelled, "Hey, folks, can somebody tell me how to get to the Piggly Wiggly supermarket?"

Chief Tackett never looked up, just said in a loud, firm, and level voice, "Take a left at the stop light, drive within the speed limit for a half-mile, take a right at the caution light, proceed forward about two hundred yards, then hit the accelerator. You'll crash into the cash registers at the Piggly Wiggly." Then the chief looked up at him and smiled, "I'd suggest you stop at about a hundred and eighty yards."

Everybody around the table grinned. Shufflehead gave a big laugh and said, "That's a good'n chief."

The man stared at us for a few seconds then muttered, "Thanks," and shut the door.

"Yessir, Ralph," Hartford said in a sarcastic voice, "we got a Piggly Wiggly market and a new town center. Sure done a lot for Kettle. Just look up and down our empty Main Street." He took a sip of coffee.

The chief spoke in a quiet, exasperated voice, "You'd've thought town council coulda figured it out." He looked towards

Ralph. "After the four-lane opened in fifty-four, everybody started complaining to me and town council." He raised the loudness of his voice a notch. "No place to park on Main Street so they could do their shopping. And all town council did was argue. A couple of councilmen wanted to tear down a building or two and put a parking lot in the middle of our old downtown. Another one had a hair-brained scheme to restrict traffic—sell parking passes for downtown Kettle. In the middle of it all a feller from Huntington come in, bought ten acres of cornfields on the east side of town, filled in some of the low-lying bottom land and put in a bunch of stores with a big parking lot. He named it the Kettle Town Center."

"I've often wondered why in tarnation didn't somebody stop it?" Pappy Roosevelt asked.

Phil answered, "You know why, Pappy Roosevelt. We don't have zoning in Kettle. All we've got is deed restrictions to keep colored folks from buying homes here. If you want to put a business, even a commercial outhouse, anywhere in town you can do it, as long as it's legal." He looked at Ralph. "By the summer of fifty-seven, Ralph, we had a second downtown called Town Center."

Shufflehead's face beamed. "I like that big sign out in front of it, next to the four-lane—a kettle with steam pouring out of it. How'd anybody think that one up?"

The Kettle Town Center, a single-story ribbon of stores with a huge asphalt parking lot, had a Piggly Wiggly supermarket on one end, a Big Hammer hardware store on the other end, and assorted small businesses in between. Before the Piggly Wiggly opened, most folks in town had heard about supermarkets but few had ever shopped in one.

"We didn't see it comin', Ralph," Whit said softly. "After the new stores opened, the old downtown stores continued to do business just like they had in the past. A year later Gruber's Department Store went out of business. Then Hartford here decided to retire and closed Wilson's Dry Goods. Before long all the stores in our old downtown had closed. There's no way you would know this, Ralph, but Gruber's and Wilson's had been fixtures in Kettle forever. Gruber's had been there since before the turn of the century. When I pass down Main Street and look at those empty buildings I feel like old friends have died."

"It was about time for me to retire anyway," Hartford reflected. "The new Town Center may have pushed me forward a year or two. My wife says we should be grateful, it's nice to have more time together."

Chief Tackett's voice carried a combination of relief and sadness, "A bunch of small shops finally moved into some of the empty buildings on Main Street—greeting cards, hand-made jewelry, and leather products, that sort of thing. But they last about as long as a kernel of popcorn in hot oil."

Shufflehead said with some enthusiasm, "I like the name of that new barbershop on the first floor of the old Gruber's Department Store, 'The Hairport.'"

"That's where the grocery department at Gruber's used to be, Shufflehead. We've moved a big step towards the modern age," Hartford said with a wince.

"One thing strikes me about those new shops," William White said reflectively. "The signs on the storefronts are all hand-lettered. It's a known fact in schools of business that a hand-lettered sign on a store is a sign of uncertainty, likely failure."

"Tell 'im whut come next, Hartford," Shufflehead suggested.

"OK. I guess we have to talk about it sooner or later." He paused and looked at Ralph, then said in a low voice, "Ralph, they came in and took away Kettle High School."

Ralph looked down at his coffee.

Hartford's words caused a sinking feeling in my stomach. The *Kettle News Leader* broke the news in nineteen and fifty-seven, not long after the birth of our son, Jackson. The *News Leader* reported that the county Board of Education would close Kettle High and build a regional high school. The new school would serve the towns of Kettle and Tipple, our archrival in football and basket-ball, as well as in spelling bees and the world series of math.

The new school would be located halfway between the two towns, about ten miles north of Kettle.

Ralph spoke softly, "That must have been hard on the town."

I replied, "At the time I didn't know which was worse—our kids going to school with kids from Tipple, or Kettle without Kettle High School. But I knew this—closing Kettle High would cut the heart out of our town."

Out of me, too. Jack wouldn't go to Kettle High School, most likely would never know a place that had meant so much to me. I wanted to believe the newspaper's story had no truth to it. But I knew James Garfield wouldn't report that kind of news without first checking the facts.

I said, "I tried to find some good in the board's decision, maybe more advanced subjects for the kids or a better football team. But whatever I came up with couldn't offset the loss I felt. Still feel. The afternoon of the day we learned about the closing, on my way home I ran a stop sign. Nearly had an accident."

When Beverly heard the news she broke down in tears. That's the day we decided to sell our home. On the positive side, that very night our lovemaking improved. We soon bought a ranch-style house still under construction in a new development about three miles west of Kettle. Later Beverly and I had a big fight over a choice of kitchen appliances—she wanted avocado green, I wanted harvest gold.

On moving day my insides got all wrenched up into knots. Living outside of Kettle? Hard to believe. I'd been born in Kettle. Momma and Daddy too, so had my grandparents. The world had come to life for me in Kettle—the place where I marked my boundaries, my accomplishments. A place that marked me. When I stood on the streets of Kettle and looked at the hills around town, I felt comforted by their broad shoulders, soft colors. I could tell the time of day by changes in the light on the hills. Move out of Kettle? I'd move away from a part of myself.

That day I went back and forth from our old place to our new home, each trip moving parts of our past, our belongings, from a life we knew to one we didn't know. And each trip through Kettle loosed a flood of memories, seemed to take hours. At the same time, when I looked at the treeless streets and the old downtown, or the shell of it that remained, I knew my memories reflected a place that had passed on.

After we loaded the moving truck with the last of our furniture, Beverly walked up to me with Jack in her arms. She pulled the three of us together in a big hug and said, "The move will be good for you. For Jack and me too." Then she gave me a warm and lingering kiss.

Bertha's round "Drink RC Cola" clock hanging beside the doorway to the kitchen showed nearly ten o'clock. "Well, folks," I said, "Phil's got plenty of time to sit and talk, but I've got to get back to work. Nice meeting you, Ralph."

I pushed my chair away from the table as a dusty blue four-door Chevrolet parked in front of the restaurant.

Ralph looked out the restaurant's plate glass window. He got excited and said, "Hang on a minute, Freddy. There's somebody I'd like you to meet."

Senator Hubert Humphrey stepped out of the car. He and the driver walked into Bertha's Place. Ralph greeted them and shook hands. He asked Bertha to please serve them some coffee. Senator Humphrey introduced himself to everybody and shook hands with us. He and his friend wore no suit coats and the sleeves of their white shirts were rolled up to their elbows. Senator Humphrey insisted we call him Hubert, and we did, but to me he continued to be Senator Humphrey. Though, with his rumpled shirt, chubby oval face, and warm smile, if you overlooked his Minnesota accent you might mistake the senator for somebody from Kettle. He introduced his friend, Orville Freeman, who looked to be about Hubert's age. Orville combed his hair with a straight part on the left side and wore round horn-rimmed glasses. A few weeks later *Time* magazine mentioned Orville's title, Governor of Minnesota.

Senator Humphrey gave us a big smile and said, "Coffee's on me." He and Orville sat down and Bertha refilled everybody's cups. She brought Shufflehead a fresh RC Cola, looked at Senator Humphrey and asked, "This OK, Hubert?"

He grinned, "Sure."

After the senator had been introduced to Pappy Roosevelt, he called him "Pappy." Pappy Roosevelt gave Senator Humphrey a wide tobacco-stained smile.

We had a little chit-chat comparing our weather to the weather this time of the year up in Minnesota, and then Senator Humphrey looked around the table. In a serious tone of voice said, "I'm glad you got to meet Ralph, he's a good listener and will fill me in on your conversation." He paused and looked around the table. "But let me ask you folks a question. What kinds of issues should the next president of the United States address in order to help towns like Kettle?"

"I reckon we've never been asked that," Hartford answered. "Until you and Senator Kennedy came along, the last candidate for president to visit Kettle was William Jennings Bryan in aught eight. He gave a speech from the rear platform of his train, right beside the old railroad station that once sat directly across the street from this restaurant. He talked a lot but he didn't ask any questions."

Hartford paused for a moment and looked squarely at Senator Humphrey. "But when I think about your question, Senator, ...er... Hubert, I think we need to figure out how to recover what we've been telling Ralph about, what we've lost."

Senator Humphrey raised his eyebrows and glanced over at Ralph. Orville asked, "What did you lose?"

Hartford spoke at a slow pace. "Until not long ago, Orville, Hubert, Kettle was a sleepy little town, just a spot on the map, but it was a place we loved. We conducted business with one another, went to school and church together, and cared for each other. One day, without so much as a 'howdy', the State Road Commission slipped in and tore down our old covered bridge, over a hundred years old and solid as a rock." Hartford went on to describe how the state dropped a four-lane highway into the middle of town, then gave town council a bundle of money to cut down our shade trees and widen our streets.

"Don't fergit the Interstate, Hart," Pappy Roosevelt said. Hartford described how the Interstate caused homes to be torn down and sealed off one side of town.

Pappy Roosevelt interrupted, "And tell Hubert about how the new Town Center went up, and all the old businesses on Main Street went down, families started movin' out."

"Now we got theft, vandalism, and a night policeman," Whit said.

Hartford continued, "And to cap it all off, one morning we sat down to breakfast, opened our newspapers and learned that the Board of Education had voted to close Kettle High School. What do you think would happen to the little towns in Minnesota, Hubert, if you took the high schools outta them?"

Senator Humphrey nodded.

After a pause in the conversation, Bertha spoke. "Well boys, you too, Hubert, Orville, maybe this's as good a time as any to tell you my bad news. With all the old stores on Main Street gone, my business has dropped off to near nothing—and has stayed there for a long time. Some days I don't make enough money to pay the light bill. Six months ago I started looking for somebody to buy the place. I offered to darn near give it away. But no takers. As much as I enjoy your company, boys, I'm too old and too poor to do full-time charity work. In a few weeks I'm going to close the restaurant."

Whit Saunders' mouth fell open. He lived alone, came here every day. Every evening, too. William White sat speechless, wide-eyed. Pappy Roosevelt reached into his back pocket, pulled out a plug of chewing tobacco, bit off a chunk and began to chew.

Phil Buckingham's face dropped into a sad expression. "Bertha, you've been…this place has been…part of Kettle…our lives."

"Boys," Bertha replied with tears in her eyes, "you've been part of my life too. But walk out the front door—look at the empty buildings up and down Main Street. I can't make ends meet."

Hartford turned towards Senator Humphrey. His voice sounded like it did when, years ago, he taught our junior high boys' Sunday school class. "Hubert, this restaurant sits on the site of the first building in this territory, the Kettle Trading Post. Bertha and the owners before her have served hospitality, good food and drink for a hundred and fifty years. Here's where our town began, came to life. The life of every dad-goned person who ever lived in Kettle has been touched by this place."

I didn't know if I should speak my mind, but decided to jump in. "Hubert, I read that you were once the mayor of Minneapolis." My voice quivered. "Maybe you can understand how a little town like Kettle is sort of like a person. It has a heart, it lives and breathes." I paused for a few seconds to collect my thoughts. Senator Humphrey took a sip of his coffee but kept his gaze on me. "And if you rip out the heart of a town, even in the name of progress, life can't be pumped in any more. We're losing Kettle— it may already be gone."

Nobody spoke. Hartford cleared his throat and leaned forward, his elbows on the table. He put both hands around his coffee cup and bowed his head, shoulders slumped. Then he looked up at Senator Humphrey, who looked squarely at him. In a soft voice Hartford asked, "If you're elected president, Hubert, can you help us get our town back?"

Jack trotted across the field towards me waving his little arms. Behind him the horizon glowed a fading pink under a ribbon of pastel blue. The dark of night rushed across the sky from the east.

"Come on, buddy, let's go home."

"Go."

I smiled and knelt. "Hey, you've really got that 'g' sound!"

Jack grinned and threw his arms around my neck, "Pig-gy back?"

After we tucked Jack into bed Beverly and I walked outside, stood in our back yard under a dome of bright stars. The crisp moist air held a faint scent of apple blossoms. I put my arm around Beverly's waist.

She whispered, "It's like the sky is filled with jewels."

After a moment I said, "When I was a kid, sometimes at night I'd hike up Tucker's Point, about where the Interstate now comes through Kettle. Half-way up the mountain the lights of the town would spread out below me. I'd think about how all the lives in Kettle were in those twinkles of light. I'd wonder if, on other nights, I'd be in the twinkles that somebody else looked down on."

Beverly leaned into me, we kissed.

"Then I'd climb all the way to the top. Kettle would become a bright spot in a sea of darkness—and beyond Kettle other bright spots would glow."